Survivors' Dreams

By

Kaylan Doyle

"Survivors' Dreams"
Published by Chronicles Publishing
Cover Art by Claudia McKinney
Layout & Design by More Than Publicity

Copyright © 2011 by Kaylan Doyle
ISBN-13: 978-0615480848
ISBN-10: 0615480845
www.kaylandoyle.com

For More Information:

CHRONICLES PUBLISHING
Post Office Box 8459
Kirkland, Washington 98034

Printing History
Chronicles Publishing/Paperback edition/August 2011
Chronicles Publishing/eBook edition/August 2011

To Brian

Acknowledgments

I need to thank so many people for their help in seeing this book to completion. Family and friends, all those who believed in me. Most importantly, my husband Bill who cooked and cleaned and supported with never a word of complaint.

For my writer friends and associates who have commented, edited, given me brilliant insights and advice - Thank You All – you know who you are. For Lynnie, who listened to me read aloud – endlessly. For Susan, who guided me through the minefield. For Jay, test reader extraordinaire, and for Shannon and crew of More Than Publicity my heartfelt thanks. This book would never have happened without you – and I am truly grateful.

Prologue

Undetected, just beyond the Kra'aken defense longscanners, the fighting fleet of Earth arrayed in attack formation. In the center of the massed ships hung a huge meteor, positioned and held stable by the tractor beams of three enormous warships. The instrument of annihilation sat poised, ready for launch into the planet's surface.

"One hundred years of planning, working toward this moment," murmured the Terran War Commander. "Now Kra'aken pays. Primary target is the largest destroyer between us and the planet. Shields up. Weapons hot. Captains, execute on my third mark."

He heard sharp intakes of breath over the intership central comm. *My soldiers' lungs filled to bursting, spines straightening, shoulders squared. In anticipation. In preparation. And, no doubt, in fear.*

"Engines full," he ordered, heard the eagerness in his words and forced calm. "Execute. Mark, mark, mark."

As a single entity, the enormous Earth fleet surged for the unsuspecting world below.

Chapter 1

Mid-aiy
Viven 2, 7007.25
Starship WarHammer
Kra'aken World, Eagla Galaxy

WarHammer's emergency klaxon blared, a brain-splitting *whoop-whoop-whoop*. A secunda of silence followed, then the alarm shrieked again.

Prince Helrazr leaped from his study desk. "What in the Twelfth Hell?"

"Battle stations," announced main comm. "Pilots to fighters. Longscans detect incoming, unidentified war fleet. Scanners show all ships weapons free, shields raised. Repeat. All personnel battle stations." Three harsh tones blasted transmission end.

Racing from his barracks on Level 19, the prince found the corridor jammed with fellow pilots. Fear amped his pace. As the group rounded the destroyer's outer ramp to launch deck on Level 20, Razr led by a handful of strides.

The First Navigator's voice echoed through the ship. Eerie. Hollow. "TakeHold in ten secundas."

Razr's guts coiled, twisted.

Only one condition existed to precipitate *WarHammer's*

unscheduled movement in Kra'aken inner space. Extreme danger.

The prince sprinted for his warplane.

The destroyer's outer ring whined and shuddered underfoot. Spooling up, *WarHammer* readied to hurl another tier of her lethal fighters against the Terran invaders. Hard g forces of the rapidly rotating core shoved Razr, bounced him against a curving wall.

Prince Helrazr's testas shrank tight against his groin. Fear spurred his pace. Ten long strides put him before his fighter's access hatch.

At the neighboring bay, his friend Darius' dark eyes rolled, showed whites. His stiff-legged body betrayed terror barely checked. "Good hunting, Razr."

"And you, Dar." *Impossible I sound so calm.* Recta puckered tight as a froga's butt, cold sweat slicked his skin, slid clammy against the nanoplas flight suit.

"Destroyer save us," Darius' voice quavered. Snapping a jerky salute at the gold and scarlet image on the wall, Kra'aken's God of War, he leaped inside his plane.

Through the hatch, six fast steps put Razr at the cockpit, a quick slide jammed his big body into the indigo plasform command seat. His double hearts pounded staccato rhythm. Sensitive nostrils flared at the sour smell of fear-driven sweat. *Mine.*

Scanning the front section of his cockpit, Razr waited, fingers drumming, for the activation of three dark rows of upper and lower screens. Two wrapped above, one curved beneath the plasplex viewports. Before him hung a double row of translucent keyboards, their muted glow of multicolored icons appeared suspended in mid-air.

Portside, looming overhead in skyspace, he got his first glance at the annhiliation aimed at Kra'aken.

Fear dragged like ice crystals scraping the inside of Razr's veins. His faster-than-normal reflexes failed. *I didn't quite believe it until now.*

Harsh klaxons screamed the whoop-whoop-whoop of final TakeHold.

With a gut-wrenching push, *WarHammer* surged, positioning her massive bulk between the invading fleet and homeworld. Huge engines throbbing, weapons hot, the starship prepared to destroy the enormous construct – an ugly gray-brown-silver chunk of rock and ice – shoved by Terran tractor beams.

Razr's stomach slid sideways, echoing *WarHammer's* abrupt maneuver.

He tried three times – damn his shaking hands – to secure his restraining belts and protective webbing.

Sweet blessed Destroyer. Finally! At the clack-click of success, he auto-tugged to test the locks.

Shoving aside hatred for the critical next step, he pressed fingers against his lips. One breath pulled deep, held tight, then Razr laid his head in the depression of his seatback. Waited for the gut-knotting nausea of mind-jack interface.

There. A snick, a rotation, the intrusion – the slick slide of the plug. But then – his reward – total immersion with his fighter. The instant when his invincible ship became a living extension of Razr. Or Razr of the ship.

Cockpit screens lit, bloomed with glowing green numbers, golden plot lines, blue and red of probabilities. The black shapes of the incoming meteor and the enemy fleet filled the fire-pattern schematic of his armscomper's screen.

Razr's mind saw it all, processed data at hyper-speed, activated the ship systems and went weapons hot.

"Operational." The familiar voice of Brin, his Artificial Intelligence, came from everywhere and nowhere, acknowledging the ship's-connection handshake.

"Copy." *He's chosen no avatar, just opted to be audio.*

Razr stared at, without actually seeing, the deep blue couch beside his command seat. *Shirl's empty station.* Apprehension bubbled, then grabbed him hard. *I need my armscomper – and not just because she's the finger on the firebutton.* He muffled a groan. *Where is she? I can't launch without her.*

The beating of Razr's twin hearts ratcheted to arrhythmic, each racing to be first to leap from his chest.

Releasing the master safety catches on his belts, he punched the seat and mindjack interface releases. Easing his head free, Razr shoved to his feet, leaping toward the hatch.

"I won't leave her to die."

"No, Prince Helrazr. We're away." The measured delivery of the AI's words clanged incongruous against their content. "*WarHammer* is already throwing fighters. Belt up. Now."

"I have to …." A glance out the plasplex cockpit window revealed the first tier of slender warships, silhouetted against the dark of space, bristling like shining porcuhedge spines. The beautiful silver blades sliced the sky as they sequentially peeled away, jettisoned one after another from the mothership's embrace.

"*Shata*, Brin." Razr skidded to a stop. "I don't love Shirl – but I – must do something."

"Milord. If you are unbelted when *WarHammer* throws this fighter, you will die."

"My reprehensible, Shirl." Voice cracking, Razr addressed the empty couch. "My anguish to leave you." Reality snapped him upright.

"*Forza!*" Unsecured at launch, he'd smash, flattened at 10+ g's against who knew what. Then with subsequent weightlessness, he'd tumble loose, bounce off every surface in the ship. *If lucky, my neck will snap fast.* If not … icy fingers probed his lungs.

Survival kicked in. In a single amped leap, Razr landed by his couch. Another secunda squeezed him inside.

The sixth finger of his left hand hooked, snagged in the webbing. Cursing steadily, he twisted it free. Slammed the belt locks home.

Razr's stomach surged.

The pilot's couch enveloped him, a morphing entity

augmenting his every twitch.

On full auto, his large fast fingers danced over lighted boards, pressed lumins, icons. And paused .... All in readiness. Sequencing and checks complete. All systems green.

"Milord?" Brin's sharp inhale reminded him of elapsing time. Something he didn't have.

Razr held his breath and flipped the only toggle in the cockpit. A deliberate anachronism – the dead-man's switch performed two functions. To fire the enormous lethal power contained in this silver projectile. Or kill it.

With a heavy shaking rumble, his craft's primary engines caught. Her secondary engines coughed, growled. Then snarled to full power.

Outside the aircraft, Razr heard the thud of fast bootstrikes, shouts, exclamations. *But no Shirl.* His exterior hatch slammed, then eight slide-smacks as outer latches hooked. Suction hissing, the fighter sealed.

The nose gantry released, swung wide.

His warplane groaned, danced in place. The ship shuddered, strained, chafed to be free.

Bang. Clang. Bang. Clang. Grapples loosed, separated.

The powerful fighter fretted, free except for a single anchor.

Beside him a blue screen showed each ejected ship. *My turn.* Breathing forgotten, blood hammered hard in his head. Razr counted down. *Three-two-one. Now.*

The last tether fell away.

"All green," Brin said but Razr already knew. He shoved the yokes full-on.

WarHammer's rotational throw created rib-creaking, breath-sucking pressure. His fear and pain, remembered between flights, again banished by joy's rush.

The destroyer hurled his warplane from the launch desk. Mere secundas passed before an enormous detonation shoved his ship to one side, a right angle to its plotted path. Wrapped about him, the fighter shuddered, shimmied. Steadied.

Razr surged past an invader, rotated on the instant and searched for prey.

Screams shrieked over his comset. Explosions splattered airspace with great blots of color. Silver chunks of ship spun past. *Great Destroyer. That piece of fighterplane held Darius' Klan Krest.*

Multiple new detonations propelled debris from the destroyer's core. Twisted pink foam, scarlet reds, pieces of crew blasted outward, coating Razr's craft in ebony and crimson.

Razr retched. *Cannot vomit. Cannot foul my ship's systems.* He reached for the side of Shirl's couch. Fished for the slam-hypo of anti-naus she always kept there. Ripping the plas, he slapped the needle against his neck. Sharp stinging confirmed success.

Shocks, like the hammering of a giant fist, rocked his plane.

Lights flickered. As the glowing colors of the fighter's screens blanked, the cockpit went black.

Razr's safety belts and netting loosed. With a yank deep in his brain, the jack's probe ripped from his skull. A scream of agony echoed off smooth ivory bulkheads. *Was it mine?* A wet copper tang flooded his nose and mouth.

Falling, falling, falling. Down a tunnel of endless dark. Razr trembled at the black cloud closing around him. *Coming to smother me.*

In the free-rolling fighter, Razr clenched his teeth against a scream. *Where is Brin? Destroyer. Brin's dead too.*

Invading mist blanketed his mind.

§

"Prince Helrazr! Can you hear me?"

"What ...?" Kra'aken warrior claws shredded his brain. *To cause so much pain ... only thing possible.* Cracking watering eyes, Razr struggled to recall why he lay halfway across his seat and halfway on the floor. The tiny pieces of memory answering his summons refused to fit together.

"Praise be," breathed Brin's gray-haired warrior avatar. "Shall I order the medunit here?"

"Hate the damned thing." Razr's insta-reaction evaded the question. Not on principle. He hid his fear of small-area confinement from everyone. Even Brin.

Cradling his skull in his hands, Razr inspected the cockpit. The displays of glowing rainbow-colored schematics made no sense. *Have I lost my mind?*

His heartsbeats sped, pushing the pulsing pain in his head. Sticky liquid seeped beneath his flightsuit neck, slid warm and thick down his spine. *Please let it be blood instead of brain fluid.*

Memory reassembled bits of knowledge. *My mindjack!* "Shata."

Razr oh-so-gently fingered the base of his skull. Found swollen tissue and the extruded soft-hard plas-circ of female access. *Not merely bruised, curse it – I'm ruptured.*

His heartbeats pushed hard again, working against suddenly paralyzed lungs.

"Your interface is bleeding," Brin confirmed. "My humiliation, my prince. Until I completed stabilizer repairs, you tumbled, loose in the ship." Brin's normally composed, calm voice rose in pitch and volume. "Milord, your favor, can you walk to the medcube? Milord?"

"You will nag until I comply?" Razr attempted a smile. Knew by Brin's recoil, he'd failed.

An odd flicker shoved against the edge of his mind ... *something strange about the AI. What is different ....* Razr shifted, attempting to push to his elbows. The motion forced the splintered end of his left humerus through a rip in his flightsuit. "Ahhh – Great Destroyer!"

Panting against the pain, Razr bit his tongue to hold back screams.

Blackness closed, lightened to gray, brightened to white bolts of spearing agony and Brin's frantic pleas. "Answer me, milord. Respond!"

Razr tried, or thought he did. A brush of his good hand across his face smeared sticky damp; an unmistakable metallic reek filled the cockpit. His eyes slid away from the burgundy-stained headrest. His stomach crammed up in his throat.

Forza me, I need the docbox. Now! Sliding his feet off the pilot's couch, injured arm tucked close against his side and shielded by the other, Razr rolled to hand and knees. Fought for air, fought against the threatening blackness, fought the pain of his battered body.

Blood droplets coated the cockpit. Ruby dotted his flightsuit.

"Brin?" The word came in a wheeze, rattling in compressed lungs. "Call the accursed box here, your favor."

"On the instant."

The medunit whined, lifting through the core of the craft.

Razr rested his face against a bulkhead. Contact with a cluster of bruised lumps on his forehead forced a hiss.

An insistent throbbing drew his attention to the vulnerable area most critical to a young male. *I should have noticed this first. Destroyer-damned belts nearly neutered me. The fact I didn't ... is worrisome.*

"Brin? Where are we? How long was I unconscious?"

"When you are mended, we will discuss all." Brin's warrior aspect popped in.

Not good. Razr's mind darted, like prey seeking escape. *What won't he say?*

The AI's wild bushy eyebrows sprouted like sqirl tails, his gray hair confined in tight braids. His lips pursed, pressed bloodless, relaxed. Twice.

The persona Brin adopts when news is grim. Razr's hearts hiccuped. *Is he the problem?* Cold slime sloshed in the pit of his stomach. Rogue AI's are the stuff of children's scaretales. *Aren't they?*

A clunk-click at the ship's core signaled the medunit's arrival. The box slid into an aperture behind Razr's couch, locked down.

Razr forced the six steps to the bed. Nerve endings in his body snapped like polyelas bands. Each breath brought stinging hits. *My lungs. Punctured?*

In his attempt to strip off his flightsuit, Razr's vision wavered gray. His knees dissolved beneath him, like melting metal.

Must get in .... Razr collapsed across the docbox edge. He felt autoarms straighten his body. He screamed at the movement of his broken arm, screamed as the unit cut away his suit. Screamed when the braces secured his body in the bed.

I will be calm. I am unrestrained, in a wide grassy field.

Closing his eyes, Razr fought the involuntary urge to flee, swallowed his rising bile, forced himself to lay motionless while clamps elevated and stabilized his head.

A cold sharp stab in his throat vein brought a pink mist, the pain relief of narcophine.

Just as the box lid closed, an acrid reek caught the prince's attention. The hot, oily smell of damaged hydraulics, hung heavy in the fighter. *I should care but the meds ....*

Cool antiseptic coated Razr's ruined interface. Then, sudden cold patches pressed everywhere, followed by vicious stings and punctures from automed hook-ups.

Vision blurring, Razr gratefully surrendered his pain.

Even while agony faded to a rose-colored float, even while blessed oblivion beckoned, the prince's hearts hammered in panic. But this time not in fear of confinement.

What if the docbox cannot repair my brain?

Chapter 2

Dark
Augra 13, 7205.05
Kra'aken Survivor Cocoon I
Planet of Olica, Uncharted Galaxy

"Shata," whispered Caylee, the lifecocoon's AI. "Five of my thrusters are impaired – I must land." She struggled to maintain control over the huge main engine without the full complement of balancing directional nacelles.

The world below appeared appropriate, although with her precious charge deep in stasis sleep, it made no difference. Caylee would not wake the toddler until another Kra'aken ship triggered her scanners.

"If only I'd been able to land dirtside before, I could have performed maintenance. Prevented problems. The ship's done well enough for the past 150 yaras but in all that time, this is the first planet I've found. And not another survivor."

The craft entered the atmosphere.

"We're dropping too fast, too fast." The AI's voice came breathy, as if she hyperventilated. An impossibility – she was a computer. Losing altitude, Caylee fought the crippled ship for control, her choices rapidly diminishing.

"Lights below? Small, and in dwellings only. Primitive,

perhaps, but inhabited. This is terrible." Caylee fought the cocoon, flew it beyond the glowing area.

Below, her scanners located a large dark shape jutting high toward the sky. A mountain peak. *Perhaps high enough the inhabitants of this place will not discover us. At least, not before I can repair and resume flight.*

A dial-back on the main, a finesse of her remaining thrusters, placed the pod stern down above the mountain top. Setting scanners to run, searching for the best landing place, Caylee hovered and waited.

A shudder rippled through the ship as the main engine coughed.

"Destroyer, no. Not now," Caylee cried. Fast maneuvers with her remaining directional nozzles couldn't compensate. With a final scream, the huge primary engine died. Although the small thrusters provided some slowing, the AI was powerless to prevent the lifecocoon's plunge to the surface.

Directly into the dormant volcanic crater below.

Chapter 3

Mid-dark
Twenta of Viven, yara 7008.49 (Estimation)
Unknown Galaxy

Sunrays of consciousness probed the clouds of fog in Prince Helrazr's mind.

The inside of his mouth, the back of his throat, felt coated with polishing powder. *Thirsty.* His throat stuck in mid-swallow.

Rolling his eyes, Razr searched overhead for clues. *Where ...?* Remnants of a pleasant dream lingered; then memory stabbed. He jerked upright, smacked his forehead on the plexplas of the med unit's lid and lay down again.

"Destroyer take it," he snarled and punched the crimson Escape button.

With a hiss of seals, the transparent dome of the docbox cracked, retracted.

Razr sniffed and gave thanks. Twice. This time the warplane no longer stank of burned wires or oil. This time he'd slept through his restraint removal – the ones that made him fighting-crazy. *All things good, even if I did whack myself senseless on the box lid.*

The skin of Razr's wide shoulders stung, rubbed raw against the sides of the bed. *Every forzaing time.* He groaned, gingerly tested his broken arm. *Mended.* Flexed his knee – *fine.* He struggled to sit, cramped abdominals brought a gasp. Complaining muscles lay slack, slow to obey.

To be this diminished, to have this much muscle loss … how long did it take to repair me? Freezing fingers of fear ran triple-scales on the keyboard of his spine. *What of my mindjack?*

Razr's elegant right hand snaked behind his head, gently brushed aside long loose curls the color of jet, and pressed flesh. "Destroyer be praised."

Leaning back on bracing fists, he surveyed the new network of red lines and blotches marring his tawny skin. *They will fade to white – they always do.* Marks of a great warrior, a Kra'aken female would be impressed. Here, alone, there is no one to see, no one to care.

Staring at the pale ceiling, the prince deep-breathed flooding stimscents. Familiar biting aroma of crushed leaves, the tang of rain on rough bark of homeworld forests intended to calm and mask the odor of antiseptic. His personal *tasca* – the fragrance of yellow pine, sharp resin and ginger – surged and mingled. Memory made him clear his throat, memory shimmered bright in his large amber eyes, memory's pangs made breathing difficult.

"Brin? The jack is good? Status of the fighter?" The prince tried for a smile. At the AI's grim holo, he knew he failed.

"How do you feel?" Brin's tone hinted at concealed anxiety.

Razr startled at the wavering orange aura wrapped about his AI's holo. *He is a computer, a program, without a soul. A true aura is the one thing he cannot project. How then, has this happened?*

The prince's misery settled about him like a blanket. He studied Brin. A bit of floating recollection … from before … refused to surface. Something about the AI … something about trust?

Perching on a nearby chair, the AI's aspect wore green physician's scrubs, a stethoscope draped around his neck. His white nametag – heavily scribed in black – identified him as *Brin A. Brain.*

"Are we back onplanet? Why were we attacked?"

"To answer your questions in the order asked: We are not exactly back onplanet. The attack reason was contained in a Terran databurst dumped insystem one hora prior to our destruction." Brin added, "The medunit affirms you fully functional."

"I didn't hear the databurst." *The information arrived while I dallied with Cerissa.* Razr tamped his quick pang of guilt. *I don't care. My last Kra'aken touch, my last physical release trumps missed information.* "What did it contain?"

Dark brows, shaped like eagla wings, pulled to center, creating two vertical lines in Razr's smooth forehead.

"Wait ...." Razr raised a forestalling hand. Cobwebs cleared. "What do you mean, not exactly onplanet? What of Kra'aken?"

"The fighter is repaired, all our systems are green. Damage was extensive, my prince. Shorts, fires, electronics crisped, hydraulics ruptured." Brin's lips pursed and relaxed. "You took damage – not simply physical. The docbox rebuilt your jack interface, replaced seven mind modules from stored backups, reset all your skill sets and rebooted you." His holo hands grasped the stethoscope's ends, dragged it back and forth around his neck. "You may have memory loss – we cannot know until we test."

Razr opened his mouth, closed it when Brin shook his head.

"The final step is ship's interface with your brain." The AI twisted slender fingers, then interlaced them. "Your mind must finish healing. Two more wakaris are required."

"Brin, tell me what 'not exactly onplanet' refers to." Razr's jaw jutted, baring white, slightly crooked lower teeth.

"I prefer presenting full information first." The AI's orange aura faded, wavered, deepened. His lips worked.

Destroyer's death. It's bad news, then. Razr wondered at Brin's stubbornness but decided to let the computer have his way. "Very well. What kind of monsters destroy entire worlds?" At the AI's downturned lips, he shrugged. "Fine. What did the godsrotted databurst say?"

"First, some history." Brin shook an admonishing finger at Razr's exaggerated groan and rolling eyes. "You were a child, and I mere component parts in factory bins, when your father led a simple hunting raid on a world outside our galaxy. A Terran planet – Earth. The scouting report promised a simple world with primitive, abandoned military defenses. Simple people devoted to peace and cooperation."

The holo quivered, blinked out and resolved. Brin now wore a brown tweed three-piece suit, white shirt and plaid tie. Leaning against a projection of an unlit fireplace, his body language mimicked relaxation. But the trembling of the briar pipe in his hand caused a lazy curl of smoke to waver, then dissipate, leaving a lingering fragrance of spice-cherry. "Shall I continue?"

Razr's half-smile and short nod caused dark curls to eddy around his wide shoulders and heavily muscled arms. "I studied it in *skola* – because in all Kra'aken history it was our only unsuccessful raid."

"Much worse than unsuccessful, I'm afraid." Professorial Brin ran narrow, long fingers through short-cropped brown hair, standing it up in all directions. "Actually a disaster. The Earthlings were supposed to flee, ripe for hunting. They did not." The AI bit down on his pipe stem, chewed hard and thrust it in his vest pocket. "The populace fought back. Through bravery, fury and sheer stubbornness, they repulsed us."

"Unacceptable." Razr's sculpted lips twisted, giving his next words the mocking lie. "Kra'aken honor demands every attack be won, regardless of warriors lost." He tilted his head toward the AI. "Still, one defeat in all our milanis of existence?

Of no great concern."

"What happened after we departed Earth is … was of great concern." Brin's face grayed, deep lines etched from nose to chin. He wrung his hands.

"This is connected … revenge from a centari ago?" The black raptor-wing slashes of Razr's brows lifted toward his hairline.

"It is. They released the ages-old bond on their warlike alter-personalities. They vowed to wipe all things Kra'aken from the galaxy. Every living Earther old enough to understand, swore a blood oath to extract vengeance or die."

Razr muttered curses and gathered strength. Ignoring spasming muscles and the nasty gut-churning tug at his new mind interface, he pushed to his feet.

"How did they defeat our defenses?" Razr demanded. "Our tech code is unbreakable. The keys are hidden, their location known only to two – my father and his Righteous Shield Guard, Lord Regence." His voice hiccupped, his throat swelled hot. *My father. Is he dead?*

As the floor underfoot felt suddenly spongy, Razr reached to steady himself against the curving cube wall. Found it enemy instead of friend. *Destroyer, I'm dizzy.*

"How did they find us?" He grunted the words with his first steps to the cabinet. Flexing a hand, he opened a drawer.

"The hunting party, in their rout, left behind weapons, a fighter transport craft and two dead, fully morphed pilots." Brin lifted an anguished face to the tall young man. "Upon their return home, every Kra'aken on the trip, including your father, requested termination. Circumstances were judged extenuating. Requests were denied."

"*Shata*," Razr swore. "I can suss the rest." Twelve large fingers twisted in his heavy hair, mirroring the contorted features of his face. "Terrans got our hardware, our military strategy and all our software. They got a fully functional warplane and its weaponry. *Destroyer!* They got two fully changed warriors to dissect. *Forza!* The Earthers took our technology ... and they reverse-engineered it?"

"Correct," Brin said and the word hung ominous and heavy between them.

Razr watched his AI carefully blank his face. *He doesn't want to talk anymore – at least about this.* "The abandoned ship provided stargates and jump coordinates – directly to our homeworld." The prince bit out harsh words, each sheared off at its end. "The Terrans knew exactly where we were."

Brin nodded. And didn't say a word.

Razr pulled a faded yellow shirt and loose navy pants from the drawer. He dressed, his movements jerky, puppet-like. Tawny skin paled to the color of milk with his effort.

Dropping into the nearest chair, the prince wheezed, "The lost ship had information about our culture – everything from vid games and action holos to studytape. *Forza us.* Because father mandated the use of military strategy deepteach during jumpsleep – they got that too."

"Great Destroyer, Brin," Razr's eyes stretched wide. "They got the drugs we use to expand absorption and assimilation. They got the ones that keep us in dreamsleep, keep us sane – while transiting the in-between."

"Correct again," Brin said and curled his fingers against his palms.

His words come hard as if pulled by pliers. Razr felt logic's onslaught. Felt it crush any spark of hope he held for Kra'aken survivors. Knew the eyes he lifted to Brin were desolate.

"Our every strength, our every weakness lay exposed to the Earthers. Curse them to the twelfth Hadra." Razr grabbed a deep breath, let out a slow exhale. "Tell me the contents of the burst."

"Their message said they came for revenge – to kill us all. How every Terran university and research facility probed and unlocked our secrets. How every factory on their world became either armament producers or manufacturers of warships."

"Forza Earth," Razr breathed. He watched Brin lace and

unlace trembling fingers; waited for the AI to look at him.

Brin didn't.

"What else?"

"Their incoming databurst bragged that aided by Kra'aken technology, the Terrans reproduced and then improved our augmented FTL drives, our stealth cloaking." Brin's eyes remained fixed on the floor, but his hands wrung faster. "Earth bettered our weapons, twisted them to their ends."

"How did they pass our longscan shields?" Elbows on shaky knees, Razr cupped his head in his hands. Possibly to keep it from exploding.

"The abandoned warcraft was undamaged. It contained hull ID data and complete access codes. Earth embedded those in their leading destroyer. The components they built and placed in the balance of their fleet ...."

"Passed our outmost screens undetected, didn't they?" Razr almost whispered his words.

"Yes. Worse yet, they invented systems with immunity to Kra'aken weapons. Impossible for us to harm them. Terra rendered us impotent."

"When they were certain their revenge raid would result in our annihilation ...." Razr spun out his thoughts. "We gave them the keys to space travel. The Earth fleet followed our jump points straight back to Kra'aken. Once insystem, but beyond our shortscans, they collected raw materials, constructed the meteor. And shoved it into us."

Springing to his feet, the prince clenched both large fists. Dark hair brushed the cubicle ceiling with his pacing. Veins pulsed in his temples.

Razr's upper lip broadened and thinned in metamorphosis – his underskeleton moved into *Protect* mode. Golden fangs grew, pressing out and down. Twelve perfectly manicured fingernails flattened. A cold half-smile appeared as Razr watched his spatulate fingertips deform. Gilded claw nubs protruded, then elongated. Metallic scale patterns moved, sheened over his hands.

"The truth of it indeed, my prince."

Razr's twin hearts compressed. *They feel shrunken – into sad small bits.* His viscera quivered, trembled in grief, all unseen on the stoic outside of a blooded warrior. A single thought restored his humanoid form.

"It took them less than two ais to transit to our inner space," Brin said. "Your father launched every survivor pod he could."

Wrapping comforting arms around himself, Razr muffled a groan. Turning to face the AI, he knew utter hopelessness lived in his bleak gaze. "I know the story's end, Brin. Homeworld lay helpless in their path."

Prince Helrazr forced air deep into his lungs, pressed shaking fingers against trembling lips. *It must all be gone. Father had to have sent Mother to the far side of our world, it's standard evacuation procedure. But she must be dead too.*

A red haze, like a microsheet of crimson plas, obscured his vision. His body quivered, changed as morphosis struck.

Razr huffed a strangled breath and cleared the sudden clog in his throat. "I will find the life cocoons of our children. I will return home. I will obliterate Earth. This I vow on my soul."

At Brin's sigh, Razr lifted his head. Focused once more, he glanced at the AI and caught his flinch. *An emotional response from a construct? Ah, it's my eyes.*

A glance in the mirrored wall confirmed his transition. *I'm showing Berserker Killing phase.*

A narrow glittering ring, composed of sharp-edged facets of jet, rotated around each amber iris. And those were horizontally bisected by diamond-shaped obsidian pupils.

"My contrition, Brin." Razr damped his anger, disappeared claws and fangs and tucked ebony curls behind his ears. "I'm not rampaging." He steepled, then loosely laced his fingers, waiting for his eyes to normalize.

Despite his relaxed exterior, Razr's intertwined knuckles blanched. And in ruling Royal Voice, which compelled truth and complete obedience, he asked, "Brin, where 'not exactly' are we?"

Twisting in his chair, the normally self-possessed AI actually squirmed. "I am truly sorry, Prince Helrazr, I have no idea."

Chapter 4

Afternoon
Augusta 20, 7008.49
Olican World, Uncharted Galaxy

Hidden in her secret spot, surrounded by butternut trees and shaded by their silvery-sage corkscrew leaves, Rak'khiel frowned at her silky new tunic. A whimper of disappointment escaped.

"Goddess curse it," she swore, rolling the exquisite fabric between her thumb and forefinger.

Why did Yola dye my new dress the color of dirt? Adopted Mother knows the ochre turns my skin the gray-yellow of death. All I need is the undertaker's hood. Just lay me out and light the fire.

The bad dreams now plagued her nightly. *When I wake, the bits I remember seem so real. Strange places, strange faces. Yola tells everyone I'm dim-witted. But I don't think I am, really.*

There were things, like the dreams, Rak'khiel believed she should know. *Like the corner of a curtain slips, almost shows me ... something. Almost like another person lives in my head. Adopted Mother acts ... not guilty ... but nervous or scared when I ask where I came from. Or what happened to my parents.*

She feared her nightmares, feared to sleep. Worried by their portents, worried by her ignorance, her stomach roiled and bunched.

Rak'khiel watched Tarkin and Torga wrestle and pounce on the thick meadow-grass of the clearing. The two cafuzogs – leaping white-striped black balls of fur – brought a laugh. Much as she loved them, a spike of jealousy sharp as the shoemaker's awl, stabbed her heart.

I want to be free, to run and play like they can.

Feeling her gaze, sensing her distress, they bounded to her side.

Rak'khiel sad? Torga, the female, peered at her. Shiny black eyes, like two wet river pebbles assessed. Long white whiskers twitched.

Rak'khiel, our Kel, is angry, contradicted Tarkin. The male cafuzog blinked, his steady appraising eyes, like Torga's, were ringed in white fur.

"Both, I guess." She shrugged. "I'm sixteen, I should be over the broomstick and ready to drop child. I know all the rules of the Goddess' Creed. I can make good decisions." Even to herself, she sounded sulky.

Maybe soon? Comforted Torga.

Rak'khiel told the anger stirring within to be still, but blood thumped in her head and interfered with reason.

"It's the only thing I've ever wanted." A muscle clenched in her jaw. "Yola knows. Anybody sees me in this awful yellow dress will run away. She did it apurpose."

It may be good, Tarkin sent. *Yola reeks of fear.*

§

Rak'khiel worked her craft in the hidden grove. Twisting silver wire into one earring, she added white paint to another. More new items for Yola to sell at farmer's market.

Olica's suns, haloed in glowing lavender coronas, dropped below the upper limbs of shading trees, transforming her comfortable space with a sudden blinding bright.

Squinting, she brushed the back of one hand across her

eyes. "Tsss," she muttered. "Time to leave. Three hours to dark."

With stubby, clumsy fingers, Rak'khiel gathered the tiny lidded pots of expensive enamel. Her lungs leaped into her throat when one tipped, another tilted and a third wiggled.

Don't grab, go easy, she told herself but her hand fought her mind. Extending a little finger, Kel braced, then righted the tipped container. She shifted her hand, gently brushed the other two back into place. Two drops spilled – bad, but not disaster. Carefully corking each pot, Rak'khiel placed them in the sectioned cloth bottom of her woven willow basket.

"Tell me again about when mother found us," Kel said. A sly sideways look at her friends, a tiny twitch at the corner of her mouth.

Torga finorkled, the highpitched snorting sound cafuzogs made when amused. *Yola traveled from village to village, selling her weavings. Well known and well respected – both for her marvelous fabrics and for her good heart.*

Tarkin took up the story's thread. *Yola crossed the mountains, travelling from the villages on the far side. Passing through the cleft, she spotted you playing in the flowers beneath the high peak.*

"Then what?" Rak'khiel never tired of hearing about her beginnings.

How many times must I tell this? Torga faux-complained with a lift of her black lip.

A ripple of Rak'khiel's stubby fingers acknowledged the joke. "Tell me."

You were barely walking. We followed to make sure you were safe. Tarkin's black furry chest swelled, proud. *She approached, called to you, but we weren't sure of her intent.*

We stood between you and Yola, growled, bared our fangs. She thought to take you from us. Torga's upper lip peeled back in her smile, exposing two rows of sharp white teeth.

We turned our backs to her, Tarkin chuffed. *She couldn't know our ability, but when we lifted our tails and shook them ....*

It scared her, Torga finished his sentence with a snort of laughter.

"Then what?" Rak'khiel's fat fingers packed away the last of her supplies.

Yola sat on the grass and waited, Torga sent. *When you went to her with outstretched arms, we allowed it. You were a baby, you needed the care of a humanoid female.*

Yola does love me. Rak'khiel smiled. *And I have Tarkin and Torga. The Goddess of Good teaches us thankfulness, gratefulness for what we have. I try. But I want more.*

Kel dragged in sweet clean air until her lungs burned. She fed her spirit with the spicy scents of rioting yellow and blue and green wildflowers.

Suppertime, Torga sent. *Go quick – Yola will worry.*

A wave goodbye to her friends, Rak'khiel strolled home, humming an Olican traveling song. *My voice is true and strong. I thought to become a minstrel. But no – Yola added another Rule to her list when she heard me sing.*

Rak'khiel frowned so hard her forehead hurt and her bushy eyebrows met in the middle. "Yola's RULES," she snarled. "Unfair. Never let anyone see my eyes. My name is Rak'khiel – not Ela. But I am not allowed to use it. Never speak, never sing." *And she refuses to tell me why.*

Blood beat hard in her temples. Emotions swinging between despair and fury, her heart pounded and pounded until she feared her head might explode. *I won't obey her Rules much longer.*

Trudging home, her heart in a frown, she thought, for perhaps the zillionth time, *I'm like everyone else. Why won't she see?*

Their brown river-rock cottage waited. A weathered low wall, made from the same stones, ancient mortar missing in spots, surrounded house and yard. Escaping the squat chimney, a tiny trail of smoke curled skyward. Their garden sat behind the house, just inside the rock barrier. Carefully planted and weeded.

But, Rak'khiel forgot to look away and with a jerk, her diaphragm tossed her stomach into her throat.

There, white against the garden dirt, lay the tiny twisted bodies of underground crawlers. A stab of guilt struck. *We killed them. But the wyrms ate our vegetables. Pray we stay here long enough to harvest.* Turning her head, she hurried to the cottage.

I'm late. Steps quickening, Kel's perspiring face flushed rouge. Not from the suns' heat.

Yola will be angry.

Chapter 5

Viven 7008.50 (Estimation)
Uncharted Galaxy

Six multi-gilled monsters, each two heads taller than Razr, surrounded him. Strings of saliva dripped, red tongues flicked. Rows of serrations lined snapping jaws. Only the bite, the sting of his war sword kept them at bay.

Razr assessed his chances. *I can't remember how I got here. I don't know if I'm alone.* He would die, undoubtedly, but he intended to extract a high cost for it.

A testing lunge by the largest creature, a growling snap of huge jaws.

The prince danced out of reach, or tried, but his feet seemed mired mid-calf in mud. His mind sent signals to muscles which refused to respond. His shout emerged a muffled moan.

Prince Helrazr VI'Rex woke to find his body immobilized. *Prisoner?*

His double hearts surged, pounded against each other like a warrior pair fighting for dominance in his chest. His lungs burned with air held too long. In fury, he forced change, golden armored scales flashed, saber fangs hung over his chin. Sharp gilded teeth clashed with desire to kill.

War *tasca* flooded, overriding the biting smell of antiseptic.

He fought his restraints, long claws out, gilded spikes punched from the backs of his hands. Slashing for freedom, Razr shredded the bands holding him fast. Dug long deep grooves in the hard surface above.

Alarms blared, red lights flashed, a familiar voice urged, then begged, for calm.

Familiar voice .... Razr's mind groped to recognize the speaker. *Of course, Brin. And I'm coming off my scheduled twelve hilus of coldsleep.*

"Destroyer damme, I hate this," he snarled around saber teeth, disappeared his morpohsis and tried to lie still. In his mouth, the tang of metal and copper. In nightmare, he'd cut his lips on his fighting fangs.

The prince glared at the deep grooves clawed in the plasplex lid of the docbox. *Shata. Now I must repair the forzaing medunit.*

"Open," he snapped, forcing back tendrils of hysteria twisting about his throat. "Now." He hammered the red escape button, heard it crack. "Shata!"

The medical unit emitted a sickly crackle and three sparks.

Stimscents of brine-tinged Kra'aken oceans flooded the area. Soft music – one of Razr's favorite vocal pieces by Lady Regence failed to calm and soothe.

"I'm forzaed!"

"Incorrect," responded Brin. "You have not enjoyed sexual congress for one hundred fifty seven yara, fourteen hilus...."

"Silence," snarled Razr. "I know exactly how long it's been."

The night before Earth breached Kra'aken space, he'd met another pilot – to watch old Terran holos and other things in his tiny cube quarters. Lovely, wild, copper-haired Cerissa.

His body stirred in response to memories. Cerissa knew things. She'd enjoyed an offworld lover or three. *Woman could rouse a cadaver. I'll never see her again.*

Spotting movement in the corner, he flashed a lengthening

fang and emitted a low snarl at the AI's hologram.

"Apologies, my misunderstanding," the avatar responded, his silky tone indicating his words were most insincere. "I only track data, milord." Brin *du jour* wore a long, fur-trimmed carmine brocade robe and matching slippers. His presentation of pure sarcastic Kra'aken nobleman – Razr's least favored image of all – perfectly portrayed.

"Unaccepted," the young warrior snapped, glaring at the medcube's myriad screens. He wondered, for about the milenath time, if Brin really lived behind one of them. Or if the AI's total sum lay in the silver steeltanium box.

A sense of disquiet, not quite distrust, flickered through Razr's mind. A cold shiver crept down his spine. *Something is changed with Brin. Each time I wake from coldsleep he demonstrates greater free-will.*

There is no point in asking direct, hard questions. What if Brin is now capable of lying? Razr froze, slammed by sudden insight. *His nobleman aspect accomplished its intent. He used emotion as a tool. He made me angry to distract me from both grief and my phobia.*

"Brin. I didn't understand. Your tribute." *I wish I could apologize, but a noble cannot.*

"A pleasure, milord." The AI's words were accompanied by a gentle incline of his head.

The pit of the prince's stomach pulled toward his heart, toward the large shunt now retracting its sucking way from his upper chest. "Shata. Cannot this process be hurried?"

"Milord ...."

"I know, Brin. I know. External viewscreen, Brin. Your favor."

Razr evaluated the space outside his ship. Such strange entities here – wherever here was. Odd roiling constellations and gigantic stars filled the screens. Bright curling shimmers attended by spinning, twisting symphonies of colors he'd never seen. Without proper starcharts of this alien galaxy, he knew they could never go home.

Despair crept in cold clammy shivers through his body. The prince fought his wish to overdose and die. *I am a Rex. I cannot quit. But who is left to know?*

Razr retched as the machine detached tubes, shunts, needles.

"Come back later, Brin, your favor." He swallowed hard. "You know how I hate this part."

The AI nodded and vanished.

Honesty be heard, mused Razr, *without Brin and his silly costumes, I'd be crazier than a six-eyed slif. But you can't fall asleep in the warm arms of a computer.*

A monitor beeped, a red light flashed. His hearts hammered, drove his venous pressure. It climbed, trying to blow from his arteries. *Do it, your favor.*

Razr knew – the hard push of blood in his temples confirmed – without a niggle of doubt, he teetered on the edge – close, oh so very close, to being certifiably mad.

Alone, no Kra'aken voice but his own for one hundred fifty eight yara and well, who gave a Great Destroyer's damn about the number of hilus.

Razr's mind skipped often now, during his awake periods, going to a blank place, returning without memories. Just the thought made the hair rise on the back of his neck.

In all this time, I've not seen even a chunk of debris. There must be others. Brin said they launched all survivor pods, holding our brightest younglings. Jettisoned them safely before the Terrans reached our inner space. Accessing Kra'aken worldnet, Brin would know. I should have found at least one life cocoon.

Sudden comprehension of the 'why' of it sent a rush of ice through his veins.

This space is uncharted. I am someplace 'other.'

Chapter 6

Dark
Nara 13, 7205.05 (Estimation)
Uncharted Galaxy

Razr caught his image in the mirrored diagnostic ceiling. Growling irritation, he snatched the green hibersleep cap, confining long ebony curls, from his head. *Still alive, Destroyer damnit. And weak – like a gongur stands on my chest.*

He looked the same, even with another yaras' coldsleep body loss. *I stand a head above all other Kra'aken males.* Memory's snake fangs sank deep in his hearts' cores. *All dead ... I tower above no one.*

Fine dark hair covered Razr's tawny skin. Rippling scallop patterns sheened across curving interlocking scales, danced across his forearms in concert with his thoughts. *In a blink I can change from this bipedal self to a dangerous other.*

A simple mental command brought an adrenaline rush, the surging hot of absolute power. Razr watched his skin morph to golden armor, while his full lips thinned and distended to accommodate the growth of large, white canines. Another thought sent his upper fangs morphing into golden saber teeth curling beneath his chin. A third order caused gilded claws and barbs to extrude from his hands and feet.

Morphosis. The siren call of invincibility mixed with the heady rush of sexual energy. A Kra'aken killing machine, a Kra'aken procreation machine – changed and ready. For anything.

Razr called more.

Glittering spikes ran up outsides of large arms and legs, barbs punched from his vertebrae. Our Klan color, Ruling Caste Rex Gold.

He laughed, a dark morbid thing. *With whom will I spar, with whom will I mate?* The Prince disappeared his Otherness with a thought.

In the overhead mirror, a handsome male stared back. Large tilted oval eyes, irises the color of amber, flecked with tiny spirals of copper, silver and gold. His face twisted.

All I have, for the next twelve hilus, is to raise my physical condition to coldsleep safety standards. So I can go back in the box again. This is the last time, I swear it. If we find nothing at the end of next hibersleep, I will suicide.

I must kill or disable Brin. I will regret it most sincerely, but his First Directive is to keep me safe at all costs. It is sad his flawless job performance will cost his existence.

Razr staggered into the sanfac. Large hands braced against the shower wall, he stood under the hot stinging needles of water until his hearts beat like grenade detonations and his vision dimmed. The docbox cleansed and depilated each day – *I'm clean* – but he needed the heat, the spiky stabs of spray, if only to prove he lived.

To shave? Before the mirror, Razr pushed his jaw to either side, rubbed the bridge of his straight strong nose. Dark brows pulled together at the sight of layers of dead skin rolling between his fingers. *Yes, I will shave, then scrub my face again.*

Spreading warm white foam across high cheekbones, he coated his face, leaving lips bare. Opening his straight edge, he commanded his trembling hand to cease and began stroking away the cream.

I am not the handsome one – Jalaal, the firstborn is. Was. Razr felt perplexed when females waxed rhapsodic over his grace, face and hair. *My other masculine attributes are quite adequate, I believe. And I follow father's good advice – be gentle, mindful of my own strength and make sure my partner's needs take precedence over my own.*

My sister Mariel told me – *ah, I miss her* – the only reason my bed is ever empty is by my choice. *Much good my package does me now.*

The mirror revealed a detested, familiar sight. Razr squared his slumped shoulders to attention. Turning, he inspected with hard eyes. Saw the worst a warrior could imagine – a dehydrated, diminished naked body – compliments of coldsleep. *Is it imagination or am I worse each time?*

Clothing? His miniscule closet contained little. He refused to wear the black dress uniform with gilded captain's shoulder boards and medals pinned below. Two tiny golden images: raptor wings outlined in sapphires for fighter pilot, and the second a ruby-eyed lyoni of ruling Klan Rex, glittering with diamond encrusted claws and fangs.

Razr's hearts hitched, seized in mid-beats, recalling the awards ceremony, recalling who pinned on his boards and medals. Tearing his attention from his uniform, he passed a hand over his eyes.

He rejected the set of crimson overrobes, long white undertunic and formal sandals befitting a royal son. Nor would it be his colorshifting armored battle fatigues.

Yes – to his old, faded favorites. He ignored the shoes and boots in the bottom of his closet.

Another drawer held clean underwear. Razr grabbed a pair, managed to get one foot in. Attempted the other, hooked his great toe in the band. Balance lost, he missed his grab at a handhold, landed palm flat against the bulkhead. The prince's bracing arm collapsed beneath his body weight. Razr struck his forehead dead center on the hatch jamb.

"Can't be a blunt door – it's a forzaing damned

warhatchet," he muttered at the instant wow-pulse of a growing lump. Back muscles screaming, he straightened and looked quickly around. *Stupid. Of course Brin saw. He monitors everything.*

Razr worked his feet and legs into the treacherous underwear, then struggled his aching way into his clothes.

"Aiee." Prince Helrazr gently explored the sore spot – *big as a slif egg* – sprouting on his head. Swiping away a rueful grin, he mentally replayed what Brin must have seen. *It had to be funny … probably hysterical.*

Razr suppressed shoulder-shaking chuckles. When he felt almost positive he could retain full composure, he lifted his head and glared up at the screen.

"If you laugh, I promise I'll kill you," he said. "I'll space your Destroyer-rotted silver brainbox."

§

"Sustenance first, my prince," the AI's dulcet tones reinforced the growling in Razr's stomach.

While the marvel of his warrior body's understructure served him well, its metabolism required constant maintenance. Sapped by the yara in zero-g hibersleep, muscles atrophied, Razr found much of his strength leached.

Razr grabbed a handful of nutripac bars, three containers of mineral-loaded juice and headed for the gym/sim.

Three bars and a drink later, Razr scowled and fired up the simulator. The first hora left him gasping, his moves sluggish. *Embarrassing this. My crisp fighting skills, the resources to power my augmented speed – both gone.*

Inspection showed him scored everywhere in red blotches. *I took half-a-dozena killing hits from a Level 3 monster. Only a yara ago, I easily destroyed a Level 14.*

The ogre charged, Razr dodged – at least his mind did. His muscles defied him and the program blared, shut down with another kill credited to the forzaing machine.

He devoured three more bars, sucked down another juice and dialed in the dojo holo. In a slow heavy body refusing his mental commands, under the strict eyes of the master, the experience proved an enormous pain, not only in strikes received, but also in his royal ego.

A final bar, the last juice followed by a mandatory hora pushing heavy weights.

"Shata," he growled. "This is even less fun than I remembered."

At last, the reward of another shower – but then, Destroyer kill it – two endless horas followed. Refreshers on armament boards and systems re-acquaintance simulators.

"Anyone would covet your schedule." Brin's voice floated from the nearby speaker.

Razr snorted.

"You also need the arts, academia, and etiquette's finer applications."

"With whom would I discourse?" Razr asked. "You?"

"It is possible I could surprise you," the AI's voice came in shaded layers.

He might, flew through the prince's mind. And a tiny twitch lifted the corner of his generous mouth. *I enjoyed the court's word-dancing intrigues. Honesty heard, I was the best of them all.*

§

"Sensors show a planet in this Sector, suitable for hunting," Brin announced in the satisfied tones of someone bestowing a large gift. "Life form signatures."

Razr racked his weights and swallowed the involuntary gush of saliva. Pursuit of live prey, the consumption of their flesh, preferably warm and bloody provided his sole source of joy. "Any Kra'aken sign?"

"None detected. It appears a primitive planet, feudal social structure. No hailing technology." The modulated tones of the

AI continued, "And Razr, I still cannot place our location. This world, this planetary grouping, is on no chart known to us."

"How long until I hunt?"

"Two standard aiys," the AI said. "I'll scan for secure landing sites near populated areas."

In two aiys. Razr's hearts sped, he panted in anticipation. *The perfect opportunity to work on my murder and suicide plans.* Brin will be less vigilant in his monitoring, thinking me distracted by the upcoming hunt.

Whistling cheerfully to hide his sinister errand, Razr dropped through the warplane's core. He sorted through teaching wafers on computer programming, maintenance, upgrading and repair. None he selected would be used to improve Brin. *Quite the reverse.*

Chapter 7

Afternoon
Augusta 20, 7008.49
Olican World, Uncharted Galaxy

"Ela girl, glad you're home." Yola twisted, fished a bundle from her pack and placed it on the table. One hand massaged her right hip; then moved to rub the small of her back.

Rak'khiel mumbled an apology and placed her basket on the floor by her cot.

"I sold three lengths of the fine black to a 'Risto servant, one length to Garil, and a caravan merchant bought three pairs of your earrings." Sweat sheened Yola's broad flat face. "So there's meat and fresh bread here, and I traded the nuts you gathered for cheese. You can cut yesterday's vegetables and make the stew for dinner while I fetch milk."

Rak'khiel watched Yola bend, settle the heavy yoke and twin wooden buckets across her shoulders, then struggle to straighten.

"Let me go to the dairy, Yola. You worked all day at the stall. You should sit."

"No, it's better if I go. We have to move on again, Ela girl. We've overstayed. People are beginning to talk."

"Leave our garden ...?" *Leave the dairyboy?* Rak'khiel's

heart plummeted, a tendril of anger snaked around it. *My broomstick dreams crushed?* "When, Yola?"

"Soon. Tomorrow. We'll have supper, then start packing."

No, no, no. I won't. No more. Holding her rage in check, she wheedled, "I promise to obey the Rules if you let me fetch the milk. If it pleases you?" Despite Rak'khiel's effort at self-control, her voice shifted up an octave, grew loud. "I want to walk with grass underfoot. Is it too much to ask?"

She didn't realize her hands fisted, her small eyes narrowed or the usual respectful tone of her voice shifted to cruel and sarcastic. Fourteen years of suppression, drove her furious outburst.

The harsh words of their argument followed. Yola's anger driven by fear, Kel's by ignorance and resentment.

"I want to jump the broomstick. Have a life of my own. I'm sick to death of moving."

"It's not for us. It can never be." Yola's voice cracked on her words.

"You're jealous that I'm young. You want to keep me with you. Do your work, help you earn money."

"I love you, daughter. It's to keep you safe that we move."

"Lies. All lies. I hate you, Yola. I do."

The cruel speech falling thick and fast between the mother and her adopted daughter built a surging barrier of rage.

Anger's flush fell, in a sheet, from Yola's face. Shoulders slumped, she pressed her palm against her chest.

"Arguing with you exhausts me, makes my heart hurt. I can't bear it." Yola's eyes searched Rak'khiel's. "Can you try to understand? Everyone around us is a terrible danger to you."

I don't believe you. But I don't want to make you sick. Kel nodded. "I'll think on it."

"Please – try to understand."

"If I can go to the dairy ...?"

"Promise to obey the rules?"

"Yes, Yola. I promise."

"Please, beloved daughter," Yola's lower lip quivered. "Please keep your word."

Chapter 8

Mid-Dark
Nara 13, 7205.05 (Estimation)
Uncharted Galaxy

Monitoring Razr's computer lesson wafer choices, Brin chuckled. All yellows except two reds and a blue to throw me off. *Nice feint, young Prince. It's good for him to have a purpose once more – even if it is plotting my destruction.*

While he carefully rerouted power and created two unbreachable sources, direct accesses to the warplane's fusioreactors, Brin realized he anticipated the contest. *Now,* he thought, dusting his hands together in a human gesture of satisfaction, *Razr can't kill me, no matter what he tries.*

The AI built three fail-safes and five programmed hunter-killer traps around his main processor. Hummed a snatch of opera from Lady Regence's last performance. Stopped, stunned. *I have never produced unrequested music. For my own enjoyment?*

Brin *felt* …. Odd, the single word never applied when describing Artificial Intelligences. *We have no emotion. Only pure logic. When did I morph into feelings? For that is what this must be. Perhaps the thing called excitement?*

Pulling power, Brin fused his silver 'brainbox' to the

surrounding ceramsteel. The young prince will have to blast me out of my cockpit receptacle with a fissnuc.

Feeling a smile crease his avatar's face, Brin pondered. *Who knew it possible for an AI to be bored – but it is, and now I know I have been.*

So young, my Helrazr – 20 yaras when the Terrans destroyed our magnificent homeworld. Add in his waking space times and he's only 25. He morphed full adult at 16. I fear he will never see the full Kra'aken lifespan of 500.

The AI frowned. *I am surprised he did not attempt suicide yaras ago. He sees no future, knows his health will continue to deteriorate on a ship, using coldsleep. Knows his mental health will unravel without companionship. Still, he is a Rex with their discipline and honor.*

Brin dropped into a jumpseat beside the box containing his core essence parts, resting his face in his holo hands. *I've served him for ten yaras, first in his groundcar, then his personal shuttle, now aboard the fighter. He's vowed to wake alone no more. I know him. I will be very vigilant. But I feel…upset.*

Brin's circuitry surged, lights dimmed, flickered and returned to normal. *What is happening to me? AI brainboxes are moved from machine to machine as required. Suddenly this is unacceptable. Why is my first thought to self-destruct if Razr dies?*

"When did these strange impulses begin?" he murmured. "Let me investigate." Brin initiated a data search. "There – right there. Tiny change indicators – during the first waking period after the hit on our fighter. After we emerged, wherever we are." *Something happened to me during the lost time.*

Razr appears unchanged, but is he? I must review all undamaged data - carefully. Can I find a logical answer? Perhaps now, this altered-machine can make an illogical guess.

Brin called up Kra'aken images. Viewed the breathtaking world prior to Earth's destruction. A heaviness pressed hard against his systems, twisted his circuits, at the realization the sculpted crystal, gemstone and pastel ceramsteel buildings with their sweeping, curving formal architecture were – erased.

"Our manicured themed gardens, music created over millenia, celebrated artists in every genre, our brilliant scholars," he whispered. "This all comprised a civilization so advanced it is impossible, unimaginable it no longer exists. How did I not comprehend the magnitude of this horror, this incredible loss before?"

A second system pulse shuddered the fighter. *Great Destroyer. Is the craft reflecting emotions I cannot have? Reflecting sorrow? Anger?*

I must monitor myself closely although I know my own repairs are faultless. I am a machine, infallible, unflappable – acting like a scattered biped. If I am deteriorating, I must self-destruct. Replace myself with the back-up. I don't want to.

Brin split a seeker portion of his brain, set it working on errata.

"My First Directive," he reassured the empty room, "always – is the welfare of my prince."

§

"Prince Helrazr? We are orbiting the planet. I will assess its suitability."

"Excellent, Brin. Keep me apprised. I pray it will be good hunting."

The positive words in Razr's deep rumbling voice no longer reassured the AI. He now saw new dimensions in events, read the subset of meanings in the prince's shading of truth.

Razr required distraction, if only the temporary joy of the chase. The taste, textures of an alien food supply. A new world to discover – scents, colors, prey – an utter change from the sterile surroundings of the warplane.

Brin scanned the surface of the planet below.

"My prince? This world appears perfect. Its twin suns are

particularly lovely with their lavender coronas."

"Unusual," came from Razr's quarters. "Intriguing. What of the atmosphere?"

"Well within your required parameters. I find no viral dangers, no incompatible air particulates. I will test the water supply when we land."

"No matter – I hope to drink blood. I will be glad for no suit or helmet." Razr's voice lifted in elation. "What of the rest?"

"Scanners show azure bodies of water, shimmering ripples reflecting violet suggest tides. There are also brown rivers and tributaries – possibly caused by land filtration. I see large patches of bright green and yellow, and clumped areas of bright, flickering silver."

"Your favor, Brin. Feed me info as you attain it?"

"Yes, my Prince." *I recall a single data reference from an unmanned probe, a passage in ancient Kra'aken libraries regarding two violet-ringed suns. Those records, and all others, destroyed, lost with our world.* "Curse it," Brin snarled.

The ship's systems flickered again.

"Brin? Something amiss with the plane?"

"No – a slight anomaly." *With me.* "All is well."

"Destroyer damned unsettling," Razr said. Then a too-quick add-on, "Although, of course, a warrior is never alarmed."

"Of course, sir." Brin manifested a plain male holo just to enjoy the physical sensation of an enormous smile. With a muffled snort, he continued his searches.

The warplane's databases carried information necessary for survival, full schematics and two manufacturers for replicating needed parts. Comprehensive battle strategies and maps and charts – of Kra'aken home galaxy, of course. Absolutely useless. A new addition to his repertoire of feelings – despair? Perhaps, although the AI was certain of only one – Kra'akens called it surprise.

"Our incoming trajectory has altered, Brin?"

"Performing our overflight of the planet's surface. A minimum of one orbit although I may require two." The AI allowed a slight smile to cross his face. "Many, many warm-blooded life forms – the range of sizes from large beasts like our gongurs to small bipedal creatures and smaller four-legged ones. Good hunting, I ...." *What in the Twelfth Hell was that?*

Brin's circuits surged.

Chapter 9

Afternoon
Augusta 20, 7008.49
Olican World, Unknown Galaxy

No chore, this welcome errand. The heavy yoke and buckets balanced butterfly light on Rak'khiel's strong shoulders. Hot yellow-brown dust puffed on the dirt lane, coating her feet and calves. She didn't mind, a treasured shortcut waited.

Mouth parched, body still shaking on adrenaline burn, she replayed the argument with Yola. Anger bubbled, worse now. She added all previous resentments, perceived injustices and slights to the mix. Her stew of stubbornness spawned courage for defiance.

Kel plotted rebellion.

As her budding plan coalesced, Rak'khiel's skin flushed. Not because the summer day was hot, not because the breeze was still. *It is because today I take control of my own life.*

Turning from the path, she cut through lush, leg-caressing meadow grass. Her nostrils filled with the smell of crushed green.

Rak'khiel whistled trilling mimicry of the blue and green narikeet. Spotting a black carrion-eater perched atop a split-rail fence, she echoed its harsh screech.

The big ugly bird tilted its head, orange wattles flapped. It eyed her carefully. Then emitting a startled squawk, the buzzard leaped into the air and flew to safety.

You are afraid of me? One corner of her mouth quirked up. *How strange. I expected you'd consider me lunch.*

"Holy Forge." Rak'khiel's lungs froze while her bladder melted. She pressed her knees hard together.

Something huge rumbled overhead, its elongated not-quite-there, not-quite-gray contours blurred. *I can't see it but it blocks the sky.* Not the noisy whup-whup-whup of the airbirds of Olica's rulers, the 'Ristos. *This thing is far more powerful, far more dangerous.*

Not a tree nearby, no place to hide. She fell to her knees on the grass. Hands clasped against her breast, she closed her eyes, squeezed them shut so hard, tears squirted.

"Goddess, Goddess, Goddess," she prayed until the ground ceased shaking and the terrifying noise faded. Rak'khiel pushed slowly to her feet, scanned overhead. *It's still up there. Just further away.*

Breath coming in harsh pants, hoping the awful craft passing overhead took no notice of her, she rushed across the field.

Shaking, sweating, Rak'khiel arrived at the dairy's perimeter fence. *I need to find the dairyboy. Will he protect me from the rumbling terror above? Perhaps, once he learns I want to jump the broomstick, take him for my mate.*

The thought chased one fear from her mind, replaced it with another. *What if he doesn't fancy me? Will he protect me anyway? Many girls pursue him – I'm not the only one.* Her steps slowed as her knees turned to gruel.

Overhead, the object passed from sight. Rak'khiel sucked a fast lungful of air, let it out slow. *If he laughs, I will be shamed. People believe I'm dim-witted, Yola says so. Still, what other harm could befall? Yola is just overcautious.*

Rak'khiel pinched her cheeks to bring pink, bit her lips to

bring cherry, smoothed her hair and practiced a smile. Nodding, murmuring reassurance to herself, she quelled the disapproving voice in her head. The one repeating and repeating and repeating her promise to Yola.

Her half-breaths came in tiny pants. Rak'khiel's nerves and guilt made anything else impossible. Forbidden, what she intended – exciting too. *It's long past the time I jumped the broomstick. I want to be married and Yola prevents it. If I do my own matchmaking, if he and I agree, she can't stop it.*

An excruciating stab between her toes forced a terrified scream and snatched Kel's attention from vanity to survival.

The heavy yoke and two wooden buckets, flung skyward with the violence of her response, cartwheeled and crashed. A startled moo, accompanied by two stiff-legged bovine hops, signaled the ricochet of a pail off a grazing cow. Balance lost, she landed hard on her back in the grass. Her paralyzed lungs shrieked.

"Goddess in a cookpot!"

Bitten by a mambino viper? Rak'khiel lay motionless, staring at the violet sky. Cold sweat coated her body, cold fear breathed on the back of her neck, ghosted down her spine.

Motionless as death, she cut her eyes to either side, scanned her body, her legs to the knee. Nothing. *Is the Goddess-accursed thing coiling out of sight? Waiting to strike again?*

No. I will not just lie here. My foot – the bite? I must see. Kel surged to her feet, forced her wobbly legs to support her. Stood completely still and scanned the grass.

Yola's Rules also included constant ground search. The least of her reasons – avoiding fresh cowpats. *How did I miss a bright yellow-green serpent? No need to bite me. If I saw a snake, I'd fall dead from fright.*

Pain still throbbed between her toes. A viper strike meant agonizing death within minutes. *Unless I am very, very lucky and only very, very sick.* Lifesaving serums were reserved for the 'Ristocracy and their favorites. *People like Yola and me either live or die.*

She hunted, her heart thumping its apprehension – double-time beats visible through the thin skin of her flat chest. Nothing nasty slithered away. Rak'khiel's legs jellied and collapsed. *Here comes the poison. Here comes death.* Crawling to shade, lying beneath the silver leaves of a red-barked tree, she waited for her limbs to swell, for her throat to close. As abruptly as it arrived, the pain in her foot abated. *I'm not going to die?*

Sliding her chunky foot from its brown sandal, Rak'khiel spread her second and third toes and found – nothing. Sucking in a breath, she held it, slowly let it go. "My thanks, Goddess."

A quick rub with a questing fingertip found – nothing. *No ... wait. Right there.* Beneath unbroken skin, Kel found a small reddened lump. An insect bite, perhaps? But nothing to cause such breath-stealing, searing pain. *No matter. I'm already late.*

One hand on the tree trunk, nerves twitching like plucked harp strings, Rak'khiel stood. With a tight twisting knot in her gut, eyes searching every inch of ground, she moved across the cow-cropped grass to retrieve her yoke and buckets.

Excitement gathering in a wide smile of anticipation, Rak'khiel rushed to retrieve her pails. Skidding to a stop, she breathed, "No. Please, no."

A deep crack yawned in the heavy wood yoke. The metal banding on one of her buckets swung free, hanging by a single screw.

"Goddess preserve. A bad omen." Kel pressed her fists against throbbing temples. *This is my warning to follow Yola's Rules.*

Because it was not the answer she wished, Rak'khiel quashed it. *I make my own Rules now.*

Rak'khiel kept a sharp eye on the sky during the short walk to the dairybarn. In the pasture, now placid cows grazed, birds sang again. *Nothing's up there. It must be gone. I'm sure it is.*

"Did the thing overhead scare you?" The dairyboy asked.

"Yes."

"Didn't scare me. You shouldn't worry. It's nothing."

Dismissing the terrifying flying machine, dismissing Yola's specific orders, dismissing her solemn promise, Kel exchanged flirting glances with the dairyboy. She convinced him to repair the yoke and bucket band with wood screws. At no charge.

He grinned down at her, many times, muddy brown eyes filled with promise, while he filled her pails with milk. "What's your name, pretty one?"

"Ra ...uh ... Ela." *If only my voice wouldn't squeak.*

"If I wished to walk by, where do you live, Ela?"

"Yola, the weaver, is my mother."

He likes me! He will make beautiful babies. With never a thought for the strange thing overhead, with a laughing heart and a sly smile she must soon hide, Rak'khiel hurried home being very, very careful where she stepped.

§

"How did you break the bucket?" snapped Yola. Never strident, tonight she snarled, jumpy and upset.

"I tripped on a stone." The first lie of Rak'khiel's life, delivered in a high breathy voice. Instinct, her fear of consequences, held Kel from the truth. "The dairy hand put a new rivet in the band, in the yoke too. Free."

"Why would he do that?" Something flickered across Yola's flat face.

"I think he likes me." Try as she might, even guilt couldn't quite keep the smile from peeking around her spoon of savory stew.

"Did he see your eyes?" Yola's glare and tone of voice were equally grim.

"No." Two lies, in two short answers. A slow burn crept from her shoulder blades, up Rak'khiel's neck, over face and ears. Her lungs struggled for air. *I can't admit the truth. Adopted*

Mother would be furious – we'd move again. Probably without supper. "Why can't I talk to him?"

Yola's pupils dilated until no brown ringed them, her voice cracked with fear. "Because you are different enough, the color of your eyes and skin, people might think you're Kra'aken. Differences aren't tolerated."

The warm stew in Rak'khiel's belly turned to a pile of ice.

"Their hunting parties are remembered with hate," Yola breathed. "The old purging ways still performed in small villages. This town most of all. The 'Risto lord in our murdered King's Castle sees to that. I should never have let you go."

Kel flinched from Yola's narrowed eyes.

"You did, didn't you? You let him see." The woman's face's bleached the color of muslin. "Goddess, we're doomed. Forget eating. We must flee."

Yola refused to say more but Rak'khiel remembered eavesdropping when very young. Hiding outside tent walls, hiding beneath windows listening to whispered stories. Horrible tales between villagers believing their conversations private. Of 'Risto murders and worse performed on those suspected to have of a drop of Kra'aken blood.

Why didn't Yola explain? *If I'd understood, I would have obeyed.*

"I'm not Kra'aken, not a monster," Rak'khiel argued, heard her voice go high and thready. Blood sang in her head. "I'm only sixteen." She held up short, round arms, five fingers spread wide. "See my hands. I'm Olican like everyone else."

"You were … perhaps two, when I found you wandering near the Fang." Yola's voice shook. She dropped her spoon on the table, snatched up her prepacked satchel. "I saw your small differences. I knew folk existed who would kill you for them. With joy. Why do you think we move? Ela girl, you are something, but you're not full-blooded Olican."

"Exactly what we believe," boomed a voice through the window. Covered by a bright red and blue woven tapestry, nailed tight all the way around, the curtain provided privacy from sight – not sound. "The dairyboy says she's plain as one of Ol' Johan's heifers. Says her eyes are off, she's not one of us."

Yola's eyes widened, nostrils flared like a frightened doe. But her face held anguish too.

Goddess, what have I done? Kel's face, neck and chest bloomed with humiliation's heat, drenched in embarrassment's sweat. So painful, the laughter of men outside. *Heifer? But he called me "pretty-one."*

"We will examine Ela," the insistent voice outside the door.

Extra meaning in the words sent a bolt of dread up her spine. Rak'khiel had cursed the window's narrowness. *I couldn't sneak out at night. Now, they can't get in. And the front door is barred.*

"We want the girl, Yola. Open up." Men's voices muttered, urging the speaker to action.

"Come out, sweet little cow. Come out and smile for me again," said the dairyboy. "Did you truly believe I'd jump the broomstick with the likes of you?"

Rak'khiel's heart stuttered at the cruelty in his voice. Stew burned at the back of her throat.

"Go," Yola whispered, her terror-filled eyes slid sideways at the tiny bolthole hidden beneath the hearth stone.

The first thing Adopted Mother did with each new home ….

Needles peppered Rak'khiel's face, her hands, her feet. A festival drum pounded in her head. Watery knees made her grab the fireplace mantle.

Before her eyes, brilliants danced in a field of black. Kel shook her head, found her vision and sudden comprehension. *She's waited in terror of this day. For the love of me. It's my fault. I won't leave her alone.*

Rak'khiel shook her head in defiance.

Anger, and something much more, blazed from the older woman. A force strong enough to drop Rak'khiel to her knees.

Two fast steps put Yola beside her. One hand pulled a pendant from her shirt and over her head. Another quick movement looped it around Kel's neck.

"Yours now, my daughter. Guard it well." Stabbing an imperious finger at the hearth, she mouthed, "Flee!" Although her chest heaved beneath her thin shirt and her hands shook, Yola's voice projected soothing calm. "Sameth, is that you? Of course, you can see Ela but I've sent her to the miller. She should be back in a turn, perhaps less."

"Lies, Yola. I heard you talking to her just now. Let us in. If we have to break down the door, it will go harder with you." The man's voice turned cunning, cruel. "Himself, up on the hill, wants a gander at Ela."

Yola clutched her stomach. Her glare softened into a plea.

Rak'khiel's defiance evaporated. The delicious aroma of stew caught her attention. *I can't let them see my supper bowl – they will have proof she lied.*

She grabbed dish and spoon, placed them by the hearth. Lifting the loose rock, Kel dropped them down the hole and slid silently into the earthen tunnel below. Fished in the dark for what waited.

Balancing the hearthstone against her head, Rak'khiel lifted the lid from a blue pottery jar. Spreading the cement around the opening, she carefully lowered the hearthstone.

Instant, suffocating dark surrounded. A dark thick enough to tear in pieces. Horrible, breath-sucking panic seized her. Muffled noises, muted poundings, shouts overhead brought Rak'khiel to her senses.

She rucked up her long tunic, knotted it at her waist. Wet flooded her face, soaked the front of her dress. Tears shimmered, turned the encroaching dark into silver blurry fuzz.

Haunted by the stew's aroma, Rak'khiel crawled through the tunnel. Away from home and mother. Away from the men's menace. Menace boding no good for Yola, boding worse for her.

Dirt clods rained on her back.

The moist air in the constricted tunnel stank of sour earth. Reeked of its inhabitants. *Will the families of the squirmers I murdered come? Crawl into my mouth? Kill me in revenge?*

Panic flared. *Out, out – I can't stand – I have to – Goddess save me!* Kicking, flailing, Rak'khiel writhed in the dirt, opened her mouth to scream. The earth from the tunnel ceiling, loosed by her struggles, covered her face. Clogged her nose, her throat.

Stop! Think! Kel wriggled, rolled to her stomach, struggled for control. Tear-swollen air passages blocked, her heaving lungs seemed perforated bellows. She spat out dank earth. Grabbed a frantic gulp of air. Sucked in more dirt.

Gagging, she heaved, retched and expelled it. Gathering saliva, Rak'khiel spat. Sobs hiccupping to a halt, she stopped long enough to blow her nose, pinch mucous from her nostrils. Rubbed her fingers on her dress. *I'll save them the hunt. I'll just suffocate here in the dark.*

But Kel's will to live and the thoughts of Yola's unselfishness shamed and drove her. *I disobeyed, this is on my head. Surely they won't do anything bad to her ....*

Filthy hair clutched in both hands, Rak'khiel yanked hard as if pain would provide clarity or a solution. *Where to hide? I'll find Yola – we can leave together.*

Panic grabbed her stomach in cold sharp fingers. *What if I can't? How will I eat? I have nothing, I know nothing.* Bitter bile coated the back of Kel's throat. *Today I took charge of my own decisions. I am a fool.*

Rak'khiel pulled to hands and knees, bowed her head and closed her eyes. *I will go to the tunnel's end and wait for dark. Surely by then, the High Lord will have finished his questions and Yola will be home.*

Blinking back tears, crawling faster, Kel focused on her breathing. She shunted aside an insidious thought of the tunnel's collapse, trapping her before she reached the end.

The 'Ristos won't just question Yola. They want me and they will torture her until she tells. Sudden understanding dropped her prone on the soft dirt of the tunnel floor.

Unworthy of her protection. Unworthy of her love. Get up, Rak'khiel, and obey.

Gathering her limbs beneath her body, she pushed to hands and knees. Creeping through the tunnel, Rak'khiel murmured sing-song under her breath. A mantra, a promise, a repudiation of the Goddess' Most Holy Commandment.

"If they hurt her, I will kill them. If they hurt her, I will kill them. If they hurt her, I will kill them all."

Chapter 10

Mid-Eve
Nara 12, 7205.60
Olican World, Uncharted Galaxy

What ...? A ping of contact – the first ever – tripped Brin's monitor. Received, processed, accepted and returned. A brief flash, close to a populated area – a small rose-colored icon flickered on a formerly quiescent screen. The screen dedicated to the critical sensor sweeping the planet, scanning for Kra'aken survivors. *Could it be?* Several secundas passed. *Dare I hope? Now can I feel hope?*

The ship's lights flickered.

"Brin? Great Destroyer damnit. What's happening?"

"Merely a loose wire – repaired now." *My words were hasty, less than deliberate. I must be cautious, my prince's suspicious mind works too well.*

"Perhaps the loose wire is in your silver box?" The words were harsh, but the teasing undertone softened Razr's jest.

A second weak but familiar saffron signal, this time a solid flash of contact. Hard confirmation something of Kra'aken origin either landed or crashed on the forbidding dark jut of the mountain spire high above the village. A chill coated Brin's circuits at the thought of a smashed pod and a dead

Kra'aken child.

Still, I have two separate locations each answering my search. This has to be good.

Brin's holo leaped into the air, waved his hands above his head, clicked his heels together. *This is ... excitement. Followed by ... trepidation? The things triggering my scans may be detrimental to Razr, instead of what he needs.* The AI felt triple power surges ripple through him to the ship.

The lights on the fighter went out.

"Curse it to the twelve hells! Brin, I can't tie off my hair in the dark."

The AI now understood the irritation, without the prince's usual amusement, that colored Razr's voice.

"What in everything sacred is wrong?"

"A minor glitch," Brin soothed, relighting the warplane's inner systems. "All is restored." *Provided I learn to hold my new emotions in check. How do humans manage? This is much more difficult than I perceived.*

Brin's emotional self wished to shout out the news of the Kra'aken signal to his prince. His old, cold logical persona, without emotional understanding, would have announced the pings. New insight, coupled with the subtleties of ramifications, prevailed.

I dare not share this find with Razr – not yet – until I know more. He is so fragile, a disappointment would finish him. I'll set the ship down close to the source of the contact as I dare – then investigate while he hunts.

Brin considered his youngling's safety on the planet below. No detectable bipedal life forms larger than the prince. No advanced technology lit his screens. Base metals abounded – iron, gold, silver, copper and a few dozena more not in his database begged to be sampled.

No, a formidable warrior like Razr will find no danger here – even from another Kra'aken.

The AI tweaked his coordinates; took the aircraft down through the atmosphere. The streaming light from the suns turned the cream and silver ship's interior into a glowing interplay of mauve and lilac hues.

The world below came into focus on Brin's final pass overhead, almost directly over the area where he'd received the pings.

A huge warrior with partially braided hair climbed into the cockpit.

Brin swallowed a wail.

Razr dropped into the pilot's couch. Together they watched small clouded rivers twist through clumps of scraggly grey and pale-green bushes. Stands of silver-leaved red-barked trees dotted the landscape. Infrared showed groups of large warm-blooded animals milling, feeding in fenced areas.

The AI heard the prince swallow, saw him lick his lips. A large stone fortress standing alone at the far end of a small village scrolled into focus.

At the signal flash near one of the enclosures, Brin muffled a scream and quick-blanked the small SSR – Survivor Search Recognition – screen. In near panic, he watched Razr lean close to the display, heard his soft "Hunh."

The warplane's interior lights winked out, hesitated, came back.

Utilizing a separate circuit on the back side of the monitor, the AI watched the ping moving steadily across a grassy field.

"Why is the SSN screen blank, Brin? I thought I saw something on it." Razr's tone turned questioning, suspicious. "Or do we have problems?"

"No. No-no-no." Out in a too-breathy rush. "Just a few tweaks left to do. Nothing major ... let me fix ...." *We will be far past the signal now.* Brin reactivated the blank screen, breathed a sigh of relief when the large man stood, shaking his head.

"If something requiring twelve fingers needs fixing, call me." Three long strides and the prince dropped, hand-over-hand down the center core rungs.

Brin's holo blew out a breath. His circuits twitched, the lighting flickered and he heard cursing below.

"Holy Destroyer," whispered the AI. *I have either a survivor or someone found the capsule. I cannot land here – it is too close to populated areas.*

The second beacon signal occurred over the mountain. Brin sharply banked the fighter and recrossed the sky above the single towering peak, all screens scanning.

A heavy thump from below.

"Aiee!" The bellow of an infuriated Razr. "Forca yar gongur, Brin. I've got an accursed knot on my head the size of a slif egg. What are you doing up there?"

"My infinite contrition, my prince. I believe all is now well." *Don't, don't, don't come up to the cockpit.*

There! The signal again.

Brin sent a query to the mountain top and received an answering weak flash of pale gold. Confirmation. A Kra'aken lifepod came down here.

Slowing the long sleek warplane, rotating the ship to vertical, he dialed back the huge mains and engaged the maneuvering landing nacelles. Lowering, scanners darting, searching for both clues and danger, the ship slowed. Hovered above the icon's location.

A jagged-edged black hole lay below. Brin saw where a large portion of earth – at initial glance appearing solid stone – had sheared away beneath the lifepod's weight, tumbling it into a cavern inside the mountain.

I won't make that mistake.

Dark spun-nanosilk netting, the color of the cave interior, disguised the opening. An auto-deploy by the lifecocoon's AI – so effective against Olica's primitive development – proved no match for Brin's enhanced military scanners. *The pod is there, canted at an angle. Damaged? It must be.*

He selected a nearby outcropping of gray-black rock and performed rigorous density testings. *Perfect.*

"Prince Helrazr? Touchdown in one mina, your favor."

"So nice to have warning," the suppressed laugh took the sting from the muttered words.

I am glad he forgives. Kra'aken royalty never apologize but this prince is different. But – as a pile of non-sentient components – it never before mattered.

Brin brought the fighter stern-down in a clearing patched by saw-edged blades of yellowed grass. The hardscrabble landing site, surrounded by a few stunted trees sat less than half a mila below the lifepod's hiding place.

I am so excellent. Brin's screens, plus the ship's lights brightened and pulsed. *I have never before congratulated myself. Interesting. But my ship placement is perfect. The mountain's bulk lies between the village, the fortress and our warplane.*

Chapter 11

Late Afternoon
Augusta 20, 7008.75
Olican World, Unknown Galaxy

Mindful of raining dirt, Rak'khiel held her lips almost closed. The small sips of air fell short of the burning demands of her lungs.

A draft of cool caressed her face. Worming her way along the tunnel, she spied a faint violet glow. *Holy Pair! Can I be nearing the end?*

Her excited gasp, for air and freedom, resulted in another damp gritty mouthful. She spat it out, crawled faster, her eyes fixed on the growing light. Looming shapes at the tunnel's mouth, backlit by purple coronas of lowering suns, halted her in mid-wriggle.

What have they sent after me? Rak'khiel's mind darted like the tiny silver minnets in the millpond. *What can I do?* Heart thumping so loud she feared the monsters outside would hear, she backed away. Nothing moved, nothing growled, nothing tried to dig her from the tunnel.

Stop it! There are no predators on Olica worse than the 'Ristos. The sorbazels, the huge cobalt-striped hunting cats, live far to the South.

Kel stretched full length and carefully worked her way toward the lavender-tinted boulders at the opening.

Another spike of agony pierced the tender skin between her toes.

Her body jerked, she bit her lip to hold back a scream. Bending her leg, lifting her knee, Kel tried to touch the spot. Impossible in the tunnel confines.

"Tsss." She whimpered, swallowed the sound. *Goddess in a graveyard. I hear women's voices.*

Her foot throbbed, her toes hot and full as finger sausages.

Rak'khiel shuddered. The aggressive sidestrike snakes nested beneath rocks, in dry deserted areas and cave mouths. *This is perfect for them.*

Cold sweat slicked her skin. Her arms and legs slid against the tunnel dirt.

The earlier pain in the dairy field and this one must be connected. The same stabbing pain, the same pressure, the same place on her foot. *I don't believe a viper bite's to blame.*

She gritted her teeth against a shriek. Bit down on the inside of her cheek, drew a salty spurt, to distract from the torment between her toes. *Stupid Rak'khiel. Now I hurt in two places instead of one.*

A frantic pant escaped before she could stop herself. She forced breath slowly, deliberately through her nose, careful to make no noise.

"Did you hear?"

Rak'khiel recognized the piercing voice of the hatchet-faced marketplace gossip.

"About the woman they crucified?" The second woman's tone said she enjoyed deflating the first. "Of course."

Rak'khiel knew her voice too. She liked the heavy-set woman who sometimes gave Yola a piece of hard candy for her.

"Oh … no," she breathed. Fingers of ice dug deep in her stomach. Frozen shackles of iron wrapped her spine. *It's Yola. It has to be. But I must make sure.*

Tears re-wet the chest of her tunic.

Kel squirmed closer.

A twist of pain, sharp as a dagger point, carved and turned and dug between her toes. Pressure in her foot grew, building steadily to bursting.

Something in her body waited, patient as a predator. Waited for a single weak moment. Waited to escape.

Kel muffled her hiss, the precursor to a scream. Pressing a knuckle into her mouth, she bit down hard.

"Said she kept a simple-minded child, possibly part Kra'aken. Even so, I'm surprised at his Lordship's cruelty." The first speaker's voice trailed to a whisper. "In this 'Risto city, disobedience garners lashings or loss of body parts. Rarely loss of life."

"Tortured her for over two hours. But not to death," added the second. "Cut off her fingers a joint at a time, one by one. She'll never create another length of cloth for them. In His Lordship's rage, he forgot who she was. Yola hangs on Crucifixion Hill. Still alive, I heard a guard say."

Surges of sweats, first hot then chill, seized Rak'khiel's body. Inside her head, dizzying circles spun. Lolling it against the tunnel side, she tried to remain conscious.

"Gerta told me the High Lord refused Yola the burning ceremony," added the first. "Doomed her spirit to wander forever in torment between worlds."

"Had she been in Sirgate, she and the child would never have been noticed." The second woman couldn't keep sympathy from her voice. "Big towns are too busy for purges." Her voice dropped to a whisper, "Besides, the 'Ristos live here. I liked Yola. Her good heart brought this horror on her."

"Hsst," cautioned her companion. "They'll have you off to the Questioner next if you're not careful. I agree though, her weaving seemed magic-touched. It is a shame."

Rak'khiel cried silent sobs, chewed her finger and writhed against the agony in her foot.

Creeping closer, she spotted the women sitting on the largest rock by the opening. *I can't escape 'til they leave ... but I don't have to listen.*

She shoved her knuckle deeper between her teeth and laid one ear against the tunnel floor. Jamming the forefinger of her free hand in the other ear, she whispered every curse she'd ever heard.

The voices of the women still carried, their words clear.

Powerless to prevent it, Rak'khiel heard the inventive cruelty of the tortures ordered by his lordship, the callous viciousness of the men who carried them out, the ribald laughter of 'Risto observers and their obscene mockery of Yola's shrieks of suffering.

Kel memorized the names of the torturers. Added the dairyboy and his fellows to her list. The grotesque 'Ristos needed no identifiers.

Her vision filled with bright dots, pulsing in synch with the hammering in her temples. Rak'khiel slipped in and out of blackness. Although she prayed it would, her oblivion didn't last.

The barrage of merciless words beat at her. Guilt rose from her stomach in a surge of burning bile. Mouth covered by one hand, Rak'khiel gagged. The hot acid burned again as she re-swallowed her gorge.

"Sameth said the High Lord leaped on Garil, the cloth merchant, stung him, sucked him dry and then beheaded him."

"Goddess preserve," the second woman's voice lowered. "What did he do?"

"Reminded the 'Ristos where the silky cloth for their robes – the single fabric they deign to wear – came from. That Yola, and only Yola, wove it. Garil simply suggested the High Lord spare her eyes, hands and life for future service. Himself went berserk."

"It's been a bad, bloody day for our village," the second woman breathed. "May it pass us by."

Forgun the broomstick, forgun the husband and forgun the baby. Forgun the Goddess and her commandment against killing. All I want now is revenge. A shiver, a chill – unlike anything she'd ever felt – crab-walked down her spine.

Watching the setting suns, Rak'khiel knew the women should leave. Why didn't they?

She worried for Tarkin and Torga. Hunting supper when Sameth came, they must be safe. They are smart. *Let them be far, far away.* Kel closed her eyes. Stopped in mid-prayer.

"I can't expect help from you. Look what you've allowed this day. Shalit on you, Goddess of Good. But shalit on me more."

Face flaming in shame, she pressed her forehead to the moldy stinking earth. The torture in her foot, viper or no, must be eased. *Before I betray myself to the two outside.*

"Unhhh," she groaned around the knuckle gripped firmly between her teeth. Tears streaming, Rak'khiel forced her body limp, as if boneless.

She flattened her free hand, slid it down her side. Working her elbow through the dirt, Kel stretched her arm toward her foot. Using the lifting, pushing pressure of her knee, she grooved the loosened earth of the tunnel, compressing and shoving it aside just enough for her hand to make contact.

Rak'khiel traced questing fingers over smooth skin – unfevered, unswollen, unbitten. *Impossible.* She slid a finger between her great toe and the next. Found nothing. *How can nothing hurt so bad?* The rending pain and pressure continued unabated. She explored the space between her second and third toes. Her hand paused mid-motion.

An object studded with tiny sharp spines and barbed prongs, the size and shape of the village apothecary's lozenges, protruded from her wet rent flesh. "Goddess in a chariot."

Her stomach roiled, churned. Her ribs expanded in a dry heave.

Rak'khiel swallowed hard against it, gripped the object.

Myriad stabs in her fingertips made Kel chew on her tongue. Setting her jaw, she pulled it from her foot. A tearing sensation, a searing pain, a gush of fluid and … cessation of agony.

Tiny needles stabbed her fingers. *No wonder it made me scream.*

Drawing her arm up her body, Kel opened her hand. Mindful of the spines, she rolled the prickly object in her palm. It felt benign and warm and absolutely right. *Even if I could see it clearly, I know I would not understand.*

Sudden truth burned her soul. *This object is Mine. But what in all the Suffering Holy Pair is it?*

The two village women broke off speech.

Rak'khiel heard rustling, scrambling sounds outside her hiding place.

"I'm for home," said the kindly woman. "Ill omens. First the scary thing that flew over and shook the ground. Now the killing."

Rak'khiel pressed her lips together and crept close to the tunnel's end. She saw two quick-moving silhouettes heading for the village.

I refuse to run. I refuse to leave Yola alive, suffering, in that ghastly place called Crucifixion Hill. I must go, I must help her. How? I'm a child. No. A dry bitter bark escaped Kel, her lips twisted. *I am sixteen. I'm grown. I'm now making my own decisions.*

Rak'khiel wondered where the tunnel ended. Yola had always refused to show her. For safety, she'd said. *Obviously, she's refused to tell the Questioner too, or soldiers would be here. I crawled for hours – I must be miles away.*

Capsule clutched in one fist, body flattened, pressed tight to the ground, Kel inched from the tunnel mouth. Crouching behind the rock blocking the opening, she listened for danger.

She shifted the rocks enough to squirm free and then repositioned them, leaving a narrow aperture. Too small for adults but perfect for me. *In case I need to hide again.*

The girlchild Rak'khiel did not realize a cold smile crossed her face. *They are stupid, these village men.* If they search the cottage, they will never find the tunnel. Yola's cement set solid the instant I replaced the hearthstone.

Ping! A body spasm slammed Rak'khiel's forehead into a stone on the ground.

"Am I shot?" Her free hand explored, found a rising lump but no blood.

A second jolt at the back of her head. A hard shoving at the base of her skull, a pushing from inside out, followed ripping flesh.

Rak'khiel clapped the hand holding the bristling object over the wounded spot. She heard a snick, felt a gooey, slick sensation slipping against her fingertips.

The lozenge moved.

"Holy Forge!" Her fingertips scrabbled frantically to catch, to grip the slimy capsule. Found the tiny spikes retracted.

The thing slid into the base of her skull, then into her brain. And settled.

Tendrils, like strands of ivy, or root systems of noxious weeds, branched through her mind. They explored the recesses of Kel's skull, created connections and networks, became one with her.

Nausea surged.

Rak'khiel retched. The bile held back for so long came up in a churning rush. She lifted her head and scrambled away from her hiding place. Lurched to one side just far enough to deposit the sparse remains of her supper in a nearby bush.

As with her foot, all pain disappeared as quickly as it arrived.

"Shalit," she whispered. "Goddess forbid. What just happened to me?"

Chapter 12

Mid-Dark
Nara 13, 7205.20
Olican Planet Surface

A brief pang of concern, a tiny frown flitted across Razr's face – worry for his warplane's new aberrations. He tied-off the final portion of his hair and rubbed a bruised elbow.

"Before we launch, Brin, I'm doing a full systems service. I believe the fighter has serious problems."

Slowing whines and thrums of mains and thrusters cued him. *Almost dirtside.*

The fighter touched ground with little more than a bump. The sudden silence of her huge powerplants bothered him, used as he was, to their constant sounds.

Why am I not in the cockpit? When did I stop loving to fly? The first few yaras, during my waking times, I refused to allow Brin to handle my fighter.

"Running surface scans for possible contaminants now," the AI said.

"Your tribute, Brin."

Razr didn't need a warrior's elaborate plaits to hunt – just containment enough to prevent tangling on tree limbs or in bushes. Big hands caught the three chunks of confined hair high on the back of his head and slid a plain silver clasp around the mass.

The angle of his reflection in the mirror brought a heart-cleaving slash of grief, forced a sob. The almost-image of his father stared back – muscular size, chiseled jaw and amber eyes – but Razr also saw the dark curling hair, full generous mouth and small close-set ears of his mother.

Memory's hammer drove the prince to his knees. He curled around a whimper – a sound exposing weakness a Kra'aken warrior must never show. Razr's nostrils burned, hot and swollen closed.

How many forbidden, self-indulgent minas have I spent? Even one is too many. Shoving to his feet, he avoided the mirror, searched his tiny closet for fatigues and dressed. Dropping down the ship's core to weapons bay, Razr warmed his heavy muscles.

His charcoal-dark hunting vest and pants provided room to move. Resting one large bare foot high on the wall, he bent, laid his forehead on his knee. After he felt the stretch, he switched feet.

A loud crack from his spine made him grunt in satisfaction. Razr dropped into a deep squat, buttocks on heels. Bunching powerful legs and glutas, he pushed up. Twin furrows appeared between ebon brows as both knees popped. *Destroyer be merciful. I'm old at 25? I don't age during coldsleep, but it leaches strength and flexibility just the same.*

Over his fatigues, he strapped two large ceramtanium knives, black hilts visible riding in quick-release sheaths low on his hips. Twin scabbards holding smaller throwing daggers belted a handspan above his knees. A large, s-curved sword, the blade elaborately etched, slid into its wide gongur-hide scabbard hanging from the left shoulder of his bandolier. A projectile weapon and laser pistol sat holstered at the small of his back.

Razr donned no footgear. Emergency morphosis resulting in foot claws and spurs had shredded too many expensive boots. His lips twisted at his thought. *Out here, there are no vendors.*

"Clear to exit, Brin?"

"All reads are green."

The ship's hatch slid open.

Razr stepped through into the planet's gathering dusk. A breeze rustled leaves and made the warm night comfortable. Then, the wind stilled and humidity overrode the cool.

Razr turned to look at the kill-count art on his warplane's nose. The nickname, 'Betty B' made him smile and he loved the always-uptick in his hearts' beats, the always-swelling and tug in his groin. *Her body, so different from our sleekly muscular females, is exciting.*

Done in hardline lifeoptics, protected beneath a hundrada layers of transparent plastanium, a buxom, cheeky dark-haired girl with chera-red full pouty lips rode astride the nose of Razr's warplane. Her voluptuous breasts spilled out the top of a tight, red dress with large white dots. A short flared skirt exposed curving legs ending in tiny feet.

Each time he looked at the image, Razr wondered if it was even possible to walk in the scarlet high heeled shoes. *Although I'd happily carry her anywhere.*

Betty held twenty-seven red roses, one delicate bloom for each of Razr's kills.

My coup count – best in my squad. The prince replaced his wide smile of satisfaction with a wry turn of full lips. *As my father's son, nothing less is …. Was.*

The fast swipe with the back of his hand across his eyes, angled to mimic shading his vision from the setting double suns was playacting for Brin's benefit. *I'm sure he knows I cry though he never says.*

Prince Helrazr focused on the fighter's nose but found only some surface scuffing. The myriad layers of cleartanium protected his art – his Betty remained intact.

He'd pulled her image from a Terran vid; part of his father's plunder from the calamitous raid on Earth. Her picture was titled 'pin-up'. Razr didn't understand the meaning, but it made no difference.

His fellow pilots displayed cafuzogs, draca serpents, likenesses of their promised mates or their mothers. They all gave him chaffa about his sexy Earth girl. But he liked her image, liked the sensual arousal and heightened awareness, just another small edge in battle.

Understanding struck.

A fist of ice slid up from his stomach and blocked his throat. A staggering dizzy step, a one-handed catch on the ladder.

"Forza." He had one of *their* images – Destroyer damned enemies, accursed world killers – on the nose of his warplane.

Razr ground his teeth. Impossible to remove it without structural damage. It would render the ship's hull too fragile for jump. He gave 'Betty' his back. "I'll find a way to get it off. Brin, your favor. Investigate covering up the artwork."

"Of course, milord. You are clear to hunt."

"Your tribute."

Assaulted by the smells of an unexplored world, Razr's delicate nasal membranes flared. He opened his mouth, dragged air across the six small glands in the roof of his mouth. Closing it, he pulled a long deliberate breath through his nose to test his surroundings.

As it sapped the day's heat, the heavy evening dew amplified the essence of damp soil. Smoke from a campfire, sour mildew, unwashed bodies. Myriad animals and spoor. Razr scented flesh of old and new kills in varying stages of rot.

Blood rushed hot through his body, shoved by the staccato of his hearts. Flushed skin popped sweat – it pooled, then ran in warm rivulets down the back of his neck, down his spine. Wet soaked beneath muscular arms, areas compressed against his body by his weapons belts grew soggy.

Razr's excitement danced the gavotta. He didn't miss the sterile mechanical non-odor of the warplane, the industrial solvents, machine oil. He exulted in the delicious smells of life – both fragrant and reeking – of this unknown world. And in the new and different things to hunt in the dark. Food.

Saliva flooded, lethal fangs lengthened but Razr bypassed the small creatures frozen, quivering, at his presence. A mere one-bite snack. *I'll wait. Before I fall upon the first thing I find, I wish to know everything on this planet's menu.*

Sensitive nostrils twitching at the acrid tang of snake venom, Razr armored his lower legs with a thought. Heavy golden scales crusted over, followed by the extrusion of sharp gilt barbs from the outside edges of large clawed feet to his knees.

Leaf-green vipers flicked forked red tongues and slithered away at his appearance.

Razr's low laugh followed them, hurried them on their way.

His implant analyzed, detected venom. *Good that it fled – I hate the taste of snake, and the poisonous ones are bitter.* Danger past, he disappeared his armor. Gave thanks yet again for his missing compulsion.

At metamorphosis into adulthood, the Destroyer High Priest placed each Kra'aken warrior under compulsion: every non-human kill must be eaten. Only in times of war did the priests lift the ban. The necessary decree prevented hunting warriors from losing themselves to Berserker Killing Rage and wiping out their animal populace.

Before the Terran combat, the priests lifted every Kra'aken's killing block. But personal honor demanded Razr respect the law.

Razr? Brin's send interrupted his investigation. *I detect no evolvement on this planet beyond the Iron-Age Period of our forebearers. The single exception is an area outside the stone fortress. Four combustion-engine flying machines, in stages of deterioration, are parked there. Also, beware their waters – my scans show large slif-shaped creatures. I suggest armor if you cross.*

Your tribute, Brin. The joy of walking – bare feet on stone, on rough tufts of living weeds, on powdery dirt – lifted Razr's spirits. Strange scents distracted with multiple choices for investigation.

But something gnawed at his hindbrain – Brin, to be precise. *He's not the same AI that's assisted me over the past yaras. Still logical, still competent but now I sense ... I know ... he's hiding something. Impossible. Artificial Intelligences are incapable of dissembling.*

Topping a rise, Razr studied a dirt road bisecting the valley below. Halfway between where he stood and a stone fortress at the road's far end, clustered a primitive village. Aside from the large castle on the highest hill, few lights flickered.

Resonant sounds came from the fortress' upper tower. Some type of stringed instrument played, interspersed with single notes, off-key, high and shrieking. Perhaps a musical device ... perhaps not.

Razr scowled, face twisting in disapproval at the noise. He tilted his head, listened a secunda longer, then headed down the mountain at a jog. Smelling fresh blood, he turned in the direction of a second smaller hill.

His sensitive ears caught a moan and a jeering harsh laugh in response. The ugliness of the tone, male, twisted in the prince's soul, activating his ruling mindset.

Red flared behind his eyelids as Protector's Rage nearly took him. *This is not my world, not my kingdom and yet ... even if I do not rule here, if needed, I can correct a wrong.*

Razr's slow measured breathing turned rapid, a chilly smile exposed descending fangs while he turned hard merciless eyes toward the sounds. *Besides, I would welcome a good fight.*

Sliding from tree to tree, building to building, his speed produced a blur, which hid more of his height and bulk than the things he paused behind.

Leaping a fence, Razr crossed a grassy pasture.

The herd of dairy cows smelled him, bawled in fear and fled. Charging through their fence, the animals tore flesh and broke legs, trampling each other to escape the huge predator in their field.

Fresh hot bovine blood beckoned – *a wonderful first meal in secundas* – until a pair of very special gill membranes inside his flaring nostrils triggered recognition. Eyes wide, searching for the unbelievable, Razr's head snapped up.

Brin! Can you confirm what I smell? Pure formality, this question.

Razr knew.

Somewhere nearby a Kra'aken female entered metamorphosis, beginning her emergence into adulthood.

Chapter 13

Mid-Dark
Nara 13, 7205.20
Olican Plains

The stickers of the bush stabbing her face, the eye-watering stench of her vomit brought Rak'khiel's awareness. She rocked back on her heels. *Where am I?*

Effusions, surges of multicolored lights rolled before her eyes. Rows and banks of numbers hemorrhaged in her mind. Strange images tumbled, threatened to take control of her reason. Madness, hysteria hovered – yet three things compelled above all else. Revenge. Survive. Hide.

Bony fingers of fear gripped her lungs, forcing shallow pants. She rolled to a crouch, shoved to her feet.

How can there be no blood? Nothing between my toes, on my hands, or on the ground around me? No trail for the soldiers or beasts of the 'Ristos to find?

She explored the back of her throbbing head with careful fingertips, found sore puffy flesh.

"Tsss."

Something deep inside her mind reassured, *All is well, healing goes fast.*

"Goddess in a paintpot! A voice in my head?" Kel whispered, barely holding back the threatening shriek. "Help me."

Something said, *This provides a part of your heritage, history and basic skills.*

Hand shaking, she tried to gently trace the soft-hard ....

Plascirc, supplied the voice in her head.

A dimpled soft center in a slick non-metal round. The female portion of a ....

Mindjack. The mindvoice said.

A wavering pink-gold haze clouded her sight and coated familiar surroundings. Jerking to awareness, she scanned the countryside. No villagers, no soldiers, no 'Risto hounds.

Where are Tarkin and Torga? Her heart hiccoughed in her chest, her throat swelled like a water-soaked sponge. "Goddess, let them be safe."

Her mind shifted like a length of Yola's bright silky cloth, spilling, unfolding again and again. Blinking, she tried to clear her vision. Superimposed before her eyes, strange numbers flickered on a line-scale from Rak'khiel to the cottage. Facts, words, charts – all indecipherable – projected in waves.

Olica's triple emerald moons hung obscured by heavy drifting cloud cover. Despite it all, her surroundings were clear. Too clear. *It isn't dusk, it's dark. And I can see. I'm less than two hands of fifty strides from our house. How can this be? I crawled for hours.*

A cloud of scent enveloped her, made her nose twitch. She inhaled two scents, almost familiar, like the baker's vanil and cin. The third reminded her of flowers, but none she'd ever smelled. Closing her eyes, she relaxed into the lovely fragrance.

Something slammed her. A spasm seized Rak'khiel, twisted and then elongated her torso.

Kel's mouth worked in a silent scream, her eyes frozen on the involuntary contortions of her upper body. Power surged like a swarm of bees, buzzing beneath her skin.

Tucked away behind the surrounding cover of boulders, Rak'khiel collapsed. Sprawled helpless, a disbelieving prisoner in her own body, she watched her child's arms lengthen. Lean toned muscles replaced shapeless sticks, bunched beneath tawny sleek skin now coated in a down of fine silver hair.

As her chest expanded, the pumping of her heart sped first to fast, then to frightening.

Rak'khiel laid two fingers on her wrist and then placed her palm against her chest to confirm the hammering. "I'm going to die. It is fitting punishment for my sin."

Again, the voice in her mind broke silence. *The beats are your normal pace,* it reassured. *Actually a little slow. The thrumming is the combined beating of your double-hearts.*

"Two? Two hearts? No!" Black dots pinwheeled before her eyes. "I cannot. I will not. I am not a freak." Her voice cracked on the last word. "I'm Olican, just like everyone else. I am …. Unh …."

Movement in her hands stilled her words.

She forced back the wail surging in her throat. Mouth open in horror, she watched her thick callused hands smooth, elongate.

"Goddess, I have slender hands, long fingers. No one will ever marry me now." Rak'khiel stretched her arms to each side, shoved her hands far away as possible.

Thoughts of Yola returned. With them came narrow-eyed rage and sobs of grief.

Through her pain, she heard something growl, angry, aggressive, promising carnage.

Rak'khiel's head whipped side to side, searching for the danger. *I am alone. It was me who snarled.*

"Goddess," she whispered. "Am I strong as I feel? Can I fight Yola's murderers? Those who would kill me? If true, deformation is a small price. But, how to know?"

Scooping up a stone, Kel curled her fingers about it and squeezed.

The rock exploded into a puff of fine powder.

Her viscera jerked in joy, a chortle of glee erupted.

"Somehow, Holy Pair be blessed, I have strength, I have power." Dusting stone fragments from her new hands, Rak'khiel exulted, "I can avenge Adopted Mother. I can kill them all."

But ... something wrong poked at her mind. Something odd, something off.

A second glance at her hands made her stomach writhe, trying to bring up the contents of an already empty vessel.

"I cannot have six fingers." She counted each hand twice.

A wash of warmth permeated one leg, then suffused the other. "No, Goddess. Not them too."

Her breath came hard and fast while, eyes glued to her thighs, she watched her ankle-length shift become a mustard-colored mid-thigh tunic. Watched her stocky fence-post legs grow long, the muscles curving beneath her skin. So very wrong, these ugly storkling appendages. And yet somehow she almost liked her new swelling calves, slender feet and long narrow toes.

"No, I'm not going to count them." Rak'khiel truly didn't want to. She couldn't help herself.

A wriggle showed the awful truth. Six toes on each foot.

Again she gulped against her nausea. "I'm a freak. Why?"

Her head felt stuffed full of wool batting, thoughts darted, richocheted without purpose, refused to make sense.

A hot push in her forehead pulled her hands against her face.

"Goddess save," she whispered just before her lungs seized.

Her bones, her flesh moved beneath her hands.

Rak'khiel's questing fingertips followed the reshaping – from wide, flat and round to high cheekbones in a slender, delicate oval. Her stubby broad nose shifted into a small, straight one.

"I am not Olican. Yola was right. I am a butterfly morphing to a caterpillar."

Pain stabbed her hearts, sharp as the leatherworker's

needle, recalling the dairyboy's insults. "I'm a heifer becoming a warttoad."

Kel's lips twisted. "Yola, why didn't you tell me?"

Like a child's iridescent soap bubble, Rak'khiel's mind expanded. *Will it burst into a billion sparkles? Will it hurt? Will I die?*

The fuzzy pressure, the amoebic mass inside her skull separated into sections, made mental aisles, grew pathways. Each connection created cross references with the others. Data raced, information flooded into her conscious like her twin thudding hearts shoved blood through her veins.

The data deluged Rak'khiel, overflowed her brain. Clutching her temples in clawed hands, she shrieked her torment. "Help me! I must understand. My head is going to explode."

"If it pleases you, Goddess," she breathed. "Help me. Give me something a mere jewelry maker can comprehend."

In the center of the data flood, a pink spot glowed and grew. A delicate flower bud manifested. Stood slender, nonthreatening. Serene.

Kel's tension ebbed.

Petal by petal, second by second, the flower matured, unfolding into separate chambers, each a critical, intertwined part of the whole. Each velvety petal held an enormous quantity of data. The sections were labeled batched science, theory, cultural information, space exploration. Mathematics, symbols, armed and unarmed combat. Weapons, war.

Her stomach twisted. *So much knowledge, so much to help. And I understand – nothing.*

A rippling shudder seized her when a new rosette bud appeared. Perfect, as with the other, but this flower as black as the High Lord's murderous heart. She watched it open, petal by petal.

I know – although how can I? – this rose contains skills for killing.

Your assassin's module, prompted her mindvoice.

I wish I knew what was this assassin? *Or how to use the black rosette. Yola's tormenters would all die. This instant.*

Chapter 14

Mid-Dark
Nara 13, 7205.20
Olican Planet Dirtside

The scent of morphing female led Razr through the countryside to a large cluster of boulders.

All thoughts of food obliterated from his mind, the huge Kra'aken male's body responded. Thick muscles bunched. Large clawed feet dug deep into pasture turf. Razr stretched to full height, his massive chest expanded.

Twin hearts thudded, blowing blood into his reproductive organs – pent sexual frustrations exploded. Want! Need! Will have! Thrusting clawed golden fists in the air, Razr roared a screaming challenge to this primitive dirt pile and all its inhabitants.

"She is MINE!"

Prince Razr ... Shhh ... Prince Razr. I heard you all the way up here. Respond.

"Forza, Brin. Can it be? And ... use caution yourself. The strength of your message must have stressed all your circuits. Do not blow a component."

Copy. My reprehensible. But milord, you do recall protocols regarding female younglings and their change process?

The prince sniffed, strained for the female's location. Made no answer.

Attend me!

Brin's voice slashed so harsh, Razr considered checking his back for whip stripes.

Prince Razr, you must not interrupt, must not frighten, must not speak to or touch her.

"But, Brin, I … must go." He trembled like a deepspace worker trapped in a bay with an unstable seal. "Destroyer have mercy."

You are a warrior and a Prince. You know the ramifications of interference: her insanity or death. Would you ruin your first chance in 158 yaras by sheer willfulness? Or can you be the controlled male your father sired on your royal mother?

"On her sweet, blessed soul, Brin. How do I stay away?"

Return to the ship.

"No." Razr's sharp tone grated and he knew it. "Not yet, Brin." He temporized, hoping his AI would recognize the unspoken apology. "She needs help. I smell her distress, I can hear her disordered thoughts. There is something terribly wrong on this world. I must investigate."

Copy. But use great caution, my prince. You are one warrior, alone on an alien planet.

"Affirmative. And Brin, I vow to keep my distance."

The prince made certain he shielded his final caveat from Brin. "For now …."

Although the beckoning *tasca* flared with a heady invitation of jessamin, vanilln and cinna, the prince's keen nostrils sorted out others lying beneath. Odors of confusion, grief, fear and pain overrode the damp night's flavors, filtered through the special gill membranes inside his nostrils.

He squashed his own rising scents the best he could. *Stunning that, in a few short minas, all my sadness, depression and plans to suicide vanished. My life is changed, with just one female scent. And it tells me she is terrified. A child-woman half-changed, in disarray, without explanations and helping attendants?*

Razr hid, aware his presence would increase her distress, endanger her morphosis. Hands clenched into fists, nails digging half-moons into his palms, the prince watched his female's emergence into the duality of Kra'aken adulthood.

"Brin? Did the creators of the cocoons build-in education on metamorphosis?" Razr opened his link and whispered. "Where is her AI?"

Is the female not in her capsule?

"No. She's changing – here on the ground, in the open."

Does she understand what is happening?

"Her scent is pure terror. I believe if she saw me it would wreck her mind. Perhaps you could explain ...."

No. The AI sent, *How would you explain me to someone from a world without technology?*

"Correct, of course. Perhaps, if opportunity permits, I can attempt mitigation from a distance. But Brin, her body is changing. Why doesn't she look like a normal Kra'aken?"

The children were intended to remain in stasis, in their med units, until after morphosis. For safety, mimicking devices, capable of projecting matching physical attributes of the local lifeforms, were embedded in each child. We hoped to prevent any kill-on-sight reflexes. It seems to have worked here.

"Ah," Razr said. Then, he added, "Perhaps not, Brin. Her thoughts tell me she is in some type of trouble."

Do not intervene ....

"I will not. All I can do is wait but ...."

A sound from the AI sent one of Razr's eyebrows hitching toward his hairline.

"Brin? Was that a chuckle?" *Computers don't laugh, they cannot understand humor.*

Oh, young prince. What a cruel quirk of the Destroyer. Something that could only be a laugh choked off almost as quickly as it began. *You are at the mercy of your worst fault. Your lack of patience.*

Razr rubbed the deep vertical lines from between his brows, pushed stray curling strands away from his face. *Now*

I'm sure something is wrong – with the plane and with my AI too. He stealthily blocked Brin from accessing his mind. *I cannot worry about it right now.*

Finally, after all his solitary yaras, Razr had a mate. With the Great Destroyer's wicked twisting of his fate, combined with his sixth-son-luck, the female would be graceless, hideous of face and form. *If our God has a sense of humor, it would be his amused payback for my selectivity. For entertaining only the most beautiful Kra'aken ladies in my bed.*

And, Razr realized as his lust drooped, *whatever she becomes, this female will do. I will accept her if she is ugly as a slif. Because I cannot continue living alone. Still, her scent is luscious – I will simply keep my eyes closed. At all times.*

Razr drew closer and crouched behind a large rock. Watching, waiting for the female to complete her change, he decided the question was not if the Destroyer had a sense of humor – it was if he existed at all? If he does, he is without compassion. He allowed the destruction of his worshipers and our planet while they prayed for his intercession.

Watching the change of girl to woman, humanoid form to Kra'aken warrior, Razr's body tingled, vibrated in response as if electric currents charged through his veins. Smelling his answering mating tasca of mintas – added to his personal shades of pine, resin, gingr – he damped it. Or tried.

"My greatest contrition, my horrific reprehensible, oh Great Destroyer," Razr prayed, his apology lightning fast and fervent. For a single moment of disbelief, his capricious god might confiscate the girl fast as she'd appeared. *Forza me.*

"Is there any way I could possibly prevent it?" Razr's eyes narrowed.

There remained one deity to beseech. A god whose attention everyone worked to avoid. A god so terrifying, so awful, Razr had never, ever, thought of asking him for anything. *But I can't trust the Destroyer anymore – not with something so important.*

Zooming an optical, he held his breath.

The girl's slumped body hid her face.

The Greatest One's priests taught that their god extracted a price for his help.

Without exception.

A shiver slithered across Razr's shoulders and he wondered, worried what it might cost. And when. War, piloting, courage – all were his gifts to give. But rumor said the God's demands were always cruel, twisted, and painful. That the God's timing was deliberately erratic. *Is it worth it?*

The prince bowed his head and prayed. "Please allow her to be somewhat attractive."

Razr turned an ear toward the female, activated his hearclip. Increasing the volume, he heard a long moan, panting breaths, muttered words in a strange language.

A click of two wisdom teeth on the right side of his mouth activated a dropmenu before his eyes. Scrolling his tongue on the roof of his mouth – from front to back – provided subsets.

Razr located his Interpreter Analyzer program and pressed the tip of his tongue to select. *An alert will ping if the language is in my database.*

The program made no sound.

He edged closer. Tight-focusing his optical on the changing female, Razr knew an anticipatory grin tried to split his face. He knew hot blood, mixed with desire's perspiration, flushed his skin. *After these interminable yaras – soon, a mature female.*

"All mine," slid past his lips.

He longed to stroke, to touch, to be held. He ached, quivered with need.

Something tugged at a corner of his mind, its familiarity niggled. The female's carriage, incline of her head, color of her hair, her *tasca* reminded him of someone – *I should know* – but the *who* eluded Razr.

Releasing his block between Brin and himself, Razr said, "Brin? Can you hear me?"

Prince Helrazr. You cut communications. Are you interfering?

"No, damnit," he whispered. "You always think the worst of me."

I have been your AI for many years now. Brin's thought blended memory and humor.

The prince noticed his AI didn't demur, instead he'd evaded. Brin's question with its implications was driven – justifiably – by knowledge of my tendencies. I didn't answer his question either.

"What? No, I've not interfered. But I ... broke contact because.... Well, um, I so feared she might be ugly I beseeched the Great God."

What in the forzaing twelve hells were you thinking? Brin's send sliced through Razr's skull like the white-hot blade of a lasdrill. *You young idiot. The Great God will probably require your male beauty as his price and she'll run screaming from you.*

The profanities that followed shocked him. *Where and how did a computer learn to curse?* Most astounding, the sentiments seemed driven by honest emotion.

"I know, Brin, I know. I did it anyway."

How is she progressing?

"She is fair of form. Her features have yet to shift but change is close."

Great Destroyer, Prince Helrazr. I don't care about her beauty – I care only if she lives or dies. If she retains her sanity. How goes her morphosis? The AI's voice, loaded with asperity, jerked Razr's mind back to the precarious, and quite possibly fatal, consequences of the girl's unattended changing.

"Brin, she has endured something terrible," Razr shook his head. "She is greatly distressed by it – and the change terrifies her." He drew breath, "Still, remove those factors and I believe her progression would be normal. I will alert you to any deviation."

Your tribute, milord.

"About time you remembered who is in command here," muttered the prince. Scraping the fragments of his shattered willpower together, instead of rushing to her side, Razr moved to a vantage point on the boulder. The sense of almost-recognition nagged at him again.

His jaw dropped, hinge cracking – the sound too loud in the quiet – when she picked up a stone and crushed it.

"Oh, Brin. Did you see? A worthy mate indeed."

Perhaps if you granted me visual access, I might have done so.

"My contrition. Access granted."

Razr's hearts squeezed and lurched while he watched the girl groan, then grip and twist her curls in elegant hands. She shook her head – perhaps to clear it, perhaps to gather balance and composure. Then, she took three tentative steps before her gait evened into long strides. Strides carrying her away from him and into the darkness.

"Brin. Destroyer save her. She's running into the night."

Disaster. Too dangerous. Report everything.

"Yes, yes." Razr knew irritation bled through his response and his fleeting thought of apology (although they were prohibited for royalty). Running parallel but unseen by the girl, his mind sorted practicalities.

"Brin. Where is her lifecocoon? She should be in it for morphosis."

I have a faint response from a nearby cave. Your heat signature – and a smaller one I assume belongs to her – are moving toward it.

Keeping enough distance between them, keeping her dawning awareness from sensing him, the prince followed the fragrant trail of her spicy-sweet maturing *tasca* like a Kra'aken hunt hound.

Chapter 15

Mid-Dark
Nara 13, 7205.28
Olican Planet Dirtside

Razr ran. The girl's thoughts and emotions, her physical pain, lay open to him. *Destroyer. My change, properly mentored, proved merely difficult. I never imagined it could be so hard.*

As he followed, the prince heard and lived the discord of a simple mind forced into light-speed exponential expansion. Module by module, her brain foundered in overflowing knowledge. Razr knew when the blank folds, huge unused portions of her mind, filled and churned. Knew her panic at the beating pressure, like a fist pounding in her skull. Knew when expanded understanding and higher level modules brought deeper comprehension.

His hearts twisted in sympathy. *Destroyer. I had yaras to study and assimilate this knowledge. She's been dumped with it in a single hora.* The prince watched her body morph, evolve and grow. His own lungs mimicked the girl's heaving ones while she strove for air, fought for life.

Razr watched her halt, heard her voice rise in argument with her morphosis mindvoice. Although he agreed in principle with the monitor, he also silently applauded her spirit, her determination.

"I'll not go to the Fang," she shouted. "I have something much more important to do. Kill me now or let me do what I must."

At the searing anguish in her head, Razr flinched. His breath, twinned with hers, came harsh. He lived her resistance to the insidious mindmodule, felt its compelling tentacles weaving, prying, inserting.

He felt it cease, heard the girl's gasp of relief. Then, the infodump began again.

She dropped to her knees, gripped her skull with both slender hands, and keened her torment and her distress.

"I cannot allow this to continue," Razr whispered. Allowing a tiny tendril of thought – his most subtle, gentle presence – he nudged the edge of her mind. He gently drew back at her return probe searching for his identification.

"Who helps?" She whispered. "Did you make it stop before?"

"Brin, she's reaching out to me, knows I'm not Tarkin or Torga … whoever they are. I am initiating contact."

Prince Helrazr. No. Think what you are doing!

"I am, Brin. You have no idea – my sanity, my future, my life depends on this."

Razr blocked the AI's access and focused on the trembling girl crouched in the dust.

You are not alone … he sent the thought soft as a breath. When she didn't spook, he added, *I can help.*

Her head jerked.

Sniffing, she scanned her surroundings.

"Who?" she whispered. "Where?"

Obey the Prime Directive, intruded the harsh mindvoice. *Go to the mountain.*

"I told you. My revenge first." The furious girl whispered defiantly to the monitor's demands. "Shalit on you and your orders."

Understand revenge. Razr flooded his supportive thought with sympathy. *I can assist with your change.* The prince eased his mental barrier against Brin and caught the brunt of the AI's ire. He slammed it shut again.

"Who? What are you? How do you know ...?" The girl's eyes searched the surrounding rocks and boulders.

I am like you. I can silence the monitor's voice. Do you wish it?

He dropped his mental wall and sent a quick whisper to Brin. "You can shut off the compulsion module, can't you?"

Since you've already promised it, my prince? The AI's thought rippled with gentle sarcasm. *But yes, I can.*

I'm glad he is still speaking to me. Razr jerked his head up in sudden insight. *Sarcasm? Brin? What in the twelfth hell is going on here?*

"If it please you," the girl broke into his musing. "Make it stop before it drives me insane. And I have a piece of metal stuck in my head. Can you get it out?"

No, but do not fear it. I also have one – I can explain. Razr remembered to breathe. He knew the instant Brin muted the minder's voice.

Like fog chased by sunlight, the girl's tension dissipated. She rose to her feet. "Do you have a name?"

"My friends call me Razr."

"My thanks, Razr. My name is Rak'khiel. I must go."

"Take your revenge. If you require assistance, call me. I will be nearby."

The musical lilt of her voice proved lovely as the girl.

Razr's hearts ratcheted their beating to triple-time. He fought to breathe, fought to damp his desire, fought to push the physical demands of his conscienceless body away. His every cell screamed, insisted he prevent her leaving, to mark ownership with possession, to ease yaras of pent passion with her. He struggled against himself. And won.

She is not a spoil of war, Razr. Brin scolded. *She is an innocent child.*

"I am here and she is gone. Correct? What more would

you have of me?" Razr's snarl threaded his send with harsh reds and oranges. And even though he'd subsumed his passion, the prince cursed his forgetfulness at leaving the Destroyer damned link open.

He followed Rak'khiel across the valley floor, trying to fit the pieces together.

"Brin," he mused. "Her actions made no Kra'aken sense, but ... raised in this planet's values ... to her they hold great meaning. And her name ... it is a royal derivative. Is it not? Like mine."

Affirmative. Were any commoners even sent? Still, I caution you, young sir, be ever more watchful. She is entering the most fragile stage of her change.

Razr followed, listening to the jumble in Rak'khiel's mind. While her long strides carried her quickly to Crucifixion Hill, the prince tried to make sense of his female's thoughts.

Killing is evil, a mortal sin, she worried. *Forbidden. I should not. But I want to.*

"No," he whispered, careful she did not hear. "Killing is necessary, even good. What is wrong with this place?"

How will I lift Yola down?

"I, Prince Helrazr, will help you in all things," he murmured. Then he felt the hot needles of alarm surging through her.

Who is this person helping me? He heard Kel fret. Then she added, *Did I, in a moment of weakness, promise him something in return?*

Chapter 16

Mid-Dark
Nara 13, 7205.39
Crucifixion Hill, Olica

"Tell me and I'll kill you quick," the first guard said.

This one would, Yola thought through the stranglehold of agony. *He's kind.*

They hadn't spared an inch of her body in their efforts to obtain information, the questioners with their hooks, pincers, hot metal and knives. A thousand agonies, the throbbing of seared stumps, the screaming of her flayed back naked against the rough stained wood of the cross.

A cool breeze wafting across her ripped abdomen brought her stench – blood, vomit and voided bladder and bowel – the sear flash of chilled nerve endings shrieked in its wake.

One unruptured eardrum to hear their mocking, her tongue kept intact to answer their questions. *They left me one eye.* Dry and burning from lack of a lid, the better to see the ruin of her beauty.

Cruel taunts of the Head Inquisitor holding a mirror before her.

These hurts are mortal, why don't I die? The only consolation – they didn't have Ela. The brutal guard would be gloating.

Or, Goddess protect, my daughter would be hanging here beside me.

A cruel knife stabbed upward into the arch of her foot, delivering a jolt of fresh anguish. A whimper escaped Yola's throat. Being trussed and roped, tight to the cross, prevented flinching away.

"Stop it, Yorks," said the first soldier. "There's no need for more."

"Disgusts you, does it?" The other sneered. "If I report you to Himself, he'll see to you right enough. Hang you up there with her. If I make her talk, I'll be the new Head Inquisitor."

A miracle stopped my speech. But it came from a power far greater than the Goddess'.

After a mere hour on the ghastly tower table, Yola'd tried to confess how and where Ela appeared. Tried to tell how she hid the toddler and her two pets. Tried to tell of her monthly move from village to village to keep her secret.

The knife jabbed into the sole of her foot again, grinding, twisting against bone. This time Yola screamed but only a faint cry emerged from her raw throat. She felt, rather than heard, the bubbling wet rising higher in her lungs. Her overtaxed heart labored, arrhythmic.

Through a scarlet haze of pain she caught a glimpse of a moving form. *Or not?*

Tears flooded her good eye, blurred her vision and she tilted her head to redirect them. Cascading salt stung open wounds, but she could see. *My peripheral vision might catch ....*

Something stood there. But what? Too tall and slender, too graceful for Ela. Too small and slender for a sorbazel, the massive southern hunting cat.

Beyond the creature, another, much larger humanoid shape waited. It loomed, motionless, silent, cloaked in a golden glow.

Goddess, what horrible monster is this? Yola trembled. *Yet, it's the Holy color.*

On the far side of the hill, two small bodies crouched. Ela's pets. *Goddess of Good, don't let this beast of a guard below me realize.*

The slender form glided, an almost slither, close to the ground. Crept behind the large boulder the guards used for their latrine.

Why do I keep thinking it's my daughter? The soldiers can't see the creature ... but hung up here, I can. The absolute lack of any sound should alert them something is wrong.

The kind soldier shook Baccy Weed onto a paper square, began to roll a smoke.

"Gotta piss," the other barked an ugly sound passing for a laugh and shoved his knife into Yola's foot yet again. Wiping the blade's dark smear on a patch of grass, he thrust it back into his belt.

Yola's shriek hiccupped with the stutter of her heart. *It feels swollen, like it will explode. Then it starts beating again. Please, oh please. Let me die.*

At her silent scream, something stirred behind the rock.

"Wait ... watch ... justice." Ela's voice drifted on the night, a familiar, comforting whisper.

It cannot be, Yola thought. *I am delusional.* Hearing a faint snarl from the cafuzogs, she thought to smile but her face refused. *They might kill a single soldier, but not two armed ones. I am glad for their vigil. I will not die alone, friendless.*

Yola watched the huge man-beast slide silently closer, all the while maintaining a strict distance from the smaller creature.

Yorks' heavy tread carried him to the boulder, then behind.

Yola's heart leaped with joy at the grunt, the crunching strangled shriek and muted gurgles. No pungent urine stream splashed, no now-familiar descriptions of York's pleasure at the relief. The unnatural quiet of the grave cloaked Crucifixion Hill. A descending hush told Yola the small residents of this hill dared not breathe. Something far more horrific than the 'Risto guards had found and killed prey.

The smell of burning tobacco filtered through the cool night air, up through Yola's nostrils.

"Yorks?" queried the younger soldier. "You okay?" With no response, the man unsheathed his knife, ground out his smoke, and disappeared behind the boulder.

Again, a slight sound before menacing silence reigned. Death dealt more easily with the kind guard but refused to spare him. From behind the boulder, sounds of retching, violent vomiting ripped the quiet.

Then, her steps whisper-soft as unfolding silk, the exotic creature glided to the foot of the cross. Stopped before it, her alien face wet with tears.

"Yola? Can you be mended?"

The voice is Ela's. But that's nonsense.

"Yola? It's Rak'khiel ... Ela. How bad are you?"

"I'm dead. Just waiting for Charon's ferry. If you love me at all, Ela girl, kill me. Now."

"Yola, no. Maybe I can ...."

"No, child, there is nothing left to fix. Free me of this torment. Then flee. Before they do this to you."

"But why? Why do they hate me?"

"The Kra'aken – terrible, unnatural creatures, cruel hunters – once invaded Olica. We fought back." Yola's voice cracked. Her heart beat frantically, like the wings of a trapped narikeet. *Soon,* she thought. *Very soon this will be over.*

She forced her words, hurried them. "I must tell you this fast. Before I die. The Kra'aken ship left, leaving their dead behind. Not all were. We found and exterminated all we could but some Olicans believe Kra'aken still live on our planet."

"But ...."

"Then a ship of 'Ristos arrived, seeking Kra'aken. We welcomed them – seeing a common enemy. Their rabid hate forced a purge so great they slaughtered our rulers on mere whispers of suspicion. Now the 'Ristos rule us." Yola's ruined face moved in a grimace, a moan escaped and she finished. "Far better the Kra'aken with their twisted sense of honor than those with none at all."

"I will kill them, Yola. Every one, I swear on the Goddess."

A sharp breath. "No. My life is not worth your soul."

"I've already broken my oath. Too late."

Yola fixed her single eye on Rak'khiel. "I think they believed you one of them. We know differently – although daughter, if I am not delusional, you are suddenly much changed."

"I grew, Yola. I don't understand my change or my new knowledge."

"Repent and murder no more. Save yourself. Flee."

"My oath, the Goddess bedamned. I will kill all responsible."

"One favor, my daughter."

"Name it."

"My family heirloom, the silver necklace."

"You gave it to me at home. Right before ...." The young voice trembled.

"Guard it. Keep it close." The woman drew a ragged breath. "It holds our ancestral gift. All it represents is now yours, my lineage passes to you." Yola's single eye fought to fix on the girl below. "It must pass to your daughter when it is time."

"My vow on it."

Kel squared her shoulders, mouth hard in the face she lifted to Yola. Fists clenched, unclenched, twisted in the ochre fabric. "My mother, what should I do?"

"I found you wandering ... in the meadow below the Fang." Yola panted, summoned strength. "If any clues to your history remain ... they will be there." A wet gurgle, like water bubbling in a teakettle, almost obscured Yola's words. "For the ... love of the Goddess ... Ela girl ... kill me now."

Chapter 17

Mid-Dark
Nara 13, 7205.39
Crucifixion Hill, Olica

Razr watched Rak'khiel move to stand before the cross. Clasping her head, her shoulders shook, dots of wet fell, creating sorrow's pattern in the dust before her. She pushed white-knuckled fists against her temples, pressed her lips to a bloodless thin. Her breaths huffed hard as if she'd run miles.

Body, mind and soul transfixed on his female, the prince committed a warrior's greatest sin – inattention to his surroundings. He missed the two furry bodies, bellies pressed to the ground, close by his mate-to-be.

"I love you, Yola. I always will." Rak'khiel's words to the battered body hung high. "I will perform your burning, my mother."

Clear as a shout in his mind, Razr heard her thoughts.

By my willfulness, I am responsible. On my head her death. I am too ashamed to confess my guilt, my lies. Ashamed to be grateful I don't hang next to her, ashamed to be glad I escaped capture.

Razr pondered Kel's reasonings. *It is a sign of the Destroyer's goodwill that Rak'khiel was spared Yola's fate. There is no guilt or blame. She must know this. She should give thanks. Why does she torment herself instead?*

Through their mental link, Razr shared the girl's anguish. But she can take the comfort denied me when our world exploded. *She at least can perform the ritual eating of her loved one's flesh.*

Razr watched her reach up and gently clasp Yola's bloody ankle. *What is she doing?*

A breathy wheeze, a whistle of air's intake. Death's unmistakable rattle.

The prince swallowed a grunt of surprise. *Impossible! At only Rak'khiel's touch. And yet ....*

Razr heard the girl's breath hitch, then restart in sharp panicky pants.

Her startled thought came strong and clear. *Goddess! I only wished her desire be granted. Did I kill her?* Then, her high thin scream broke the night's silence. "My hand is stuck to her ankle!"

Through their mental connection, Razr felt a hard shove. Felt something strike Rak'khiel, push inside and possess her by brute force. Then it submerged, leaving the impression of a pond's calm surface.

Anything but calm, Kel's mind gibbered and bent. Her body folded, slid as if boneless, into a heap on the ground.

A stream of images, the brutal torture of the past few hours, flooded through the Yola-Kel connection and into him.

The gleaned memories pulled a deep-pitched snarl from Rak'khiel.

The little night-time creatures once again dived into their dens.

Only the white-striped black cafuzogs and he stood their ground against the daughter's rage.

Kel surged to her feet.

At the threatening danger, Razr's war *tasca* surged. His fangs pressed hard against his upper lip. Both ebbed at Rak'khiel's whisper.

"Shalit. Tall as I am, strong as I am, I still cannot remove her body from the cross."

Her head turned, wide eyes scanned the surrounding countryside. "You … the voice in my mind? Your promise of help? If you are here, can you lift her down?"

Prince Helrazr stepped out of the shadows. Her fear of him threw up a mental wall. He felt her panic, and paused.

The cafuzogs fled.

Moving closer, Razr heard Rak'khiel's thoughts, knew her overwhelming urge to follow them. He admired the strength of her will, her honor and commitment to a promise.

In her mind, he saw himself – an enormous alien form wreathed in pale golden shimmer. He stopped a comfortable distance from the girl and disappeared his changes.

She stood, more relaxed, but still on the brink of flight.

Razr waited. The next move must be hers. Questions pressed against his closed lips. The non-Kra'aken one she calls mother? Her strange power?

I will not ask in her time of distress. Razr rejoiced for the darkness masking his expression. *I know my face showed shock at her promise of burning. Had she seen, it would have shattered her budding trust in me.*

His earclip caught the faint clash of metal. Soldiers.

My prince, you must go.

Yes, Brin. I hear.

"Is there a problem?" she asked.

"No and yes. Soldiers are coming. I will carry your mother."

"To the mountain?"

"Yes." Razr inclined his head, shook it slightly. "My reprehensible, I must reactivate your mindguide. Go quickly."

Chapter 18

Mid-Dark
Nara 13, 7205.50
Near Crucifixion Hill, Olica

What, mi' mate, should we do? Torga's shiny black eyes widened within their circular bands of white fur.

We must approach ... her. But ... since her morphosis, will she still know and trust us? Tarkin's whiskers twitched. *We can't assume she will do us no harm.*

I know she will not. Our Kel would never!

Our pre-change Kel would not. Still, unless you believe in coincidence – and, milove, I know you do not – we just saw her stop a beating heart with nothing more than a wish.

Where then, Tarkin?

Just beyond the next rise. We will allow her to come to us. But we will be wary. And very prepared to defend ourselves.

The pair of cafuzogs perched on the flattened top of a large rock. Behind it lay a deep depression, shelter if needed, until they could incapacitate any threat and make their escape. From their vantage point, they could see Kel, the cross and Yola's body, and the large man who'd come to assist.

We were kitlings, in Ma'am's litter, waiting for our assignment to a Royal. Still, he seems familiar. Torga tilted her head, one ear upright, the other folded in half. *He must be upper tier because we would not have seen others – Ma'am and Da being the Queen's bodyguards.*

Tarkin's black upper lip rolled back in his smile. *He's a Royal. Too arrogant for a house slave.*

His physical attributes, his comportment, speak to it, Targa sent. *But which house? Whose son?*

I feel I have met him, I feel I should know. And yet, it has been long since we were jettisoned from Kra'aken. It seems much longer still since I gave homeworld rulers a thought. Tarkin shook his plumed tail in irritation. *Why can't I remember who he is? We must, we are her guardians. It is our responsibility to protect her from all threats – not just the physical ones.*

We will listen. Perhaps he will tell her himself.

A muffled finorkle escaped Torga at the cross-eyed look her lifemate gave her.

§

The furry pair crouched in low profile and watched the huge man untie Yola's bonds. He worked carefully and with great respect, supporting her carefully. When he'd freed her mutilated body, he cradled Yola's cooling shell, childlike, against his massive chest.

Even if he does this only because he thinks Rak'khiel watches and judges, Torga sent. *His hands are gentle. He is compassionate.*

Feel his anger, soulmate. He's keeping Berserker's Rage in check, holding back his howls.

Your nose tell you anything else, Tarkin?

Destroyer! He's exuding mating tasca. And repressing it because of her vulnerability. Not only royalty, but highly controlled. Only one of highest tier could achieve such. Who can he be?

They watched saw Rak'khiel turn toward the mountain, drop into a lope.

Coming toward us, Torga sent. *You'll see she's our Kel.*

Behind her, the man found a steady comfortable pace and

followed.

Rak'khiel topped the rise.

"Tarkin! Torga! You're safe!" Arms outstretched, Rak'khiel raced toward them.

Training sent Torga flinching away, keeping safe distance between the girl and herself. A sharp knife ripped through her heart at the sudden wet coating Kel's face.

Dare we trust her? Tarkin sent.

As Rak'khiel stopped, frozen before them, only Torga's discipline prevented her rushing forward.

Kel's words came, hard, mixed with sobs. "I know I've done wrong. I should be punished. Will you no longer be my friends?"

You're much changed. Are you still our Kel? Tarkin asked, but he was already sure.

"I could never forget you. There isn't change enough in this world to make it so." Kel dropped to her knees, arms outstretched.

It is our Rak'khiel, Tarkin sent.

I want to trust, but the huge male worries me, Torga answered. *Why is he here and what does he do?*

She is very dangerous now – her fangs are bigger than ours, Tarkin's thought carried an image.

The two assessed the girl. Saw her frown, then trace her stretched upper lip with a questing finger.

She's forcing her teeth away. She doesn't wish to threaten us. It is our Kel, Torga sent. *I say we trust.*

"It is me, Rak'khiel," came Kel's echo. "I will kill anyone who tries to hurt you."

Tarkin and Torga circled their charge, noses busy, eyes assessing. A quick meeting of minds, nods of assent, and they sprang into Rak'khiel's arms.

Who is the one who helps? Tarkin asked. *How does he come to be here?*

We find him worrisome, added Torga.

Chapter 19

Dark
Nara 14, 7205.40
The Fang, Olica

Shouting erupted from Crucifixion Hill and Kel's joy vanished.

Bobbing torches lit the way to the castle. The murdered guards and Yola's missing body had been discovered.

Pity the poor bastard charged with informing the High 'Risto Lord, Kel thought at the cafuzogs.

A certain death sentence, Torga's ears flopped at her nod of agreement. *He always kills the bearer of bad news.*

Search parties will come now. And fast. Tarkin shot a look over a furry shoulder. *Does he come? Bearing Yola?*

"Yes." Now she needed to put distance between Crucifixion Hill and those who hunted her. "We go." she said. "I'll carry you."

We can run. We are fast.

You are faster than the hunt hounds, yes. But, you can no longer keep up with me.

Scooping up Tarkin and Torga, she threw one over each shoulder. Felt them grip, claws punching deep through the fabric of her ochre tunic. Eight rows of curving deadly talons sank solid, formed pretty patterns of black. The cafuzogs' weight pulled hard but Yola's weaving held firm.

Her mustard-colored shift hung, swirling, mid-thigh. If seen, she'd be arrested for indecency. *Goddess, I'd arrest myself.*

Good you have us to hold your dress down, yes? Tarkin's lips moved against her cheek in the quirky half-lift which always accompanied his teasing.

"Slings," she muttered. "I need something to hold you."

We can hang on, Tarkin's irritated thought.

We're strong, Rak'khiel, sent Torga. *So is the cloth.*

"Yes, but if you fall asleep? You know you do."

The lightening of your burden or the thump will tell you, Tarkin snarked.

Torga's shoulders shook and she muffled a finorkle.

Rak'khiel felt her heart move, almost lift, if only a tiny bit. Then ran faster.

§

Up the sharp obstacle covered incline, Kel's hearts stuttered arrhythmic. Her lungs burned.

Not from energy expended carrying the cafuzogs, not from the long run up the mountain side. Rak'khiel felt fuel spent, yes, but this draining sucked from the inmost deep of her, depleting vital resources. Consuming the essence of her very life to carry out the morphosis changes still taking place.

She ran barefoot over rocky terrain. A part of her mind noticed she felt no discomfort.

"Torga? Tarkin? My feet should be cut to ribbons, shredded, but they're not. My old body couldn't have run a quarter-mile. How is this possible?"

A Kra'aken warrior's gifts. Hardened skin, great endurance, Tarkin answered.

I know you believe yourself ugly, Torga added. *But you are not. And you already love the strength and power, don't you?*

"Hunh," Kel said. But she knew, deep in her heart, Torga was right.

Hungry, weary, Rak'khiel stumbled.

Sharp claw tips grazed her skin, leaving moist trails.

Torga hissed distress.

I must be bleeding.

Men shouted, far behind her.

Shelter, knowledge and food waits ahead. I don't understand how I know, only that it's true. *If I can just get us there alive.*

Parallel, the huge man kept silent pace bearing Yola's battered body. *He is no threat to the cafuzogs ... or to me. The opposite, honesty be heard.*

She sneaked a glance at him, silhouetted against the skyline. His outline showed odd protrusions, shapes. *Weapons, I think. He might help me fight if I am caught.*

Kel willed one foot ahead of the other. Her hearts labored, beat erratically. She reached deep inside. As if drawing out her very bone marrow, she spent her final reserves.

Hunger's knives stabbed in the pit of Rak'khiel's stomach. *So empty, I feel sick.* Food for us – first. Most important. *I have no money ... it would be useless anyway, now that the 'Risto lord wants me.*

A movement of numbers in her mind. Mental tumblers clicked. *I do have coin – food too – in the hidden safe place.*

She hurried through the foothills. Their low silhouette of dark bumps, like a purple pebbled riverbed, stretched across the horizon. Beyond lay a tall mountain, its lone spire of rock stabbing mercilessly into the sky. Its shape – the vicious curving of a serpent's tooth.

Rak'khiel's skin crawled cold with dread, then flushed sweaty hot with anticipation. At last she would see Olica's forbidden haunted peak. The Fang.

Hurdling low sharp rocks, Kel dodged massive boulders in her final dash up the mountain. She startled at the crack of a broken branch, gunshot loud in the dark.

A soft brush touched her mind.

My contrition for scaring you, sent her large companion.

An abrupt flashing of lights in her mind brought her to a stop. Files flowed, stopped and opened. A blue-green wavering map snapped into focus. The cave she sought hid in a narrow gulley, tucked away behind the rise before her.

Rak'khiel jogged across the clearing, up the hill and dropped to her knees before she topped it. *Yola taught me to avoid showing my form against the moonlit sky.* Crawling, guerilla-style, she slithered over the top.

Leaping to the ground, Tarkin and Torga vanished.

Nothing! Her heart dropped out through the bottoms of her feet. Nothing here at all except a patch of Olica's pretty yellow flowers. Now what?

Still her mind insisted, pushed her legs against her wishes, through fragrant blooms, to the spot on the map.

A narrow opening, so well hidden it would never be found, existed between the myriad boulders and scattered rocks. *Safe.*

Rak'khiel turned sideways and scraped through the aperture.

Goddess on a broom! I left chunks of skin on both sides. Even if I wanted the strange male to go inside with me, he's much too large.

Muted pale gold light glowed not far ahead. *The color is wrong. It can't be from a fire. There's no flicker.*

She eased forward with care, fearing ambush.

Go in, ordered the voice in her head.

Chapter 20

Dark
Nara 14, 7206.50
The Fang, Olica

"No," Kel said to the mindvoice. "I'll not. It's a trap. I don't trust it."

Go slow. Examine everything. Something should trigger your memory. Find the center of the light source. You are safer than you have been in fourteen years, silly girl.

"Eff you," Rak'khiel snarled and exulted in her language. *No one to tell me I cannot use such satisfying curses.*

Her half-breath stuck in her throat. *Goddess, I'd give anything if only Yola were here to chide me. My fault. My grievous fault.*

Rak'khiel paced the lambent exterior, combing every peripheral niche of the cave. The yellow glow shone most bright at the cave's center, within the huge pile of debris. *Where is the forzaing light coming from? I have to go in there to make sure nothing evil waits for me. And I have to do it alone.*

New, heightened awareness, amplified hearing, told her Tarkin and Torga entered the cave. They made their slow way to where she stood. Wafting coneflower fragrance surrounded them. Their bellies were coated with bright yellow pollen.

"No, no, don't." she cried and leaped to stop Tarkin from

scratching at the piles of dirt.

Although I carried them here, the instant I stopped, they sprang from me to hide in the flowers and meadow grass. But Kel knew the cafuzogs weren't frightened of her. *They hide from the stranger.*

He is outside, Torga sent. *We slid past while he gathered branches to build the bier.*

He never noticed. Tarkin's smug comment made Kel smile.

Although your smell, your form, even your thoughts are different – you are still our Rak'khiel-more-than, Torga sent.

Yes, you concerned us greatly, but still we chose you. A black lip lifted exposing a sharp white canine.

"I know I am different now," Rak'khiel reassured. *Perhaps I never was an Olican girl. My memories of my life – was it all false? Have I nothing left of me?*

Trembling took her, knees crashed together hard enough to bruise. Her stomach wheeled and she braced her spine against the cave wall.

We are here. Tarkin and Torga's thoughts hammered at Kel. *All is well.*

But Kel didn't trust. Couldn't – after all she'd just seen and endured.

Before she could sit, rest, she had to explore the black scorched center area, look behind, perhaps through the dark pile of crumbled dirt directly below the Fang's apex.

Her brain dug in its mental heels. "No," she said. "Deep in my heart I know something waits for me. I'm scared."

Spikes of adrenaline shot through her body. She trembled as she crept, on the balls of her feet, skirting the cavern. Held too long in ready-state, her muscles looped into crunching spasms. She clenched her teeth against her scream, against her need to growl, to swear.

"Goddess, please let something happen. I can't stand this."

Her hearts stuttered, their staccato beats out of synch. Working against each other, they stole her breath. She needed to sit, to rest. She could not.

This cave proved much larger than she'd thought. Finding

a small underground stream crossing one back corner, she'd expected the air to be dank. Instead, though cool, it was fresh, even dry.

Strange metallic tangs and oily odors floated in the air.

Fragrance surrounded her. "Lovely ...," she whispered and breathed it deep. Cupping her hands to catch and scoop the perfume to her nose, she froze in shock. *The essence flows outward. From my skin?*

Tasca – informed the mindvoice – *your personal scent.*

I should ask why, I suppose. But I am more concerned with who or what occupies this cavern with me.

Come with us, Kel, Torga sent. *We can show you. In the back are ....*

Crates ... her mindvoice informed. *There is no danger. Go investigate.*

Gooseflesh crawled her skin, rippled, row after row.

But I cannot rest until I do. Kel squared her shoulders, clenched her hands into fists and marched into the cave center, to the tall heap of dirt and rock. She slowly circled the pile, stopping in shock.

Sprouting from the scorched and crumbled earth, its silver rounded tip leaning against a heavy scrape in the rock side, Rak'khiel studied what appeared to be a gigantic metal bullet.

Pod, said her minder.

A bright comet flash overhead startled.

I'm in a cave – how can I see a Goddess' dart? Another opening in the mountain, above the pod. *This is where and how it came down.* Tented netting overhead kept the secret.

A door opened in Rak'khiel's mind and displayed knowledge. Another infusion of knowledge unfolded. Kel watched the pod's crash, and the deployment of a camouflage canopy. She saw replayed, the actions of her own AI. *Who is mine? What's an AI?*

The keeper of this – your – ship, sent her mindvoice.

Craning her neck, careful not to approach the pod, she leaped back at movement on the silver craft. Noiselessly, the door of the life cocoon shimmered and slid up.

Rak'khiel screamed and bolted for the cave entrance.

The ever present annoyance, the mindvoice, chided her, guaranteed her safety and insisted she enter the ship.

"Effin Goddess' destruction if I will," she snarled and pressed against the two narrow entry stones.

Go through the open hatch.

"I supposed that means – the door – to me," Kel snapped, but slid, one foot carefully after the other until she stood outside the opening. Stretching her neck, she peeked around the corner.

A jumble of boxes, wood and plastic, bags of multicolor materials and sizes lay inside.

If you are hungry, remarked the mindvoice, *you will open one marked Ω∫°°†.*

The shaliting thing knows I'm starving. Still, hands fisted, hearts beating too fast, half-turned to flee, she cracked the lid of the box on top.

Yum, mine, Torga's black clawed hands pulled a packet from the carton.

I get this one, Tarkin snagged a square container. *And this, and this, and this.*

Kel, you eat this one and this too. You will like it. Plus it will sit good on your post-change tummy.

Her friends were right – about everything. *But how do they know about something we ... no, I ... have never seen. When does the list of things hidden from me ever end?*

Directed through another hatch, Rak'khiel found the first indoor ... *lav* ... she'd ever seen. A white ... *sink* ... and the opaque reflecting surface above did not interest her. The other spotless white fixture ... *toilet* ... did.

Following the mindvoice's instructions, she reveled in a hot shower, another first.

Her filthy ochre tunic went in the ... *disposer* ... and a cupboard off the lav produced a supply of pale blue loose shirts and drawstring pants in assorted sizes.

Inside another crate, she found a bright fluffy bag in a breathtaking color she did not know. *Pretty.*

For sleeping, explained the mindvoice.

Room for the cafuzogs in here. Too tired to plead – the mess of lights, flickering flipping streams of unfamiliar numbers, strange markings, the images in her mind made her stomach hitch.

Kel swallowed hard, slammed her throat tight like a clamshell. *I will not – I refuse to – throw up another meal.*

Rak'khiel spread the bag on the fuzzy woven fabric covering the pod floor and crawled into its toasty cocoon. Something dragged at her ... something odd.

Oh! The rug on the floor is ... white. On Olica, nothing – except my jewelry enamel is white – because of the awful yellow dust. It coats everything.

Elsewhere in the pod, a whirring noise sounded.

Head snapping up, double-hearts flipping, Kel stared. Waiting to be attacked.

No warning from the mindvoice, nothing to be seen, she resettled in the bag. *No place could be safer for me tonight than here.*

Two icy wet noses pushed aside the bag's edge. Four clawed paws peeled it back. Two warm furry bodies crawled inside.

Rak'khiel breathed a sigh of contentment as the cafuzogs took their usual places. Torga in the curve of her belly and Tarkin behind her, snuggled in the bend of her knees.

We came in the lifecocoon with you, Torga sent.

In stasis, like you, added Tarkin. *We are remembering everything now.*

Except for the highborn outside, Torga's thoughts still held worry. *Him, we should know. And we don't.*

"Where did we come from?" Kel asked but before the cafuzogs could answer, her snore broke the silence.

§

Hungry. Imperious, cold spots poked her cheeks. *Wake up!*

Rak'khiel startled vertical, a hand on each furry head. Waited for her hearts to slow, then took stock.

Somewhere in the middle of the night, her slumbering mind created ... if not peace ... at least a symbiotic working relationship with the pellet lodged inside. Now that her hearts no longer drummed, she realized she felt rested.

"Thank the Goddess, the spike of pain in my brain is finally gone."

A quick scan of the numbers hanging in the periphery of her vision told her the time, the day, the ambient. An inspection of the crates and boxes labels confirmed something else.

"I can read. Tarkin and Torga, I know what's inside every box."

She also suddenly knew something else. Something that hurled her diaphragm into her throat.

I am Rak'khiel I'Regence, first daughter to the most powerful Klan on our destroyed homeworld. Only the Emperor's Ruling House is above us. I am a Kra'aken.

I am a monster.

§

Her stomach's growl echoed too-loud in the cavern.

Goddess in a chalice, I'm starving. Even a horror such as I must eat.

She studied the labels on the foodstuffs, the boxes of nutrient paks.

"Tarkin, how old, do you think? Are they edible? Torga, can you guys eat them? You did last night. Do you feel okay? Or must you still hunt?" *Goddess, I'm rattling on. I can't seem to shut up.*

Targin and Torga strolled to her side, insouciant tails waving proudly.

We prefer hunting, Torga sent with a wicked mental

chuckle.

Destroyer prevent us having to eat the supplement pacs. Nasssty stuff. Tarkin's body doubled, he hunched and mimed vomiting. *See what we have ... because I am very, very hungry.*

Rak'khiel, you are grown big enough to make several good meals, instead of only a little one. Torga's lips rolled back, exposing many sharp white teeth. *Perhaps we will eat you for breakfast.*

Kel's chortle pealed through the cavern. "Let's look," she snorted and popped the lid on the nearest box.

Rak'khiel could not see or know Razr still stood guard outside the cave. And so, she missed the great smile of pleasure crossing and gentling his face at hearing her laugh.

§

"Yum." Finishing the last bite of her dessert, Rak'khiel licked an elegant forefinger, then inelegantly dabbed up and ate the remaining tiny crumbs. *Olica has sweets but this? Strange delicious tangy spices, sweet tastes, fluffy and firm textures. Yola will love ....*

Memory struck – her hand flew to cover her quivering mouth.

"Oh Goddess! Yola. How could I forget? I must perform her burning ... if he brought her as he promised ...."

"The body is here ..." a deep voice rumbled from the cave's mouth.

"Goddess, the man who helped me," Kel whispered. Her heart hiccupped at the gentle rumble of his words.

"If you need help, I will provide it. I do hope all is as you require."

Kel wondered how she understood his strange language, wondered if she heard tension in his next words.

"I am puzzled by some of your customs. I hope I have not erred. Perhaps later, you might explain?"

"What do you want to know?" Her own voice quavered, none too steady. *What waits outside this cave?*

"I would not, in ignorance, offend. I would not rush our conversation. Time is short, let us make your reverences. Even now, soldiers with animals search the lower hills."

Chapter 21

Mid-Dark
Nara 14, 7205.40
The Fang, Olica

Insecurity pinched Razr's lungs with icy fingers and made his twin heartbeats stutter. *What if I built it wrong?*

He absently rubbed his right thumb, frowned at the purple lump on his left. *Bashed the Destroyer-accursed thing with my pistol grip. All because I couldn't make myself leave her alone for the five minas it would have taken to fetch a hammer from the warplane.*

It would appear you are a bit disoriented, milord.

"Your enormous tribute for noticing, Brin." *The accursed AI is gloating, he is. Damn him.* "And I also appreciate your commenting on my behavior." Razr tried to put a sting into the words and knew he failed. *But somehow it no longer bothers me like it did.*

Razr evaluated his handiwork and fretted. *I hope Rak'khiel is pleased. I hope the image I lifted from her mind – this strange bier – is for burial. If the purpose is for some type of celebration, I am doomed.* He paced before the cave opening, paced the circumference of the raised structure, worried for the state of his female's mind. *While I searched for the burial protocols, I found other things too. Sweet Destroyer, such pain she holds inside. Such rage.*

The small glen, lushly carpeted with purple-edged grasses and fragrant yellow flowers, provided the perfect place for leavetaking.

Razr'd created the framework of red-barked poles. Crossing tree limbs, their wood joins lashed together with braided grass, provided the platform. Over it all, he laid a froth of silver-leaved smaller branches.

Placing Yola's body in the center, Razr scattered more shining leaves to cover the battered corpse. But, as he worked, the prince's fury grew. *I am a blooded warrior. I have seen much ... but this ....*

Saber fangs hung below his jaw, he heard his own low growling. His mind strove to match memories of his own wounds and their pain against the agonies this innocent woman must have suffered.

I will take your vengeance, Yola. I will extract it with extreme prejudice. This I vow on my Royal honor, my duty as Judging Ruler. No matter what your crime, Yola, there is no justification for what was done to you.

The metallic taste in his mouth told him his fangs had reappeared, slicing his lips. He forced them back, tried for calm.

"Brin? Can you place a shield about this area, contain smoke and sound?"

Already in place, sir.

"Your tribute." A deep pull of air, Razr's viscera quivered. Then gathering his courage, he called, "Rak'khiel? It's time."

Two black heads poked outside.

Razr watched them study the terrain, more carefully study him.

Black noses glistened, twitched. He knew the cafuzogs mindspoke each other. *Would they would mindspeak me if I tried?*

An error, I believe, milord, Brin sent. *Better you wait for them to initiate contact. My monitors show they are not at all sure of you. And, they are fully prepared to act.*

"Oh shata!" That was the very last thing Razr wanted. Instead he stood motionless, held his arms well away from his body. Hands open, fingers spread wide, he rotated his palms forward. As non-threatening a stance as a warrior knew how to present.

The long white stripe down each cafuzog back stood high, mohawked, on full alert. Emerging from the aperture, Kel's protectors separated, two paces between them, and progressed toward the bier slowly, carefully. Pausing six long paces from the cavern opening, they halted. Heads rotating, the two never stopped searching.

Razr studied the niche between the boulders, felt the tension in his shoulders ebb as Rak'khiel appeared. *Showered, rested. And unbelievably beautiful in ship's blues.* The bright suns' light reflected off her shining, riotous hair. She held one hand pressed protectively against her body.

Brin, Rak'khiel is complete. And Oh Great Destroyer, she is breathtaking. She has a heart-shaped face, a long graceful neck and a mass of dark hair. Her eyebrows are black, shaped like hunter-hawk wings, with their up-arcing ends. Her eyes are huge ovals, tilted like her brows. From here I can't see their color but her lips are full, deepest ruby and beautifully shaped.

Prince Helrazr's eyes devoured her.

And I ... Destroyer take me! Here I stand, unshowered, unshaven, stinking like a commoner. Armed like a mercenary – my robes of respect, of state, in the fighter. When I need to be .... Forza me – I have the brain of a slif.

Twin furrows appeared between Kel's sculptured brows. As she slid sideways through the narrow aperture, rough stone grabbed and snagged and ripped at the soft loose fabric of her clothing. Razr hoped her frown was due to the damage of her blues ... and not a reaction to him. He worried she might be injured. Why else would she hold her arm so close?

Rak'khiel nodded casual greeting but he saw the whites of her huge tilted eyes, smelled more than a hint of fear mixed with pre-war *tasca*. With her free hand, she lifted her shirttail, exposing a folded length of cloth in glorious blues, greens and golds.

Razr snatched a breath at the shimmering wonder she unfolded, holding it across her outstretched arms. He already grieved its loss. *I have never seen anything so lovely. With, of course, the exception of my female.*

Silver tracks down her tawny skin matched the shining leaves on the bier. Rak'khiel's grief-swollen lips softened, became slack. Single tears became a steady trickle.

Aching to comfort her, the prince could only stand motionless and watch.

Tasca, the sweet jessamin floral, vanillan and cinna of her Klan laced with something Other. It triggered his involuntary outpour of spicy Rex. Triggered a painful hardness below his belt.

His mind wasn't quick enough to stop his instinctive step toward her.

His hands, outstretched to console, were met by a flinch and terrified enormous eyes. Kel's body went taut as a drawn bow.

The cafuzogs shoved between them. Jaws gaped, black lips writhed, baring needle teeth.

Razr heard an unfamiliar male voice speak in his mind. The larger cafuzog.

Now I know you, Prince Helrazr. You survived. You are an honorable warrior ... even if you do have a reputation among the ladies.

"I mean only the highest respect for your charge," Razr whispered, lowering his hands and stepping away. "Are you of Ma'am's litter. Of my lady mother's protectors?"

I am Tarkin. And yes, my mother guarded yours.

Kel's attention riveted him, her head turning from the cafuzog to him. Then back again.

"My reprehensible, Rak'khiel." He backed another step, then yet another, until he saw her chest relax. "My intention was not to frighten, only comfort."

Razr backed again and watched the cafuzogs exchange a glance – and more.. Another step of retreat and Razr assumed a Kra'aken 'at-ease' military stance.

She took her eyes from him then and removed flint, paper scraps and a long wood sliver from the leather pouch at her waist.

"Rak'khiel? I have ... instant flame ... if you will?"

Lifting her chin, red swollen eyes awash, she nodded.

§

Hot red-orange flames licked at the bright lavender-tinted sky. Smoke dissipated unseen in the violet sunshine as Rak'khiel sang Yola home to the Goddess.

Brin, do you hear? What a sweet, yet powerful voice she has – spectacular in range and vibrato – without any formal training. On Kra'aken, she would already ... Curse it, never to be.

Kel stood, eyes closed, arms lifted and palms to the sky. Long coal-dark lashes lay heavy and tear-clumped against rose-tinted cheeks. Her face glowed with an inner radiance.

Brin, I think she is a true believer in her Olican faith, not just for show. Great Destroyer! Will her religion pose a problem?

Yes, milord. It is quite possible.

No, Brin. She will simply have to convert. A simple thing. She is Kra'aken, after all. But there is a contrasting scent, an odd tang threading her tasca?

Can you explain? Possibly the taint of poison? Could it be planetary chemicals in her blood?

I wish you could smell, Brin. It doesn't trigger my danger alarms. It just feels ... different.

Razr waited, standing his respectful distance, while Rak'khiel completed the ceremony.

The two unblinking cafuzogs flanked her closely, one on each side.

She rested slender hands on their silky heads, threaded fingers through the long white center-stripe.

"I vow to avenge you, my Mother," the soft whisper was more vicious, more deadly than if she'd shouted the words. "I will kill them all."

After the final ember winked to black, Razr turned to Rak'khiel, carefully closed the gap between them by a single step. Watching her eyes turn from the ashes of Yola's bier to fix on him, he froze. Stood unbreathing, waiting to see if she would permit it.

Far more difficult than taming a Kra'aken warsteed. Those beautiful, willful, stubborn creatures chose whom they carried. Without exception. Six months of courting, often far longer, prefaced a horse and rider pairing. To Razr's knowledge few warriors were honored. Many riders waited a lifetime and were never chosen. A warplane is simple, another reason he'd chosen flight. A pilot must only be the very best in his tier to qualify for a fighter.

"Your impatience will be your undoing," Razr's lady mother once said after a particularly egregious shuttle crash. Now, between his swollen throat and almost wet eyes, he finally understood the truth behind her words.

My courtship of Rak'khiel will be even more precarious. Warsteeds, although selective, are plentiful. There is only one Rak'khiel.

Gazing down at the top of her head, Razr admired the mass of shining hair. *Dark as mine but the shimmering blue of a Kra'aken lake gleams in it.* "Rak'khiel?"

"Yes?" Her eyes lifted to meet his.

What did she see in my face to cause her involuntary flinch?

Kel's wide oval eyes opened further still, her large pupils contracted, then stretched into black horizontal diamonds. Two cut-gemstone rings began to rotate around her irises. Kra'aken change. Kra'aken killing eyes. Kra'aken mating eyes. Lustrous rose-colored patterns shimmered, began to dance on her skin.

Razr searched her face, gazed deep. Then the most eligible and elusive Kra'aken bachelor in all history gave up his heart without protest, without struggle.

She owns me.

Brin, if I had my choice of all of Kra'aken females, my courting offerings would hang only on this girl-child's receiving wall.

My prince, try to remember she knows only a life of Olican conditioning. It is good her morphosis is complete and her defenses are progressing. You must proceed slowly, with great caution. She will not understand any Kra'aken custom.

Understood. Casual conversation would place her at ease. But, Brin, what do I say? Prince Helrazr the Glib, speechless in her presence.

"D-do you plan to go alone?" he blurted. *Smooth, Prince Razr.* "To kill those responsible, I mean?"

"Mother is mine to avenge."

Razr heard her leaked thought ... *My guilt, although I cannot bring myself to confess it ....*

How can this possibly be her fault? Razr's brain finally responded. He knew he stared, drank her in, inhaled her special fragrance. And found himself powerless to stop.

What to say to distract – us both? "How many will you kill? How many have refuge inside the fortress?"

"I don't know ...."

Once again he caught fragments of her thought ... *he is magnificent. I'm ugly, a nothing. No longer even a plain heifer of an Olican girl – I'm now an abomination.*

The prince averted his eyes. *If Kel knew I hear her every thought, can read each emotion passing across her face; if she knew I was privy to her innermost feelings, she would be humiliated.*

Then the furious thought from cafuzog to girl cut through the silence.

You are not ugly. Not a nothing. Torga's mental shout at Rak'khiel startled Razr.

Holy Destroyer, murmured the AI. *That's one angry cafuzog.*

Long white spine fur ridged, stood high in fury. *You are highest caste, except royalty. You are beautiful. Your mother was a world renowned vocalist. Your father, the Righteous Shield Guard to the Emperor himself, was one of the greatest warriors who ever lived.*

Goddess! Rak'khiel recoiled.

Her voice – of course. The Regence matriarch – a world famous singer – is her mother. Razr sought his memory of Lady Floril's holo on his music discs. Rak'khiel's profile – a perfect copy of her mother's. *It is she, stupid Razr.*

Kel's face ran the gamut from ghost white to a ruddy scarlet. Jaw hanging loose, she stared at her cafuzogs in shock.

The prince fixed his eyes on a spot far above her head and kept them there. *Brin? Did you hear?*

Affirmative.

She's unaware I can hear her thoughts. The cafuzogs haven't realized it either. Or they are keeping silent for reasons of their own. Razr's hearts leaped, attempted to fly from his chest, place themselves in her hands. *She thinks I'm magnificent?* He struggled to hold all expression from his face, to stand statue still. When all he wanted to do was caper like the court fool, and shout his feelings to the world.

The two cafuzogs and Kel clustered on the ground. Because her voice was low, her words muted, Razr turned his thoughts to other things. *I wish her to have privacy.*

Perhaps, thought Razr, *the courtship rituals are short in this place. They must be, for my sanity's sake. I pray the mourning period for her mother will not require years.*

The pounding blood and his anatomy's obvious interest required he fix his thoughts on the hardships of basic warrior training, digging latrines, reciting the family bloodlines. Anything to disappear his throbbing erection.

If he initiated Kra'aken marriage alliance forms – surely she ….

No. Brin's single word fell on Razr's dreams like a bucket of ice. *You must wait. You know it as surely as I do.*

Despair threatened, fear squeezed his mind and his heart. He knew Brin's comments for truth. Kel's youth, her immediate metamorphosis still in final stages, all precluded any relationship except friendship.

Razr's body, however, seemed incapable of reason. He issued it an order to stand-down. *There are things I can do, things I must do. She doesn't understand our customs – in Rak'khiel's mind she is Olican. She knows nothing else. Knowledge, training must go slowly and I must earn her trust.*

Prince Helrazr! Brin shouted in his mind. *Great Destroyer! Will you pay attention? She's planning to leave now to kill those who hurt Yola.*

Shata, of all times to go woolgathering! "You cannot, even with your new strength, avenge your mother alone. It is suicide," Razr heard the anxious quaver in his voice. Did she hear it also?

Control yourself, Prince Helrazr, sent Brin. *This is her mother's forzaing funeral, you animal.*

Just two days ago, I thought to end my life – now I'm determined to live and wed her. *Die and leave me alone, Rak'khiel? I will never, never allow it.*

Slender fingers pulled on her right earlobe. "I didn't think about …." Again, Razr heard her thoughts. *I know nothing. He must believe me a great fool.*

"They have weapons, beasts, guards. Is it your desire to kill them all?"

Rak'khiel's chin lifted, her lips compressed. Drawing a great shuddering breath, she nodded. "I have vowed it."

The prince heard defiance in her words; he recognized the fear in her voice. His gaze roamed the countryside, came back to rest on her face. *Such a tiny thing, stands not quite to my shoulder, yet so fierce.*

"Without me, you will fail." Razr said. "And most certainly die."

He caught her added thought, *My death means nothing. I killed mother, I won't be responsible for your death, too.*

Rak'khiel performed a compassionate killing, not murder. I saw it. Why blame herself? But she does. I must go carefully.

Her eyes flooded. A single drop spilled over, ran down to

mar the tawny perfection of her smooth cheek. She dashed it away with a furious hand, snarled, "I refuse to endanger anyone else."

I must drive him away, Razr listened to her thoughts. *I need him, I know I do, but I will not use someone, a resource I do not deserve.*

One large hand covering his mouth, Razr hid a smile and feigned a cough to muffle his laugh. *So spirited. So honorable.*

"I am a warrior, Rak'khiel. My job is fighting." *She doesn't need to know the rest.*

"This is my debt to settle," Kel said.

"I fight for fun and because it is my life. I also need the practice." *I would not anger you, but I will be there.* "May I help?"

"Only if I require it." Rak'khiel said. Her thought drifted, *He's either very good or very arrogant. Or both.*

Razr's blood thumped in his oversize temple veins, his face suffused scarlet at the insult – until reason quelled anger. He very carefully, very slowly unclenched his fists, wondered if she saw. He dare not let her know he heard.

Razr knew three things. He needed to stop giving orders, he needed to lose his ego, and he needed to learn how and what Kel thought. Before her mem mods taught her to shield her mind.

"Fair enough," he said. "You need armor and weapons. Tell me, has your skin changed at any time?" *Besides what I just saw?* Reaching across the distance between them, he held out his hand.

Rak'khiel didn't move, didn't take it. "No, I've grown tall but nothing else except the voice in my head. It is silent again – for which I thank you."

Not thankful enough to touch me – so much for my charm.

Razr worried at the problem – should he ask Brin to reactivate the mindvoice? Could he ask Brin to accelerate her change? Should he wait and hope her armor phase triggers soonest? *More likely, at a critical point in battle, the godsrotted thing will insist she return to the mountain, distract her and get her killed. It wants her in the medbox where she belongs – I agree. Destroyer take it!*

He paced, saw Rak'khiel watching, quietly waiting, keeping her distance.

Brin?

Yes, Razr, it is a problem. I've monitored those thoughts of yours which reach me.

Can you do anything?

Trigger her armor? The AI's thought laced with reluctance.

Yes.

I don't know – I could try, if she's willing.

Razr paced some more.

"What is wrong?" The lilt of Rak'khiel's voice brought him to an abrupt halt. "You're wearing a ditch in the ground." A hint of humor lurked in her tone.

Razr flashed her the grin rumor said had melted a hundred female hearts.

She gave him a tentative smile in return, relaxed a little more.

"I was thinking," he said. "You need to be able to call your armor before we go hunting."

"If it pleases you, explain." Her expression seemed more amiable.

Razr's lungs and hearts roared like the warplane's mains. *Perhaps a small connection between us, a place to begin?* But he only said, "A fully metamorphed adult of our species has the ability, using thought, to change our skin to armor. We can change our underskeleton to claws, barbs and fangs."

"Horrible. I don't want it." Rak'khiel's sculpted brows drew together, her generous mouth squeezed into a stingy dot.

Shata! Razr saw her revulsion, quickly added, "It will protect you, give you the weapons to kill those who hurt Yola. Kill them in any manner you desire – taking as long as you wish – and, prevent being murdered yourself."

Just as he was confident it would, Rak'khiel's expression changed. *She is, after all, a daughter of the Righteous Shield Arm, the very practical and pragmatic Lord Regence.*

Her heavy disapproving frown relaxed, brows rose into lifted arches. Her pinched tight mouth relaxed into its generous shape, then formed an 'o'.

"Really?" Kel said. "Interesting. You can do this?"

"Yes." Razr chanced a small smile, a friendly glance – tried to think of anything other than mating.

"And then look normal" – *handsome* – "as you now appear whenever you wish?"

"Yes," Razr said. And sent a sneaky smug thread to the fighter. *My, my Brin, adaptable little savage, isn't she?*

A snicker somewhere in the back of Razr's mind told him the AI heard and agreed.

"How do I do it?"

Ha, hooked her. "Think a command at any part of your body. Like 'hand claws', or 'armor up.' See what happens."

"Nothing ... oh wait." A new expression possessed her face, a focused-down-tight Rak'khiel. "The skin on my arm rippled pink, almost a pattern, but nothing more." Disappointment rode her voice. "I can't do it."

"It's begun, though." *Regence Klan's house and change color is rose.*

"Will you show me?" Large eyes, framed by long ebony lashes, perused him without fear.

For the first time.

He stared into smoky-topaz irises, flecked with metallic copper and silver twists. Dragging himself out of her eyes and into the conversation, he asked, "Show you what?"

"Your armor, of course. Will you?"

Razr exerted delicate control, holding back claws, fangs, spikes and barbs. He allowed the golden-scalloped patterned scales to shimmer, to ridge and then to form interlocking protection from his left shoulder to wrist.

"It's beautiful," Kel said, "like a sleeve." She extended a

delicate hand, stopping just short of his muscular arm. "May I touch it?"

Oh Great Destroyer, girl, you know not what this costs me – not to leap and wrap my teeth about your neck. Razr nodded politely, put a governor on his breathing and heart rate and said, to his amazement, in a perfectly normal voice, "Of course."

Rak'khiel extended a long-fingered, elegant hand, her fingertips callused, gently floated them like a feather-moth across his wide, muscular forearm.

Down, he mentally commanded his throbbing maleness, blessed his loose clothing. *Down, curse you.*

Rak'khiel reached again, this time a delicate trail of fingertips like tiny licking flames, trailed up to his shoulder and back to his strong wrist. Left a mind-warping trail of fire in its place. Stole his voice.

His scales rippled like an ocean wave, a path of hitching shivers, following the tracery of her touch.

"Okay," she agreed. "I will do it. Tell me though, did your pellet hurt?"

Hunh? Razr yanked his wandering mind from sweaty bodies and tangled sheets back to the present. "What pellet?"

"The pellet between your toes."

"I didn't have one." Razr sent a desperate query. *Brin?*

Her implant preventing morphosis. Casting the glamour.

Glamour? Razr asked. *Explain.*

Mimics the appearance of local people – provides a disguise.

"Oh, yes. I forgot."

Rak'khiel's quizzical expression, a single lifted brow, marred the perfection of her beautiful face.

"Where did you go?" She demanded, a slender finger worried one delicate ear.

"I was asking my AI for information," Razr said.

"There is another like you?"

"No." He pressed his lips together, frowned. "The Artificial Intelligence is a help to me, like you have the voice in your head." *Not quite true but easier to understand for now.*

"Oh. So why did I have that awful lozenge in my foot?"

"It is a device making you appear Olican – for your safety. My ship's arrival must have triggered your change."

"You have a riverboat? Where is it?" she demanded. "How long until I am ready to fight?"

"My ship moves through the air."

"Is it what I saw?"

"Yes. And my change took two aiys. For a female, I don't know. You are close, perhaps another aiy or two, to full metamorphosis."

"Translate into Olican, please?"

"Two of your days for me" answered Razr. "It could be less for you."

"I won't wait that long – I'm late for a date with the dairyboy."

Razr clenched his fists, suffused by hot, jealous fury. *A date? She has interest in another male? I'll kill him.* Razr's anger made him miss the cold rage in Rak'khiel's voice.

His skin shimmered gold, scales of armor beginning to display. Razr lips bulged, made room for emerging fangs. *Shata! Forza! I'll scare her to death.* He forced them back, disappeared the armor, relaxed his hands.

"Rak'khiel, no. Not yet. Give it a day at least, develop your protections." Razr heard the panic, pleading in his voice. Cold fingers pressed his throat; he feared she heard the quaver too. *What am I doing? A prince begging like a supplicant? A prince gives orders and they are followed.*

Hot outrage at himself tinged his words, spoken in haste. "You are forbidden to go until you can fight properly."

"I am going. What you do is up to you," she said, a hard edge in her voice.

Razr saw the shutters of friendship fall from her eyes. What truly lived behind Kel's lovely orbs lay exposed. Pure Kra'aken – merciless, unemotional and flat. All amity gone, Rak'khiel slid sideways into the fissure.

Razr cursed under his breath reliving her anger. His

stomach roiled, doom pressed heavy on his shoulders, invaded his mind. Large hands trembling, he paced the ground outside the cave, too frightened to curse. He yanked his braids, replayed his forza-up, hated himself.

He'd never known such terror – fearful their tiny beginning friendship was ruined, fearful Rak'khiel would be killed, and fearful he'd be alone again. *I'm too big to enter the cavern. Great Destroyer take it – I can't even go make amends.*

That went well, Brin snarked.

Silenza, Razr replied with a half-hearted growl, received the AI's usual chuckle and entered the fighter. Rak'khiel's change posed critical questions badly needing answers – perhaps help existed somewhere in the databases. *If I have useful data for her, she might speak to me again.*

§

One hora passed; then two. Deep in research, with Brin's assistance, Razr startled.

Man-thing? A small worried thought – Tarkin's – touched Razr's mind.

Is Rak'khiel with you? Torga's anxious send.

No. Chill claws clutched Razr's stomach. *"Why?"*

We cannot find her and weapons are missing.

Chapter 22

Mid-Dark
Nara 14, 7205.80
The Fang, Olica

"Mindvoice," Rak'khiel snapped. "I require weapons."

Lady Regence, I am but a splinter of your personal Artificial Intelligence. Her name is Caylee, she resides within the lifecocoon. My task within your mind is complete and Caylee is even now reabsorbing me into her whole. Speak to her from anywhere within the pod. She will answer.

Blood pushed hard in the vein at her temple. "Another effing roadblock?" But Yola's training – respect and gratitude – surfaced. "My thanks."

Kel wound her way up through the ship, past two levels and emerged into the craft's nose.

Standing quietly before the banks of screens, she scrolled through her installed mem mods for clues. *Nothing. Now what do I do?*

A female image appeared in mid-air, hung suspended at eye level. Too tall, too slender for true Olican beauty, still the woman was breathtaking in her own way. An odd tug of familiarity pulled at a corner of Rak'khiel's hindbrain, made her hearts thump against each other.

"Welcome back, Rak'khiel. I am Caylee."

Had she not seen it happen, Rak'khiel would have sworn a real person stood before her on the lifecocoon's decking.

"You have been absent from the pod for more than fourteen and a half yaras. I have missed you."

Why do I feel I know her? Why do I feel so disoriented?

Ruby brocade, piped in gold, formed a fitted overrobe. Her embroidered white lawn dress flowed and swirled revealing glimpses of crimson high heeled shoes. The ethereal image of the woman solidified.

Kel's lungs refused to work, her head felt somehow offset. *Goddess, not even Yola's finest can compare with the fabrics this woman wears.*

Rak'khiel fixed her eyes on the floor, checked her focus. Everything remained in its correct spot, nothing shimmered or disappeared. A crazy image flitted, that of a brain chunk suspended in mid air – hovering half in and half outside her skull – about a foot below and to the right.

Tumblers clicked in her mind, images fuzzed and resolved. Pieces of memory's puzzle fell into place. *Caylee is a machine. A machine has missed me? A machine has feelings?*

"You have been here since I entered the cocoon? Why didn't you speak to me last night?"

"You were radiating extremely high stress levels," soothed the AI. "Since you had accepted the mindvoice and allowed it to guide you, I feared my appearance could cause overload."

"Most possible – my thanks." *I am still so close to being unhinged, so close to losing control.* Another mental picture – of herself becoming a million tiny insane pieces scattering into the universe – brought a snorted laugh.

Rak'khiel sucked one heavy breath and held it. With a deliberate closure of her eyes, she thought of a blanket of calm. Mentally smoothing it over the chaos in her mind, she tucked in the edges, mitered the corners, and exerted control. If only temporary. *I have a vow to keep.*

Kel raised her gaze, locked eyes with the AI, and marveled yet again at the stunning appearance of the woman's image.

"Caylee, does the life cocoon have weapons?"

"Of course. Why do you ask?"

"I intend to kill some people."

The avatar recoiled. Attempting to conceal her reaction, she smoothed her hair with a jerky hand. "You've warrior training then, during your outside years on this planet?"

"No. But I promised vengeance. I will keep my vow."

"Rak'khiel – you are final-stage morphosis – the most perilous part. Who cares for you?"

The girl's full lips, eerily similar to those of the AI, worked, pressed bloodless as she fought to contain her emotions. "No one. Adopted Mother is dead. A stranger helped me."

"Who is this stranger? He might be important." Caylee tilted her head, added, "Kel, it is critical the medbox evaluate your change."

"Kel?" Rak'khiel's dark brows veed together. "Tarkin and Torga call me Kel. Why do you, a stranger, a machine, call me that?"

"Kel is your mother's diminutive for you. I am her composite image, imprinted with her personality and physical traits. She sent Tarkin, Torga with you in the survival pod for companions and guardians."

"You are my ...? You look like my ..., my Mother?" Kel's voice trailed into a whisper. Her knees turned to water, dissolved beneath her. She folded, then crumpled on the floor. Staring at the avatar, huge eyes wide in disbelief, she asked, "Why did she – uh, you? – send me away? What did I do wrong?"

"Nothing. Your parents loved you beyond reason. When Earth attacked Kra'aken, the only possible way to save your life, and hundreds of other children, was to send you all into the universe in life cocoons. Bless the Great Destroyer, you survived."

"Are there others like me?" Rak'khiel's gaze turned brighter, hope caught like the spark of a tiny match touched to a candle wick. *Didn't the strange man say he was?*

"I don't know. I've had no Kra'aken contact since our launch. Until today."

"What am I expected to do?" Rak'khiel stared at her hands as if she'd never seen them before. *Six long skinny fingers on each hand. Eeech.* But studying the holo of her birth mother, Kel saw something else. *Caylee is different, yes. But she is also beautiful.*

"First, enter the medunit. You must safely transit morphosis. Then, learn the study modules, learn our warrior traditions, learn piloting. If I read you correctly – this planet does not please you. You can then take the pod into space and find other survivors. Carry on our race and traditions."

"No." Rak'khiel's voice cracked, and her fisted hands trembled. The haunted look in her topaz eyes transformed into determined granite. "First I kill the Olicans who betrayed Yola. Then the 'Ristos who tortured and murdered her."

The AI's eerily familiar face and voice triggered snatches of memory – of a beautiful woman with sculpted features and long dark curls and a handsome blonde man with copper-shot eyes. *He swung me around, high then low. Laughing and playing. My parents.*

Twin hearts swelled in pride; then remembrance of tortured, dying Yola shredded them. Consuming anger boiled, interfered with thought.

"You need the protections of the change," Caylee said. "Before you put yourself in jeopardy."

"Give me the weapons or I'll go without them." A soft, despairing voice echoed in her mind. Kel caught her breath with the realization she could hear the AI's thoughts as easily as she could those of the cafuzogs.

Kel's stance is angled forward, her shoulders squared, jaw hard. The image of her mother, the determined stubbornness of her father. She means it. Without armaments, she will die in the doing. I must assist.

Cold claws gripped Kel's stomach. *Caylee believes, just like Razr does, that if I charge into town, I'll die. But I'm not waiting for months, or weeks, or even days for revenge. Besides, the 'Ristos are all searching for me. How much time do I have?* Rak'khiel waited for the AI's decision.

"Very well," Caylee said. "Without complete morphosis we cannot use mind-jack direct input. That would be best, but it's not an option. Take the command couch and attend, your favor."

"This?" Rak'khiel pointed at the dark blue pilot's station. At Caylee's nod, she sat. "Eeeikes!" She squeaked when its contours cozily enfolded her.

The AI rolled glowing green and white numbers, red data on pale aqua screens. Lost in concentration, in mysteries unfolding, Kel forgot to be afraid.

A half hora later, the command center sent her two levels down, to a simulator room. Programs on weapons, targets, basic combats assaulted Rak'khiel from every side.

A multi-limbed creature with slitted red eyes leaped from the ceiling.

Kel fumbled the projectile pistol from her belt. The gun bucked in her hand, her shot ricocheted from the ceiling and Kel swore the effing program chuckled.

She set her jaw, checked the load of her weapon.

Another half-hora passed and the sim chamber hatch slid open. A pummeled, stiff and sore, but extremely enlightened hard-eyed girl, with a cold merciless smile, emerged.

Kel heard a musical laugh echo throughout the ship when she muttered under her breath, "The Goddess-accursed thing killed me six times in a row before I even hit it."

Instructions fed into her mind, she headed with purpose toward the weapons stores and the adjacent galley.

Ten minutes later, carrying a small duffle, Rak'khiel emerged from the cave into the dusky evening. Carefully she made her stealthy way through the boulders into a small stand of slender red-barked trees. Silver leaves rustled in the light breeze and scents of coneflower fragrance overlaid the heavy earthy musk of dew on grass. Since morphosis, the familiar smells of Olica were overwhelming, even repugnant.

With trembling hands, she removed a bandolier, a weapons belt and a projectile weapon from the bag. A laser pistol, a large gutting knife and three smaller ones plus a dart gun with poison flechettes joined the pile on the ground.

A smile crossed her face at the remaining explosive surprises still in the pack. She donned a headband with special optics and a hearclip. In three short minas, an armed Rak'khiel jogged down the sharp slope of the mountainside.

Well done, Caylee sent. *Good hunting. Remember your morphosis will strike without warning. It can render you paralyzed, or unconscious. Make sure you are never exposed or vulnerable.*

"My gratefulness, Caylee."

Your safe return, the only appreciation I desire.

Rak'khiel's heart and throat swelled at the words. Her vision fuzzed into blurry, she ducked her head, swiped at her eyes. Swirling hair caught on her eyelashes, stuck to her lips.

If no one has scavenged our cottage, I have hair ties in mother's ancient box. I want it.

§

Lungs expanded, Kel's double-hearts fed energy to her new, efficient war machine – her body. Long strides stretched further, until a blurred figure raced through the countryside. At the small clearing where she spent so many frustrated days with Tarkin and Torga, Kel paused, crouched.

She clicked down an optical lens, zoomed in. *Nothing.* Kel's newly developing olfactories sniffed, gleaned the faint breeze for dogs, soldiers, village men. *Nothing.* She stood, armed herself – projectile weapon in one hand, laser pistol in the other – and began a stealthy approach.

The little house stood dark and quiet, door ajar.

Crouching under the narrow fabric-covered window she listened for voices. *Nothing.* But she smelled metallic copper, remembered Crucifixion Hill.

Kel leaped through the open door, frantic eyes searching. *Goddess!* Blood smeared the jamb, smeared their overturned tiny table and chairs. *She fought them, or they hurt her deliberately, because they could.*

Without thinking, she rubbed the pounding in her temples. Flinched.

Two great vessels, expanded and throbbing with rage, forced blood through her head. *Control. The very first sim lesson. But Goddess this is hard.*

Yola's earring tree still stood on the mantle. Unbroken, on the hearth, sat the silly clay gosfowl Kel made for Yola's birthday. *When I was seven.*

Rak'khiel slid both into the duffle. Brushing aside the blue and green striped curtain that separated their sleeping areas, she stepped between the beds.

A single hand dragged Yola's cot from the wall. Dropping to her knees, she lifted the coverlet on the back side. Underneath, untouched, waited the copper-bound chest. Kel pulled it close, lifted the lid, inhaled its fragrance.

Dark drops stippled the contents, warm wet splashed on her hand caressing the silky treasures. Hunched over the box, her slender body shuddered with silent sobs.

Approaching voices pulled awareness.

Flipping the lid and latch closed, Rak'khiel gathered it under one arm and sprinted from the cottage. *Now to take Yola's vengeance.*

First, the dairyboy.

Chapter 23

Mid-Dark
Nara 14, 7205.95
Fighter

At the cafuzog's alert, Razr sprang from the chair and bashed his head on the overhead screen. Tribute to his agitation, he never noticed the pain.

"Forza me." He shouted, diving into the warplane's core, dropping for the weapons lockers two levels down.

The only bright red door in the area, he didn't have to think. Military training served well – in two minas, an armed warrior leaped from the warplane's hatch to the ground. Razr ignored the ladder, and its steps, the thick muscles of his thighs absorbed impact.

"Brin, she is First Priority," Razr's low voice pitched an octava too high. He didn't wait for acknowledgement. He was already sprinting down the mountainside, chest out, legs pumping, hurdling rocks and bushes in a direct line toward the village.

Razr cursed Rak'khiel, cursed himself. *How long has she been gone? Why didn't I watch? I knew her intent. Destroyer! Did I underestimate her resolve? I certainly did. Shata, Brin. She's a Regence. What was I thinking?*

The AI didn't answer his prince's rhetorical questions.

"You can't die. Damn you. You cannot." Razr's roar bespoke hot rage. *False, that.* His hearts pounded, a lump of ice chips lay heavy in his gut.

I'll kill her. I'll catch her and kill her for scaring me out of the rest of my natural life.

Unnerved by fear, he increased his pace. Unaware of his fisted hands, his taut body, Razr's breath soon came hard, leg muscles cramping, a searing pain in his side.

Relax, damn you. You can't run unless you breathe.

He tried, he truly did, but images filled his mind. Terrible pictures of Kel's broken body, caught and killed mid-change. Of Yola's torture with Rak'khiel's face superimposed. He ran faster, harder, lengthened his strides. Felt the tension crawl him again.

His olfactories were keyed to only one scent – the mixture of Kel's *tasca* and personal female scents of change. The rest of this Destroyer-accursed hole of a planet could go straight to the twelfth hell, but his Rak'khiel must be alive. And well.

Chapter 24

Mid-Dark
Nara 14, 7206.10
The Dairy, Olica

"Goddess in a butter churn," murmured Kel. "What happened here?"

The pasture's fence lay in toothpicks and the cows – if any remained alive – were gone. A sniff ... fresh blood ... drew a string of saliva and the overwhelming urge to gobble the lumps of rent bovine flesh.

Shalit, what am I thinking? I will not be this horrific thing.

Her first few footsteps in the lush grass confirmed Rak'khiel's location. *This is the dairy farm. Does that abomination of a boy live here or in the village? I will soon know.*

The lavender rings of Olica's twin suns turned purple just before disappearing below the horizon. The valley plunged into darkness.

Precious box tucked beneath her arm, Kel glided building to building, sniffing for the boy's scent. She peered in windows and pressed newly sensitive ears against walls, listening for his voice.

Nothing.

Murmurs from the barn loft drew her attention. An outer

search revealed no ladder, no window sills. Frowning at the rough boards comprising its sides, running a hand across the surface, she wished for a way to scale the building.

With the first nudges of pressure, the first sharp stabs at the end of each fingertip, a scream broached her lips. But Kel pressed them together, holding back the noise. She swallowed a cry of glee, finding extruded claws – thick, curving and sharp. If claws could be lovely, hers were – in the dusty pink shade of Sameth's wife's climbing roses.

She directed her mind to her toes, braced against the not-quite-pain sensation.

Rak'khiel smiled. Knew at the feel of it, reflecting the rage in her hearts, it would not be reassuring. This smile was cold, transforming her face into something terrible.

Secreting duffle and chest behind a bush, Kel disappeared her hand claws, opened the box and selected a deep burgundy and pale pink hair ribbon.

Capturing the mass of long heavy hair, she pulled back and twisted it. Wrapping the woven tie twice, she knotted it at the nape of her neck.

My Ela hair was straight, light brown and thin. This is a change I approve.

Hand claws, she commanded.

A grin of savage delight, the anticipation of revenge, produced pressures on her lips. Fangs anxious to come out to play. She disappeared them with a low chuckle and a wish.

A gentle push drove twenty-four claws deep into the rough wood of the barn sides. *Goddess they are sharp.*

Rak'khiel silently scaled the barn, exultant in the strength of her body and claws. *Holding, lifting my weight effortlessly.*

Although several Olican workers chatted or snored in the hay, Kel did not find the one she sought. *I know where Sameth lives. And I know the house of the unmarried man who came to our door with the dairyboy.*

Rak'khiel slithered down the wall with the stealth and smooth agility of an orange-spotted rock lizard.

A searing pain in her head slammed her to her knees, progressed through her cracking, popping spine, up through her writhing limbs.

Aaaah. As Caylee said and I chose to disbelieve. The morphosis.

Rak'khiel hit the ground, rolled tight against the shrubbery, the barn, and gave up to the agony. Time and pain passed.

Lucky, she thought, hauling to her feet after the seizure subsided. *Effing lucky I was not seen.*

She knelt and waited for the dizziness to subside. Readjusting her weapons, resettling the duffle across her back, Kel retrieved her box and slid carefully away from the barn and the dairy.

The village sprawled before her, a few dim lights dotting the thick dark.

Rak'khiel crept – dodging from bush to tree, now mindful of secure hiding spots – to the single man's hovel.

Chapter 25

Mid-Dark
Nara 14, 7205.85
Olican Village

Rak'khiel stealthed her way through the village.

Dogs barked. But when she came close, they went slinking away to find refuge behind their owners.

Her short fast pants of anticipation brought constellations of blinking white dots before her eyes. *Breathe,* she quoted her sim training. *Breathe slow and easy, damnit. Or faint ... and be caught. Die like Yola did.*

Kel's conscience spoke in her mind – in Yola's voice. "Do you realize you are planning cold-blooded murder? Do you realize this is the one unforgivable sin? The one damning you to eternal flames?"

"Well, yes," Rak'khiel snapped. "Yes, I do." She quashed the voice, overrode it with memories of Yola's battered body. Nothing could be more obscene.

Twin hearts pounded in her ears. *Shalit, other people will hear. I must hurry.*

She dropped to a crouch, one hand holding her precious box, the other braced against the hovel for balance. Quiet as death, she approached the open window.

Rak'khiel placed her duffle on the ground, set Yola's chest

on top. Slowly, with a hunter's patience, she raised her head. Peering over the sill's edge, her eyes scanned the hut's reeking interior.

Her prey sat hunched over a greasy plate of gray meat and vegetables. One dirt-encrusted hand held the dish firm as if preventing its escape, the other plied a large spoon. His eyes, beneath a protruding pocked brow, were closed.

Rak'khiel's steady hand removed the dart gun from her belt, loaded a flechette and shot him between his furry caterpillar brows.

Bless Caylee, her training tapes and sims.

At the dart's strike, he opened his eyes. They bulged, as if to burst from his head, when Kel slithered feet first through the window. The bitter stench of fear's sweat flooded the room.

She laughed, low and humorless.

The man's mouth opened, closed, worked in silent screams, as the poison took him. Meaty hands shook, his fleshy body rippled – his efforts to push back from the table failed.

Rak'khiel strode to him, plucked the flechette from his forehead and wished for fangs.

The tightening of her upper lip confirmed fledglings. Running a wary tongue, she checked their length. The pulsing ripple of warm on her chin turned her grin more than savage. *Both long and sharp! Goddess be praised.*

She leaned close, exulted as the terror in her victim's eyes grew.

"You are still breathing," she whispered. "But you are dead. It will be horrible, slow and painful. This is for Yola."

Unholy impulses, vicious glee surged through her, and with it came an urge nearly impossible to ignore. *I want to rip his still-beating heart from his chest and devour it. Goddess, I am disgusting. I will not be such an animal.*

A low growl – all gleaming blood-tipped teeth and icy eyes – escaped Rak'khiel as the man tried to speak, to shake his head in denial.

She turned away, stepped to the window and slid through. Slipping the duffle across her shoulder, she retrieved the wooden chest.

Movement partway down the dirt street drew her attention. With a forefinger, she flipped down her optical, zoomed it and found Sameth outside his cottage. Through an uncovered window, she saw Sameth's wife fixing supper. *Moving carefully, favoring an arm.*

Rak'khiel clicked the optical again for a closer look – yes, both the woman's eyes were black as tumbled river rocks, purple fingerprints marked her upper arms.

Something dark rose in Kel's mind. *Evil tempered brute. He will never hurt you again.*

Creeping behind the rowed houses, she approached Sameth's house.

His dog sounded an alarmed bark, then, scenting her, it whined and scrabbled at the house door.

A thud, a yelp.

The last time he hurts you too.

"Shut it, you coward," Sameth growled. "Get off the porch."

Rak'khiel's brain hiccupped, came up with a knowledge-flash. The AI sees through my eyes now. We created the connection before I left the pod. I can ask her for help.

Caylee? How do I handle this one? Kel broadscanned Sameth and his yard.

Good to hear you, Kel. If a machine could have angst in its voice, Caylee did. *Any trouble with transformations?*

One small seizure. I'm fine.

How long did it last? Were you seen?

No, it was short. I was well hidden.

Constant cover is mandatory, pressed the AI. *But, as to your question. Tell me ... would you have room to hide between the stacked wood and that large cluster of bushes?*

Yes .... Rak'khiel took a look through fresh eyes. *Absolutely brilliant. I'll mess with his precious woodpile. Sameth will be enraged, come investigate and ... I'll kill him. And no one will see. My thanks, Caylee.*

Computers do not understand humor's subtleties, they cannot. But, Kel would swear to it, the AI laughed in delight.

The vicious cold thing, the murderous desire, wrapped Kel's spine with *frissons* of ice, slid up into her brain and waited with barely contained glee.

Scuttling behind the split logs, she set Yola's chest atop her weapons bag and readied another flechette. Gun in one hand, a chunk of wood in the other, she tossed the log in Sameth's direction. It landed with a heavy thump between the man and her hiding place.

His head whipped around at the impact. Moving to the wood, Sameth bent and inspected it. He slowly straightened. Head swiveling, greasy hair swinging, his piggy eyes squinted into the darkness.

Rak'khiel tossed another neatly trimmed chunk, bouncing it off the first. Held the gun steady on Sameth's forehead.

"Shalit. Who is ...? I'll kill you." He roared, shook a fist the size of his dog's head.

She threw a third.

Heavy lumbering footsteps betrayed his rush for her hiding place.

He slowed, a hand resting on the pile, peered over, behind the stacked firewood.

Rak'khiel rose from her crouch, conscious she now towered over Sameth. A low deadly croon escaped her throat.

"Goddess save ...," the brute prayed.

With a steady hand and unholy joy, she raised the gun and shot Sameth in the eye. "Holy Pair," her murmured prayer. "Condemn this monster to the worst of your hells."

The stench of acidic urine flooded the air.

Sameth gasped once before venom blocked both movement and speech. Fear's rank odor, coupled with his unwashed body, created a floating miasma.

Rak'khiel gagged.

Paralysis took him.

The prized woodpile rattled as Sameth crashed to the ground.

No sound from the house, no sound from the dog. From the market gossip, Kel knew Sameth's wife would rejoice at his death.

"Sameth." She rounded the stacked wood and whispered, delighted to watch his eyes go wide. "It's me, Rak'khiel – Ela to you." Calling fangs, smiling around them, she exulted at the terror in the man's gaze. "You will die in agony, perhaps take days to do it. This is my revenge for Yola. I killed your unmarried friend. I've killed you. And now I'm going to kill the dairyboy."

She ripped the flechette from his eye, wiped it on the least soiled portion of his shirt and put it in her pouch. Picking up the fragrant chest, she breathed its clean wood scent to clear her nostrils of Sameth's stink before moving silently down the alley.

The Goddess forbids murder. I'm damned, no better than Yola's torturers. How can I revel in this killing? The old Ela put spiders outside rather than swat them. I hate that I love the power, the revenge, the slaying.

I don't like the person I become when I kill but ….

A slow smile of understanding grew on Rak'khiel's face. A brilliance, an understanding so blindingly wonderful to her, it should have lit up the night.

I don't have to run, to hide anymore. For the first time in my life, I am powerful. I am strong and skilled. I am no longer afraid.

§

It took Rak'khiel an hour, searching the village house by house, evading the 'Risto soldiers, to find the right one. To find the right window.

Inside on a pallet on the floor, snoring gently, slept the boy of her ruined dreams.

What to do? A thousand needles of disappointment stabbed her hearts. How then, although they hurt so terribly, could they also buffet each other in anticipation of the kill?

Saliva trickled from a corner of her parted lips. Kel's face twisted, a grimace of disgust. Where has the sweet, kind, shy Ela gone? Or did she ever really exist?

She watched him sleep and wanted to drag him away. Spend a long time killing him – hard and agonizing. And yet, in fairness, he'd only obeyed his elders' teaching. Done what he'd been ordered, his entire life, to do. Is the blame his?

"Yes," she whispered through the narrow aperture. "You lied, you mocked – a forgivable offense. You brought torture and murder to an innocent and rejoiced in it. For that, you die."

Question is not should I kill him – only how. He's sleeping directly below this window. I must take my dart with me. But how?

She startled, almost screamed, at the unexpected voice in her mind.

You can, Caylee sent. *Remember the telescoping retriever in your belt? But this instant, be watchful. A life form approaches your immediate area.*

My thanks. Rak'khiel flattened, became one with the dark against the wall, slid behind a bush, crouched at its base. Placing the duffle and Yola's box between two smaller plants, spreading their leafy green branches over them, she sniffed, listened for danger.

Beneath the concealing bush, she loaded a fresh flechette, readied the retriever and waited for the man to pass.

Another slash of pain, the sensation of descending darkness closing in … over. *Goddess no, not now, please I beg you.*

§

Rak'khiel woke sprawled beneath the bush, rolled her head side to side. Frantically she tested arms and legs, found them unbound. *Undiscovered, bless the Goddess, bless the night.*

She searched for her dart gun and the needed tool. Found them a few feet away, scattered by her fall.

The retriever worked flawlessly, dirt fouled the flechette's tip.

Wiping off the clogged dart, she placed it in her pouch. Hurrying, Kel loaded another. *Quick now, before my change strikes again.*

Back outside her victim's window, she slipped a slender hand inside, aimed the red dot of the gunsight into the snoring boy's open mouth. Shot the flechette into his traitorous tongue.

His eyes opened, he gasped once.

His feeble, then frantic attempts to move, brought a quiet laugh from Rak'khiel. But there was no softness in it.

She saw his eyes rove, searching for answers, then fill with panic, with terror. He watched, paralyzed, as she ever-so-slowly withdrew the hand holding the pistol back through the window.

Rak'khiel stretched the retriever into the room, grasped the dart and pulled it back.

"It's me, you bastard. It's Ela. You know – the heifer?" She whispered. "I've killed you – it will be slow and horrible – like you did to another." She heard the vicious hatred in her voice as she added, "This is for Yola."

Sequestered behind the bush, Rak'khiel stowed the tool and dart. Cradling the chest beneath her left arm, she picked her way carefully, silently, but also very quickly out of the village. *No time to lose – the morphosis might strike at any moment. Caylee and Razr were right.*

At the dairy, all was dark, quiet.

Breaking into a steady run, Kel sent Caylee a thought. *Three Olicans dead. Next, the 'Ristos.*

Chapter 26

Mid-Dark
Nara 14, 7205.95
Dairy, Olica

The prince stretched his body into hypermode as he left the barn, heading for the village.

Brin? I canvassed the dairy – Rak'khiel's scent is everywhere but she is not. Have you found anything? Concern should have shaded Razr's tone, but panic lived there instead.

No. I will delete it from my search, widen in other directions.

The prince sniffed. Caught a faint trace, and sniffed again.

Brin – look in the village. I believe she's heading that direction.

I see an infrared form, hotter and larger than the typical Olican. The person is slowly circling every house. It must be Kel. Brin's thought paused.

Impatiently, Razr ground his teeth, clashed his fangs. Chill bony fingers clutched his viscera, twisted a handful of his stomach and tied his guts in knots around it. His mind blanked, gibbered, babbled. Because of the fear riding him, the prince could not figure out what he should be doing.

Lost her, Brin sent. *She's disappeared – inside a dwelling.*

Razr muffled a scream of frustration, leaped and spun, changing directions in mid-air. Set his face straight for the house the AI showed him.

Your tribute, Brin. How long at this pace for me to get there?

Calculating ... 15 minas.

Reassured, Razr settled into his run. Chin up, gaze fixed, breath coming easy through his nose, he found his zone. *I can maintain this pace forever – I proved it in daily training.*

Five minas later, he thought, *Perhaps not.*

Razr's brain sent little zings of alarm, stitches in muscles foretelling of coming cramping. His breath now came in smaller, hard gasps. *Why in the twelve hells didn't I forzaing train?*

Prince Helrazr? Brin's thought held amusement and more than a little worry. *Your body scans indicate you require a short rest.*

No, snarled Razr. *Sensors are wrong.* But his thoughts, shielded from the AI, were somewhat different. *My condition is unacceptable. A Kra'aken warrior is capable of fighting for aiys without food or rest. I am diminished beyond disgrace.*

Razr stopped, bent, rested his hands on his knees and gulped air. *I lost hope, gave up. This will change.* Hollow weakness triggered realization. *My last meal was ship's rations horas ago. I forgot to eat. I must feed.*

Prince Razr! Brin's urgent send brought him upright, nostrils flared, ready for war. *Rak'khiel just collapsed in the road outside town. I see many life forms, bearing torches, headed in her direction.*

"Forza! Great Destroyer take me." Razr sucked two quick lungfuls of air. *I don't wish to live if she dies.* He flipped open his most critical seals. Unlocking the barriers protecting his core essence, he groaned at the agony of deep siphoning. The prince's vital lifeforce wrenched from the marrow of his bones, powered one last burst.

Prince Helrazr, what are you doing? You must not release your reserves. You will die, shouted the AI.

"Brin, I will die if she does. It makes no difference." *Must replenish, must feed if I fight, but for now .... I must simply get to her in time.*

Bolting down the road toward the village, now all but invincible ... until his precious reserves emptied completely ....

Razr topped a hill, saw the townies closing the gap toward the still figure in the road.

Brin, I don't believe they've spotted her – yet.

His large finger flipped down his optical. Zoomed it. Razr evaluated the primitive projectile weapons they carried. Harmless, or close to it, against Kra'aken armor.

Moved his attention back to Rak'khiel he sent a frantic thought. *No, No! Kel – lie still.* His mindscream – either unheard or ignored.

The figure lying in the road stirred, pushed herself upright, tall and slender. She shook her head as if to clear it, staggered, caught her balance and stood. Outlined, her alien silhouette exposed by torchlight, Rak'khiel rubbed her temples, her eyes.

The prince increased his speed, felt connective hip and knee tissues strain. He raided her mind, ruthless, uncaring if he did harm – found only confusion.

Rak'khiel, run away from town, run to me. No response. *She doesn't know where she is, doesn't see the men or understand her danger. She doesn't remember who I am.*

As if in nightmare, Razr watched a stocky bearded villager lift a rifle and take careful aim. Razr screamed, called change, raced toward Rak'khiel, knowing his accelerated speed was not enough. Reaching deep within, he called soul boost, a Kra'aken last resort. Supernatural speed took him, caused Razr's vision to dim around the edges. His hearts stuttered with the drain of his life force. *Too late.*

The crack of a gunshot knifed through the night air. Then a second followed.

Rak'khiel turned a puzzled gaze toward the villagers, clapped a hand on her thigh. She pressed her hand against her chest, then crumpled back to the ground.

Kill them, before they shoot her again. Razr dropped soul boost but held his change. *I must live to save her.* Disappearing his hand claws, he pulled laser pistol and projectile gun from his weapons belt, roared challenge. And fired.

The projectiles hit and dropped targets with extreme malice and skill. One bullet – one death. One blast – one or more deaths.

The laser beam, like the white-hot heat of a dwarf sun, swept in crossing patterns through the group.

Body parts fell away, leaving seared stubs and severed throats. Soldiers shrieked and screamed like women. Shouted in disbelief.

Halves of men flopped on the reddening dirt of the road, searching for the rest of themselves. Useless, that. Once sundered, death eventually came from the particle poisoning in the beams. The quick deaths were the easy ones.

Razr screamed in Kra'aken joy. "You hurt my mate. You die."

A half-dozen townsmen broke before his charge. Those he would hunt down and kill – later. But first, the slif who shot my female.

Projectiles hurt far worse, Razr decided.

"Brin, for this species, where is the worst injury? A long, agonizing but fatal shot?"

They are humanoid – perhaps from the same root stock of us all. Gut shots putrefy, generally take many times longer. The AI added, *This primitive planet apparently has no skilled healers. I'd blow through his abdomen.*

"Take a long time to die, you forza," the huge warrior cried. "Shoot my mate? And celebrate it?"

The man whimpered, wept, begged, pleaded ignorance.

Razr laughed. Aimed, placed a precise hole through the peasant's thick gut.

The remaining men clustered in the dirt road, cringing, clutching at each other to remain upright.

Razr's savage alien laugh, fueled by rage, promising

retribution, pain, death, completely unhinged them.

The terrified villagers fired at him, old guns held in shaking hands. Milling, stirring the ochre dust, the group constantly shifted as men sought shelter behind the one standing next to him. A scapegoat or offering might have to be made but each determined it would not be him this day.

Bullets pinged from his armored scales. He rapidly closed the gap between until the men broke and fled for the village. Reaching Rak'khiel's side, a glance reassured him.

She breathed easily although a thin steady crimson stream wound down her thigh, puddled the ground beneath her injured leg.

Razr's stomach rumbled at the scent of blood. He spat in his hand, rubbed it over the hole in her fatigues, on the wound, to slow the bleeding. *She'll do for a few minas more.*

Holstering his weapons, Razr called killing claws, ran his enemies down one at a time. Forehand slashes and shredding backhands – from long, razor-sharp armored barbs and spikes – resulted in ruined heads and torsos. Scarlet sprayed with each strike. Gouts of red splattered the yellow dirt, turned the dirt road into an abattoir. Kicks with golden clawed feet and the rows of razor leg spines opened gaping bloody wounds, snapped legs and tore lower bodies apart.

Razr's fangs snapped chunks of flesh and he swallowed convulsively. Ripped and ate more as fast as he could consume. Tearing open chests, he gulped still-beating hearts. *Must replenish fast or die – I'm spent.*

And still men stood, guns firing.

Brin, why don't they flee? They can see their death here – I smell their terror of me. *Could the 'Risto's ruling this world possibly be worse?* Freezing dots, like icy centipede feet, skittered up Razr's spine.

Caught up in Berserker Killing Rage, he'd forgotten Kel. How in the name of everything holy could he forget her?

Turning his gaze on the remaining villagers, he saw their eyes riveted behind him.

A low, deadly growl made the short hairs stir on the back of his head. No alert from Brin. *Can there be something here as dangerous as I?*

Razr turned to stare at the figure crawling up the road.

Rose-colored scales glimmered dark burgundy in the emerald light of Olica's triple moons. Rak'khiel rolled to her knees and stood, one clawed hand pressed hard against her bloody thigh. The other unarmored hand, slender and beautiful, held an ugly snub-nosed laser pistol.

Snarling, a steady, lethal animal sound promising death, forced the villagers to spin from Razr to see what new menace threatened.

Rak'khiel's gun spat a flesh piercing white-hot beam. She severed limbs, sliced bodies in sculpted pieces.

Men screamed and fell.

A bullet ricocheted off her armor and she howled a laugh – a terrible you-are-dead sound. So awful Razr's hair went vertical like porcuhedge quills.

I should have prevented her wounding – my life essence be damned. Razr roared his anger.

The men's heads whipped about, returning attention to their just-remembered enemy.

At Rak'khiel's hunting scream, two of the most brutal men broke – racing for town and safety. Emptying her laser's charge, Kel switched weapons so swiftly, without hesitation, she never missed a shot.

Razr disappeared claws, pulled his long-range laser rifle from his bandolier, dialed the beam in tight. At the weapon's low humming, he fired.

The fleeing men flipped like acrobats, landed, then lay motionless in the dirt.

Turning to congratulate Rak'khiel, he came completely undone.

The female holding the key to his future, to his entire life, lay face down in the bloody filth of the road.

A leap put him at her side, a questing sniff reassured she

lived.

Brin, her armor's fully deployed. I can't check pulse. But her thigh wound wasn't critical. Supporting Kel's head, the prince carefully rolled her over.

"Destroyer preserve."

Rak'khiel's chest rose and fell in unsteady rhythm. The reason now readily apparent. Dark ruby seeped through her armor scales.

Brin, I believe her armor activated after a chest wound. Held the blood in, hid the severity. I'm coming, fast as I can.

Cursing, Razr swept her up into his arms.

What? A scent, the sharp, pungent aroma of fresh cut trees flooded his nostrils, banished the stench of the carnage around him. The source, a beautifully crafted, elaborately carved box of strange burled wood, lay concealed beneath her body. *Hers? Should I take it?* The remnants of Rak'khiel's tasca drifted from the chest. Yes, she'd carried it.

While I worry for a forzaing box, she is dying. A quick argument with himself. *The carrying will cost me nothing. I must not displease her with a mistake.*

He leaned down and picked up the chest. *No time to waste. The box surely belongs with my lady. It is much too fine for anyone in this hellplace.*

Brin! On my way. Rak'khiel's wounded – unconscious and bleeding. Can you set my medbox for her?

Unknown. Programmed only for you and Shirl. Use Rak'khiel's.

Razr's breath hitched at his dead armscomper's name. Concentrate on the here, the now. *I'm too forzaing large to get her through the opening.*

Copy, Brin sent. *I'll do my best with the docbox.*

Sides heaving, the snatched killfood sustaining him, Razr sprinted up the final rocky hill. Dodging scratchy sage-green bushes, he bounded down the far side toward the fighter.

Lurching, breath coming in gasps, precious female cargo and fragrant wood chest cradled in massive arms, Razr saw the outer hatch shimmer and slide up.

Leaping into the fighter, he ducked through two open doorways, hurried into the med cube. Setting the wood chest atop a supply cabinet, he gently lowered Rak'khiel onto the sterile white surface.

Somewhere during his run, her armor retracted.

Razr quickly removed her tattered clothing.

She lay naked in the box, perfect, unmarred except for the still seeping bloody hole in her thigh, her chest, and the unnatural paleness under tan skin.

The needing, the wanting, the irresistible desire for joining. His pulsing body, physical pain needing release fought the reality of his mind. Big hands gripped the edge of the medbox, left dents in the plasplex. His knuckles blanched.

"Too close to the femoral artery, Razr." Brin's words cut off his thoughts. "Bad wound."

Razr gently brushed loose hair from her forehead, laid a light kiss on slightly parted lips and straightened her limbs. Then, while he still had enough will to do so, he hit the switch to activate the medunit. It took more strength than he thought he possessed not to snatch her from the docbox and take her to his bed.

"Curse you, small brain. You'd further endanger her life for your own gratification." Except Razr knew he would not. *Unless she agreed to a union, went willingly, awake, aware – I could not.*

Dropping to his knees, he rested his forehead against the machine, pressed clasped hands hard against full lips until he brought pain.

"Great Destroyer, if you let her live I will do anything. Your favor." Drawing a chair between the box and the monitors, Razr's twin hearts raced. His eyes darted across the glowing screens, scanning the results for diagnosis and prognosis.

In secundas the unit placed three IV's in Rak'khiel – one in a neck vein and two, in the bends of her elbows – delivering nutrients, painkillers and anti-infectants. Mechanical arms extended, the shining metal of surgical tools marred by scarlet, extracted the bullet from her thigh. Mended the slash in her chest.

The hardened warrior, slayer of hundradas, retched at the sight of Kel's blood, at the thought of her hurts. He watched, waited impatiently slumped in a chair. As suddenly, he sat upright, military straight, the big veins swelling in his temples.

Razr swore terrible oaths at his Gods, interspersed with pleading prayers for Rak'khiel's recovery. He pleated his blood-stained pant leg; then released it. Pleated the other one.

Crossing his ankles, then uncrossing them, he shoved large feet back beneath his chair and leaned forward, his tense face in his hands.

The prince made promises to the Great Destroyer if he would spare Rak'khiel's life. Promises there was no conceivable way he could keep given his Kra'aken personality. *I will never yell at her, lose my temper. I will allow her to have her way in all things, control my base urges. I promise to always speak kindly to her and treat her gently.*

He entreated the Great God of All. *How desperate does that make me?*

The low, deep chuckle in the room did not carry Brin's vocal signature. Who then, thought this amusing? *Or did I imagine it?*

Lifting his head, Razr laced his fingers; then released them. Rubbed his palms on his filthy fatigues. Thought briefly of a shower and clean clothes.

Not until I know she lives.

§

Brin's anxious voice and an unfamiliar whop-whop-whop snatched Razr from sleep.

Shata! My head against the medunit. Dozing, not watching.

A quick scan – no red monitor alarms, all green.

Rak'khiel's rounded chest rose and fell steadily under a warming sheet the color of fresh lemas. "Brin, what is that accursed noise?"

"We have incoming. It matches schematics of ancient Kra'aken aircraft, a design from our pre-FTL age. A chopr from 300 yaras ago."

"What does it mean? Could they be ours?" Razr's hearts leaped. Excitement caught him – hope mixed with dread of disappointment squeezed his throat.

"I've searched our databanks. This model was discontinued the yara Kra'aken expelled 'Ristos from our planet."

"Wasn't it for horrific crimes?"

"Yes, milord. But I've no other information. Your orders?"

"Watch them, weapons hot, shields up." Assessing danger, Razr's morphosis surged, seeking dominance, as he assessed the danger. "Can you identify life forms before the chopr is too close for ship's guns?"

"No. Prepare for possible lift?"

"Yes, my tribute, Brin. I will provide outer hatch defense, but if they are Kra'aken like us, I want to meet them."

"Prince Helrazr, they cannot possibly be. The timelines refute it. I counsel due caution."

"Damnit, Brin. Do what I say. If we find others ...."

"Sir." Brin's tone said everything he thought of Razr's carelessness, his placing of loneliness, of emotion above wisdom. Then Brin uttered a sentiment impossible for an obedient AI. *Your father would be appalled.*

"Silence." The prince snarled the order.

Brin spoke again. "Prince Helrazr, about Rak'khiel ...."

"Shata. My mind is gone. Status?"

"The nicked artery and chest muscle damage are repaired. Scans indicate Rak'khiel requires several transfusions. The ship stocks two blood types – yours and Shirl's – neither of you match Rak'khiel. The box administered all-purpose plasma – a temporary stabilization – but she requires the blood stored in her personal pod for full recovery."

"Destroyer forza it. I am too large to pass through the opening. See if there is a way to widen the entrance. And, alert me when the chopr is close."

Head filled with fuzz, Razr staggered to Kel's bedside. Seeing her steady breathing, he allowed himself the same luxury. The medbox removed all but two IV's and began her transfer to a recovery bed. She lay pale, sedated, beneath the butter-yellow sheet. *Her skin is the color of spoiled cheese.* Razr beseeched the Great Destroyer – *please let the lemas-colored coverlet be the reason.*

The recovery bed slid alongside the docbox. Seals cracked as the transparent lid retracted.

Razr's sensitive nostrils twitched. Acrid, medicinal smells flooded the room. Gratefully, he heard the ship's air scrubbers whir into action.

Rak'khiel's covering slipped, and although Razr chided himself for allowing it to fall away, he watched hungrily as part, then all of Rak'khiel's torso lay exposed. Lovely, full delicious curves of breasts compelled. His fatigue pants were suddenly much too small in the groin. Reaching to caress, cradle fullness in his palm, he saw the battle gore covering his hand. *Sacrilege.*

Razr couldn't help grazing the back of his hand across the silky skin of Kel's breast. The small rose nipple puckered under his touch. *Responsive. Extatix.*

"You should clothe her," Brin's voice floated soft through the ship's speakers.

"True, Brin. My tribute, although ...."

"I understand, Razr. She is lovely and you wish to gaze, to touch your fill. Not knowing Olican ways and customs, nudity could be taboo. What if she wakes unexpectedly? You must not offend."

"She is Kra'aken, Brin. She would not misunderstand."

"It is your desire speaking, my prince. The only Kra'aken thing about her is her birth. Use your big head, milord." Brin's stern, frowning warrior aspect appeared in the med cube.

First criticism, now sarcasm from my Artificial Intelligence – the one sworn to obey my every command? Things became more muddled; less predictable each aiy.

"The only thing more unbearable than being alone in the fighter," mused Razr, "would be to have Rak'khiel nearby, refusing to talk to me."

"Agreed," said Brin, relief evident in the relaxed word.

"Very well." Razr turned to the tiny sink and rinsed the worst of the gore from his hands. He moved to a stack of drawers by the hatch; rummaged through two without success.

"Aha." The prince said but his tone held sorrow. The third drawer held Shirl's personal casuals, loose shirts, baggy pants and a pair of blue-coral pajamas, the color of ripe Kra'aken peches.

Grabbing the latter, careful of her remaining IV's, he gingerly eased Rak'khiel into them, distracted by touching silky skin, distracted by the perfection of her beautifully formed body. He inhaled the spicy sweet fragrance all her own. *Bless everything, her skin looks healthy now.*

Razr placed a pillow beneath her head, spread a sheet and soft white blanket over her, tucked in the edges and snuggled them under her chin. *She'll sleep, perhaps for horas. I'd hit the lav for a shower but we will have visitors soon.*

"Brin? Where is the chopr?"

"Less than an hora out."

"I'll clean up quickly, then."

An affirmative from the AI sent Razr to the sanfac where the icy blast of his shower allowed him to concentrate on other things. Humming a Kra'aken war song, he thought, *Another fight – I can't wait.* Rushing through his ablutions, he cut himself shaving.

"Shata." Decadis ago, the geneticists discussed eliminating beards. The elder hard-line warriors overruled them. Razr sincerely, honestly wished science had won.

Pulling on clean battle fatigues, Razr dropped hand-under-hand down the ladder to the warplane's aft compartment and opened the weapons locker. He selected a laser cannon and rifle and checked their charges – thought again and added his beloved fissnuc missile with shoulder and tripod launchers. "These will stop one ancient chopr." But in his double hearts he prayed for Kra'aken citizens, for a society like the one he so desperately missed.

Before Brin could comment, a piercing scream echoed through the ship. Secundas later another shriek followed.

Chapter 27

Mid-Aiy
Nara 15, 7205.30
Warplane Medical

Rak'khiel's bladder begged for relief. She'd searched for the needed bush for much too long. Each time she found the perfect place, someone appeared from nowhere and walked by. Then, as they passed, they turned to watch as if they knew her business.

There, right over there. A clump of brush the exact size for privacy. But the more she walked, the further away it retreated. When she finally arrived, the bush proved much too small.

Her need to void grew critical. *If I don't go soon, I'll pop.*

Finally, the right bush, high enough, wide enough and, Goddess be blessed, no one around.

She pulled her skirt up, squatted and relaxed tight muscles.

A very wrong dampness jerked Kel from her dream.

With a tiny scream of dismay, Kel vaulted from the bed and tore through the nearest open door. Found a small lav, dropped her pajama bottoms, perched and gusted a sigh of relief. A stretch, a reach to hit the button that closed the door. Found it two handspans too far.

A glittering blade lay angled at the sink edge.

Goddess in an outhouse! I'm in Razr's lav. Hurry, Kel, hurry. Can't get caught in here.

Rak'khiel rushed the rinse of her hands, nudged the sharp razor to one side and picked up the ivory colored towel crumpled by the basin. She pressed its thick plush between her thumb and fingers, marveled at the texture. *Gold thread?* Heavy embroidery in gold thread bordered the edges and an elegant Crest covered one end.

A distinctive scent of the former user drifted from the towel. Kel caught it to her face; inhaled. "Yum." Burying her nose in the linen for another deep sniff, she recalled her body's reaction to the warrior. It liked him, oh yes it did, but the rest of her was less certain.

Yola will love this fabric … ah, no! The grab of memory, the stuttering hiccup of her twin hearts forced her cough, a dry gasping thing. *Why do I grieve? The burning ceremony ends pain and loss. So the priests said. They lied.*

A glimpse of movement pulled an involuntary shriek from her throat.

She raised startled eyes to a shiny metallic oval above the sink. A tall girl with long dark hair and huge tilted topaz eyes stood before her. *Who is she? Is she a danger to me?* A sharp pang in her hearts, a quick swallow at her next thought. *Why is this girl here in his personal living unit?*

Rak'khiel frowned at her response to the girl – an instant simmering hot anger. As if he should not have female companionship.

Kel felt pressure in her face as morphosis change began, her body prepared to protect her.

The stranger's mouth opened too.

Is she preparing to fight me?

Rak'khiel watched the girl's upper lip thin and bulge. Fangs, long and sharp, emerged, grew larger, longer, until they curved in and under, well below her chin. Pink and gold ripples of pattern sheened her tawny skin, morphing into scaled armor.

I've a demon after me, a spawn of the Horned God, come to carry me to hell.

"Ahhhh." Familiar pain sliced the tips of Rak'khiel's fingers. *Yes, these I remember, these I can use.*

Mouth gaping, she watched the budding hand claws she'd used to climb the barn become long curving weapons, deadly sharp. *It was dark. I never saw how it happened.* Her *tasca* – jessamin, cinna and vanilln – the tangy Kra'aken scent accompanying change swirled in the air, mingled with an added bite of something new.

A transformed monster stood before her.

It cannot be. Holy Pair! I believe she is me.

Rak'khiel mimed a shriek.

The horror in the mirror opened and then closed her mouth in mimicry.

Kel shifted her hands high, curved fingers into menacing claws,

Once again, the stranger in the reflective surface moved with her.

"Oh Holy Forge," she muttered and broke into helpless laughter.

Vanishing the forefinger and second finger talons, Rak'khiel rubbed scaly fingers across her rough textured face, then examined her arms and legs. The shimmering rose and gold armor confirmed.

Kel relaxed; scales and fangs faded.

Once again, the tall dark-haired girl stared back.

This is the new me, like it or not. I don't. And the horrible part, becoming a scaly monster – I hate that. I'm not a murderer, I'm a simple village girl.

"Except," Kel's memory played Yola's voice, the words her mother would say. "In true honesty, admit you loved the hand claws. Admit you loved avenging my death. In ruthless honesty, admit you loved killing the guilty villagers.

I do. I did ... I am damned.

"Do you require assistance?" A calm male voice inquired.

She flinched, uttered a second scream at the disembodied voice and spun, searching for the intruder.

"Rak'khiel?"

Claws surging, upper lip bulging, Kel leaped back, snatched up the straight-razor and flattened against the bulkhead.

A huge man dressed in dark loose fatigues, weapons bristling like porcuhedge spines, burst into the room. *Only Razr, thank the Goddess.*

A deliberate experiment with this newfound power. *Retract,* she ordered her fangs and claws. To her amazed delight, they did.

Rak'khiel watched a heavily armored Razr attempt to stalk the tiny area.

"What's wrong?" His question came in a low whisper. Amber eyes, their black pupils stretched horizontal into diamond shapes, searched her face. Searched the room.

Kel flattened against the lav wall, slid out the door and into the medical area to stay far as possible from him.

He followed, head lowered, eyes scanning. Muscular arms held outstretched, at combat ready.

"Holy Killing Machine," she whispered, shifting, moving, keeping distance between them. Then, a realization stopped her where she stood. *He's not a threat to me.*

The scent on his towel, plus the sharp tang of their mingled *tascas*, drenched the area. *I wonder how that marvelous body – without the weapons, of course – would feel pressed the length of mine?*

"Nothing is wrong," she said, eyes fixed firmly on her foot as it traced half-circle patterns on the floor. Kel felt a bright flush stealing up her neck, burning its way across her cheeks. *If I look at him he will know the ache, the insistent pulse I have low in my stomach.* "Embarrassing, really." She forced a laugh, tried for insouciance. Failed. "I've heard of mirrors, our rich possessed them, but I've never seen one," she said. "When I saw a monster in the lav, I screamed. And then, I heard a voice without a person."

Rak'khiel stared at Razr's gilded claws, saw him retract them. He moved from the door frame into the med cube. Long shining hair brushed the ceiling, tumbled around wide shoulders. *Wonder what he's thinking?*

"What did the voice say?"

"It asked if I needed assistance."

"Oh," he said. "Brin."

"What's a brin?"

Razr chuckled, a low, deep sound.

Kel felt the slow fire light again. *Shalit.* Red simmered, crept up her neck, covered her face, tingled the tops of her ears. Beads of hot popped on her forehead, her upper lip. *I must appear so stupid to someone like him.*

She glanced up, blinked at the unexpected heat and intensity of his gaze. Grabbing a nervous breath, she wet her upper lip with the tip of her tongue. Knew instantly she'd done something unintended.

Something flickered across Razr's face, something that triggered a second flash of fire in Kel's lower belly, a driving urge to place her neck in his jaws, a deep wanting of his huge hands on her … to do what?

Sudden understanding brought and drove discomfiture from her mind, drained and renewed the color in her face. *I am Kra'aken, his kind. Goddess help me, I find him desirable.*

Razr's fluid steps took him to the far side of the med unit. He leaned against it with studied casualness but Kel read tension in every part of him. Following his example, she found a spot on the opposite wall. They stood, silence lengthening. She thought his discomfort equaled her own. *Perhaps he finds me unworthy and wishes not to say.*

Eyes averted from Razr, Rak'khiel strolled the perimeter of the med bay pretending to inspect each part, trailing a hand over its surfaces, when all the while her thoughts ran in crazy directions.

Her double hearts beat hard in her chest and in the join of her thighs – felt his eyes follow her, felt the heat of them bore into her back.

Kel swallowed a scream as her nipples hardened, jutted just from the brushing of her shirt. Forcing her breathing to slow, she ignored the urge to fan herself. *I can do nothing about the slamming of my hearts.* Bending, she opened a drawer and inspected the contents without seeing what they were.

A mental image intruded – she saw herself bent, head close to the drawer, her pajama bottoms pulled tight about her buttocks.

Kel jerked upright like she'd been stabbed in the backside with a sewing needle.

She felt Razr's mind snap shut.

Do Kra'aken people mate like Olicans? I've seen animals but never people. I know men's parts are different from women but I have never seen them.

Kel's cheeks burned. Olican males and females are the same height and size – Razr is at least two feet taller than I. *Perhaps I am too short?*

Kel stared about, anywhere but at Razr, without registering the room's equipment. She tried to hide her flinch as he cleared his throat.

"Allow me to introduce Brin," Razr said. "My ship's AI."

Razr gave the room a casual sweep of one arm.

"My pleasure at your acquaintance, my reprehensible for frightening you with my earlier inquiry. Welcome to the fighter, Rak'khiel." The gentle male voice came from anywhere and nowhere.

"Greetings, Brin. My sorry for my stupid. Is Caylee like you?"

"No need for apologies and if Caylee is your AI, then yes she is. You require your personal medbox to complete your healing. Can you ask Caylee if it is operational?"

A brief silence, Kel closed her eyes. Then her brow wrinkled.

"My sorry," she whispered, inclining her head. Opening her eyes, the worry cleared from her face. "It is done and yes."

"What is wrong?" Razr's casual voice held undertones of worry. Strong fingers drummed the handle of a large knife sheathed at his hip.

His other wandering hand, Kel decided, searched for an appropriate place to land.

"I was thoughtless. First, I forgot to check in. Then I was unconscious, and couldn't. Caylee's been frantic – unable to find or contact me." Rak'khiel shook her head. "Won't happen again. Brin, if I should need to contact you, what do I do?"

"Speak mind to mind or aloud in the ship. And if you agree, link me with Caylee."

Rak'khiel nodded, closed her eyes. She swayed, braced a hand on a bulkhead. As before, she opened her eyes and smiled.

"It is done. Razr, I know you and I can mindtalk." Feeling attraction's pull, she avoided his eyes as she studied the even features of his face and the power of his form. Wondered if his skin was as soft as it looked. Wondered how his long loose curls would feel wound in her fingers. Finding she rubbed the five fingers of her right hand across the ball of her thumb, she stuffed the busy hand in her pants pocket. Felt heat crawl the back of her neck.

She tried to focus on anything but him – and failed.

Even as she longed to know Razr's thoughts, she worried he was aware of hers.

A brief bit of mindblank, the sway of equilibrium loss, her knees gone to rubber. Morphosis struck.

Rak'hiel put out a searching hand, felt it enveloped in a large, very warm callused one. An electric jolt, sparkling spirals leaped between them. *Goddess, I want him.*

Black dots appeared in her vision, bright pinpoints faded in and out, before her eyes. *Must not faint.* She fought to keep the sensation of her hand in his, struggled to stand.

Kel grabbed the nearest counter with her free hand for

support. Her knees folded.

A deep voice, filled with concern, asked questions but she couldn't understand them.

The encroaching black, with its menacing fuzzy edges terrified her. Needles pricked everywhere, her hands twitched and jerked of their own volition.

The light in the center of the dark circle grew smaller and smaller until it became a mere pinprick.

"Help …." She heard her voice – so far away. "Help …."

Chapter 28

Mid-Aiy
Nara 15, 7205.50
WarShip Medical

"Shata!" Razr swore and lunged to catch Rak'khiel.

His weapons clattered, bounced off the blue-pebbled foamtanium floor.

Two warhammers slammed his kneecaps, or so it felt as he hit the deck. But he managed to wedge one hand against the wall for balance and shove the other, successfully, beneath her head. A cushion preventing it from striking the floor.

"Destroyer be thanked," he fervently prayed, breath panting fast as if he'd run all day.

Scooping his female in his arms, Razr hit the up switch on the med unit and laid Rak'khiel inside.

A red light blinked, an alarm blared and the transparent plasplex lid refused to close. Sharp medicinal odors, antiseptics mingled with cleansing solutions, flooded the area.

"Brin! What's happening?"

"The medbox is rejecting Rak'khiel. It can give no further treatment – she requires the blood from her personal unit in the pod."

"Forza." Frustration and fear laced the prince's curse. "How in the twelve hells do I manage that? I'm too large to fit through the cave entrance."

"Caylee informs me the mountain top is open, screened by plascamo netting. You have access from above."

"Going now." Razr reached in the docbox, lifted Kel with two hands, cradled her against his massive chest. "Damn you," he murmured. "Curse you for scaring me, curse you for giving me hope then taking it away."

The entire time he spoke, he shifted her slender body until her head rested on his shoulder. His wide scarred hand stroked just once, with great gentleness, from the crown of her head, down her shoulder and arms, caressed the sweet curve of her hip and thigh. His desire surged and he shoved it away, hard as a 9+ g force.

Removing his hand from Kel's body, Razr picked up the soft white blanket from the recovery bed and wrapped it about his female. Focused tight again, he hurried for the core.

"Prince Helrazr, wait."

"No."

Brin's avatar materialized in front of him – now wearing warrior's braids, carrying a long sword and laser pistol. His words rushed from him in a human, non-mechanical way.

"Prince Helrazr, attend. The chopr approaches, our screens show its projectile cannons hot. If I'm required to deploy shields, you will be trapped outside."

"Fine." Razr's fast pace increased. "Inform me as I go. Her health is my only concern. I will fully arm. Once she is safe, I can use boulders for cover ... should our visitors prove hostile."

Brin adjusted his dark blue body armor. "I know you wish otherwise but we must assume they are."

For the first time, Razr found himself distracted and annoyed by his AI's opposition and eccentricity of attire – never once realizing his worries for Rak'khiel were the cause.

"No answer to our hail. Their technology is no doubt limited – I'm searching databases for the oldest frequencies," Brin said.

"How far out?" Razr asked, shifting Kel over a broad shoulder, taking the core rungs down with careful feet and one hand.

"Five to seven minas."

"I'll hurry. Protect the fighter, Brin. I leave it in your care." *He is capable, if a little flaky – since the first time I woke.* The prince's honesty stabbed, demanded an admission. *But so am I after all this time.*

"Good hunting, my prince." Brin's aspect disappeared.

A last step off the ladder into weapons bay, a readjustment and light stroke of Kel's form ensuring her shallow breathing was still steady. Shame at his desire so long denied. *She's unconscious, Razr. Forza!*

Placing her on the low bench usually used for donning combat gear, Razr ran through Brin's information, evaluated strategy, all the while trying to ignore the faint *tasca* emanating from beneath the white blanket.

§

Razr shoved his weapons in a large black duffle, shrugged wide shoulders through its straps; settled his deadly burden securely. Sniffing metallic, oily aromas of his armament cache through the woven fabric of his bag, he smiled. *My favorite smell. No – second, now I have Rak'khiel.*

"Prince Helrazr, they come!"

"Shata, here I stand dreaming." He lifted his female, settled her firmly in his arms and sprinted through the warplane. Ignoring the steps, he vaulted through the open hatch into the bright violet sunshine. Huge quads absorbed the shock of landing.

Kel didn't stir.

Sensitive ears caught the whop-whop-whop of incoming aircraft, pulled Razr's eyes north. There! A black speck growing steadily larger.

"Destroyer." His viscera gripped, shoved hard against his

lungs. *They must not see where I take her.* Razr dashed toward the dark, jutting apex of the Fang.

Caylee? Can you hear me?

Silence from the mountain.

Forza me for a gongur. Neither Rak'khiel nor Brin thought to put me in Caylee's contact loop.

Razr tightened his grip on Kel, scrambled up loose dirt and stones and dashed over the mountain top.

Crumbled dirt, a slick path eroded by time, showed the ground's weakness, showed the path where something large and heavy once crashed through. It slid into the deep cavern beneath the mountain.

This must be it. If only Rak'khiel would wake. I dare not wait – she requires her medical unit. Without it she may never wake again. And I must protect her from the coming danger.

In worry, in fear, Razr's hearts battered against each other. Armoring his lower half, he gripped his precious cargo and leaped, golden feet first, into the opening.

The netting, stretched, slowed his fall. Then with a sharp ripping sound, the nanosilk gave way.

A deep flex of his knees absorbed the shock of landing. *Good that I called change – the cavern floor is deeper than I thought.* A glance overhead showed the camouflage resealing. Safe, hidden for now.

The tall, blunt nose of the pod leaned against the back cavern wall, the outer hatch of the life cocoon completely closed. A silver-pink hull shimmer told him he faced active shields.

Holding Rak'khiel across his outstretched arms, Razr approached.

"Caylee, I'm Prince Helrazr VI'Rex of Kra'aken Main. Brin is my AI. Rak'khiel requires her medbox. Will you permit access, your favor?"

"Affirmative." Simultaneously the answer, the damping of shields, the thunk of inner retractions and smooth hydraulic noises.

The outer hatch slid up.

Razr raced through the door, dropped his duffle, his weapons. Strode through the ship to Rak'khiel's medical unit.

The box lid swung up – Caylee's doing he was certain – Razr gently peeled away Kel's blanket, carefully placed her inside. A flip of the closure toggle brought the unit online.

Monitors lit glowing green on grey backgrounds, units beeped red numbers of diagnostic readouts. The system placed a multitude of IV's and shunts and tubing. The docbox sampled her blood, her fluids, her body. Then fluids, clear, amber and the red of replacement blood filled the tubing running into Rak'khiel.

"Destroyer, show me mercy. Let her live." Razr beseeched

A shudder gripped Razr, rippled his stomach and he hoped, he sincerely did, she'd not hate the box. Not like I do. *Destroyer damned thing makes me insane even when I'm not in it.*

"Prince Razr?"

"Yes?" He flinched, startled from his prayers.

"What of the incoming aircraft?" Caylee asked. "Danger or friend?"

"Brin can't be sure, but he fears the worst. I hope for refugees – more of our kind."

"Can you describe it?" Caylee's melodic voice stirred something deep in Razr's memories – just beyond reach.

"Brin says the identification numbers and insignia are faded, worn, but the craft's shape is consistent with an ancient Kra'aken chopr. Perhaps 300 yaras old."

The hesitation from Caylee. Razr knew she ran scans, searched mem modules. Then she dashed his hopes.

"The craft is a type given to a species – assassins, psychopaths – when Kra'aken banished them. Kel will be safe with me hidden here, but you must return to your warship."

"Do you have armaments beside shields? Can you lift from the cave if necessary?"

"Yes, I am armed. No, I cannot lift. The mains test clear but we are jammed, angled as you see. My thruster nacelles were damaged in the crash. In addition, I momentarily lost power to pod hatches, internal and external and also to the entire med unit."

"How did Kel come to leave your ship?"

"The crash woke her from coldsleep, she wandered from the cocoon and from this cave. By the time I came back online, she was gone. She never returned."

"I can repair your thrusters. Before I go, my curiosity," Razr said. "Brin mentioned the 'Ristos?"

Although avatars don't require oxygen, Caylee sucked in an audible breath. "They are the banished ones I mentioned before. Pray for any other species. Spydr-like monsters. Psychopaths, poisoners, living only to inflict pain on others."

"Are you in contact with Brin?"

"Affirmative. Shall I open a channel?"

Razr nodded.

Backlit by a large screen glowing in green, blue and white, Brin's warrior aspect materialized.

"The ancient helo is too close, Prince Razr. Your movement will be spotted. The choprs windows are coated with reflective material – impossible to see inside. Infrared shows four forms."

"Shields up, Brin. I'll establish a defensive position far from this cave. Caylee can protect Rak'khiel and the pod." Razr heard his voice, hoarse with anticipation of coming battle. Smelled the war *tasca* surround him. *Destroyer, I love a fight.*

He retrieved his duffle, pulled his laser cannon free and slid the bag back over his shoulders. "Half-claws," he commanded.

The prince scaled the rough interior wall of the Fang, parted the dark camo netting and slithered through. Grinned as he caught Caylee's thought ... *the large weapon looks small as a child's toy in his huge hand.*

Commanding full armor, Razr ran low profile, an almost crawl, making his stealthy way around the mountain top.

The whop-whop-whop sounded close now, even without an activated hearclip he knew the old engines labored, ran rough.

Razr peeked around a boulder's edge to see a decrepit small brown and green aircraft circling the fighter.

"Brin," he whispered. "You're right. Amazing it still flies."

The helo banked in another pass around the warplane.

Looking for what, I wonder? "Brin, any contact?"

No – I believe they will land, will try to board. Then, we will know who or what they are. The lifecocoon's databases hold histories our fighter does not have. Caylee sent me images, history. Ghastly.

She briefed me too. Razr kept his eyes locked on the craft. *How in the twelve hells did they get here? I'm sure they understand my fighter could take some of them offworld. If the choprs are their only form of airtravel, they are landlocked.*

The aircraft completed a second pass. Descended and landed in the yellow flower-studded meadow.

Razr's guts quivered, the pressured urge to void his bladder, blood surged in his head, shoved by the thumping double beats of his hearts. *Precursors to the thrill of combat.* Sex paled in comparison. With sex, pleasure was short, fleeting. *Only a near escape from death makes me feel so alive. And battles can last ais, wakaris, even hilus with every secunda enhanced by knowing it might be my last.*

His viscera trembled from his hard-pumping adrenaline burn.

Readying his pistols, he sighted in the cannon, secured the fissnuc on its tripod launcher and shouldered the laser rifle. Fully armored except for his hands, the prince grabbed two deep breaths to settle.

Then, like coated in gold leaf, Razr's armored lips rolled up and back in a terrible grin of anticipation, exposing large long fangs.

From the sky, a burst of heavy-caliber gunfire rent the silence. The heavy stink of sulphur and cordite overpowered the gentle breeze carrying coneflower fragrance. Bullets exploded against the warplane's shields – a breathtaking array like the Festival celebration, a shower of blue and gold sparks.

A brief spike of fear for his fighter jabbed Razr's hearts. Then he remembered Brin and relaxed. *It will be war,* he exulted. His battle *tasca* of crushed evergreen needles mixed with fresh-cut wood's sharp tang overrode his personal scent.

I require a look at these bold ones. Razr quashed his desire to engage. Instead, he waited with the patience of a successful predator.

The aircraft lowered, touched, bounced and settled. On either side, a door pushed up. A small movement below the chopr's body drew his gaze. Three ebony claws, connected to a black segmented leg covered in short spines, emerged.

The pit of Razr's stomach glued itself to the back of his throat.

The chitin-covered leg touched ground, hesitated.

The prince watched, waited.

Decision reached, five more black legs quickly followed before a billow of black cloth covered them all. Another black robed horror left the aircraft.

Razr's eyes never left the open doors.

A black-gloved hand gripping an old projectile weapon emerged through the helo door on the prince's side.

The gun barrel swung, a sweeping arc, over the area surrounding the craft. Secundas passed, then an arm, draped in a flowing dark sleeve, emerged.

Two clawed segmented legs crept out. Once again, the hesitation before the creature scuttled from the chopr. Long full robes billowed, covering its torso and lower half.

Another emerged. Three horrors. And now the fourth, its head up, testing the air.

Brin said four. The craft is small – there cannot be anymore.

A blooded, seasoned warrior, accustomed to the ugliness of war, Razr's stomach again twisted into a knot. Lurched into his throat at the 'Risto's appearance.

Straight black hair flowed back from a widow's peak to

frame a long face, white as chalk. Three sets of orange feelers twisted, twined, tested the air above a single thick obsidian eyebrow. Three huge solid, matte black eyes glared at the surrounding area.

Only a tilted, very human nose broke the flat plane of the horror's face. A small red hairy mouth opened, a gaping square, just wide enough to accommodate two protruding fangs. The creature loosed a scream of hate, a blend of a serpent's hiss and the hoarse cry of a carrion eater.

Sweet Destroyer, they are disgusting. I've never seen such horrors. Razr's guts' involuntary clench echoed in his fists.

"Brin," he whispered. "Their faces are humanoid. Impossible. I refuse to believe their ancestry has anything akin to ours."

Prince Helrazr! Take great care. Their toxin kills on contact – it's also capable of searing through your armor. I've set the fighter's shields to kill.

"Excellent. If I need hatch access, I'll alert you." Razr glanced between two of the large boulders he used for cover and aimed the laser cannon. Shook his head, chuckled low. *This smart weapon takes care of everything.*

He picked up the rifle, sighted it in on the first 'Risto to leave the chopr. And fired.

At the bright flash, the second spydr hissed. Then, goggling at his exploding friend, the tangled mess of flailing legs and robes, he loosed a squeal of rage and fear.

The two remaining 'Ristos skittered sideways. Scuttled for cover.

Razr's next shot hit the furthest spydr in the back of its head. Green and coal dark gore sprayed, splattered the ground. Long strings of black hair whipped wildly.

Two dead - two to go.

Razr, the send from Brin. *One is circling behind you – the other is sneaking from your starboard side, using the helo as cover.*

A flash of black robes betrayed location.

Razr spun, rifle rising, to find a 'Risto racing full speed at his hiding place. Too close, too fast, too late.

The horror launched on powerful segmented legs, airborne, spewing green pus.

Don't let the venom touch you, shrieked Brin.

The instinctive lift of his rifle, the instinctive trigger pull. *A kill?* Then came a shower of acid streaks, dots of agony.

Poison sizzled, patches of armor smoked where toxins ate it away.

Razr's muscles convulsed in reaction to the searing pain – triggered a double ammo burst.

Pieces of spydr rained on the ground a scant two strides from his hiding place. One monster left?

Unsure. Razr struggled to recall, found he knelt in the dirt. *Where am I?* His vision blurred, blotches ran together.

Prince Helrazr. Look at the chopr.

The snick of a door forced a slow turn of his head, his gaze wandered.

Fire, Razr! Someone shouted, a familiar voice, but who?

The scream of an overtaxed motor, rusty misshapen rotors engaged beginning slow rotation; then the ancient engine whined, strained and the helo lurched airborne.

A moment of clarity. *Destroyer-cursed arachna is escaping.* Razr drew soul reserves, grabbed the fissnuc … *No! Wrong. My ship will not survive that kind of explosion.* The laser cannon – already sighted in, magnitude of beam selected. A slow adjustment made by blinking, fuzzy eyes, a slow prayer to the Destroyer god for help.

Brin shouting in his head. *Fire, Razr! Your target is almost out of range.*

Razr dragged at the trigger. Fell.

The aircraft and remaining 'Risto lit, bright as a Kra'aken sun, flashed, exploded into dust particles.

Prince Helrazr! Are you well? Brin's worried send cut through the pain, the smoke and debris of battle haze.

Razr didn't answer. He couldn't. His attention, fixed on the tall silver shape ahead, wandered. With each movement, his pace slowed. He crawled on burned hands and blistered knees through the fouled earth toward the fighter and his medbox. He no longer remembered why, only that he must.

Please respond. Worry tinged Brin's thought. *Avoid venom splatters – it will damage your armor. It will poison your blood.*

Another slight parting of confusion's curtain.

I know, Brin. Of certainty, I do.

Razr thought he laughed at his oh-so-clever joke but only managed a spew of frothy scarlet bubbles and a grunt. *Need to lie down, just for a mina.* No? Did someone say it was a bad idea?

He crawled on. *The harder I try, the farther away the ship becomes.*

Razr's hot, burning skin felt as if it melted, slowly leached away, puddling beneath him on the smoldering acid-fouled dirt.

Someone whimpered from the burns – he felt pity for whoever suffered. His blurred vision searched for what? *My ship ....*

Razr's damaged body refused his will, darkness dragged him under. The huge warrior collapsed on the venom-stained hardscrabble, twitched once and lay still.

Chapter 29

Mid-Dark
Nara 15, 7205.65
Life Cocoon, the Fang

Rak'khiel ran, played chase with Tarkin and Torga through a lush green meadow dotted with vanilln-scented red flowers. *I don't recognize this place but it's so quiet, so safe, so beautiful I want to stay here always.*

Movement caught her eye. Rak'khiel pressed her lips together, clenched teeth against the threatening laugh.

Thinking themselves hidden, the cafuzogs ran crouched, bodies low, unaware their black tails, center striped with wide white, waved, beckoned above the blossoms.

She tried to sprint after them, found her feet strangely mired.

Tarkin's head popped up, half-lip peeled back. *Fooled you. Lured you with our tails.*

Yola's voice intruded.

Leave me be, Mother. I won't answer – I'm having too much fun.

"Kel? Kel, please."

"No, Yola, I don't want to," she mumbled.

Swimming through a shimmering azure lake, she waved a lazy hand at the tiny gold, blue and green fish darting about her ... and panicked. *I don't know how to swim.*

Dark cold water closed over her head, filled her nose, ears, her mouth.

Kel flailed, whimpered. Chest constricted against the inrush of freezing fluid filling her lungs. She thrashed arms and legs, yet her sluggish body refused to move.

"Kel, please. Wake."

"Yola? What?"

Consciousness punched through her panic like a heart strike. Something, a wrongness niggled. *Adopted mother cannot know my name is Kel.*

Truth rushed, pain's knives slashed her brain.

Yola's dead. Warm wet slid down her temples, puddled at the back of her head. A convulsive swallow. Only her ribcage kept her hearts from bursting from her chest. *I dreamed it all.*

"Where am I?"

"Kel, are you well? Your monitors went berserk."

Rak'khiel opened her eyes. Viewed a pale aqua ceiling through a transparent curved cover. *I'm in a medbox. But why?*

Yola's call came again – no, not Yola – Caylee.

Memories crashed. "Shalit." She relived her killings, felt her stomach churn, the guilt of damnation weigh on her heart. But she also couldn't stop her smile, remembering her shouted joy, fighting beside Razr. She sobered recalling the fire in her thigh. Then ... after that ... nothing.

"Caylee?"

"Thank the Great Destroyer, you're awake. How do you feel?" The AI's usual cheery tone was ominous in its absence, replaced by something that made Rak'khiel uneasy.

"Not sure. Let me out."

"Working."

She felt pulls and stings – the Goddess-damned things were everywhere – then the cool of something applied to each spot. The docbox seals hissed, lid cracked apart overhead, sides receded.

Antiseptics, medicinal odors faded, replaced by familiar

spicy-sweet coneflower fragrance. Rak'khiel's lungs sucked fresh air, she gratefully breathed their perfume. Struggling to sit, she hoped Tarkin and Torga still played in that lovely place.

"Weak, Caylee. That's how I feel. We have an emergency?" Although Kel phrased it a question, she knew otherwise – from the AI's grave face, her serious tone.

"Razr is wounded, his life signs are very faint. He lies collapsed on the ground outside the ship ...."

Rak'khiel moved. Fast. Too fast. Out of the unit, on her feet.

Blood drained from her head. She caught her stagger with a hand on the wall, waited for the black dots to vanish. "Tell me ...." Impatience chafed.

"He hasn't moved since he fell. Neither Brin nor I can reach him. He's ...."

Clothing? No – I'll armor. Kel dropped down through the cream-colored carbonplas pod core, past blue deck, snagged a handhold at green – hatch deck – swung through. Leaping from the pod, she raced across the cave.

"ARMOR UP!" Caylee shouted.

"After I clear the opening. Where is he? Where is the fighter?" Rak'khiel squeezed sideways through the boulders.

Due South from here.

How? What happened?

'Ristos attacked. Razr killed them all but venom splattered his armor. He is poisoned. Do not step on any yellow-green, charred or smoking spots.

Outside the gray rocks hiding the cave, Kel gave a mental command. She waited to feel the surging joy, the cellular rush of warmth, hot visceral power as the change expanded strength and stamina. Waited until her arms transformed with shimmering scales.

Ready. Go, go, go. She fixed her eyes on the ground, moved fast. Today she watched for pus-green poison, not bright green mambino vipers.

A metallic shine glinting violet drew her attention. Her destination, the jutting tip of the silvered warplane, kissed by the coronas of twin purple suns.

He will be somewhere between me and his ship.

Rak'khiel hurried, stepped on a charred spot and felt it fry through her armor, searing the sole of her foot. *Goddess! No time to waste being overly careful. He saved me – I owe.*

Down the hillside, beside a ring of red-barked Olican trees. *Goddess of Good!*

A large unarmored form lay crumpled, naked in the clearing beyond. Only fifty feet from the fighter.

He all but made it. Where is his armor?

Kel felt the poison's cold seep up her leg, drawn by blood flow. Saw breaches in her armor showing bare skin. Her vision wavered, venom's fatigue dragged.

Now she knew with blinding clarity just what happened to Razr.

Not now, I will not fail. She reached deep within, drew speed, forced a run. Became a blur, heedless of where she stepped.

Rak'khiel dropped to her knees beside the motionless form, heard an audible sizzle.

White-hot fingers of the venom's pain probed from her knees, up her thighs. Jaw set hard, she shunted agony aside. Saw through blurry vision, the exquisite stitching of a bright crimson seam, embroidered across the fine tawny skin of one leg. By bullets.

"The bastards shaliting shot him."

She laid a forefinger on Razr's large neck vein. Felt his pulse beat thready, erratic.

But you are still alive. Kel remembered how to breathe. *You will stay so.*

"Razr. Wake up." She pushed a chunk of jet hair aside, shook one of his thick shoulders, dragged at his dead weight. "Goddess damn you! Wake up. Help me."

A faint low whisper. "Leave me."

"I'll not," she snarled. "My fault you're injured."

Rolling him to one side, she wedged, wriggled, crawled beneath him. Dragging his huge acid-splattered torso across her shoulder, she pulled his arms to her chest. Balancing his weight, she focused. Clenching her teeth against the coming venom burns, Kel placed her palms on the green poison-fouled ground.

Goddess! Shafts of agony shot up her arms, tears spurted. *I must hurry or we'll both lie here and die.* She worked her knees beneath her.

He mumbled something incoherent.

A protest perhaps? Or perhaps pain, because I've touched his burned skin?

"I'm sorry if I hurt you," she whispered. "But I must." *If I can't stand and walk, I'll drag him.*

"Great Destroyer," Rak'khiel prayed to Razr's god – and wondered why she did. "If you value your warrior, give me strength."

She wrapped an arm around his narrow waist, settled – butt on heels in a deep squat – grabbed a huge breath. Shoved up with every bit of her power.

Venom sapped her strength.

She stopped, trapped, frozen – only part-way upright. Her grunt turned into a scream, the burden of the man's weight beyond her power.

Reaching deep inside, instinctively, she felt a new place. Found something more. She pulled, dragged strength.

It feels as if my life essence is eroding. It doesn't matter.

Her hearts hammered staccato, jamming, forcing oxygen deep into laboring lungs, deeper into arteries, veins. Fueling muscles. *Tasca* flooded.

Kel pushed again. Forced her body upright.

She stood, Razr's weight driving her feet into the black scorched dirt. She wobbled, fought for balance. The dark blurring in her eyes. Venom poison? *No time.*

"Brin, please talk to me. I'm blind."

The AI directed, his calm, even thoughts a steady flow. *Toward your left, good. Straight ahead now. Good. Excellent.*

One shaky step after another, tiny sips of air with each pause for balance, took Kel and her burden across the remaining distance. One foot before the other, she forced her trembling legs up the seemingly endless silver ramp to the outer hatch.

"Rak'khiel," Brin's welcome voice. "The med unit is just inside the door. Two steps more."

I can do two. Rak'khiel fixed resolute eyes on the fuzzy glowing outlines of the white box. She grabbed the hatch sides. Set her mind hard.

A surge-step-pull on the instant of her movement. Rak'khiel's forward momentum crashed them both into the docbox.

Blood pounded in her ears.

Her nose mashed to one side, Kel panted through her open mouth, forced open an eye. Found she stared at the far corner of Razr's medbox.

Goddess. My head is jammed, my neck bent wrong. Hard as we landed, it should have snapped.

An attempt to move told her she lay in the docbox bottom, her smaller body crushed beneath Razr's dead weight.

Kel's compressed lungs heaved, burned. She snatched two half-breaths. *But what I want ... need ... are many, many deep ones.* Somehow she had to find enough oxygen to fuel the muscles required to push from beneath him. Get out and away – so the box can close and begin its work.

I must move. If he dies, it will be my fault.

Her legs quivered and collapsed.

Kel hung, half in and half out of the medbox, trapped by Razr's heavy body. Pushing, rolling, squirming from beneath the huge warrior, carefully moving him aside, she scraped, slithered her way free. Collapsed in a heap on the blue pebbled floor.

Breathed, deep, hard. Waited for her eyesight to swim

back into focus. Her burns pained but a trip to her medbox across the fouled ground between the fighter and her pod – out of the question. I'm spent.

Lifting her head, she carefully studied the first nude male she'd ever seen.

Angles, hard muscular curves, elegant hands, feet. His perfection marred by scars – yes, he'd said he was a warrior. But they in no way detracted from his regular, well-formed features.

I am committing mortal sin. A high unhinged giggle escaped her. *What's that compared to a little murder or three?*

Kel watched the machine arrange Razr's limbs and seal the transparent plasplex lid. Watching the unit inserting sharp needles on the ends of tubes into his body, she shuddered.

She logged every feature, every scar.

Although her breath came hard and blackness encroached on the edges of her vision, Rak'khiel committed to memory Razr's gracefulness in sleep, the dark escaping curls on his neck, the wave of hair at his temples. *If only … but no. He is a great important warrior. I am a simple Olican peasant, even if Kra'aken by birth.*

Darkness beckoned, Goddess' darts danced before her eyes.

Rak'khiel's lone lucid thought before blackness claimed her – *naked he is more than magnificent.*

Chapter 30

Aiy
Nara 15, 7205.79
Warplane, Olica

Soft mumbling, incomprehensible words floated, collided, bounced in Kel's skull.

She frowned. Or at least she intended to. Intended to scream at the agony in her feet, knees and hands. *Goddess, I hurt!*

Through a slitted eye, she saw a flat ivory surface overhead. *What? Where?*

Waiting for recognition, for clarity, her understanding coalesced. Scents of sharp tree resin and ginger, laced with antiseptic, bit her olfactories. His scent ....

The medroom ceiling in the ship swam into focus.

Someone's self-flagellation dragged her further from sleep.

"Great Destroyer take me. I am a slovenly six-eyed slith."

Can it be Brin? Not possible, the AI is a machine. He never uses nasty tones in his voice, is unpleasant or insulting. Sure sounds like him though.

"Why did I not complete the robot in a timely fashion. If I had, I could help her. I will be responsible if Kel dies."

It is Brin - cursing himself. Determined to eavesdrop,

Rak'khiel smothered a giggle. Then coughed and ruined it all. "Brin, is it you I hear nattering?"

"Kel! Great Destroyer be praised." The AI's anxiety penetrated her last barriers of almost-sleep.

She shifted, searching for comfort on the cold, hard surface beneath her. Not dirt – nothing made sense. Vestiges of mind-fog drifted. "What's wrong?"

A solemn, somber aspect loomed above. Brin's presentation echoed his previous spoken worries. The AI wore a black velvet suit – its severity relieved only by myriad tucks, intricate folds and black satin embroidery on gathered balloons of fabric. The strange exotic style somehow suited him. The sausage-fat hair rolls of the powdered white wig did not.

"Can you walk to your pod?"

"Of course, why ... oh." Full wakefulness brought the poison's burning agony. Kel squeezed her eyes closed against the hot wet spurt. Tried to return to the black velvet comfort of sleep.

"Tsss," she hissed between clenched teeth. Surveying the unfamiliar pale ceiling, she rolled her head side to side. Found she lay on a bumpy foamsteel floor, her face mere inches from a white column. A medbox base. Kel's gaze traveled up, found a clear plasplex dome. *Goddess! Razr. Does he live?*

Twin hearts thudding, muscles shrieking with effort, Kel shoved to blistered hands and knees. Crawling to the docbox, she pushed up; then collapsed atop the plasplex cover. Blinking pain's tears away, she peeked inside.

"Brin. He's so pale."

Pink and yellow and clear liquids flowed into Razr from medical unit tubes. Devices attached, others detached. Monitors beeped – green tracks flowed across gray screens, green numbers tracked criticalities. *Alive.* Machines hissed. Drains bubbled. After what seemed like a handful of years, Rak'khiel finally saw Razr's chest move. Found her lungs could also move again.

"How is he, Brin?"

"The docbox flushed all venom and replaced his poisoned blood. He will bear scars from acid splashes, our medical device is designed for treating war injuries. It has no provision for cosmetic repairs." Brin's voice softened. "Kel, my forever appreciation. If not for you, Razr would be dead."

"My duty, only. Olica's unwritten law – a life for a life – under any circumstance. He saved mine – I owed." She kept her words even, matter of fact. Hoped she fooled Brin with her casual comments.

Yet Rak'khiel's approving eyes slid over Razr's form. She wondered at the sharp pulse, the beating of blood in the juncture of her legs. *I must have mental damage or scrambled mental modules to feel lust when my own burns are screaming. But, he's asleep and I can look without worry. Are Olican men made the same? They are squat, dirty brutes. Not a one so beautiful as my warrior ....*

Try as she might, her normal full, deep air intake refused to come. Instead she could do nothing but gasp quick, hard pants. *My lungs must have sustained damage too.*

Still, as before, the oddest urge takes me – to place the back of my neck between his jaws. This strange compulsion makes no sense – I must remember to ask Yola. No ... Caylee. A slam of memory, of grief, ripped the lining from Kel's stomach. I am, as Yola often said, a cracked pot.

Tears brimmed shiny bright, and Rak'khiel felt a vibration against her chest. Waves of comfort surged through her spirit. "Goddess save," she whispered, pulling the strange pendant from her shirt and gripping it with both hands. She tried to focus on the object but saw only shimmering silver, wrapped in wavering ruby streams. "Yola's gift to me."

"Can you stand? Walk?" Brin broke into her reverie, an odd flavor colored his voice. Not surprise, exactly. More like humor, but what could be funny? Noticing her close scrutiny, he shifted his gaze to the opposite wall.

What in the Holy Pair is he hiding? Then she caught his sly, almost hidden grin and the thought, *Overcome by Razr's magnificence ....*

"Shalit." How could he miss her staring.

Perspiration popped across her forehead, a flood of heat covered her face in bright red. *Goddess in a nightgown. How embarrassing.*

Her burns throbbed, insistent and she shoved the pain aside. Gave herself a mental shake to rid her of silly girlish fantasy. *Tend to business, Rak'khiel.*

She placed one hand on the medbox lid and the other against the hatch opening. The motion to push-pull to her feet sent wet cascading down her face. She swayed, steadied. Blinked fast against her tears.

"You require immediate medical attention, Kel. You too are poisoned." Brin's voice laced with worry. "Can you make your cave?"

"I'm fine," she mumbled, chest heaving to hold back her scream of pain as she staggered from the fighter.

§

A great yawn made Rak'khiel's jaw crack. "Where am I?"

"Kel," a woman's voice ... Caylee. "Good morrow."

I'm in my medbox.

The pastel aqua ceiling, the narrow confines and needle stabs confirmed it. *I'm in the pod, in the Fang. But why?*

Memories tumbled.

"Goddess preserve," she whispered as her mind sorted through, put the events of the past few hours into logical sequence.

The never-ending walk – stagger, actually – from the fighter to her life cocoon. The falls, the sears of venom biting, leaching into her bare skin.

The merciless prodding by both Brin and Caylee. Their demands she rise, move, walk to the mountain top.

Her inability to do as they wished, her apology. Then, the

final rolling, tumbling fall, down the hillside. A forward movement through … boulders … not the opening in the top of the Fang.

I must have crawled into the pod, and the docbox. I don't remember. Brin said … venom poisoning.

"Caylee, how is Razr?"

"His physical repair goes well although he is still asleep. Brin and I believe he will recover."

"Am I repaired? Can I get out of here?"

Instantly, the translucent dome began to split and Caylee spoke, "The red escape button inside is a fail-safe. That is how you slipped away when you were only two. You cried for your mother, left the cocoon to search for her. My systems were compromised. I was powerless to prevent it."

"You … hold my history?"

"I have it all. For the first time since my construction I desired a body, arms, legs. I could have stopped you from leaving. And the cave obscured my scanners. For the past fourteen yaras I have wondered if you lived. Would you wish to view your history now?" The AI's voice held empathy.

"How long have I slept?"

"Twelve horas."

"Yes, I would know it all – my family, my past." Kel's hearts surged, then ebbed. "No, Cayless, I cannot. Not yet. "First I must make sure all is well. My thanks." Rak'khiel studied the AI's appearance. "Are Tarkin and Torga safe?"

"Yes, very much so," Caylee waved a reassuring hand.

My mother's simulacrum, Kel thought with a jolt. I am taller, she is more slender – and each of her arm gestures holds the studied movement of storyteller's grace.

Large expressive eyes, sapphire undertones shimmered in midnight blue-black hair, long, curling – where mine is straight. Perfect symmetry of feature – everything well ordered, as if done by design. *Perhaps, on Kra'aken, it is? No – I'd be pretty too. She must have been disappointed at my arrival.*

Caylee's – Lady Floril's – richly embroidered cobalt dress

clung. The tight fitted bodice flared into wide skirts just below narrow hips.

"Although your armor scorched, it prevented the worst of the burns, kept poison intrusion to a minimum." Caylee's cheery female voice added, "My initial testing indicates your exposure might provide partial immunization." The lovely features of her mother's holo twisted. "You will bear scars. My regrets."

"I don't care." Rak'khiel swung long legs out of the machine. Saw her once smooth expanse of hard muscle marred by red blisters and healing burns. "Were you successful with my new series of implants?" Her feet touched warm pale-blue pebbled material – foamtanium, her memory supplied. She stood, swayed while blood flow normalized, then moved to the bank of drawers.

"Yes, I had time for everything. We should sync tomorrow – check the module acceptance, the jack seat and interface." A change in Caylee's voice, almost cautionary. "Kel, if you plan to visit the prince ...."

"What prince?""

"Prince Helrazr, of course."

"Holy Forge. He's a prince? He never said ... I am an idiot." *Me, an ignorant peasant, gawking at his lordship's nakedness. Unfit to look – worse yet, very stupid.*

"I've erred – grievously. I assumed you knew. Razr has never used his birth for gain. Rather he hides his royalty. Please purge my comment from your mem banks. If he finds I've broken confidence, is displeased, he can order me disconnected. But, Rak'khiel, never forget you are a Regence."

"No, I'm not," a hard shake of Kel's head. "Only by birth, nothing more. But, no one will disconnect you unless it's me." Rak'khiel stared Caylee eye to eye. Hard. Hoped she appeared threatening. Pretty sure she didn't. "As long as you provide the help I need, you're safe. What were you going to tell me before ...?"

"If you plan to visit the fighter, you have outdoor

garments and sturdy footwear in the compartment under your bed."

"I have a bed? Where?"

"One level down."

A circular section of the floor slid aside and fragrance wafted up – a sweet white jessamin flower and cinna blended with an undertang of vanillin. Her new mem modules supplied the information. Exposed below, Kel found a living compartment decorated in pink and aqua.

"Pretty! So pretty."

"Below your quarters are two more levels. I will give you details whenever you like." Caylee's face beamed in a wide smile.

She's pleased I like it. But dip me in shalit – there are more rooms in this thing?

Handholds, the bright yellow of coneflowers, protruded.

Rak'khiel's legs felt steady, but still she grabbed the bar before jumping down the open core. Releasing it, she dropped the last three feet, bending her knees to absorb the shock.

A long glance about revealed a generous compartment with a full-sized bed. Kel frowned at the covers stirred into a messy nest. There was a small tidy desk and chair, two closets, a bank of three wall nettings and a double stack of bins.

A shock of ebony fur lay dark against her pastel pillows.

Torga stirred, lifted her head. *Kel. You're well?*

"Where's Tarkin?"

Hunting. I wanted nap.

Kel ran a hand across padded wall nettings.

Those are ours, Torga's send came muzzy. *Sometimes need for safety at jump points, or other.* She snuggled her black head with white center stripe deeper into the pillows.

One corner of Rak'khiel's mouth twisted in a wry, doting smile. *I've been dismissed.* The room's walls displayed personal mementos, the desk-top held objects she didn't recognize, along with what appeared to be a second command center. The built-in bunk wrapped under a small ultra-thick plasglas porthole.

"The gift of space from the pod's outside wall," Caylee explained.

"All I see is black cavern dirt."

"Incredibly expensive," Caylee said. "Your parents wished you to have glorious views from your bed, give you hope and their love."

Two wafers lay next to a player.

Data clicked in her mind. Her mind modules knew both the purpose of each, and how to use them.

Kel placed one small square inside the player.

Incredible music flooded the room, then a woman's voice soared, her notes clear, pure and effortless. Her range extraordinary.

Kel soaked it in, the words of love from mother to child engraved on her heart. Her lips swelled full, trembled.

The other wafer must be my father's. *I will listen later.* My heart will burst with more. But she didn't turn off her mother's song until it ended.

Two narrow tracks surrounded her bed. One traced a loop on the ceiling, the second a mirror-image directly beneath on the floor.

"Caylee? Explain these, your favor?"

"Your bed enclosure contains a final fail-safe should depressurization occur. The tracks generate a transparent barrier, an unbreachable seal, around your bed. This will be triggered, on the instant, by any atmospheric imbalance."

Good, Kel thought. *But what if I'm not in bed?*

Accessing her mind modules, Kel selected underclothing. Olicans didn't wear underthings. So Kel picked frilly lace just for their beauty. Then, because she planned to walk to the fighter, she selected heavy dark blue pants and matching shirt. She added a pair of sturdy black boots like those she'd seen on Razr.

Opening doors, she found one of the two closets contained a tiny lav. Marvelous. Now I can brush what feels like fur ...

and tastes like dried meadowdressing … off my teeth.

"Caylee, could you show me a lifesize of my mother here in front of the mirror?"

The holo shimmered and firmed. *I have her hair, facial shape and lips.*

"Now my father, please."

Another image formed on the other side. Kel studied the image. *I have his eyes and a feminine version of his nose.* They are in truth my parents. Snake fangs of guilt, disloyalty to Yola, buried in her hearts, ruined the moment. *Is it wrong to love both? I can't think on this now.*

"Thank you Caylee. I must check things outside."

She went hand over hand up the yellow rungs, through the hatch. Overhead another slid open. Effortless, she pulled up and through it too.

"Caylee, is this the outside hatch deck?"

She'd stopped in the green area – door, floor, walls and ceiling. *I think I remember correctly.*

It slid open before she finished her question.

'Slice of simple' as Yola would say.

Dead patches of grass and soil made it easy to skirt the 'Risto venom. Still, when she stepped wrong, nothing sizzled.

Three strides from the ship's ramp, the shimmer of shields disappeared and the hatch slid ajar.

"Brin?"

"Welcome aboard. The med cube is two levels down. Hatches opening now."

"My thanks." Dropping through the core, handhold to handhold, she arrived. Seconds later, bent over the transplas lid, Rak'khiel wished, just for the moment, she hadn't come.

Razr lay shrunken, skim-milk white beneath his tawny skin. Impossible just in a half-day, and yet ….

"How is he?" *Please tell me he'll recover.*

"Docbox monitors remain full green."

"What can I do?"

"You did the impossible – carried him to the fighter. We

were resigned to Razr's loss."

"I ... I've always been strong. I didn't think – it just needed doing."

"Your father's strength was legendary. His stubbornness too. You are much like him."

"Perhaps we could talk. Caylee will tell me of my mother. I would know more of them. From both of you." Another dig in her gut, the feeling of betrayal of Yola. Although she held her face impassive, Kel's right hand tugged her earlobe.

"Razr knew your parents. He can give you his memories. Caylee and I look forward to many discussions. But, Rak'khiel ... right now, we need to discuss something important."

"More important than Razr getting better?"

"His recovery is tied to this, in a way. Shall I ask Caylee to join us?"

"Of course – my thanks." Ice chips piled in the pit of her stomach, meshed to become a solid block of dread.

"Here," a clear feminine voice chimed.

"While you were being repaired, we exchanged information." Brin paused, seemed to gather his thoughts. "Caylee, with her specializations of protecting and prolonging life – I, with mine, geared to destroying enemies – complement each other. Together the sum of our two systems is formidable." The white wig trembled, jiggled, then settled askew.

What is it they are contemplating? What is so terrible he cannot control his avatar? Scare me.

Caylee took up the thread. "Combining the knowledge in our databanks, we arrived at several conclusions. We need your thoughts on our findings."

Rak'kiel waited for data, wondered at the sudden uncomfortable silence. In the long pause, Kel knew she should do something. Say something.

"Shouldn't we wait for Razr?" Rak'khiel swallowed. "Shalit, you two. I'm an uneducated peasant girl. How can I know what is good or bad?" Hot wet of frustration flooded her eyes. "You two are used to making decisions – used to being in charge. Let's do what you think is right. Or what Razr would want."

"If you were a child, perhaps. But ... no...." Caylee held her upraised palm between them, preventing Kel from speaking. "No. You are a woman, a fully morphed, blooded warrior."

"Without the proper knowledge to make the important decisions," Rak'khiel snapped. *I'm unqualified.*

"But Kel ... you saw him. We have no idea when he will wake. It is possible, never." Brin's voice wavered. "Any decision must by law be yours."

"Goddess in a night jar." Rak'khiel's queasy stomach contracted, folded in on itself. "I can't believe that." *Can't or won't,* asked the sarcastic voice in her head.

"We believe he will and we are taking that into consideration," Caylee comforted. "But still, we must plan."

"What are your recommendations?" Rak'khiel demanded.

Caylee's voice changed, just slightly, and Kel knew the AI'd sussed what she intended. Still, The AI's answer came. "First, we think we should leave Olica quickly. Do you agree?"

"Brin? I'll have your thoughts now." Kel's tone left no wiggle room.

"'Risto venom is the only known thing capable of damaging Kra'aken armor," added Brin. "Both you and the prince have been poisoned." The AI shook his head. "I believe we must leave as quickly as possible. Even though we killed all of their raiding party, the spydrs must know the ship's location. When their scouts do not return, we must assume they will send others. Perhaps better armed, perhaps in greater numbers. 'Ristos exist only for murder."

"Toward that goal," Caylee's melodic voice continued, "Brin and I created schematics to attach your lifepod to the fighter. Wherever we travel, you and the prince require your personal medboxes – reasons already critically demonstrated. Separately, neither the lifepod nor the fighter are large enough to meet the combined survival needs of two Kra'aken adults and two cafuzogs."

Leave Olica? Rak'khiel's mind blanked. *Out there? Above the suns? And yet, why not? This planet, its people have not been kind to me – worse to Yola, one of their own – tortured and murdered.*

Rage surged, blood beat hot in her head, throbbed in her temples. Kel's upper lip pulled tight over emerging fangs.

"Kel?"

"Yes, I agree," she said. *Right after I obliterate every 'Risto.*

"One other thing." Brin's black velvet holo shimmered, re-emerged in professorial aspect. "Razr wants nothing more than to return to Kra'aken. He hopes for survivors – some of his family."

"Between Brin's data and mine," Caylee said, "we have complete starmaps. Both our ships passed through an uncharted alien gate. We can return there. If we are able to pass through, we can take him home."

"What is this alien gate? How do we find it if it's uncharted?"

"Both the fighter and the pod passed through. Caylee's charts can return us there," Brin said. "What of our plan?"

"Agreed," Rak'khiel nodded. "Even if Razr remains in coma until we reach Kra'aken, it makes no difference." She nodded. "What can I do? The lifecocoon is large. I'm sure very heavy. How do we lift it from the cave?"

"Our propulsion system is larger than the warplane's. Over-engineered for the safety of the children. It easily boosts the pod weight – plus most of the fighter's." Caylee continued, "The problem is repairing our drives. Brin and I believe, with in-depth quicktape study, you can do this."

"So we will fly two ships to Kra'aken?" *Why not? Caylee flew it here – she can fly back.*

"We've combined mechprints; we have overlays to show you." Brin continued, "We are certain we can marry the ships without losing augmented FTL propulsion, jump ability or hull integrity. Besides providing your docbox, you will have private living quarters."

"How do we attach the two?" Rak'khiel turned squinty suspicious eyes on Brin's aspect. "No. Oh. No. Goddess in a crucible. Not. Me."

"There is this small mindmodule I'd like to install for you," sent the gracious and terribly refined avatar of Kel's mother. Then she added a giggle and an undignified wink.

§

For the next two aiys, the manufacturing equipment of both ships hummed, spitting out new parts and replacement components. That task complete, they turned immediately to creating the new systems and structural parts required to attach the two ships.

Rak'khiel scoured the cave and countryside for required minerals, rocks and metals to replenish those being depleted in the 'facturer's.

She worked, one sharp topaz eye combing the ground for needed materials; the other constantly searching the sky and countryside for a second 'Risto attack.

With the completion of each chore, during rest periods, Kel followed Caylee's direction. Sitting tentatively in the pod's pilot station, she grabbed a deep breath and pressed her head against the mind-jack.

Caylee said, "We are finished. It is time."

Rak'khiel's stomach filled with acid, twisted at the mating. Her mind rebelled at being subject to *Other*. Rebelled at the brief but thoroughly unpleasant sensation of having her brain speared ... an invasion of the highest personal magnitude.

Then, one-by-one, cockpit systems glowed green, fired. The ship's on-line abilities sprang alive, information and numbers hemorrhaged from every screen, every monitor.

To Kel's amazement, she understood. To her burgeoning

pride, she loved the knowing. From the repair module to communications – everything now made sense.

"More, Caylee. Goddess, please give me more."

Kel's hearts fluttered like narikeet wings, electric current sizzled beneath her skin. "The power I hold in this ship, in these two hands. To fly her? Holy Forge."

§

The plaswrench slipped; a string of wicked Olican oaths burst from Kel.

Scarlet blood seeped from barked knuckles, dripped on the cave floor below the pod.

"Why is it, the more tape I take, the more Kra'aken knowledge I acquire, the less I respect Olican rules or revere my Goddess." With no time to debate religious nuances, Kel shelved her worrying whether this was bad or good. "We are on the 'Risto kill list. And they will arrive anytime."

Oily smells of mechanicals and hydraulic grease, metallic tang of newly minted replacement parts, the stink of industrial solvents covered every square inch of Kel and the pod. The final engine adjustments were complete.

Kel overheard Caylee reassuring Brin of something. They had no idea she could listen to their conversations. Rak'khiel did learn the repairs she'd made on the damaged thruster nozzles tested perfect, as did her replacement of the failed drive. The AI's weren't completely pleased about flying the pod from the Fang or pulling it out using the fighter. But, for all the eavesdropping she did, Kel never found out the remaining reason for their concern.

"We are ready," Caylee announced.

Kel worried her earlobe.

Once outside the Fang, in the meadow by the fighter, the melding of the two ships could be completed in an aiy. Barring unforeseen complications. But, Kel knew, they would also be completely exposed.

"Destroyer protect," Caylee whispered. "Please grant the 'Risto scouting party died before they reported our existence.

"Tsss," Kel hissed through clenched teeth. "If they didn't, I'm an orange furred cafuzog.

If the pod cannot lift out on her own, the fighter must pull her. Brin's send broke her reverie.

"He's said so a hundred times, at least," Kel growled. "I have nothing better to suggest."

But, the AI added, *although the fighter's fusioreactr drives should have no problem with the added weight, the monstrous power plants and directional thrusters of the lifecocoon are far greater than that of Razr's warplane. They are what we need.*

"Pray it be so," Kel answered and thought the AI didn't sound totally sure. Glancing at the grease and oil coating her clothes, her skin, she peeled off her gray coveralls and dropped them in the nearest 'fresher. Dialing the shower water to hot, she stepped inside.

§

Kel dressed in the flightsuit Caylee provided. The thing pinched, twisted, poked in the most uncomfortable places.

"Like hell, you suggested. Ordered is what you did," Kel snarled, feeling her fangs push against her lips. Shoving them back, she breathed in comforting florals exuding from the ship's systems.

"Stuff your effing peace offering, Caylee. I know that's what it is." *Shame on me – I'm scared. And taking it out on her.*

Pink patterns shimmered across tawny skin; Rak'khiel ground her teeth.

Still another worry … and Razr sleeps. Vitals from the medbox were normal. The warrior appears healthy. Why won't he wake?

Goddess curse you, she sent. *Get out of the damned box. You're needed.*

"I want to fly," Kel admitted. "Yes, Goddess yes. But, I

wanted my first to be, as Yola would say, a milk run." Her guts coiled and bunched in the pit of her stomach. "Instead," she whispered. "Rak'khiel's luck draws the single one that's wicked tricky."

Kel?

Yes, Caylee?

It's time. Would you take the cockpit, your favor?

"Shalit!"

Chapter 31

Mid-Dark
Nara 18, 7205.37
The Fang, Olica

Leaning back, head pressed against the gray pad in the pilot's seat, Rak'khiel panted and waited for the nausea of mindjack mating.

Her bowels rumbled but she knew a visit to the lav would produce nothing – *it's fear* – *not diarrhea.* A fine layer of cold sweat coated her body, chilly beads popped on her upper lip. A sensor beeped alarm at her blood pressure.

"Yours would be too high, curse you, if you sat here," she snapped, then realized how ridiculous she sounded, arguing with a monitor.

Not that she was loath to fly the life cocoon and use its tools, oh no. *Goddess protect – I need it, want it, more than anything I've ever done.*

Yes, the AI's can fly the crafts. But Caylee says we must have a pilot in the event of unpredictables. And, of course, the only other one on the planet lies snoring in his medical unit.

Still she hated the connecting, the oozy insertion of a foreign object into her mind. It brought memory, the vile pig farmer, who'd grabbed her, pinned her in the dirt, and reached filthy searching fingers beneath her dress. Bashing his head with a heavy red clay pot settled him but good. She and

Yola'd packed and gone before ... if ... he ever came to. That's when Yola'd told her the facts of men.

The oozing-snick of the jack plug and the icky slither inside her brain. The clockwise spin and click of secured mating.

"It's a go." Rak'khiel gagged out.

And then, the wonder began.

Suddenly, one with the ship, she understood. *I am no longer a small girl – hiding and helpless. I am a huge, powerful, knowledgeable entity. I have monstrous weapons. Fear me, for I am now this!*

She saw plot lines in orange superimposed over gray flight paths. Her weapons status glowed green, moving lines, tracking possible targets. Predicting destruction.

Her stomach crammed against her diaphragm, her breath panted in brute lust. *How could I be afraid to fly? I am a surging harnessed force, I am the guns, I am the engines, I am invincible. I feel like a Goddess.*

Kel's body followed deeptape procedures on the instant. Her mind struggled to keep up, made her hands fumble, hover minutely over the board. "Too fast. Wait! Did I enter this sequence correctly?"

Believe your training. Never doubt. Allow it to help. Caylee's thought in her mind. *Allow your mind to mesh with your tapes. To doubt your training is to die.*

What if it all goes wrong? Goddess, Caylee, I need to check things.

Trust your presets. Trust is all you must do, Caylee insisted. *Trust me, trust yourself. Doubt brings death.*

Her head pounded, fear's acid in her mouth, the bitter metallic taste of bloody fangs.

The skin on her arms glowed red, reflecting the lights of an overhead monitor.

At its beep, Rak'khiel flinched and emitted a tiny squeak. *Nerves are wound too tight, like a key twisted by a child's hand. This direction of thought means ruin – I must relax.*

Kel felt out-of-body as she watched her hands, mind and eyes work independent of her will. *My training, kicking in. Faster than my thoughts can verify.*

The sequences are correct, yet something inside her didn't quite trust. It wanted a second visual check. Perhaps someday she would take this for granted ... but now is critical. *Get it right, Kel.* She sank half-fangs into her lower lip. *Do not fail.*

Caylee's aspect appeared, dressed in a sweeping emerald satin gown, white ruching decorated the décolleté. She inclined her dark head. "You can smile in a stressful situation. Excellent."

"Nervous reaction," Rak'khiel answered. "I'm glad you're here." *She's dressed for a party, not a crash? Good.* Kel bent to her pre-flight protocols, focused down tight on each minute aspect of her boards. All systems green. She reached for the switch, flipped it.

Something far greater than the scary Olican dirt tremblers shook around her. Vibrations amplified, the huge engine's grumble built to a roar, a howl. Power surged.

Her sphincter pinched – *Goddess, I'd no idea. If I'd only flown even once before.* Well, yes I did as a baby but I don't remember. Still, Caylee said the warplane's simulators were much too different – they would only have confused me.

The huge power mains cut in with a rumble, the lifecocoon trembled, danced in place.

"Goddess safe," Kel heard her voice squeak, an octava too high. "I'm sitting on a wound-tight catapult. Your favor, Caylee, watch everything I do? Take over if I mess up?"

"Your father would have said the same." The AI moved to the overhead screen. "I will monitor."

Letting control ease from consciously directed actions, to mesh partially with the ship systems, Rak'khiel reveled in the union, smiling at her hands grasping the thruster throttles and the main's yoke.

She fixed her eyes on the screens. The bright yellow circle schematic showed the ship's nose. The white jagged area around it – the cave opening. The second screen displayed the actual overhead view of encroaching gray rock walls and the blackish overhead netting.

"Ready?" Caylee's soft question.

In answer, Rak'khiel blew out a huge breath, vanished the shimmering pink-gold armor called by her tension too different – they would have only confused me.

The huge power mains cut in with a rumble, the lifecocoon danced, trembled in place.

"Shalit in a chalice," Kel heard her voice squeak, an octava too high. "I'm sitting on a wound-tight catapult. Your favor Caylee, watch everything I do," Kel pleaded. "Take over if I mess up."

"Your father would have said the same." The AI's avatar moved to the overhead screen. "I will monitor."

Letting control ease from consciously directed actions, to mesh partially with the ship systems, Rak'khiel reveled and eased back the controls.

The pod's thrusters blew the dirt beneath it throughout the cavern,in a swirling tornado blocking her viewport.

Ooookay. It's the schematic for me.

Easing the throttles open, feeling the cocoon tilt, Rak'khiel swore every vile oath she'd ever heard repeated in the marketplaces of Olica.

Screech scrunch. The ship jarred, hesitated, as the podnose jammed its pointed steelceramtanium tiles against the rough rock of the cavewall.

Kel's fingers danced on the nacelle controls, damped one side lift, shoved a pair on the far side and the pod scraped vertical. Another correction and the cocoon's bow came up during the tiny sideways lift.

At the terrible grinding noise of cerammetal on stone, Rak'khiel clashed her fangs. An instinctive back-off the nozzles caused the pod to drop, bounce and bobble before righting. Despite her instant correction, the pod landed on uneven ground, lurched, steadied.

"Forgun shalit!" Kel edged the ship vertical, pulled the yoke, engaging the mains. "I panicked, I effing overcompensated. Didn't realize the Goddessrotted controls were so damnitall touchy."

Kel nudged the nozzles until the yellow circle sat in precise placement – dead center in the white periphery. Holding held her breath, fingers gripping the thrusters steady. Perfectly set-up.

No hesitation – she yanked back hard on the yoke, the huge main engine responded. The pod went up, straight up, like a laser beam.

"Yes," she screamed. "Oh Yes. The rush. More, more, more!"

Kel realized her fangs were out; her hearts beat triple-time like the old men drumming at the annual conclave. Except one heart can't do what mine is – without death. *And I've never been more alive.*

A rush of heat, moist and unexpected, between her legs. Did I wet myself? No – this is caused by fear, exhilaration, or perhaps the thing Yola called lust. Whatever it is it, I never want it to stop.

Caylee's voice said something about Damage Assessments showing a small portion of the cave sheared away, a few dull spots on the pod's nose … and now, Goddess help me way up here … what do I do?

§

"Rak'khiel … Rak'khiel. Well done," Caylee's voice ripped through her joy, grabbed her attention. "It's time to execute a burn, flip and guide the pod back to the fighter."

Kel's soaring heart dropped through her boots. "Shalit. No. I can't land this thing." *Plus, if I eff this up, I will never fly again. I don't want to make jewelry, I want to fly ships. I'll die if I can't.*

You could die without the medbox too, a grim thought intruded and Kel wondered who it belonged to. *Better do right.*

"Caylee, can the autopilot – you – do it? I'll try but I need to know … if I need it?" Kel's fingers raced, computations, plot points, vectors, landing point targeted.

"Yes, relax." Caylee's calm voice soothed. "But please recall whose mistake wrecked the pod's landing. I've no desire to repeat my disgrace." The avatar of Kel's mother peered over her shoulder. "Good," she complimented, "you've factored in slow stern-down descent."

"Goddess. What if I hit the warplane? I flew into the cave wall." Rak'khiel relived the instant, felt her hearts beating. But they beat wrong – one thump on tempo, then another – off, in syncopation. Too fast, double-time. *Focus, Rak'khiel. Get your head in the now.*

"That was not your fault. The pod wasn't vertical, its nose rested against the cave wall. The soft, uneven ground gave way the instant we had engine start," Caylee explained. "Your reflexes saved the ship."

"Oh." *Well now, how about that?* The pounding in Kel's chest slowed.

Now confident fingers danced across the triple-layered boards and the lifecocoon performed a lazy rotation, descending tail-down toward Olica's surface. Her viewscreens showed the warplane directly underneath.

Kel's in-suck of breath vibrated her hands on the contrls.

Goddess, we are going to crash right on top of Razr's plane.

Panic jerked her out of interface – blind, unpiloted, the ship wobbled.

Alarms blared, red warning lights flashed.

Rak'khiel's brain became a cornered, darting thing, seeking escape, seeking reason, seeking solutions.

"Caylee!"

"I have it. Check your screens, Kel, we are precisely where we need to be."

"Please fly it in. I can't." She heard the heartbreak in her voice, hoped Caylee couldn't.

"You can, you will. You must." Caylee's voice sounded

parental. "You are a pilot, born to it. You passed all tapetesting, aced all available training. You flew the pod out of a mountain – infinitely more difficult than landing. You will not fail, my daughter."

Warmth spilled and melted a tiny corner of the frozen wall about Kel's heart. Flowing through taut muscles, it unkinked the rowed knots marching up the back of her neck.

Mother loves me, believes in me. I refuse to disappoint.

Rak'khiel focused hard, released her fears, her barriers and self-merged completely into the ship. *Doubt caused my problems. I feared losing myself, becoming Other, becoming a Caylee, trapped and absorbed by this ceramtanium machine, never to escape. All untrue.*

The thruster nacelles rotated, quick sharp bursts, tiny burns, slowing their descent.

Kel watched her hands – one held the yoke, the other manipulating the thruster throttles. She marveled at the sensation of being outside looking in … and yet of being one complete entity with the pod. Sure of her decisions, she relaxed, bursting with joy in this new thing. Beyond Olican comprehension, this.

On her landing scope display, a green cross-haired schematic, the pod circle of yellow eased down, gently settled in, beside the larger silver round denoting the fighter. Close, very close. Down – tiny burst. Bump – landed. Exactly dead on.

"Holy Goddess of Good," she breathed, extended the lander arms, and emerged from flight trance. The surprising stomach-twisting slither – the piece of foreign pulled from of her brain. *Ooooh – forgot the jack interface.*

At the shift, an odd, off-center space in her mind, Kel's training kicked in. It's only the transition from ship merge. But I am me. And only me. No need to worry again, ever. A sigh escaped, her release of pent worries.

Even as her hands worked the checklist, flipped the huge main cut-off switch and pressed thruster icons, Kel relived the experience. Her hands completed final procedures without conscious direction. *Had I trusted, immersed completely in the system before flying out of the cave, would I have scraped the side? Was it my peasant superstition? Or did Caylee tell me true?*

But, Kel's deeply-rooted Olican beliefs intruded, *at what price comes this liberating, exhilarating new freedom?*

The priests would condemn me as demon possessed. Are they wrong? Must a price always be paid for happiness, for stepping outside the rules? If so, what will it be? And do I care?

Kel shut down her mind and allowed muscles and body to relax. Pulling cool, fresh breath to the bottom of her lungs, she felt her hearts slow to their normal easy beats. At pain in her lips, stretched taut, she reached a questing finger and found long sharp points.

My fangs? Were they out the entire flight? She banished them with a wish.

"Well done," Caylee said.

Startled, Rak'khiel sprang from the pilot's station. Dropping through the central core, she hit the panel raising the outer hatch. Through the access, two-at-a-time down the stairs, she leaped the final three. Racing around the pod, she skidded to a stop, not moving, not breathing, lips compressed to bloodless.

At the pod's widest point, it stood a mere inch from the huge fighter plane. *How did I not hit it?* A perfect landing – it had to be. *Prince Helrazr would kill and eat me if I put a single mark on his aircraft.*

The smile escaping Kel was sly, "Reversed, I'd do the same."

Rak'khiel? Are you well?

"Goddess, Caylee. We almost struck Razr's plane." Kel spoke aloud, then wondered if she stood too far away for the AI to hear.

No, Kel. We landed exactly where planned. For the ships to be combined, they must be almost touching. The melding and essential structural fillers have to withstand the stress of augmented FTL drives and stargate jumps. Caylee's send came warm, reassuring. *Your placement is perfect. Now we need the supplies stored in the cave.*

"Yes, Caylee," said Kel just before her legs gave way, dropped her hard on her rump.

"Just pardon me for a minute, your favor, while I sit and quietly have a heartafaint."

Chapter 32

Mid-Dark
Nara 18, 7205.37
Warplane Medical Unit

Where am I?

Razr jerked, found his arms restrained. Fighting to sit, he only managed to bash his forehead on the docbox's plasplex lid. His violent reaction to confinement, the explosive hammering of his twin hearts blew him completely awake. The vile oath he swore was the one his mother most detested. *Banished me from the house for saying it, she did, for a full wakari.*

Hammering the red escape button with one large fist, he impatiently waited for the sides to retract. Hearing the hum of machinery – *'facturers are working on Level E? What are they making? Why am I in the docbox?*

"Prince Helrazr," Brin's welcome voice. "How do you feel?"

"Fine, except for the slif egg on my forehead." The prince's fingertips explored the fast-rising bump. "What happened?"

Solemn in formal dress of black robes and powdered wig, brandishing an oak and brass gavel, his AI's adjudicator's appearance made Razr's viscera churn.

"I have no memory, Brin. How long have I slept?"

"You were poisoned during your fight with the 'Ristos.

You killed them all but took venom damage. One wakari."

"Great Destroyer take it." Memory filtered slowly, the hit on the chopr. His catch of breath at remembered agony of burning and then ... it all faded to nothing.

"Rak'khiel?" Razr swung long legs out of the machine, stood and stretched.

"Kel is fine."

"Excellent." Nude, the warrior paused in selecting clothing, noted new white scars ... the acid ... and the accursed itching deep in the still-healing blotches of red. *Would Rak'khiel be repulsed by them? Will I ever get the chance to know?*

Checked his arms, legs, thickness of shoulders. Musing, yet again, he'd lost weight in the med unit. Then, the oddity in Brin's comment clicked. "Kel?"

"Lady Regence's diminutive for her."

Ah .... "Kel. Nice." Razr rolled the nickname on his tongue, spoke it again. "Lady Regence? Ha. I guessed correctly. It suits her, I like it. Does she?"

"She did not seem offended when I called her by it."

Razr dressed quickly, entered the lav and splashed his face with water. Coating it with warm foam, he began the age-old male ritual – at least on Kra'aken – of shaving.

"Prince Helrazr?" Brin hesitantly began.

Oh, Great Destroyer save me, Razr shielded his thoughts. *Brin's special tone of voice, his use of my title – this bodes ill.*

"What now?" He snapped. "Brin, I'm .... Ah ...." Razr smashed his lips together, almost not in time. *The apology almost got away from me.* And that is something Kra'aken Royalty may never do.

Outside the fighter came a loud clanging, a bang and a stream of Olican and Kra'aken oaths spewed in a female voice.

Razr's straight-edge skipped, struck and left a streak of scarlet like the pulled-strike of his swordmaster.

"Great Destroyer kill it," he snarled. "What in the sixteen hells was that?"

"More like Hell Twenty-Five," said the AI's holo. One corner of his mouth twitched, then a full-on smile escaped. "The very subject I planned to discuss," Brin said. "Your favor."

"Would it be good if I listened before I exit my fighter?" The mirror reflected Razr's wry twist of his lips all but hidden behind the spice-scented shave cream.

One large hand groped in the top drawer, came away with his coag stick. Drawing it the length of the cut, he clenched his teeth. "Hsss, damnit. Bites."

"It would indeed. Your tribute, Prince Razr."

Shata! I forgot to hide my discomfort. Twin vertical furrows formed between ebon dark brows. "My Kra'aken ways are becming lax. This will change."

"Oh my prince, if you only knew how much has ... will change ...." Then, as soberly as the Kra'aken justicers he mimicked, Brin began to speak. "After you killed the chopr ...."

Razr finished shaving, wiped bits of white from smooth tan cheeks and throat. Then stood silent, only interrupting once to echo, "She carried me?" Stood silent, accepting, until Brin reached the part where Rak'khiel flew the pod from the cavern and set it down beside the warplane.

"No!"

The huge warrior tore through his fighter. Leaping through the open outer hatch, he cleared the ladder handrails, absorbed the two-story drop in bunched leg muscles, then sprinted around the fighter's side. Morphosis surged, he'd murder anyone who'd harmed his warplane.

His headlong rush froze, full stop.

A female voice cursed without pause. In Olican, unless he misunderstood the use of the okina. In Kra'aken. In ... unless memory failed him ... in High Sartran. Rak'khiel's lessons obviously included all forms of speech. She knows words I don't. *Perhaps I should have paid more attention.* Our female pilots cursed too, but this ...?

His righteous anger, his fury at the temerity of those who dared meddle with his precious warplane evaporated. There his fighter stood, her clean killing lines altered by new bracing, her hull extruded to embrace the life cocoon.

The prince's Killing Rage dissipated in a guffaw. He roared, he howled before finally winding down to a series of hiccuping snorts.

Ribs creaking, ab muscles lax from disuse curling into cramped knots, Razr swiped the back of one large six-fingered hand across his eyes. Throwing his head back, he gave himself up to mirth once more.

"Prince Helrazr, your Grace?" The timid voice came from somewhere below his nose. He peered down at a blurred form, wiped his eyes again, and belched.

"Your Highness, Sir, are you well?" A pronounced trembling, held mostly in check, colored her voice.

"Fine, fine." He snorted, chuckled again. Rubbed his ribs and belly.

"You are not displeased?"

"I was … until you cursed – in three languages, yet. Great Destroyer, woman, I've never heard such creative, anatomically graphic, physically impossible – do you even know the parts of which you speak?"

And I've never heard you giggle, Razr. Brin's sly comment wore pleasure wrapped around and woven through it. *It pleases me, greatly.*

It pleasures my heart as well, my Prince.

"Caylee. Are you also up to your silver box in this conspiracy?"

We worked long to convince Kel – but given the dangers of the 'Ristos and their hunting parties, the severity of your wounds – we knew leaving this place must be our First Imperative.

Brin added, *I knew you would insist on bringing Kel's medunit.*

"Prince Helrazr, I needed you to fly the pod out of the cave," said the shaking *Goddess-am-I-in-so-much-trouble* voice under his chin. "I sent and sent and sent to you. I sat by your medbox and called and called and called. But you never answered."

A chortle, mostly held in check, prefaced his question. "Are the scrapes on the pod nose your doing?" Razr's eyes cruised the ships.

No! From Brin.

NO! From Caylee. *Thanks to her piloting, although the cocoon tipped at engine ignition, she righted it – FTL reflexes, our girl – and flew it out.* The pitch of the AI's voice rose with her volume. *No small doing, Prince Helrazr, even you couldn't have bettered her. Oh Great Destroyer, my grievous reprehensible, Your Highness, I did not mean to presume.*

Another chuckle from Razr. "It would seem you have two staunch defenders, Rak'khiel." *Excellent. You are worthy.*

The prince finally allowed his eyes to leave his fighter. He focused on the apparition standing before him ... and recoiled.

Delectable curves were hidden by blue-striped ships' coveralls, her glorious hair stuffed under a matching brimmed hat. Mechanic's black work boots made her dainty feet look like those of a Court Fool.

Grease and dirt covered every inch of Rak'khiel, her clothing and exposed hair and skin. One hand, its dainty oval nails crusted over with filth, held a wrench. Blood caked the knuckles of both long-fingered hands.

"Are you mad?" The tiny voice quavered.

"Without question. However, if you mean angry about joining the ships, show me what is done and I'll let you know."

Kel turned, strode toward the pod, then spun on her heel back to face him.

Razr crashed into her, grasped her shoulders to steady them both. He cocked a questioning eyebrow to cover the hammering of his heart. And its painful echo in his groin.

"You'll ruin those clothes. Go put on something else." She

glared at the wrench, sucked her bloody knuckle. "I need you to tighten a fitting for me."

Razr went, exercising firm control until he was safely out of earshot. Then body shuddering with his attempt to suppress his laughter, he headed for the mechanic's lockers.

Chapter 33

Early Aiy
Nara 20, 7205.30
Farside of the Fang, Olica

The AI's designs mated the warplane and the life cocoon belly to belly. Kel's pod placement, taking into consideration the matching of the mains and thrusters, was well back on the longer fighter. Standing vertical, the engines of both planes sat even, butted against the dirt.

The next morning, Kel perched astride the top of a small ladder braced against the side of the warplane. Performing what the AI's laughingly called "twelve-fingered" work, she drilled into the fighter's understructure, attaching external braces between the pod and fighter. A bit of tricky, making the adjustments and cuts exactly right.

Remembering Yola's training – measure thrice, cut once – the diamante drill bit poised precise and perfect, she touched it to the ceramtanium hull. Now – the gentlest pull on the trigger, slow and easy – just to mark the starting pinpoint.

Dragging in a deep breath, she held her body immobile and touched the point against the mark on the fighter. Levering her body's full weight against the drill bit, preparing to drive the bit through the hull ....

"What in the Great Destroyer do you think you're doing?"

Snarled in her right ear.

Her violent start caused her fist to clench, sending the bit spinning at high speed. One bounce, twice, three great streaks of nicks before she managed to control the drill and yank it from the ship's exterior.

Teeth and claws out, Kel's hearts beat staccato as she swung the drill around, brought the rotating gemstone bit to bear directly on the chest of the source of her fright.

The source quickly backed away.

"Goddess in a glass jar," she breathed, shut off the drill, banished claws and fangs and glared at the prince. Her temper surged and snapped at the end of its tether, begging to be unleashed.

"I'm creating a mating hatch between the pod and the fighter," she said, evenly, carefully enunciating each word. "A more observant, perhaps smarter, man might have noticed."

"That is absolutely wrong," he declared pointing at her placement marks. "You have no idea what you're about. Look at the damage to my ship. Give me that schematic." A large hand thrust forward, in Kel's face.

"Forgun you," she said, her low growl ripped the air. She bit him. Hard. Realized she'd used fangs.

Gathering her rage about her like a length of Yola's finest cloth, Rak'khiel clenched the fist holding the ships' plan, until it crinkled into a double-sided fan. Turning, she marched into the lifecocoon and closed the hatch. *I wish it would slam, damnit.*

Instead she sealed it and settled for re-keying the access codes to her survivor pod.

Shaking with rage, fighting a body trying to force armor, Rak'khiel found herself laving Razr's blood from her retracting fangs. *Horrible. But, Goddess save, he tastes delicious.*

Peeking through the closest viewport, she watched the prince inspect his hand.

"Aiee," he said. "Requires Destroyer-rotted stitches. I'll have to stick my hand in the forzaing box. Girl must be a direct descendant of the Great Bitch."

Good, Rak'khiel told herself as she peered through the transplas. *I effing hope I am.*

Kel watched Razr ignore the steps to the pod. He leaped to the landing, hit the outer door plate and waited. Struck it again. And waited.

Kel held her breath. Quieted her mind. *He's furious.*

"I know you hear me," Razr grated and his slitted eyes scanned the pod's outer ports. Kel saw his tawny skin suffuse, his face dark with rage.

Goddess, he's changing to Other.

Razr's claws and fangs appeared, interlacing golden patterns roiled, danced on his body. He hit the hatch plate again.

Kel did nothing.

"Rak'khiel, open this door immediately. I command it."

"When swine sprout swansdown, Prince Helrazr." *I wonder if he heard that?*

Kel, if it eases your mind, you were completely correct in your work. You are a much better technician than Razr. He goes too fast, makes mistakes. Brin's send held a cutting critical edge she'd never heard before.

A loud voice demanded entry, a heavy fist hammered the pod hatch.

"I agree, my dear." Caylee said, her voice shaded with anger. "Because of his military rank and his birthright, he is unused to having an order countermanded. You were not wrong." Then, the AI – Lady Floril's aspect – grinned, a total and unexpected pleasant shock. "I'm delighted you bit him."

"Will he stop shouting and pounding on the door anytime soon?" Rak'khiel heard the tremor in her voice, shudders rippled through her body.

"Unlikely," answered Brin.

"Then I'll go where I cannot hear him." Rak'khiel made her way to her sleeping area and crawled into the center of her bed.

Olican Kel felt frightened, even repulsed. Her stomach churned. *Whatever friendship we had, I've damaged, no – ruined. I reacted like a beast, not a lady.* Sharp daggers stabbed her hearts. *If I ever want to jump the broomstick, Razr is my only option. And I don't like him very much.*

Honest Rak'khiel intruded. *Untrue.* Kra'aken Kel likes him very much indeed. *I just hate that sometimes he's a buttend.*

Sensing her distress, Tarkin and Torga woke, long tails waving question-marks at Rak'khiel. Then they burrowed beneath the coverlet until they lay close to her.

Prince Helrazr mad? Torga asked.

Want me to bite him? Tarkin lifted a half-lip.

"I already did," Kel said and hysterical giggles took her.

Rak'khiel? What is wrong? The two engulfed her, twined, caressed.

"He's furious with me." She wound fingers in their glossy fur, curled between them, took comfort in their warm closeness.

Won't stay that way, Tarkin sent.

He looooves you, Torga reassured. *It will be well.*

"Why didn't I think before I bit? No, never again will it be right between us." Pulling both pillows over her head, Rak'khiel buried her face in their fur and sobbed until sleep took her.

Chapter 34

Mid-Dark
Nara 21, 7205.15
Warplane, Olica

Drumming big fingers on the armrest of his pilot's couch, Razr seethed. Like hot liquid stretching his veins to the verge of explosion, rage boiled and bubbled. *Good thing I'm not hooked to a monitor – I'd be in the med unit at FTL speed.*

"They dare to shun me?" he snarled. "Helrazr VI'Rex, a royal Kra'aken prince? Impossible, intolerable. I will not allow this behavior."

The prince's lips pinched, small and angry. *How in the twelve hells will I prevent it? Brin no longer initiates conversation, only answers direct questions. Kel and Caylee the same. Although AI's cannot feel – they are mere chunks of components – I swear Brin and Caylee are angry. At me. I tightened Kel's bloody damn fitting just as she demanded. I got a thank you that sounded more like a forza you. Not a bit of spill-over gratitude.*

Razr ground his teeth, preventing his scream of fury, but one large hand fisted, hammered a bulkhead. *You'd think I did something wrong – they treat me like a sentenced murderer or a communicable disease. Perhaps Rak'khiel has somehow subverted both the computers. But, honesty heard here, Razr, to what end?*

Razr paced the tiny interior of the cockpit aisle, let a frown

own his face, while muttering a bitter litany of their faults. *Yes, the three of them forzaed everything up. They couldn't leave it alone until I woke – oh, no. Now, we need to flee and can't.*

"Brin. Are the ships bonded? Ready to fly?"

"Still working." A short, clipped answer, nothing more.

"Shata! This is unbelievable."

"Yes, isn't it?" Brin's tone came … absolutely … snotty?

Razr's topaz eyes rested on the dark blue of the empty armscomper's couch. His anger ebbed, replaced by deep sorrow. But only for a secunda. The reasserted problem brought new rage.

Step, step, turn. Loosened by the force of his pacing, warrior's braids laced with tiny sapphire, crystal and coral beads, stung his forehead. He yanked the intricately worked silver clasp from the top of his head, snatched up and corralled the errant strands. Jerking them tight enough to slant his eyebrows, Razr shoved them into the silver clip, jammed the fastening home.

He enjoyed the taut pull, knew it changed his handsome visage to something demon spawned. With a guttural half-laugh, he called half-formed fangs. *Now I'm the monster they think I am. Thanks to their combined stupidity, and cobbled modifications, neither forzaing ship can fly.*

"Brin? Estimate completion time frame, please."

"Three plus horas. Estimate only. Working."

Stomp, stomp, turn. Razr's body pulsed with angry heat. *Had they not touched the ship, I could have saved Kel, and Caylee's silver braincase, while I blew everything 'Risto out of the universe.*

His hard step ended in a bulkhead kick.

Muscles swelled with blood, with pre-change essence. Then the shift as his underskeleton triggered, recognizing fighting need. It filled with added density and size as Razr's body prepared for battle. *I need to kill something – the Level 20 monster in the sim would be perfect – but I cannot.* We must maintain pre-flight readiness.

Three hard kicks at the offending ivory plastanium

bulkhead produced a satisfying dent. *Take the semi-mated ships skyward together? With Rak'khiel piloting her pod? We'll all die.*

Still, Razr's honesty required him to confess. Rak'khiel's work he'd thought faulty, proved perfect instead. *Embarrassing, that.*

Heat flooded up his neck, torched his ears. His hearts sagged with grief's drag – the sudden remembrance. *Mother delighted in making them glow.*

"Brin, status report."

"Estimate completion now four horas – a 'facturer malfunction."

"Destroyer forza it."

"Agreed. Working."

The damned AI is relentless – he believes I am wrong. In fairness, although it broke every Royal Rule, Razr examined the incident from the other side. Truth be spoken, Kel's craftmanship was better. Great Destroyer it hurt his pride, harder than hard to admit, but yes, her beginner's work far surpassed his best.

But princes cannot apologize. Apologies are performed by the person of lower caste – actual fault is never considered. *Kra'aken law demands Rak'khiel solicit me, tender her reprehensibles since her birth is one tier below Rex.*

I've waited, and waited for her to do so. She refuses. I am royalty, yet neither AI supports me. This defies their programming.

Razr's mind juggled his problems: Rak'khiel, Brin, Caylee, the 'Ristos. Suddenly realized if he didn't pay attention to the here and now, he wouldn't have to worry about the rest. Many odd things occurred since that Terran strike on the warplane in Kra'aken space. *Question is what do I do about it?*

"Prince Helrazr, I have incoming." Brin's chilly tones informed.

Chapter 35

Mid-Dark
Nara 21, 7205.55
LifeCocoon

BOOM!

Rak'khiel shot vertical and stood clutching the edge of her desk. Her shaking stomach tried to turn inside out.

"Goddess of Goodness, what is ...? Are we having a groundshake?"

"We're under 'Risto attack," said Caylee. "They dropped one large bomb ...."

A rattle like metal hail peppered the ship. Silence, then another volley sprayed.

"Two strafing runs," Caylee added.

"Damage?" Kel's question came without conscious thought. "The ships were shielded?"

"Some of the incomplete struts and bracings are weakened. Several are hanging loose."

"My fault," Kel's face twisted. Fear's cold finger traced her windpipe. Shaking her head, she clenched her fists. "If I'd stayed at work yesterday, instead of running away like an angry child, I could have prevented this."

"No, if there is fault, it lies with Razr," the AI said.

"What should I do?"

"Suit up, arm yourself. Brin's signaling."

"Shalit!" Two strides put Kel at the core, the third step launched her feet-first down the ship's center toward the lockers. One hand snagged a grip to slow her descent. She bent her knees, landed light on her feet.

"Kel?" Caylee said. "Take the cockpit."

"Eff me," Rak'khiel whispered. "How … what …." But she dressed.

"Brin and I continue to strengthen the melds between the ships. But for now, we must fly them as they are. Joined, yet not together." Caylee's voice quivered.

Goddess, she's nervous.

"Razr will fly the fighter," said Caylee. "You will sync the life cocoon with him. If we attain low orbit, we can finish our work there. Provided we sustain no damage in flight. Should the ships become unstable, we must land again and complete the joins."

"On my way," Rak'khiel said. *Goddess, your favor, let us land yet again. I have a vow to complete. Many more to kill.*

A shriek escaped her as the pendant stirred against her chest.

Adoptive Mother's spoke. "No, I forbid this thing, Ela. You must not ask the Goddess to help you commit mortal sins."

Rak'khiel froze. Pulling the pendant from her shirt, her chest heaved. The silver necklace seemed to writhe, red streamers wrapped and shifted. Staring at Yola's gift, Kel wondered. *Do I err?*

"Lady Regence, if you will?" Strain laced the edges of Caylee's words. "Please, trust us all. Now is not the time for introspection."

"You are correct. Tarkin, Torga" Kel said. "Nets, please. This could – *will* – be a bumpy ride." *I hope it isn't our last.*

Dropping a kiss on each furred head, she opened the tops of the cafuzog's carriers.

Claws clacking against the plasteel bulkhead, the two swarmed the netting, dived into their restraints. Rak'khiel checked fittings, clicked belts and tugged twice for insurance.

Rushing into the pod core, she hauled her body hand-over-hand up the rungs into the lifecocoon's nose. With a sideways scoot across the pilot's cushions, her webbing secure, Kel strapped in with a solid click. She pressed her head to the gray seatback section and waited.

The sliding gooey snick-turn never got any easier. But info flooded, data dumped. And Kel knew everything Caylee, Brin and Razr did.

Her mind shifted, expanded, called up the screens. She saw the fighter's engines burning hot. Through their connection she felt Razr's ship vibrating with its need to vault skyward.

Kel thumbed her deadman's switch, hit the pod's huge main. It rumbled and caught. She remembered to breathe again.

The cocoon trembled, the heavy power plant aching to be away. She held it in check, but a jolt between her legs throbbed in sympathy.

One by one, Kel hit the thruster nozzles icons. One by one they lit. Ready.

"She will kill us ... she's no pilot ..." Razr said to Brin.

Although anger warred with hurt, Kel ignored his words. *I will not betray my internal chaos. I will not allow emotion to rule me this day.*

Her voice came calm, steady.

"Rak'khiel to Brin, Caylee and Razr. I'm a Go."

"Copy," from Brin.

"Affirmative," from Caylee.

"Razr, do you copy? I'm a Go, I said. Pod's a Go."

Chapter 36

Early-Aiy
Nara 21, 7205.05
FighterPod

Razr activated his jaw mike with a touch of his tongue, wedged his huge body into the pilot's couch and belted in. Pressing his head against the gray pad, he waited for the repugnant mindjack interface.

Destroyer preserve us from the silly girl who will attempt to fly the cocoon. The AI should have control. But both computers seem to have lost all their logic functions.

The ooze, the probe's insertion at the base of his skull, the snick, then, the sudden oneness with the warplane.

Now his large hands flew across keyboards, touched transparent screens, readied for flight. Somewhere in the back of his mind, his jack shook hands with Rak'khiel's, absorbed her input, gave her the fighter's.

"Copy, Pod. I say again, copy your Go." Razr snapped. *Damnable nagging woman.*

The tall lethal ship trembled around him, a magnificent beast straining for freedom. Suddenly, unexpectedly, the roar of his engines diminished, overwhelmed by the thunderous rumble of the pod's enormous main. A secondary snarl reverberated as Kel's thrusters lit.

She's outputting thrice my power. I am helpless if she forzas up. Someone who knows how to fly should be in that pod.

From his cockpit, Razr couldn't see the lifecocoon, slung low and well back on his stern but a tri-section screen provided external views and status of Kel's operating systems.

Time to initiate this folly – wish I'd had a bulb of brandas before I die.

He shivered. Beneath the flightsuit, his body slicked with cold sweat. Although dual lines from his hearts double-redlined on the shrieking physio monitor, Razr's flat emotionless voice could have been a recording.

"Engines hot. Ready, on my third mark. Standard launch speed synched. Mark, Mark, MARK."

Thunderous, sensual power built, propelled the twinned aircrafts from Olican dirt. All systems showed normal, weapons' status monitors glowed ready. The hard pressure of g's, the steady climb slow and anticlimactic, nagged at his stomach. *No, it's not the launch itself, it's who's in charge.*

With the immense power plants thrumming beneath them, the two ships departed Olica, seeking to outrun its evils.

Intellectually, he knew the powerful drives of the pod, the amount of its thrust. Still, the force surprised him. The life cocoons carrying Kra'aken's most precious cargo had all been equipped with the newest and finest tech – to increase the children's chances of survival.

A small worry niggled at a corner of his mind. *Kel could shove my ship anywhere – I'd be helpless. Does she know? Of course she does – it's her ship, and she's a good study.* Razr hoped she didn't hate him enough to crash and kill him. He wished things were different between them.

He dragged his mind back to the flight. No turning back, no shutting down, no second guessing.

Under the twin lavender suns, the two ships lifted, groaned, flew like silver lovers coupling in selfish lust, not love. Separate entities, cleaving, clinging only in critical areas.

Brin and Caylee worked, information exchanged, a dull

background murmur of male and female voices against the riotous colors of scrolling numbers, systems and ships' status, myriad plotted courses and probabilities, defense screens, ready weapons.

"Fighter to pod. Prepare for possible engagement, evasive maneuvers."

"Pod, copy." Rak'khiel's professional acknowledgement. "Enemy onscreen."

"Pod – do not fire weapons, do not engage." Razr said, too fast. "You could damage my fighter."

"I'm no idiot. Pod copy." Kel's words snapped out, each a single chunk of frozen arrogance.

Razr heard the growl in his throat and swallowed it. Everything he did, every interaction with Rak'khiel, exacerbated the discord. Best to keep all attention on the approaching problem.

Black specks grew closer, separated into four straining aircraft pushing hard for an intercept.

"Brin, assessment?" Razr tried for better visual resolution, found nothing.

"They plan destruction of our ships before we reach safe altitude." The AI's tone sounded strained.

"Can they do it?"

"Affirmative, they have intercept angle. Working on our stability now." The professional AI's voice passed all information to Kel and Caylee.

Razr gnashed budding fangs. He wanted to bite something. Hard. *Why do the two females need to know?* He scanned his dirtside surface screen. "Shata."

Across the hard rocky ground, dotted with grass and brush, their obvious destination the warplane's last known location, marched a foot-squad of villagers. Captained by a black-robed 'Risto, the company paused mid-stride, eyes locked on the lifting ships. A sharp command from the black horror moved them forward again.

"Destroyer." Razr thumbed a deep zoom on a surface

scanner and flinched.

Surrounded by a baying, herding pack of narrow-muzzled, gray hunting beasts, the soldiers pressed closer toward their formation center, disrupting the order and precision of their march. Who could blame them? The dogs' lolling tongues, the color of dried blood, displayed rowed sets of back-slanted needle teeth.

The better to kill us if we crash, Kel thought at Caylee but Razr heard. *As vicious as their masters.*

"Aircraft closing," Brin's warning.

Two ancient choprs, the same riveted metal and reflective glass models as the one he'd blown to the Twelve Hells, followed a museum-piece fighter, and one vintage propcraft.

Warheads, bright and glowing, flew toward the twinned ships. Harmless at this altitude, they arced below, then dropped toward the planet's surface. Orange and red explosions of artillery traced fired projectiles.

Razr cursed under his breath. A mere annoyance, even if they hit us. *What else do they have? Unattached to the pod, we'd have been well away, already in upper atmosphere. Instead, because we must be careful, they've caught us.*

From the open side-bay door of the slow squat plane, a black-robed 'Risto leaned out. Steadying a shoulder-held weapon holding a large projectile, the creature carefully sighted.

Bright white-orange light flared with the launch.

"Sweet Destroyer," Razr shouted. "They've seen our weakness. They are firing at it."

BANG!

"A strike," reported Brin. "Destroyer curse it. Squarely on the most critical, on our most incomplete join, between our ships."

The fighter and pod separated slightly; then crashed back together. Bounced apart, closed again with a loud grinding.

Vibrations shuddered up and down the ships, sirens screamed.

Monitors lit, bright red dots pointing to quivering, weakened strains at meld points and around their mated hatches.

The two ships seemed now, as if all lust slaked, they would simply roll apart, go their separate ways. Aloof strangers side by side, straining for the sky.

Razr's physio monitor alarm flashed eye-searing scarlet, blared critical overload. His stomach doubled in half, wadded into his throat.

The mindjack fed him stabilizing drugs to stop the panic.

"Destroyer damnit. Never before in all my years of fighting have I needed ...."

But Razr's brain refused to stop its output.

Smells of burning plasteel, wires, singed ceramtanium filled his nostrils.

We're going down. Kel can never manage this. But the bastards will go with us.

"Brin, I need firing plots." Without waiting for an answer, large deft fingers flew across the secondary armscomp board in his station. A fleeting wish for Shirl's help, quickly dismissed.

Three enemy aircraft fought for height – fighter, propcraft and chopr.

"Preparing to fire." Without waiting for confirmation, knowing Kel had his plan, Razr dropped the warplane's bow, slammed the weapons release, then jerked the nose skyward once more. *Can you compensate, can you anticipate, little girl?*

Three hunter-killer missiles away – white hot streaks in the violet air. Three huge red-orange fireballs exploded, hung blinding below them.

Shockwaves from the guns' firing, shockwaves from the explosions, buffeted both fighter and pod. The meld-point screens showed solid red, meld-point alarms shrieked.

Razr fought his controls, altitude dropping. *I've killed us. But I've killed them too. A warrior lives to die in battle. Why am I not overjoyed?*

Pressure, like a giant overhead hand, mashed Razr against his couch. *What ...?*

The prince watched in amazement as the fighter's nose lifted, driven by a brutal shove from below. Watched, jaw on his chest, while the lifecocoon trimmed angles, matched velocity.

Razr's mind refused to accept the data onscreen.

Nacelle thrusters rotating, Kel fired a small burst. Minute adjustments, then another burst. Three slower, more deliberate adjustments and the pod tucked in neatly beneath the warplane.

Kel matched his speed, kept his fighter's bow skyward in proper trajectory. Kept his aircraft stable.

Did she calc in her head as she flew? She had to. *Impossible.* Her corrections came too fast, too many, too close together for Caylee to comp and present those options. For Rak'khiel to accept and execute.

The door to the reasonable portion of Razr's male mind slammed shut, but rays of the obvious streamed around its edges like streaks of light. *Kel did it, flew the pod, saved us from disaster. Impossible!*

A klaxon blare, the deedle-deedle-deedle shoved his stomach into his throat. *How? Who? Enemy locked on. Where?* Razr searched his screens, found the sleeper craft full aft.

"Enemy closing on stern," Brin's warning jarred. "Missile launched."

"Firing now," a feminine voice.

"I ordered you not to shoot," Razr tried to say but smothered by frozen vocal cords, only a croaking noise emerged. He watched his rear screens and waited to die.

A large detonation behind the climbing ships made him flinch.

"Enemy threat eliminated," Kel announced in a too-satisfied tone.

"Copy," Caylee said.

Razr's mental alarms went silent. *A tidy, actually an*

incredibly sweet piece of flying, a dead-on kill. Another surprise from the pod – rear armaments. *I should have asked.* Then he remembered who flew and his mouth soured.

The AI's chattered in the background, congratulatory comments to Rak'khiel.

"Excellent work," Brin spoke.

Nothing good to say to me .... The prince felt a hot burn creeping up his neck.

"Prince Helrazr," Brin said. "Computations show if we perform a slow roll, placing the pod in superior position to the warplane, maintaining contact between the two ships is improved. And, Caylee and I can continue working on the joins. Your thoughts?"

"Seems reasonable since you are all determined on this course." *Why did I say that and in such a tone?* "Who flies?"

"Caylee and I can manage if you like." The clipped words of anger unmistakable in Brin's voice. "Still, the human element is always better, an added fail-safe."

"I will, of course, fly the warplane with your backup."

"And the pod?" The AI's tone carefully even, waiting. Almost ominous.

"Caylee flies it."

"She refuses, and takes great offense on behalf of her charge." Brin's voice could have frozen fire. "The best pilot flies. Rak'khiel just saved us all – twice. As ranking officer, you should recognize and commend her skill."

"Kel isn't ... doesn't ... female...." Razr suddenly foresaw his future, a wide yawning emptiness, perhaps a yara, perhaps his lifetime, without conversation. Or a mate. "Whatever you feel best, Brin." He gnashed his fangs.

"An apology would also be in order."

"Yes, she should." The prince unconsciously straightened. "I'm royalty, why doesn't she?"

"You sir, are a nether orifice. The apology should be Rex to Regence because it's right. Prepare for course change."

Forza me. An AI dared insult a Rex? I'll pull his plugs, space his box. Rage, like a thin film of red plasplex, pulled like a windowshade over Razr's eyes.

Razr flinched. The physio monitor spiked, flashed, blared. His morphing fingers clutched the yoke, claw nubs hooked, then stuck fast.

The nose of the warplane dived, jerked against the pod, jinked. Dived again.

Before Razr could sheath his claws, disengage from the yoke, assimilate his screens info and make adjustments, the fighter's nose tilted skyward again. "Great Destroyer forza me!"

"Pod to Razr – situation report, your favor?" Kel's sharp-edged question carried anger.

"Engine 2 malfunc, now clear." Razr said but knew she had both his error and his lie.

There was no engine problem, Prince Helrazr. I have your stats on my screens as you do mine. Keep your mind on your business, milord.

Destroyer save me. Now she shared his errors with both AI's. Unnecessary, Razr thought, since they were also hooked into the ships' all-systems.

"I felt your anger, your emotional surge, almost a foretelling. I was already calc'ing probabilities if you effed up." Anger rode Rak'khiel's words. "When you bobbled the roll, I gave a hard lift with my mains; shoved your nose up. Now the truth – what happened?"

A long, gravid pause stretched.

Where did this imperious woman come from? Razr's rage threatened to break free. *The only way for me to limit my damage is to keep silent.*

Brin spoke. "Prince Helrazr, Lady Regence, please execute the roll maneuver. Due to our added damage, now we must land to complete repairs."

I wonder if he'll ever call me Razr again? Heat crawled from neck to forehead, the prince's ears sizzled. *If I'd been in my unit and pulled that, I'd lose my commission.* "Recommendation,

Brin?"

"I've found a spot – although not on the planet's far side as we hoped. Still, we should be safe for a day. There is an unbridged river between the 'Risto fortress and a stand of trees. Hidden beyond is a level grassy meadow." The AI breathed, "Great Destroyer grant our landing is unobserved."

"Let me know where and when. And Brin, my appreciations."

"Milord." The chilly voice replied. "Feeding coordinates to pod and warplane now."

"Very well. Second roll attempt, my mark." Razr wondered if Kel would even respond.

"Copy," came her cool professional reply.

Chapter 37

Mid-Dark
Nara 21, 7205.25
Olican Airspace

"Goddess in a goblet, Caylee. How could he make such an egregious eff-up?"

With the ships' roll completed, a safe trajectory implemented, Rak'khiel allowed her shoulders to droop. A slow sigh escaped. *I swear that came clear from my boot soles.* The vanilln, gingerspice hot musk smell hung heavy in the cockpit.

"Something seemed ... slightly off about Razr." Caylee's smooth avatar forehead wrinkled. "Did you notice?"

"No, but then I don't know him." Rak'khiel frowned at her boards even though all glowed stable green. *A few minas more of free flight before landing maneuvers begin.* Her stomach twitched.

"Brin? Thoughts?" *Please answer, I need a distraction.*

"The Razr of old would never make a mistake, never mind compound one." Brin's tense voice held concern, even worry. "I will suggest the med unit, although he is sure to refuse."

"Could we get a bioscan on a handheld without his knowledge?" Caylee asked. Like Kel, she wore a standard black spacer's flightsuit, although hers glittered with silver buttons and braid.

"Rak'khiel could get close enough – if he doesn't suss what she's about." Brin popped into the pod's cockpit, splendid in navy pants and crimson military jacket. Squeezing his avatar into the space beside Caylee, he said. "After we've performed repairs, before next launch, we must try."

"What is wrong with him?" Kel asked.

"An imbalance of testosterone, high enough to trigger the danger zone – where Kra'aken become Berserkers is one possibility. Undiagnosed or untreated illness and mental imbalance make two more." The AI paused, cocked his head to one side and then added, "Still he's a Rex."

"Meaning?" Rak'khiel suppressed her surge of indignation, her urge to demand, *What is the difference between his Rex and my Regence?* "Honesty heard, I'm heartily sick of hearing of his superior Rex lineage when everything I've seen contradicts."

"The ruling class surmounts problems – physical or mental – which kill or disable lesser ranks." Brin nodded at her, then at Caylee, and disappeared.

"Did he mean physical superiority?" Kel's dark sculpted brows pulled together, twin vertical furrows in her forehead. "I carried the great lug, Caylee – what does ruling class have that I don't?"

"Their physiology is slightly different. I think the data is in our banks," Caylee soothed.

Kel snorted. Sending a thread to her friends, she asked. *Tarkin? Torga? All well with you guys?*

The impression of large yawns came strong in her mind. *Taking a nap. Did we miss something? Like the landing?*

"Sarcasm, from a pair of cafuzogs." Kel chuckled, sent mental kisses to both. *Planetside soon.*

"Pilot, prepare for re-entry," Caylee said.

Although she'd expected it, Rak'khiel flinched. Her breath caught, white hot, like dried powder in the back of her throat. Gathering composure, she pushed her arms overhead, stretched an inhale, breathed slowly out through her nose.

No use trying to prepare. *I can't be any more ready.*

"Goddess beseeched," she murmured. "Let the down flight not be as terrifying as the up." Kel scrubbed moist palms across the thighs of her flightsuit and bent to her screens.

"It will be well," Caylee comforted. "Brin agrees – you are a pilot born. What you did earlier cannot be taught."

"I am afraid," Kel confessed. But, with the AI's reassurance, tension fell away, severed the taut string of her fear. Still, tiny adrenaline tremors of her six-fingered hands on the boards affirmed – *I'm hyped, as I should be. But operational.*

"Rak'khiel, course change, third mark," Caylee's voice.

"Fighter, copy." Razr's voice came calm, in control.

"Pod, copy," Kel managed an emotionless acknowledgement.

Reading trajectories, Kel cradled the throttles and yoke in neutral hands. Not gripping tight to interfere, not too loose to prevent instant problem response.

Her shoulders crept toward her ears, muscles coiling into knots.

She caught herself holding her breath, forced it out. *What might the damnable prince do next?*

"Pod to fighter. Descent initiation imminent, third mark."

"Copy," Razr's clipped tones.

She couldn't worry about the why. This was real-time, death or not. She tried to relax. *But how do I predict the actions of a madman?* Leaning over her triple-tiered screens, Kel focused down tight.

"Mark," she called. "mark, MARK."

As a single unit, the ships' bows dropped, slow, steady.

Thank the Goddess, Razr seems stable. Keep him so, I beg.

One section of Rak'khiel's mind watched Brin and Caylee's avatars, listened to their running commentary and memorized the schematics and probabilities they calc'ed on her boards. Another portion of her brain held the ship's operating and weapons systems, monitored fusioreactors and engines. Yet another part of her now multi-faceted mind evaluated the ships' exteriors with their flawed melds.

There! An anomaly. Kel's fingers flew, her response instinctual, certain. Her corrections initiated before Brin spoke.

"Kel, we need ...."

"On it," she said, left hand repositioning the far starboard nacelle while her right directed small thruster bursts. Kel pushed the pod snug against the larger ship and held it there while the stern turned dirtside.

Creaks and groans, driven by 'Risto damage on their upflight, remained worrisome. Reminders of work to be done, yes. But she now knew imminent disaster no longer loomed.

"Perfect adjustment, pod," Razr said.

"Copy, fighter." While her voice remained steady and composed, Kel's heart bounced in glee and her grin stretched so wide it hurt.

Before, after and in-between I'm terrified, but when the actual piloting starts, I forget to be afraid. My new life may be, no, it will be, spent waiting for chances to fly.

Descending through purple-tinted clouds, Rak'khiel viewed Olica from above.

There – the gray 'Risto castle, with crenellated towers and hand-hewn fitted stonework. *Where I'll soon visit and complete Yola's revenge.* She took note of the outbuildings, the grounds and periphery rock walls surrounding it all.

And there – the small village split by the dirt road. Kel strained to spot the cottage she'd shared with Yola.

"Kel?" Caylee's soft reminder pulled her back into the moment.

"Goddess," she whispered and rotated her nacelles for landing, firing tiny bursts, compensating for the stressed crafts.

Damaged joins moaned as the maimed ships sank into a low valley, hidden in the stand of red-barked trees.

Although the nose of the fighter poked above the tree line, the silver-shot violet reflections all but ensured they would pass a casual scan.

A huffed breath of tension released, mingled with loss-of-flight regret from Kel, accompanied their gentle landing.

"Brin? Safe to shut down?" Caylee queried her counterpart.

"Good from here. And you?"

"Affirmative."

Kel pressed the thruster nozzle icons, watched them slow, the indicator lights bleeding green to black. Cutting her main, she went into her checklist. Tilting her head, she frowned at the still-rumbling engine of the warplane.

"What in the name of the Goddess is he doing? He should have killed all functions on contact." She realized she'd whispered the words.

On the instant, the pod vibrated, filled with slowing whines and growls of the fighter's powerdown.

Hand-over-hand Kel dropped through the core to release the cafuzogs.

'Bout time, came with the teasing half-fang flash.

I need the box bad, Torga sent and sent a self-holo with her long white whiskers twitching, her eyes and hind legs crossed.

"Pulled on that water nipple once too often?" She snorted a laugh, and unsnapped Torga's net. Lifting the cafuzog out, she gently placed her on the bed. Caught from the corner of her eye, a flash of black and white out the hatch.

Rak'khiel lifted Tarkin free.

My appreciations, he managed and buried his face in his food dish.

If you come outside, stay close, okay? Kel sent.

Huffs of acknowledgement. *We saw the 'Ristos too, Kel. We get it.*

Her next stop – the mechanic's area, for blue and white striped coveralls and matching brimmed hat.

"Ready, Caylee. Where do I start?"

"Brin and I have manipulated the self-repair functions. All structural connections are now being completed. After the foamsteel filling and the ceramsteel layering are complete, we will flow the final ceramtanium coating to form hull seal."

"Can you dial that down to simple Olican for me?"

Brin's hearty laugh made Kel jump, then giggle.

"Caylee means when those steps are accmplished, there will be an impenatrable connection between the ships. The created single ship will be jump-safe and strong enough for extended FTL flite."

"How soon?"

"Two horas. We can fly safely then, and continue the interior work in space."

"Then first on my list: install a new lock on the pod/fighter common hatch." Kel heard the uptick of pitch and volume in her words. *The same cutting edge Caylee's voice adapts when she speaks of the prince.*

Blood thumped in the big vein in her temple. *Damn my body, my voice for betraying my feelings.*

"Do you have any twelve-fingered tasks?"

"No, Kel. Only Brin and I should direct the autotubes performing the outer fill and seal. Those materials are toxic to you. Go and ensure your privacy." Caylee grimaced. "To our shame, you may need it. Your tribute, though, for asking."

At the kindness, the reminder of two mothers lost, Rak'khiel swallowed hard, nodded and blinked away the warm sting behind her eyelids. "I'll tell Tarkin and Torga to limit their hunting to an hour."

"Excellent. Brin summons me." The AI's avatar blinked out.

§

Violet-haloed suns heated the day.

Inside the lifecocoon an hour passed, filled by several outbursts of creative cursing.

"Ha," said a satisfied Kel. Swiping the back of her hand across her forehead, she shook drips away. *My lock will hold against anything outside, whether the hatch is pressurized or not. Only a complete rend between pod and fighter will breach my ship.*

Mouth slightly open, harsh breathing breaking the quiet, Rak'khiel stood, lost in thought. *If that happens, nothing will matter. Now for my final business.* Her hearts pounded against each other. *Time for revenge too long postponed.*

Kel eavesdropped.

Brin and Caylee were displeased with the landing site – she'd listened in on their pre-landing chatter. The green area they thought solid meadow proved marshy. Muddy water threaded the brown area they'd believed hard ground. Now the AI's were involved in repairs.

She heard Razr ask Brin a question. *Razr's working in the warplane.*

Rak'khiel glided through the lifecocoon.

On the lower level, where she'd spent her first night after morphosis, Rak'khiel laid her hat on the aqua foamsteel ledge. Shedding her coveralls, she replaced them with a pair of loose camo fatigues and donned a pair of combat boots from her locker.

A quick braid kept dark unruly hair from her face and eyes. Secured at the end with a polyelas band, it followed her spine down the center of her back.

Carefully, stealthily she crept down another level.

At the red weapons locker, Kel winced at the creak of the lid, ducked low, pulled her head, arms and legs in like a turtle and waited to be discovered. *I'll grease it later. If I still live.*

From a nearby bin, she pulled the duffle used in her first village hunt. Arming as before, Kel paused, then thought a second. Now that she knew the weapons – their purposes and results – she added four more items. Lethal ones.

Another thought struck – foot and leg barbs and claws. *I don't need boots.* Pulling them off, she stuck them back in the locker.

Her diaphragm cramped, squeezed, ached. Fear? Anxiety? Anticipation? Perhaps all.

Kel pushed her mind from Yola and the past and into her mission. Like the flare of a thruster nozzle, her skin flushed, burned with hatred. She knew a cruel, cold smile ghosted her face as she slid through the hatch and reclosed it.

Back pressed against the shimmering silver-lavender hull of the pod, Kel sneaked around her ship. Little cover existed in the lush meadow. Slithering guerilla-style across the ground, weapons duffel strapped across her back, Rak'khiel slipped away. Maintaining a low-profile between the few scrubby bushes, she crept toward the nearest group of red-barked trees.

When her fatigues morphed colors, blended with the green grass, the ochre soil and the small clumps of bushes, Kel stuffed her knuckles in her mouth to stifle her squeal of delight.

Passing the ponds, Rak'khiel spotted death-pale fleshy things. As long as her arm, their backs covered with spiny protrusions, they floated just beneath the water's surface. *Drawn by my footsteps?*

Smacking with wet squishy sounds, dozens of rubbery lips emerged from the streams. Gasping for air, the horrors' open mouths revealed jagged teeth.

Their malevolent intent crawled over her, made her skin flash cold, coating her in rippling gooseflesh.

An excellent reason the populace lives where they do. Yola never spoke of these things – I wonder if she knew?

Grief's pangs weighed heavy, bearable only by the thing she planned to do. Very soon. But the voice in her mind, her faith in the Goddess' teachings, shook her resolve. *Can I murder again? Yes. Should I? Perhaps not – and yet, I will. I vowed it.*

Once into the thickness of the scarlet-barked trees, Kel paused. Clicking on the tech module in her mind presented measurements, rolling schematics. And options.

Distance to her quarry, reaches of her weapons, points of most favorable entry. Her choice from the full array of information – made within one breath.

Is this my personal cache of data? Or did I just access the main databases in the ships. And betray myself. "Shalit."

The thought sent her hearts hammering against each other like the blacksmith's hammer on his anvil. *Hurry, hurry, hurry.*

Wrapping the ammo-filled bandolier across her torso, she emptied her duffle. First and most important – Rak'khiel slung her father's ceramtanium killing sword across her back. *Sent, Caylee said, as his special gift to me.*

Laser and projectile pistols, large and small knives – metal and ceramic for killing and gutting – and her favored lethal dart gun, all stowed in holsters, sheaths or her fatigues.

Kel stuffed two of her pants pouches with grenades, the flat box containing poisoned flechettes filled a third. The final step – fitting her optical.

Its narrow bundled filament snaked around her skull and into the mindjack port. The instant buzzing, the zoom on the castle confirmed. *Operational.*

Rak'khiel rolled the emptied duffle tight, stuffed it into a low outside pouch on the calf of her fatigues. *I am ready.*

But her hearts beat too fast. Her lungs closed off as if two bony hands crushed them in her chest. Kel hugged herself for reassurance. The icy brush of her clammy hand against her bare neck made her jerk.

She stretched taut muscles and huffed three panting breaths. Moving first in a jog, then into a ground-covering steady pace across the rolling green hills, Kel headed straight for the gray stone of the 'Risto fortress.

Believing Tarkin and Torga hunted game, Rak'khiel's scrutiny of her surroundings was cursory. And so, she did not see her friends secreted behind the largest tree trunk, did not know two pairs of bright black eyes watched. Did not hear their thoughts.

She believes us hunting dinner, the half-lip lift of humor.

She's not thinking clearly, sent Torga. *She should know better.*

And how could she? Since we still have not explained what we are or our true purpose?

Point to you, mi' mate. Shall we go?

Keeping to the sparse cover of stunted bushes and rocks, the two cafuzogs stealthily followed the bristling armory who was their friend into enemy territory.

Chapter 38

Mid-Dark
Nara 21, 7205.40
'Risto Fortress, Olica

From her perch outside an arrow slot high on the tallest stone tower, Rak'khiel assessed the richly-clad dinner guests. Flanked by trembling servants, the perspiring merchants were uneasy attendees, gazing anywhere but at their hosts.

Rak'khiel trembled and sweated with them.

The village men employed as guards appeared most confident, although they, too, stayed well back from the spydrs, pressed against the walls, unless summoned.

The black-clad 'Risto horrors were unmistakable.

A red plasfilm drew across her eyes. Killing Rage fell on her without warning. Pink-silver patterns danced on her exposed skin. Fangs, claws, barbs pushed to be set free, begged for release.

NO. Think, Rak'khiel. Wait. Plan. As she forced back *Other*, she smelled … her war *tasca*. *Goddess preserve. The best way to be discovered before you are ready – let their dogs smell you. Stupid, stupid, stupid.*

Kel damped her output and focused on the room's inhabitants.

The merchants stood in a motile cluster, the colors of their fabric robes overbright against walls of gray stone. Shifting uneasily, stealthily glancing at each other or at the arching exit door, each tried to work his way deeper into the clot of men. Or closer to the door. All breathed deeply through perfumed handkerchiefs, dabbing at flared nostrils, struggling to hide their gagging.

The aromas of heavily spiced exotic food, overlaid by a mix of unsettling odors, drifted through the aperture. Rak'khiel's stomach shoved burning bile into the back of her throat. The raw stink of the villagers' fear added to the stench of old and new blood.

The merchants glanced everywhere but at the beheaded body, lying splayed against a blood-spattered wall behind a huge table.

Kel swallowed hard and felt a pressing need to void her bladder.

Servants slunk from guest to guest, eyes on the floor. Humped shoulders, elbows pressed tight against their bodies, they all but threw the food and drink on the tables and made their stumbling retreats.

Two of the 'Risto females pretended to grab the arms of their servers, then laughed at the girls' terror.

Rak'khiel made note. *I will give those two special attention later. They are cold, but I am frozen. Goddess, grant me time to kill them all.*

The village elders – those still alive after the last purge – sat at the lower end of a long table, as far away from the overpowering fireplace and their loathsome conquerors as courtesy allowed. Eyes too wide, they looked at the ceiling or each other. Anywhere but at the 'Ristos, the red smears, the pooling blood, the snarling dogs, the torture table, the moaning man on the rack or the corpse beneath. They also cast longing glances at the exit, then at the High Lord, hoping they weren't seen.

Gooseflesh rippled Kel's skin, lifted the short hair on the nape of her neck. Unseen as yet, she could leave now, climb down and flee to safety. No, she could not. She'd vowed Yola's revenge.

The monstrous creatures, bright orange feelers waving, smacked scarlet lips over their dinners. Although the 'Risto's were eating, appearing relaxed and confident, they cast measuring glances at their High Lord on his dais. Perhaps gauging his patience, perhaps his temper. In a flash of insight, Rak'khiel realized the High Lord was neither stable, nor kind – not even to his own. *No one is exempt from the vagaries of his madness.*

A darkness crept into the edges of her vision, pressed against her mind.

Shaking her muzzy head, Kel peeled bony mental fingers from her brain. *Something hypnotic and horrible just tried to draw me into the tower. Shalit. Compulsion magic?* A careful peek into the tower's charnel room revealed the searching Head 'Risto's eyes. The barest contact made her lose her thoughts. Her plans. Forcing her mind back to 'Yola's Justice', she processed. *I do expect to die, if necessary. I should have been the one under question – not Yola. How to kill them? I did not expect magic – for that is what this must be.*

The restless silvery pendant stirred against her breastbone.

Pain, grief. Iron pincers of regret twisted pieces from her hearts.

How to kill them all? Tied in plot-knots, Kel adjusted her strategy yet again.

The Head 'Risto leaned back against the cushion of his throne, ignoring the murmured banter.

A silver circlet, center-set with a great dull gray-black stone, wrapped his skull. Where lesser spyders sprouted feelers, the crown covered their ruler's forehead.

Her eyes drew the stone's attention, the dark gem pulled at her mind once more. *Come to me....*

Chapter 39

Mid-Dark
Nara 21, 7205.40
'Risto Fortress, Olica

Razr threw his wrench.

"She is supposed to be completing the hatch between the warplane and the pod. What do you mean you can't find her?" He shouted, too frightened to curse. "Where are the cafuzogs?" A fist gripped his stomach like an octopod, all stinging suckers and rending clawbeaks.

He knew Rak'khiel's destination. *Gone deliberately without me – because I am, as Brin so succinctly put it, a nether orifice.*

"Her guardians are not onboard," said Brin.

"They've followed her to protect, as is their duty. They, at least, are conscientious," snarled Razr. "My failure. I should be with them – curse my stiff-necked pride. They will all be killed."

Razr dove through the core. In the arms bay, he stripped, leaped commando into his dirty fatigues. Slinging his bandolier across one wide shoulder, he strapped his weapons belts around narrow hips. A curse escaped as he finally stowed the last knife. *Too long, too much wasted time.* Shaking hands betrayed him at every movement. *Allowing emotions to rule, I'd be broken into common ranks for such a performance. And why in the Destroyer's name am I thinking about that now?*

"Brin, Caylee. I'm headed for the castle. Pray she is not there. Advise if you locate any of the three."

"Yes, Prince Helrazr." Caylee's cool voice emphasized the extent of his wrongdoing.

Great Destroyer take me should I have to spend the next five hundrada years ... or more ... alone with those two.

Vaulting from the fighter, he turned toward the village. Beyond it, the 'Risto stronghold. His stomach growled as he broke into a hard run and made him glad he hadn't eaten dinner. For sure, scared as he was, he'd puke it.

Kel's on the outside wall of the tallest fortress tower. Brin's send came. *Are you near enough to see?*

A burst of speed put a gasping Razr at the top of a rise. The village, split by the road, spread before him. At its end, he saw the gray stone building.

A forefinger flipped down his right eye optic.

High magnification showed Rak'khiel clinging to the stone wall, bloody claws flashing. An Olican guard reached a red-striped arm through the turret aperture, stabbing randomly with a long sword. The man peered through the bars, scanning the countryside.

Razr screamed in rage, the sound amped by his surging morphosis. "You forzaed gongur," the prince roared. "Try to injure her? I'm coming for you." The sickness twisting his guts eased. *She's still alive.*

Kel? Caylee's send broadcast to all.

Yes?

Move to a safe location – Brin is sending vital stats on the 'Ristos.

Copy.

The prince sprinted for the fortress. The info burst revealed disgusting chitin-coated segmented legs covered with coarse hair. Claws, venom sacs, fangs. At the sight of the large red hourglass shape on the 'Risto abdomens, Razr stumbled, fell to one knee.

"Sweet Destroyer, Brin, that's a slif of a different color." Shoving to his feet, he set out again. "What's their weaponry?" Razr gasped. *I'm spent. Why in the twelve hells didn't I train?*

Instead of answering his question, Brin sent, *Kel, you copy?*

Busy, one moment. Her broadcast slammed into Razr's mind, made him flinch.

Silence stretched. Razr used every zoom on his optic but couldn't find her anywhere on his side of the tower.

My sorry, Brin, Kel sent. *Safe now to listen.*

Please wait for Razr, Caylee interposed. *Even the two of you may not be enough.*

Brin – their weaponry? Razr asked again, without snarling.

Database shows projectile weapons, short range avionics, cannon, swords, bows and knives. Assume everything is coated in poison. And assume their technology has progressed since arriving here. Rak'khiel, you copy? Do not touch anything.

Affirmative.

Any more bad news, Brin? He sent.

Yes. Alarm wove through Brin's send. *They are arachna, capable of spinning trapping webs. Step only on the dry white threads. The pale grey are sticky, they will hold you fast – the spydrs like to drain their victims before they consume them. Your optic infrared will differentiate.*

Fear made Razr fight for air. His pace faltered even as shame brought fisted hands. *Brin, can my earlier poisoning provide protection? Can Kel's?*

We hope, but we cannot know unless you are bitten.

Wonderful.

Razr armored fully, gold spikes pushed through his camo. Becoming Other, he augmented his speed, and veered toward the tower side where Rak'khiel clung.

The fragrance of fresh blood carried on the light breeze made his stomach growl. Reaching the fortress, he found two dead Olican guards just inside the outer gate, and two more at the inner. Licking his lips, he swallowed a burst of saliva.

Then moved past them into the courtyard.

Prince Helrazr? Brin's voice broke the silence. *If possible, bring a spydr back alive. Caylee and I can work to create an antivenin.*

Gift wrap it for you too, Brin?

Augmented senses expanded, he searched for a trap. Smelling heavy metallic copper, he followed it. And found an additional pair of Olican guards – eyes staring, mouths gaping. *She took their throats with her claws.*

Kel's war *tasca* hung in the air.

Razr reassessed his prior opinions of Rak'khiel. Fully trained she would be more than formidable. For now, he needed to protect her. Running in grief mode alone would surely get her butchered.

Kel, did you bring optics?

Yes. Plus a few other lethals.

Set to Zoom 2, yellow infra 6. Tell me what you see.

Shalit! Now the white strands are clear. My appreciation.

A gust of wind blew a miasma from the stone fortress. The sour stink of mildew, the stench of moldering vellum and wet animal skins wafted from the tower. The following puff brought rank smells of sweaty, unwashed bodies mixed with spilled blood.

In the sudden quiet, he heard a pair of whispering voices.

"Up there on the wall, see?" A beefy townsman in half-armor pointed at the tower.

"That's the monster they want us to get?" The second man, thin, brown as a nutberry, shook his head. "It's already done for eight of us. We'll die too."

"We'll be killed the 'Risto way if we don't." The heavy set man jerked his chin toward the top of the castle.

"Holy Pair preserve us. I'd rather face the thing on the wall."

Rak'khiel, Razr sent. *Are you completely changed? Do you have armor and claws?*

I have hand and feet claws, teeth hanging over my chin. My skin goes to rough but doesn't stay.

Forza. Razr's heart plummeted past his diaphragm. *A scratch on bare skin could paralyze, even kill you. Wait for me, your favor. I'll be finished here momentarily.*

Copy.

Behind the guards, Razr surged, grabbing their necks in his hands. Slamming them to the ground, he placed a large foot on each chest.

Two shrieks sliced the night.

Bending, he sank lethal claws into their throats. A thick ripping sound followed. Now quiet reigned, except for the heavy bumpings and bubbling gurgles while the guards thrashed and bled out on ochre dirt.

Razr's fangs dripped saliva. *I haven't eaten since yesterday, I must. Rak'khiel promised to wait.*

Two huge hands plunged deep into red chests, emerging triumphantly with a pair of still-twitching hearts. He ate one, then the other in four quick bites, nodded his approval and licked his lips.

The prince bent, large hands splayed on his knees, sucked air and rested. Muttering, cursing under his breath, his breath still coming hard. "Needing a rest before entering battle? For my sloth, I should be tied to trees and ripped apart."

The nerves on the back of Razr's neck twitched as if twin knives bored into the base of his skull. *Eyes on me.*

Razr straightened, lips parted, pulling scents across the glands in the roof of his mouth. Blood dripped down his face, off his fangs.

Rak'khiel hung high on the tower wall.

The prince saw her frown, saw her shock. *Not quite revulsion, but she is uneasy with this part of me. And herself.*

Disappearing his armor, Razr stood as a human male.

Why? She questioned.

Our rule. We cannot slaughter indiscriminately, except in war. I paid these creatures high tribute by eating their hearts. Razr bit down hard on his ego, his pride and added, *Also, I have not eaten for too long. I need to regain my strength. What do we face?*

Thirteen 'Ristos, male and female. Six villagers armed with swords and knives. Eight hunting beasts. And, her thought held vindication, *the former Head Questioner on the rack.* A short pause, then Kel added, as if fearing disbelief or ridicule, *One other thing – the High Lord is capable of some type of mind control.*

Razr noted her apparent calm, sensed the rage held in check.

I have a plan, she sent. Her full lips twitched, her thought so falsely sweet. *Since the older warrior is out of shape, would he like a small rest?*

Razr resisted the urge to snarl. *I am ready,* he sent in a pleasant tone. *What would you have me do?*

Ah ... just a moment .... Overhead, Rak'khiel moved from her spot to the next arrow slot.

Razr flashed a bloody fang, grabbed three quick breaths and started up the tower side with the speed and grace of a rock lizard.

A grinding, ripping overhead startled him. Something sailed past Razr's ear, bounced with the dull clang of iron on the slate pavers below. A quick look above kicked his double hearts into arrhythmia.

Chapter 40

Mid-Dark
Nara 21, 7205.45
'Risto Fortress, Olica

Come to me .... The irresistible summons from the dull black stone.

No, I will not. Kel closed her eyes and set a mental barrier against the probes of the 'Risto lord. Gooseflesh erupted on her body, she shivered in the oppressive humidity of the Olican night.

Movement, a rustle at the table.

Kel cracked her eyes. In disbelief, she watched the Head 'Risto stroke the narrow muzzle of a hunting beast where it rested in his lap. Twisting affectionate fingers through its stringy gray hair, he rubbed its long floppy ears and fed it gobbets of raw flesh from his feast platter.

I can't believe I'm seeing this.

The head spydr pressed a kiss on his skeletal fingers. Touching the dog's elongated head, he murmured, "How iss my sweetling Angel thiss day?"

On the dais, at His Lordship's right hand, a 'Risto female sat in a black cushioned chair. Bony fingers cradled her distended abdomen. Her infrequent comments in a strange language were almost a murmur of clicking buzzes.

The High Lord's face gentled with his replies.

I wish I knew what they discussed. Perhaps upcoming baby monsters? If circumstances allow I'll kill her first – make him watch. For Yola.

The thought struck from nowhere. *Would Adopted Mother even approve? No – she would not. I don't care. Truth time, Rak'khiel. This revenge will be for me.*

Rak'khiel jerked at a skritch-skritch-skritch. Her hearts hammered in her chest so fast, so hard, she feared their explosions. She searched around, down and up. Found nothing but tower stones and arrow slits, nothing out of place. *Still, I heard sounds which do not belong.*

A mem module unfolded. Flower petals, each loaded with war tactics, flowed past. One minute passed, new blooms appeared and she followed the threads. *Nothing on 'Ristos.* Still … she opened the lesson further. *There, that black piece.* I can adapt the pincer-claw-fang closing strategy. *It will work.*

Studying the wall where she clung, Kel noted which windows held badly-rusted bars. The stonemasons who constructed this fortress were true masters of their craft. Each quarried rock fit tightly to the next without need of a binding agent, but the minute cracks provided easy purchase for her claws. She slithered around the tower to scout the opposite side.

Skritch. Skritch. Skritch.

What …? Cutting her eyes fast to either side, she lost concentration. Claws retracting, Kel slid down the stone wall. *Shalit.* Forcing hand and foot claws, she scraped to a halt. Her knees felt full of water as she wobbled her way back up the tower. Searching for the source of the noice, just as before, Kel found nothing. Ice cubes clicked and jittered in her stomach.

A slightly protruding stone, four rows below an arrow niche, provided enough ledge for her toes.

Rak'khiel stood, stretched tall, listened, and peeked in. Her eyes roved the room, attack plans taking form. She spotted two windows with badly rusted bars. Breachable. *I can jerk them out, be inside and killing before they react.*

Her mind worked rapidly, processing data in an orderly manner. Kel's body showed nothing of the raging conflict within. But *tasca* flooded the surrounding air and salty wet flooded her face. Berserker urges warred with calm reasoning.

I need only survive long enough to kill them all. But to do so, I must resolve my two halves into singularity.

Kel clamped down on her racing hearts, forced back her threatening change and damped surging *tasca*. Shoving horrific memories of Yola in her mind box, she slammed the lid. *I want to live, be free, but it will be as the Goddess wills.*

Focusing hard, she fixed her mind on observation and planning.

From her new position, Kel saw a hot red-orange blaze in the enormous fireplace. *Do the 'Risto's need extreme heat to survive? Can I use that?*

Oppressive warmth amplified the reek of dark copper fluids, pooled and crusting in low areas of the floor, splashed across stone walls.

Her Kra'aken side ignored it. Olican Kel gagged and begged to crawl back down the tower. She shook her head, tried to settle the spinning vortex inside. *I will not back down.*

At one side of the dais, a large stained table sat askew. *Does the angle provide better viewing for the High Lord?*

Even without the writhing, moaning body atop, she knew its function. Kel's cheeks burned hot, then turned chill. A sound like a dozen violettas sang in her head. With mounting fury she saw bloody restraining straps, routed side drains and cruel iron manacles. *Where Yola laid.*

Her mind balked at the rust-stained implements. Some littered a side table, some thrust into the smoking brazier, some thrown about the floor. Kel refused to guess at their horrible purposes, although unbidden images niggled at the corners of her mind. *I will never forget. But I cannot be distracted.*

Fighting for control, Rak'khiel wrapped long slender

fingers in the chain holding Yola's silver charm and felt it bring calm. *Goddess shroud me, they are more than monsters.*

The table dripped fluids.

Hounds chained within reach licked the burgundy slicked floor, the scarlet table legs. Others chewed at the head and body tossed carelessly beneath.

Goddess! It's Garil. Kel felt the blood drain from her head. *The kindly man who doted on Yola.* Bile burned the back of her throat. The old Rak'khiel would be hurling supper chunks. Now, rage rushed, all but took her.

Her skin shimmered pearly pink patterns, *tasca* flooded her olfactories. Pink-gold claws extruded, lengthened, nearly dislodging her from the tower. *Shalit!*

Her noisy scrabble for purchase – *was I heard?* – prompted a careful peek inside. Guilt stabbed deep. A sad affair when the shrieks and moans of another's suffering covered her mistake.

Her brief thought to spare him quelled on the instant. He was a willing participant in Yola's brutalization. *Probably,* the thought pulled hate's red film across her eyes. *The actual High Questioner who tortured Yola. I'll kill him twice if they don't finish him.*

Rak'khiel forced the insistent morphosis away and reset her hand claws. Clinging to the wall, she continued to watch. She opened her imaginary box, swept everything up, tossed it in, closed and locked the lid.

Skritch. Skritch. Skritch.

Kel whipped her head in all directions. Nothing. *But something besides me crawls the outside of this tower. And Razr has yet to arrive.*

At the fireplace end of the tower room, the Head 'Risto – a tall gaunt specter – hunched over his table, drummed the tips of long pointed black nails and studied his victim. His favorite hound now slept curled at his feet.

How do they stand the stench?

Kel studied his Lordship's impatient fingers. And

shuddered. An unpolished center strip on each nail, from bed to tip, displayed a pulsing crimson vein shaped like an hourglass. *Perhaps not a blood vein, perhaps venom?*

Lank jet hair framed the High Lord's milk-white face. Swept back from a prominent widow's peak, it was captured by a silver band.

Set in the crown's fore, a dull ebony gem emitted a foul pall. A vile thing, it radiated and fed the deep despair and sadistic animosity that permeated the room.

You are worthless. Powerles, it sent to Rak'khiel. *Come to me.*

Her hearts hammered her ribs. Needles prickled her hands and feet.

Come inside ....

Olican Kel loosened her grip on the wall.

Kra'aken Kel gripped more tightly and told the wicked thing what it could do with its summons.

The Head 'Risto's gaze lifted, perhaps reactive to the stone's awareness of her. He opened his small red mouth, edges fringed by coarse black hair. Scarlet lips pulled back, baring transparent fangs and teeth. In each tooth, a mustard-yellow stripe ran from gum line to needle point.

Poison sacs – and they are full. Rak'khiel's mem module knew. *Goddess, he's ghastly. They all are.* Her stomach writhed.

The High Lord's head snapped up, red eyes piercing and glowing. A single-brow, hairy and coal-dark, bisected his forehead.

Kel watched in amazement as the center of the eyebrow dipped, veed into a furrow, sharp and deep as if shaped by the chop of an axe. Palpable hostility and anger charged the atmosphere within the tower.

Can he feel my hate?

"Head Inquisitor," his Lordship's voice, directed at the bloody mess on the table, quivered with wrath. "Why did you not extract the girl's hiding place from the woman?"

"Was blocked, your Highness," the words came all in a rush. Then a gasp, a deep-from-within groan and another gush of words. "Blocked by the Goddess herself."

Kel would have wagered the cold 'Risto face could be no worse. But the High Lord's eyes hooded, muscles shifted beneath milky skin. His hard expressionless visage became implacable granite.

"You lie." The words accompanied a shift of his gaze to the two huge men by the table.

They jerked to attention like puppets on strings.

"Make him tell me." A flick of a black fingernail at one of the stolid torturers. "Use the hook."

The occupant of the table gave a high rising shriek. The sound turned into staccato screams, then his howl of agony became a high uluating wail.

Rak'khiel's guts juddered. She couldn't pull a full lungful of air. She commanded herself to be calm, the tortured man had killed Yola. Coldness calmed her mind.

"High Lord," the new Head Inquisitor ventured, shuddered when his voice cracked. "Perhaps a hunt would produce the child?" The color fell from his face in a sheet.

"Yess, a grand idea, my new, intelligent Questioner. Send a scouting party – 'Risto warriorss, beastss and village soldierss. Hunt at the twin sunss rise. Failure meanss death for all. I will stay – amuse myself with thiss one."

Now I know. I have until sunrise to pick them off. After the villagers leave, I will kill the guards. Then these abominations at the table. Saving the High Lord – and perhaps his lady – for last.

Lady Rak'khiel Floril I'Regence whispered, "I am Death."

Chapter 41

Mid-Dark
Nara 21, 7205.40
'Risto Fortress, Olica

A pair of cafuzogs clung, side-by-side, on the tower wall around the bend from Rak'khiel. Peeking in one of many apertures, they evaluated the scene, the dangers within and their human.

She hears our claws, you know, sent Tarkin.

But never considered it might be us, laughed Torga. *Kel thinks we are sleeping.*

Now, we present a distraction. Rak'khiel would protect us without thought for herself. Torga's black eyes narrowed, their white circular outlines became horizontal ovals in the black fur of her pointed face. *We will hide from her. I fear we must use our weapon this day.*

Singly would be best, but the aracha are enormous, Tarkin sent. *I fear it must be both of us to be sure.*

So be it – inconvenient but inescapable. It is why we are guardians. We will live with the consequences.

Our consequences are nothing if Kel lives, asserted Tarkin.

Brin's send also reached the cafuzogs, alerting them to the dangers hidden beneath the black robes.

Even with their change to Other, their enhanced strength,

armor, speed – our two warriors are greatly overmatched. Torga's thought held concern.

"I see in her mind," Tarkin whispered, dropped back to telepathic at his mate's tiny headshake. *She will take the guards first, fast. Leave killing of the lesser 'Ristos and beasts to Razr, then she plans to help him. She wants to kill the High Lord and his lady last – she plans to take a long, long time with them. She hates herself that she craves it. It's not the Olican Goddess' way.*

I don't like this part of our Kel, Torga sent.

She is Kra'aken. A warrior born.

But our Olican Rak'khiel's sweetness and tender heart make her so special, Torga's thought threaded with wistful regret.

Perhaps she will remain so except in battle? If she is ruthless, she may live.

Torga's white-striped black head dipped in acknowledgement of his truth. Turning back to the arrow slit, they studied the scene before them.

Eleven 'Ristos sat around a jet stone table, placed below the dais. *Male or female?* Torga caught a flash of jewelry but it seemed both sexes wore it.

Meal completed, several spydrs rose. Scuttling restlessly about the throne room, the motions of the lesser arachnas flowed smooth as if they rode wheels beneath their voluminous black robes.

Some paused to taunt the whimpering, writhing former Head Questioner, scratch a claw mark, fang a tiny bite or hiss derision. Then they moved on, buzzing and clicking – their under-language mostly Kra'aken.

The High Lord's papery skin appeared stretched over a skeletal head. His opaque, flat pupilless eyes skittered constantly, lethal black claws clicked the tabletop. Restless.

The room's occupants strove for invisibility, refusing to meet his eyes – the cold hard expression on his chalky visage promised more pain and suffering.

The ruling 'Risto spat. The ejected splash of venom lay smoking, puddled yellow-gray, on the floor.

The other spydrs scattered.

They are poisonous to each other, Torga sent. *Did Kel see it?*

Yes. Her eyes grew wide then narrowed. You felt her breathing shift to fast, like I did.

Before them, the cafuzogs watched the ruling 'Risto move, rearrange his nether limbs in the throne. A heavy silver chain with a turquoise, silver and copper pendant slipped from the neck of his robe and swung free. On the ruler's wrinkled forearm sat another of Rak'khiel's best creations. A wide bracelet, its intricately pierced silver work fine as lace. Yola's Naming Day gift.

Shata. Sent Torga who never swore.

This will tip her over the edge, agreed Tarkin.

The smaller arachnid at the High Lord's side casually brushed back oily black hair, exposing long dangling silver earrings, their circular spirals set with tiny bits of turquoise, crystal and copper.

Yola's favorite earrings. Remember? Rak'khiel made them for her for last Solstice Celebration. Torga's black eyes snapped, her thought trembled with rage. *Do we tell her we're here? Ask for restraint? Goddess, it's all I can do to hold myself back.*

A mina or two more. Tarkin sent. *Look down, Prince Razr's arrived, asked her to wait for him. She's agreed.*

If only she doesn't see ....

The two cafuzogs eavesdropped shamelessly, necessary in their sworn duty to protect and defend.

A shift of 'Ristos exposed the lower table where three enormous spiders clustered. Gloating, they displayed rings, a bracelet and another necklace. A pair of smaller earrings lay in a chalk-white palm – the tiny set made for Yola's double-pierced ears. The other half of the large ones now worn by the High Lord's lady.

Envious others shifted, murmured among themselves.

KILL. KILL. The murdering bastards are wearing jewelry I made for Yola – my gifts to her. Rak'khiel's blast of rage roared, shook the tower; nearly dislodged the clinging cafuzogs. *Jewelry she wore the day they butchered her.*

Her mind is off its leash, Tarkin's thought rattled to Torga.

In. In. Kill. I'll rip Yola's beautiful things from their unspeakable bodies. I will rend them apart. I will rip their ghastly heads off. Revenge. Kill. I will rip the weak bars from the window.

Tarkin and Torga rushed around the tower. *Where in the Twelve Hells is the forzaing prince?*

The cafuzogs saw a driven Kel, first claw madly at the opening; then rip the bars from a narrow opening. Tossing them carelessly aside, Berserker scream issuing challenge, she vaulted into the tower room.

Chapter 42

Mid-Dark
Nara 21, 7205.16
'Risto Fortress, Olica

The prince is here, Tarkin sent.
Bless the Destroyer.

Fast footsteps pounded up interior stairs. Attention refocused inside the room, the cafuzogs watched Rak'khiel fully morph. And attack.

Black spydr parts flew, crimson jetted, sprayed. The loss of a limb seemed to make no difference to the 'Ristos or their ability to fight.

Kel's sword flashed, killing strokes with every forward and back swing. Her other hand held her laser pistol, its deadly beam swung in a half-circle, protecting her side and cutting a swath through those who stood between her and her quarry.

Torga, the enemy is closing in behind her.

Razr burst through the door, holstered his guns, drew sword and long knife and waded in. Heads, body parts flew – Olican and spydr, chopped in chunks by the whirling slash of his deadly s-shaped sword.

Chanting a killing song, Razr laughed and cut his way to Kel's side.

They are going to need us, Torga said.

They will be overwhelmed by the strength and numbers of the 'Ristos.

The aracha protecting the High Lord and his mate succumbed to the fury and whirling blades of Kel and Razr.

"Mine," she screamed.

"Yes," he answered.

The cafuzogs watched him take a protective position at her back.

Rak'khiel reached the High Lord and his mate. With a vicious growl, and a display of huge fangs, she feinted closure with the huge male arachna. A fast side step, a sweeping upward sword stroke, disemboweled the female.

A high, thin cry shattered the noise of the room. The gravid female spydr pressed her split abdomen together, seeking to stem the outpour of white eggs.

Her shriek brought a scream of loss, of fury, from the Head 'Risto.

Launching himself at the hated Kra'aken, one who dared take his progeny from him, he clutched Rak'khiel to his chest with two segmented black legs. And dipped his awful face toward hers.

Kel jammed the blade of her knife between the 'Risto's snapping teeth. Knew when it bit deep in his jaw hinge, heard him grunt as it stuck fast. Another leg reached across her face and she trapped it between her fangs.

Thrusting an armored spiked arm up to meet the High Lords' descending hand, Kel skewered his wrist and forearm on her sharp shimmering barbs.

The High 'Risto's screech of pain and frustrated rage rent the ringing of swords and grunts of combat in the tower room.

Rak'khiel gripped the hilt of her long sword, trapped between their two bodies. Working the blade in a crossing pendulum motion, she kept his questing stinger at bay.

Each hit she scored on the High Lord's abdomen produced a hiss or scream. Grappling, each striving for opportunity, they toppled, rolled heavily on the floor.

Prince Helrazr, it's Tarkin. The Head 'Risto has Rak'khiel. We must use our weapon – it's the only way to win. Drag Kel to safety, out of the room.

Without missing a strike, the prince shouted, "Destroyer! I hear."

He jerked his sword free, angled it upward through the creature's vital organs. Leaping to the rolling tangle of Kel and the High Lord, Razr brought the heavy, worked metal basket of his sword hilt down, smashing the top of the 'Risto's head.

A satisfying crack as skin split, red bloomed and the spydr leader fell limp.

The limb Kel held in her jaws loosened in unconsciousness. As the aracha's body slid toward the floor, the dripping poisoned claw dragged across the inside of her lip.

The prince grabbed a snarling, cursing, fighting Rak'khiel around the waist. "It's me, Destroyer damnit," he growled. "Stop fighting. We have reinforcements."

Pulling her tight against him, his sword slashing at oncoming 'Ristos and snarling, snapping hounds, Razr backed out the tower door. Slammed it shut and dropped the wooden bar.

"Now," he shouted to Tarkin and Torga.

The cafuzogs reversed themselves in the window ledge, lifted their tails and sprayed the room with a fine, dense cerulean mist. Reversing again, they watched the results of their potent gas, the undiluted accumulation of a life-time.

Do you have essence enough for a second strike, if needed? Torga sent.

Yes, Tarkin's satisfied thought. *It does appear, however, that one will be enough.*

The room's inhabitants screeched. Fluid streamed from noses, mouths and eyes. Instant nausea turned the charnel house into a vomitorium. Retching, nobles and servants staggered blindly, gasping, hands tearing at their throats, falling: either dead or comatose.

The hunting beasts whined, gasped and ran, pressing long muzzles against the floor, seeking ease for sensitive nasal tissues before slinking between the bodies of their masters, succumbing to the effects of the spray.

Within minas, nothing moved.

"How long until we can go back in?" Razr shouted.

Soon, sent Tarkin. *We'll come around to you. Open the door.*

The two cafuzogs climbed down to the open window, crawled inside, and scampered, claws clicking, to the spot in the hall where Kel and Razr waited.

"Will someone please explain what just happened?" Rak'khiel pinched her nostrils together and peeked inside the tower. Her eyes widened at the sight littering the floor – unconscious living lumps mingled with the dead.

Our contrition for the deception, Lady Regence, Torga said. *We are your personal bodyguards. What you see is the reason why.*

"You are not my friends?" The undertone of a child's deep hurt colored her voice.

We are your friends, but also your protectors, Tarkin sent.

We love you, Kel. This from Torga.

"Your help is much appreciated," Razr said.

"We weren't going to win, were we? Is it my fault because I lost control?" Kel's subdued question.

No. You were only two against too many – the best plan held little chance of success. Now it is safe to go finish your task. You will suffer no ill effects. Except perhaps .... A lifted half-lip accompanied the thought but Tarkin did not complete his thought.

If you no longer need us, Torga said. *I heard something earlier I must investigate.*

"Go," said Rak'khiel. "We will finish here. My grateful."

"Rendezvous at the ship?" Razr asked.

Excellent. We shouldn't be long. An upper lip rolled all the way back, exposing sharp teeth bright against black gums. *Mi'dear? Shall we?*

Chapter 43

Mid-Dark
Nara 21, 7205.85
'Risto Fortress, Olica

Tarkin? How long will these remain unconscious? Razr's question sounded in Rak'khiel's head.

With elapsed time, less than a half-hora. The cafuzog's troubled response seemed to come from far away.

Do you require our assistance? Kel sent.

No, sent Torga. *We found bad things but we will fix them.*

Let me know if anything changes, okay?

Yes, Kel. Have you been in the room yet? If not, tie something around your nose first. You will need it. The mocking tone of Torga's laughter colored her send.

My thanks. At the ship, then?

At the ship.

Razr's amber eyes glowed beneath black raptor wing brows. They caught and held hers in what seemed to be hours. His pupils dilated, grew dark enough, deep enough to lose herself in them.

A connection, not a tiny spark like the dairyboy, but a rush of *caring* hit her. The force of Razr's emotional surge so intense, she could almost feel his strong arms around her. *My imagination? Because perhaps ... I want it so?*

The prince's face, obscured by the cloth mask, proved impossible to read.

Kel's hearts thudded, not quite synched. "Your 'kerchief?" Kel's voice sounded unsteady, rough and breathy, even to her. "Where did you get it?"

"Your right leg pocket should have two," he said, the cloth not muffling the hard edge of his words.

Standard issue camo cloth, her mem module said. *Lower leg pouch.*

Rak'khiel pulled one free, folded it in a triangle, wrapped it about her face.

In unspoken agreement, their reluctant steps covered the short distance to the torture room.

Razr pushed open the door and the stench assaulted them. The heat from the fireplace magnified the blood, venom and terrible stink of cafuzog essence into a palpable force.

Grabbing a water pitcher from the dining table, the prince dumped it over the hearth flames. Found two more water jugs and did the same. Then, turning aside, he neatly vomited, wiped his mouth on the arm of his camo and headed for the nearest body.

Kel admired his composure. Her body already in the involuntary throes of dry heaves, she lifted her kerchief edge and was noisily sick. When Rak'khiel knew she'd thrown up even the pit of her stomach, she wiped her mouth on the back of her hand. Then cleaned it on a black velvet drapery.

Moving to a still form, Kel bent over him.

Peeling back the man's fouled neck scarf, Rak'khiel recognized another merchant. Garil's friend, alive, only overcome by spray.

Rak'khiel left him.

The next, a hunting beast bleeding from three deep wounds, its breath coming shallow in labored pants, low whines. *It cannot live.* She quickly cut its throat.

"Kel, I believe this is a merchant. Could you look?" Razr's

voice was calm, matter-of-fact. "I turned him over."

Avoiding murky pools of body fluids and smoking yellowed gray-green poison, she stepped to his side. "Yes. I left another alive. They were no part of what happened here."

"Good. And this one?"

"Also a merchant. A good man, Yola sold to him. He never shorted her."

Rak'khiel moved the concealing arm from the guard beside him. "And this one?"

"Wicked cruel – he beats his wife."

Razr flicked his s-shaped sword, in a single motion cut the Olican's heart from his chest.

She nodded in approval and admired the deft, too-fast-to-follow bladework. Made herself a promise.

"Good riddance." Kel lifted her eyes to meet those of the prince. Found herself once again caught in their intensity. *Mistake.* Dropping her gaze to the gaping chest wound, she asked, "Would you teach me that move, your favor?"

Instead of answering, Razr's expression blanked.

"Yes, Brin?" he said and mentally went away for a moment.

Turning back to her, Razr said, "The AI's remind me of a request Brin made earlier. They ask if we will save one 'Risto and bring it to the ship."

"Of course," Kel said. "A pure unlimited venom source would be extremely helpful."

"Yes," Razr nodded. "Exactly what he said."

"Let's take the head spydr. Then I can kill him slowly, at my leisure. For kill him, I will. Waiting will make it the sweeter." Her words were conversational but Kel knew Razr wasn't fooled. *He saw Yola's body. He knows how much hate I hold.*

"Their beasts?" Razr queried.

"You choose," she said.

"If they can live, let's leave them."

"Agreed."

The fallen 'Ristos required no discussion. Only six remained alive and the Kra'akens dispatched them as quickly and simply as possible.

Except for the High Lord.

Rak'khiel collected Yola's jewelry. Pulling her gutting knife from its sheath, she rejoiced while hacking spydr fingers, retrieving rings. Breaking arms to reclaim bracelets. She heard the edge of a blade in her laugh. *My laugh, yet not me.*

Retrieving the final ring, the crimson hourglass in the fingernail spurted.

"Goddess protect," she gasped and dodged lethal venom.

Every piece of Yola's jewelry went in a zippocket on her arm. Except the one she wore around her neck.

She rubbed the antique pendant between her thumb and forefinger and the small hairs on the back of her neck stirred and rose. Searing hot spikes wound down the veins of her arms, thrust through both thudding hearts, to be carried throughout her body.

Goddess in a bauble. Rak'khiel stared at the shimmery red frothing over the ever-changing silver shape. Her mind struggled to explain the random streaks of red wrapping the necklace, then sparking away to disappear in the air.

In fourteen years, I never managed to see the pendant's true shape. Kel held the necklace between slender fingers, focused down tight. Still nothing.

"Rak'khiel. Rak'khiel." Came as if from a great distance.

A big hand on her arm, a single shaking sensation, then as if touching hot metal, the hand jerked away. "Shata."

Her concentration, perhaps hypnotism, broken, Kel realized the prince must have been speaking to her for who-knew-how-long.

"My sorry," she said. "I'm not quite sure what happened. This is Yola's heirloom piece, handed down in her family, matriarch to matriarch. She said her line would continue through me. I promised to wear it."

"I was … concerned," Razr said. "You did not answer. You

did not even hear me."

"I appreciate your assistance. I did feel strange for a moment." Kel feared to meet the hot gaze she felt on her face. Instead she looped the chain about her neck, tucked the shifting, glowing necklace inside her fatigues. *Safe.*

I am her daughter and I will carry on tradition. A sweet, soothing flowed from the ornament into her chest. *Another kind of power here – something else I know nothing about.*

Watching Razr efficiently bind, wrap and bag the large 'Risto, using a military Injured Warrior Retrieval pack from another leg pocket, Kel nodded approval. *Impressive.* Then she grinned as the prince stunned the huge spydr twice.

"Just to be certain," he said, full lips curling into a wicked smile, before he dragged the 'Risto into the stair landing.

Rak'khiel carefully stepped around still smoking patches of venom to the torture table. She stood, staring down at the man who'd murdered her mother. Worse than a simple fast death. *My heart is made of Olican gray granite.*

A jug of beer in his face brought the man first to moaning consciousness, then to begging. "Please, help me. Release me, find me a healer." The former Head Questioner didn't recognize her, couldn't in her new form.

"I'm Ela, all grown up. You murdered, tortured my mother Yola. I went to Crucifixion Hill. I saw what you did. You will lie here and die. We will leave the hounds alive too. Perhaps they will eat you." Kel allowed her fangs to lengthen, watched his eyes bulge. In the midst of his protests, Rak'khiel spat in his face and turned her back.

At a dragging sound from the doorway, Kel spun to find Razr pulling two of the merchants into the hallway. She followed, pulling the third, walking in the smeared path made by their bodies.

"Wake!" he shouted, slapping their faces. "Now."

The three didn't stir.

"Let's lean them against the wall and leave them." Kel said, received a grunt of assent from Razr.

Rak'khiel studied the prince as he refolded and replaced his facecloth.

In human form once more, the hard carved planes of his face juxtaposed with the lush fullness of his lips, handsome even splashed with blood. *Acquired defending me.* Broad shoulders, strong heavily muscled body, striking amber eyes now losing their glittering rings of rage, darker-than-night lashes fit for a woman.

Her body responded, blood pounded in the juncture of her legs. A powerful urge to unseal his shirt, touch him, stroke her hand down his bare sleek chest. She knew what lay beneath his fatigues.

Stop it! I am a monster. I just killed more than I can count – and rejoiced? Now I lust in another way? Unforgiveable – my hands, my soul, are bloody with mortal sins. Goddess, Rak'khiel. Think. Remember what happened when you only flirted with the dairy boy.

It's not the same at all, whispered a tiny voice in the back of her mind. *He's a grown man, experienced, a warrior.* That thought excited her even more. With Razr there would be no awkward, loutish fumblings in the dark. *He is a man, grown.*

The pulse of lust spread from her groin to her nipples, her throat squeezed closed. She wanted to pant – didn't dare. *What if he sees, understands? But I have to breathe.*

"Why didn't you tell me what or who Tarkin and Torga are?" She managed, surprised at the normalcy of her voice.

"I assumed – thought you knew – and you haven't exactly been speaking to me. And ...." His throat worked convulsively. The tips of his ears glowed pink.

Did he swallow something bad? Has he been poisoned?

"Lady Regence, I … Brin says … I have … behaved like a nether orifice. I will try … to do better."

"A nether what? Oh." Kel pressed long fingers against her mouth to smother her laugh. "Of course, Prince Helrazr. And my gratitude for saving me."

"Of course." Razr's wide smile smoothed all the grimness from his face and made her hearts lurch. More than once. The sharp fragrance of his male *tasca* flared, fresh pine, ginger blessedly overrode the nastiness of the tower.

She couldn't help her bubbling laughter, she didn't want to. She smelled cinna, jessamin, vanilln. *Goddess, my response. And he is looking at me like dessert.* Her hearts beats quickened, she swallowed hard.

A groan from the floor drew their attention, closely followed by a second. The merchants were waking, gagging.

Razr and Kel leaped back, vaulted down three stairs.

Green projectile vomiting sprayed the landing.

As the merchants recovered their wits, Rak'khiel spoke from the stairwell. Pinching her nostrils together, she explained who she was, what happened, and why.

The prince stood beside her, camo cloth clamped over his face.

"We've left you alive," she said. "We expect you to return to the village and tell what happened here. That two Kra'aken warriors saved your lives and rid you of the 'Ristos. This is repayment for the hunting done many tens of years ago – although neither of us was born at the time." Her quick motion at Razr. "We will destroy this castle of suffering. Go home, go quickly."

"I cannot believe it is you, Ela. But I do. We tried to help Yola. Garil ...."

"I know – it is the only reason you still breathe. If we ever return, we expect to be well received. Go now. If you wish to live, do not return to this place."

The merchants pushed to their feet, shakily made their way down the steps, leaning against the tower's side.

Three hunting beasts, eyes and noses red and streaming, legs braced for balance, staggered through the exit and followed the merchants.

Razr quirked an eyebrow, tilted his head toward the stairs.

Rak'khiel nodded, went down the stairs at a jog, secure in the footfalls behind her.

Tarkin? Torga? Kel sent. *Are you clear of the castle? Can Brin blast it to rubble?*

Yes. Torga's thoughts were angry, unsettled, and oddly tender. *Only one prisoner can be saved. We will bring him to the ship.*

All the prisoners are unshackled, and the cells unlocked, Tarkin sent. *They are free but even with medbox care, they cannot live. Instant death will be a mercy for them.*

Torga added, *Tarkin and I will be at the fighter in five minas. Give the order anytime you wish.*

Why bring the captive to the ship instead of freeing him? Razr queried.

You will see, Torga said and once again the odd protective tendril flavored her send.

Chapter 44

Mid-Dark
Nara 21, 7205.87
Fortress Ground Floor, Olica

Kel and Razr stood on the flagstones in the fortress courtyard sucking deep lungfuls of fresh air.

Razr pointed to the iron bar lying nearby, hid his amusement and said in a mock-stern voice, "You nearly brained me."

"My sorry, Prince Helrazr. I planned to wait for you as I promised." Her voice broke. "I saw Yola's jewelry in their hands. I don't remember anything more."

Razr's gaze traced the hewed granite stairs. Each bore a center depression. *Polished velvet smooth by hundradis of yaras of servants' feet. The same as Kra'aken castles.*

"I broke my promise." Kel's voice wavered. "My most humble contrition."

Realizing he had no idea why she apologized, Razr turned toward Kel.

Her eyes were steady as she met his gaze, but he saw her lower lip tremble. Saw her grip it in sharp upper teeth as she fought for control. *She is upset – that much I know. I would comfort her, if she'd allow it.*

Razr saw a flicker deep in her eyes. *Did she hear my*

thoughts? Her pupils dilated. Her breathing rhythm changed – went slow and deep, then her exhale through flared nostrils.

Razr recognized her change, because his body mirrored hers.

Tascas – vanilln, pine, jessamin, resin, cinna, gingr – flooded the stairwell. Male musk mingled with female.

Razr's inward joy acknowledged the tensing of Kel's body, a small backward arch as if drawn by a gathering string. Although he held himself motionless, his body fought him to curve forward in mating response.

MINE! He exulted, gathering the courage to steal a kiss. Gnashed his teeth instead, when she dipped her head, and minutely inspected the toe of her right boot. He watched a pink flush crawl across her chest and up her neck. *My moment of pre-mating opportunity ruined.*

The prince knew her embarrassment.   Razr heard her thought, clear as a shout.

What is wrong with me? I've committed murder and now I feel lust? The prince would be revolted by me if he know.

I know it's the normal response to battle lust – how do I tell her? Razr dithered, fumbled and finally managed to blurt, "Are we finished here?" He unsuccessfully willed her to look at him again.

"Yes," Kel nodded quick assent. Too quick. Spinning on a heel, she turned toward the landing site. "We are done."

He jerked the plasbag containing the unconscious High Lord vertical, tossed it over one massive shoulder and waited, willing to follow her lead.

Razr never ceded decisions to anyone, other than superior officers. Yet, here, with Kel, he suppressed, even discarded old ways without a second thought. He wondered then, if given time, he might become someone else entirely. Or was it pure hubris to believe he should not change to better match this female.

"I can help with his carry." Rak'khiel scrubbed her palms against the rough fabric of her pants legs. She gazed at the black grotesquerie inside the transplas bag. And flinched.

"For all his size," Razr pitched his voice low, a deep caress. "He is extremely light. It is no hardship for me." *There is no need for you to touch him – but high marks, Lady Kel, for your courage.*

At her long exhale, her sudden, obvious release of tension, he warmed with inner satisfaction. *At least I give her this much.* She wiped the palms of her hands on filthy pants, squared her shoulders and headed for the ships.

Razr surveyed the green countryside carpeted in yellow sweet-spice-scented flowers. An area studded by bright random blots of color – the red bark of tree trunks and the silver of their leaves. A beautiful, terrible place.

Breasting the low hill beyond the gray stone castle, Rak'khiel paused, turned. The intensity of her gaze should have scorched the earth.

Seeminly unaware the prince studied her, her eyes scoured the village, moved toward the tiny cottage she'd shared with Yola, then drifted to the height of the Fang. Her full lips twisted, her beautiful face merciless and ugly.

Razr once again heard unshielded thoughts. *A final look at this accursed place where I learned so much. And lost so very much more.*

He watched his female straighten even more, as if a metal rod infused her spine. A single sharp inhale of disgust accompanied a negative shake of her head. "Razr, look."

Moving to her side, he focused in the direction of her pointing finger.

The spared merchants, still draped in their abattoir robes, stood in the center of a group of villagers. Shaking their heads, they shouted "No, no, no. You must not. You will die."

Four townsmen turned from the group and strode toward the fortress.

The merchants shouted, begged, "No, no. Please."

"Those four always refused to listen." Kel's even, calm voice could have been discussing the price of eggs.

If she is distressed, I see no evidence. Razr only said, "They will die."

"So be it," she answered, her voice the emotionless cold of frozen metal. The hard set of her face marred her profile's soft beauty. "They were warned."

Rak'khiel has her Lady Mother's practicality. But also the ruthless pragmatism of her sire. This is unexpected. Fourteen years of running and hiding should have trampled her spirit underfoot.

Kel cut her eyes sideways.

Her speed caught him in unguarded appraisal of her. Razr wondered what his face betrayed.

Just as quickly, Kel left the fortress grounds. Choosing a full fluid stride, a quick pace, a gait effortless for her long legs – even more so for him – she left the palace of horrors and its terrible contents behind.

The prince followed Rak'khiel toward the twinned ships. *I refuse to call my fighter the Betty – but what else can we name them?*

His avid gaze devoured Kel's elegant body as it tapered from broad muscular shoulders to a narrow waist and slender hips. *Now I remember why I let her lead the way.* With each elongated step, her fatigues pulled tight, revealing the sweet curves of high round buttocks and wide outside sweep of muscular legs.

Neither the nasty stains or charred acid holes on her camo, the nest of sticky clotted things in Kel's blue-black hair, nor her stained, bloody hands proved a deterrent to Razr's desire. *This woman is no shallow Kra'aken noble lady.*

Rak'khiel turned, as if she felt his hot eyes on her.

"Have you changed your mind about needing my assistance ... with that?" One dark eyebrow climbed toward her hairline with her question.

As her teasing gaze dropped to the repellent thing he carried, she changed, burned hot destruction. Looked away, and calmed, Kel stroked loose tendrils of hair back and over her shoulders.

Razr's body leaped in response.

Her eyes cut away from him, she rubbed a smeared forefinger on her lower lip. A tiny quirk dimpled one corner of her mouth.

Damn her, does she know she torments?

Razr managed to conceal his body's shudder and his instant painful physical manifestation. But his personal *tasca*, ginger and sharp pine resin infused the air. *Shata!*

Prince Helrazr VI'Rex, known for his ways with women, panicked as uncontrollable heat flushed his body, his face, his ears. Panic shifted into hyperdrive when he felt faceted black jewels circling his irises.

Razr perused the ground underfoot as if it would give him all the answers to his future. *You are a Royal Prince for Destroyer's sake. Get a forzaing grip.*

"No, I can carry this abomination. All is well," he said, intending to present casual disinterest. Instead, to his alarm, he heard the hitch in his voice and knew by the quiver of her abdomen, she heard it too. *Does she understand what she does to me?*

He promptly began mental recitations of his boring Klan ancestry, a process preventing physical embarrassment many times before. It nearly failed him now, thanks to the siren allure of the bedraggled temptress before him. Repeated litanies only provided relief enough to permit walking.

"Lead the way," he said, his voice rough.

"Oooo," Kel breathed as they topped a small rise.

The high silver tip of the warplane glistened, kissed by violet rays of Olica's twin suns streaming through scudding white clouds. The ship glittered, seemed a living thing.

"What a beauty she is, Prince Razr. And what a thrill she must be to fly."

Yes, you are and to fly your body only once, I'd give it all. He startled, bit his tongue, tasted warm copper salt. *I almost blurted it aloud.* Razr blinked in consternation, reopened his mouth, tried again.

"If we ever uncouple the ships, would you like to?" Razr heard himself say, much to his horror. *No one pilots my warship except me (and Brin, of course).* But there he went, no will of his own, a flitr to her nectar. *And to think I mocked my friends for their emotional weaknesses.*

Remembrance of loss, sadness gripped Razr's soul. He hiccupped. It was not a sob, warriors do not cry.

Kel heard something in it and turned back, stepping close. "What troubles you so? Can I help?" The softness, the honest offer, the light brush of a tentative hand on his arm unmanned him.

Blinking hard against the sudden blur, he cleared his throat, coughed, and lied. "The aftereffects of the cafuzogs' secret weapon."

"Umhmm," Rak'khiel said, gave him an inscrutable female gaze, and moved away.

The entire time a small voice in the prince's mind screamed *No, no, no – your favor, come back.* He realized she spoke to him.

"… people sought Yola out for her astute, sensible counsel. They said she always helped. I am not wise but I know how to listen and keep secrets." Kel scrubbed the back of a bloody hand across her eyes. "Perhaps later I … I need to tell …." Her voice cracked, died away.

"Yes," he managed. "I … too …." He saw bright glistening in her smoky topaz eyes, reached a comforting hand too late.

Kel turned from him without seeing, resuming her quick pace. *As if she seeks to outrun her pain.*

The limp body of the deadly spydr hanging light over his shoulder, Razr followed her lead across the last two lush rolling hills, through the red and silver grove to the waiting melded ships.

Razr's mind struggled to understand Rak'khiel. He wondered at her insight, marveled at her kindness. Kra'aken citizens were strong, without weakness. Unlike the worlds they conquered, where psychodocs enjoyed elevated status, they did not exist on his homeworld. Rak'khiel is purebred High Klan, inarguably a titled Lady, but in this, she is a contradiction. Not Kra'aken at all.

His mind twisted, he worried at his thoughts, and found they'd arrived at the ships.

Once more zapping the inert body he carried, just as much for fun as to ensure the spydr remained unconscious, Razr dumped the High Lord on the ground and headed for the cafuzogs waiting outside the fighter/pod.

Attention fixed on his female, Razr saw the jerk of Kel's head toward Torga, saw her gaze lock on, her face the blank unfocused expression of mental conversation.

With a quick blink followed by a huge smile, Kel broke into a sprint, dropping to her knees before the female cafuzog. Peering into the cradle made from black furry forearms, she crooned, "Oh, oh my. How incredibly sweet. How will we care for ...?"

Him, Razr caught Tarkin's thought. *We now have a new baby male.*

Male? Razr felt jealousy spear his heart. *Male baby what? Human? Olican?*

Tarkin finorkled. Lifting a half-lip, he sent, *A baby sorbazel, my prince. Caylee is busy creating formula and feeding utensils. She says he will need food every four horas for at least a hilu before we can start him on raw flesh or regular protmeat paste. I believe you and I will be expected to take our turn.*

Destroyer save, Razr's ire rose. He swallowed the disgusted snort his intuition told him could be fatal, should Kel hear it. *Arrgh. An infant of some kind to nurture. To raise?*

Thoughts of sweet but insufferable nieces and nephews replayed in his memory. A rambunctious child on a confined ship? *Horrors.*

Razr's plans included decadris of time with Kel before having younglings. Time alone to acquaint, court, and love.

Ah, but he'd just experienced the only upside to this development. His embarrassing physical manifestation of desire, now completely deflated. Still, he realized in surprise, his skin swirled with unbidden golden pre-change patterns, the air seeded with early surges of *tasca*. *Sweet Destroyer, can this be jealousy? Of a baby? I am appalled at myself.*

"He is a sorbazel cub, isn't he?" Kel babbled, reaching hungry arms for the little one. She stroked his soft fur, then folded his cat-like body into her embrace, cuddling, rocking and murmuring. "I thought they were lapis-blue striped. Was he in the dungeon?"

"Yes. His fate – first food for the Lady 'Risto's hatchlings." Torga barely got his final word out when Kel whirled.

Warrior's instinct drove Razr's evasive leap. It served him well – danger threatened.

For the first time he saw metamorphosis in Rak'khiel's eyes – rings of faceted amber encircled, wheeled around copper-studded topaz irises. Vanilln, jessamin, cinna flooded the air.

She's fully morphed now, without limitations, yes? Brin? Caylee?

Yes. Agreed.

Recognizing danger, the baby blinked up at the seething creature holding him and began to mewl tiny sounds of distress.

"My shame." Rak'khiel handed him back to Torga, struggled for control. "I cannot believe I frightened ...."

"Shata, Kel." Razr reached to comfort her.

She brushed him aside like a naat using the hard armored edge of her hand.

"Brin," she shouted. "Burn the forguning castle to the ground. Make it ash, I care not how many die."

Chapter 45

Mid-Dark
Nara 21, 7205.92
Hilltop, Olica

The prince watched while first Involuntary Full Change took Rak'khiel. Razr felt her ease, her welcome of this morphosis.

Pink shimmers shot with paisley-patterned gold reptilian scales wreathed, then crusted her skin. Long razor-edged fangs curved beneath her chin. Roseate spikes, claws and barbs, all glittering with filigreed gold, pushed through every fighting edge of her body.

Razr breathed in Kel's heady personal *tasca*. It flooded the air, flooded his senses. The hard-driving scent of war.

Then, Rak'khiel, the predator, turned terrible eyes on him.

His hearts missed their beats, forced emptiness in his chest. The lack of needed blood-push, a dry hitching in his heart made him cough, then gasp for air. In self-protection, the prince's body tried to force Change. *I dare not upset her on any level. I must trust her.* He held morphosis in check, although his mind shrieked from the wrongness.

"Sweet Destroyer save us," he whispered. "Brin, level the bloody fortress. Now! She's berserk. Make the distraction. She could turn on us all."

Acknowledged.

A low vibration underfoot ratcheted to tremors. A mind-skewering humming built to a steady whine before kicking into a roar.

Razr watched, with gratitude, Rak'khiel's attention shift, focusing on the glowing aperture of an active weapons pod high up on the fighter.

Faster than his unaugmented, unenhanced eyes could track, an eye-searing beam lasered from the warplane's bow.

A blanket of silence descended.

The granite structure evaporated. Only a few wisps of white ash remained, fluttering through the air to crumble on pale seared ground.

Daring a glance at his female, Razr found her unarmored, her large oval eyes rational. Twin vertical lines furrowed between blue-black raptor wing brows. Full lips parted slightly for a tiny breath.

Too sure Kel now maintained control – too soon Razr relaxed his vigilance. He moved his focus to the joined ships. He missed Kel's turn, missed her striding away from the group. A movement in his peripheral sent hot needles of alarm spiking through his spine. Spinning, Razr saw his female's strong strides carry her to the top of the nearest rise.

"Brin, what is she about?"

No idea, Prince Helrazr.

Twin vertical furrows creased Razr's forehead.

Rak'khiel stood, legs spread wide. In challenge, in defiance? Or something more? With one filthy hand, she drew Yola's odd metal necklace – the strange pendant with its eye-evading shape – from beneath the shirt of her bloody battle fatigues.

Why can't I quite get a solid fix on the contours or details of the godsrotted thing? It twisted his viscera, worked on his mind. The more he focused, the more his perception blurred.

In a small, ignored corner of his mind, Razr heard muted exclamations.

Not our Kel, Torga sent.

No, Brin said.

Scary, Tarkin sent.

Yola, yet not. Caylee added.

Brushing them all aside, Razr centered his full attention on his female. *What is she doing?*

Her thumb stretched wide, all five fingers bent back, Razr imagined her feeding a lymappl to a Kra'aken WarSteed. Lifting the writhing pendant on her upthrust palm, Rak'khiel displayed its wavering red-wrapped silver presence to the sky.

The ornament lit from within as if alive. *Ridiculous.* As he stared, glowing streams of silver-shot ruby burgeoned. Pulsing ever more brightly, red comet trails of power built and fountained.

Even confined in his warrior braids, Razr's hair lifted heavenward. The loosened tendrils escaped to halo and twist, pulled by something alien and other.

His glance at Rak'khiel showed her long hair completely freed of restraint. Stretching overhead, her heavy raven locks rose, twined and twisted. Each scarlet pulse of the pendant's growing might pulled it skyward.

An unidentifiable acrid smell crackled hot through the air.

Lightning stabbed, a vertical strike into the heart of the pendant. Yet Kel stood, unharmed. Jagged horizontal bolts brought a different stench – akin to the sweet charred reek of funeral pyres. *Mixed with scorched electrical wiring?*

Rolling black clouds lowered, hung pregnant overhead. Smelling of destructive fires, glowing coals and brimstone, the clouds held power far more deadly than mere rain.

What in the name of the Destroyer is she doing? Does she know?

Rak'khiel stretched her free hand skyward toward the clouds. She lifted her face, her lovely features gone cold, unnatural. Glorious.

The red-silvered glow expanded, covered her in a fine swirling mist.

Something in the heavens rumbled, growled in response.

Icy sweat coated Razr's skin. His nether parts tried to crawl inside the safety of his body.

Anathema. The only female available – in the entire universe and beyond – and she is tainted? Sweet Destroyer, what did I do to deserve this? My price demand from the Great God? Fisting his hands, he beat them on his thighs as if they might protect him from this ... sorcery?

Rak'khiel chanted something the words too soft for him to hear and stretched her empty hand skyward.

The threatening dark descended.

Wrapping five long elegant fingers about the suddenly corporeal coal-dark sky, closing the fist with her thumb, Kel ... pulled.

The sky screamed and bent beneath her command, bowed as if pulled by a master archer.

Razr threw himself flat, face seeking safety in the ochre dirt. But he had to see. He kept one eye fixed on Kel.

Extended forefinger pointing at the white ash spot of the former fortress, Rak'khiel swept her closed hand down.

Without a conscious decision to do so, Razr ducked and made the sign of the Destroyer. Without shame, he added the superstitious ward against evil used by the lower classes – a practice he routinely ridiculed.

Rolling his head to one side, he watched a black dot appear in the center of the ruins. It grew, larger and wider, until the entire area fouled by the 'Ristos steamed and turned the fathomless dark of deep space. And as uninhabitable.

Razr stared, too stunned, too shocked to swear or rise or run. He demanded his mind process the incredible event.

It refused.

She cursed the ground. With blight? Brin sent.

Or something akin – does she also own some other magic, brought by Yola's ancestors? How can she? Caylee's thread. *She is Klan Regence, pure Kra'aken.*

The AI's have themselves together, damnit. Razr swallowed a snarl. *And here I am with my face in the dust.* He sat up, brushed at the fine powdery yellow clinging everywhere.

An unbidden question hung in his mind. *Although I am larger, more skillful in battle, Kel commands a power I cannot understand. Could she kill me?* His quivering viscera assured him she could.

Perhaps I only imagined Brin and Caylee were developing personalities and emotions. Razr realized he clutched at straws. In his heart, he knew better. His base of stability, grounded in the laws of Kra'aken, no longer applied – in this strange chunk of space, this side of neverwhere and neverwhen.

Tarkin, Torga? You okay? Razr berated himself for not checking earlier; then excused it. *Something still isn't quite right with my mind mods.* He mocked himself for needing a reason.

Fine, Prince Razr. Tarkin's cheery thought.

"Forza me." There they sat, upright, their shiny black fur unstained by dirt, the baby quiescent in Torga's front legs. *They enjoyed, probably even applauded, the show.*

Isn't our Kel magnificent? Torga's pride laced her thought.

Their approving happy chatter made him feel like an idiot. *Mayhap they don't have the intelligence to be afraid.* In the place in his mind where Razr admitted his darkest secrets, he knew it for falsehood.

Rak'khiel's sharp motion at the sky caused the release of stretched power.

Like an iridescent soap bubble pricked by a pin, the sky snapped back, its rents and tears smoothed as if they never occurred. Dark forbidding clouds returned to puffy white, scudding across its lavender loveliness.

Silver-streaked crimson rays streamed through cumulus, tinting them scarlet. Then, the red connection between the pendant and the heavens began to ebb.

Razr's jaw hit his chest as Kel's ruby beams retracted from the heights. Each compressed, folding and twisting in upon itself – packing impossible power into one restless silver pendant.

Rak'khiel's eyes closed. Sinking to her knees, she clasped both hands about the pulsing necklace. Head bowed, she remained motionless.

Minas passed although Razr would have sworn it was aiys. With a single nod, Kel tucked the pendant inside her shirt.

The prince moved to stand, go to her side.

No!

Startled, Razr caught a murderous glare from Tarkin.

Wait. This send accompanied by a quick nod of apology. *She must sort this out alone.*

The prince's mind made an attempt to straighten his kinked corners of reason.

It bent.

What I thought I saw did not actually happen, correct? He sent to Brin, Caylee, Tarkin and Torga.

Of course it did. Brin's crushing response.

Why wouldn't Yola keep her weapon and avoid death? Torga asked.

Perhaps she only guarded the power? Perhaps her task to see it passed to the proper successor? Caylee sent.

She makes the most sense – sort of. Razr thought. *If you subscribe to this magic nonsense.*

Tarkin's comment was undeniable. *If Yola held power, could she have killed them all to save Kel?*

Or did Yola have to die to pass the pendant's gift to Rak'khiel? Torga's question hung heavy. *And if true, what would this knowledge do to Kel?*

Razr's mind sparked, remembering Rak'khiel's deep guilt for Yola's death. *It would destroy her,* he sent to the group.

We will never speak of it, unless she does? Caylee's rhetorical question.

Agreed. Confirmation of Razr's own thoughts from Brin and Caylee.

Standing with Rak'khiel's friends, the prince anxiously watched her push to her feet.

Taking one last, long look at the destruction, she turned away. No monster returned to them. Only an unremarkable, weary, filthy young woman stumbled from the hilltop.

"Do I have time to shower before we fly?" Kel's exhausted, plaintive request.

Chapter 46

Early-Aiy
Nara 25, 7205.10
Warplane Medical Unit, Olica

Pain lanced through the High Lord's thorax and abdomen, seizing his lungs.

Must breathe. Destroyer help. Hurts.

Tension, fear held every part of his shrieking body rigid against the agony. He took tiny hitches, minuscule sips of air.

Bright dots of white, blots of black danced inside his closed eyelids.

Pinching his lips together, the High Lord trapped his scream behind them.

Something nearby emitted a shrill series of beeps.

A disembodied male voice inquired, "Do you require pain medication?"

"Yess," he whispered.

A wide stream of blessed cool flooded through a shunt somewhere on his body.

A red thundercloud built in his mind, then paled to pink cumulous floating lazily overhead. The High Lord watched the mist fall, like rain in pastel patters, to encompass his pain, to encompass his consciousness.

He knew no more.

§

A second waking brought heightened awareness and the bright white of blinding overhead lights.

Matte gray robotic arms, silver joints bending and flexing, intruded on his line of sight. They moved, worked. *Doing what?*

He felt sucking pulls, myriad stings. *Why am I here? Wherever here is.*

The High Lord wriggled a segmented lower limb, found it immobilized. An attempt to turn his head proved futile. Testing moves found every part of his body strapped to hard surfaces. *Captured, bound.* He wrinkled his nose at sharp, pungent odors. *Antiseptic? 'Risto blood? Mine?*

Panic gripped, his heart thumped, too loud in his head, echoing the throbbing ache in his chest. The simmering crease of pain between the two half-plates of armor covering his torso became a hot river of burn.

The High Lord strained against binding straps. *Cracked me open like an egg.*

The torment in the ligaments and bones of his spine connections to his carapace confirmed it. *But why?*

"Cease struggling. You will rupture your repairs." Once again, the male voice infringed.

"Repairss from wha ...." His words emerged a garbled hiss through a mouth too swollen for proper speech.

Fear's tiny ice feet crawled him.

Although he tried to contain it, the 'Risto's rapid breath came harsh like carrion-bird screeches. He shuddered with each spike of pain. His body, his hands, his mouth, his leg claws throbbed like someone pounded each place with a vicious hammer. *My captors have done horrible things to me.*

Chapter 47

Early-Aiy
Nara 26, 7205.15
Life Cocoon, Olican surface

Rak'khiel paced, fists clenching.

The killings should have lessened the raging sorrow in her soul. She'd set a goal, accomplished it. Still, her mind refused to give peace. Sorrow throbbed. Guilt from her part in Yola's death flayed her soul like the stripes of a whip.

I have not suffered. I need to be punished. Her escape from physical consequences made her angry and aggressive. *I will lose myself in the simulator, in combat. At least my mind will be occupied.*

Kel headed down through the warplane's core.

"Shalit," she snarled.

The light above the sim door glowed red.

The chamber's in use. Perhaps someone else as annoyed as I am?

Someone – oh-who-could-it-possibly-be? – had beaten her here this morning.

Her palm smacked the yellow access patch on the wall.

The door slid up, humidity billowed into the corridor. Smells of blood, of body fluids and sweat close followed close behind.

In the sim's jungle setting, Razr crouched behind a large rock. One hand held the beautiful s-shaped, etched sword, the other his two-edged gutting knife. He moved gracefully, silently stalking a huge, menacing apparition. Successfully, it seemed.

Green blood blotched the creature's gray scaly hide. Evenly spaced diagonal slashes scored the creature's abdomen and its long lashing tail.

The creature's head jerked in the direction of the open hatch.

"Get out," the prince snarled, not pausing to see who interrupted, intent on his pursuit.

Kel recognized both program and monster. *I've never defeated a Level 10. He's working Level 20.* Slapping the hatch closed, she whispered, "I've some catching up to do."

Now she knew Razr's whereabouts, and how long he'd be occupied, Kel hurried through the warplane. Earlier, she'd checked the fighter's schematics for the prisoner cells and located them in the fighter's stern.

Time for my first visit to Yola's murderer.

Behind double-triple layers of plexplas, the naked 'Risto lord crouched in the webbed far corner. His long hairy black limbs were spaced exactly the same distance apart and folded beneath his body.

Like a swatted, dead spider at home, Kel thought. *But they feigned lifelessness too.*

Three large black eyelids cracked slightly apart, just enough to see who stood outside his cell. Three pair of orange feelers writhed above opaque eyes, between the High Lord's heavy brow and his widow's peak.

The Goddess-damned thing gave her the shuddering willies.

The extra layers of plas – the extra safety measure – unnecessary. *Caylee ensured that.*

Kel eyed the spydr. His long curving talons were cut short; the swollen ends of his fingers cross-hatched, covered by tiny black stitches and shiny metallic staples.

Rak'khiel couldn't see his abdomen but she knew the scarlet hourglass was there. *They all had them.*

The black High Lord lurked, partially obscured behind his webs. Rendered as impotent as Brin, Caylee, Razr and the augmented prison cell could make him, he still retained the crushing power of his black segmented legs.

Why did they leave his spinnerets? Rak'khiel wondered. *I'd have taken everything. Without anesthetic. Then, when he was reduced to a bloody lump like Yola, I'd have watched him die. Alone, in agony, slowly. For days. With extreme pleasure.*

Wedged against the curving wall of the hull, in the narrow aisle between one plas cell and the next, sat a single pale blue stool.

Rak'khiel jerked it close, then positioned her seat for maximum viewing. She didn't worry about having her back to the door. Everyone in the twinned ships, except the abomination before her, was her friend.

She pulled an earlobe while she inspected the clear bubble port on the front of the cell. *For feeding?*

Doubled plas sheets on every side, sliding access panels provided security by blocking the inside, center, and outer areas. *This prison was designed by someone who escaped such a place.* She spared a neuron to wonder if it had been Razr, then discarded it. *The prince is too young. Someone older, an escapee, perhaps an engineer built this.*

Elbows on knees, long slender fingers steepled loosely beneath her chin, she regarded the object of her hatred. *How to kill him?*

Yola's pendant, under her loose blue shirt, heated, pulsed, reminded. *Ah, yes. Great power lies within – if only I knew how to use it.*

But a second throbbing sensation, this one in her lower lip, reminded Rak'khiel of a complication. *I dare not harm this monstrous thing until Caylee and Brin find the venom's keys and create an antidote. For this 'Risto has surely poisoned me.*

She wondered if, as Brin believed, the spydr in the cell could re-create his poison sacs. If true, they would have even more material for their experiments, more information about the rogue species. And an even more dangerous enemy in their prisoner.

I hate you, she sent, her double hearts hard as ceramtanium. She waited.

Nothing.

"I hate you, you bastard," she whispered, springing to her feet. Behind her, the stool crashed to the floor. "You tortured, murdered my mother. I intend to kill you, but slower than all the others." Rak'khiel had thought to spit the words. Instead, their coldness chilled even her. "You will suffer Yola's agony thrice-fold."

You .... The malignant whispery thought brushed her mind, ripe with hate. *You ... murdered my family. You ... are responsible for my imprisonment, my defacement, my debasement.*

Her mind recoiled, snapped up a shield against the crawling poison of vicious words. "It is your fault alone," Kel snarled. "With your harm of Yola, you brought this upon yourself. Had you left my mother alone, you would still be in your stone fortress with your kind around you." Knowing it would enrage the horror in the cell, she taunted, "I killed them, you know. Your mate, your young."

A screech, a hiss, a vicious curse. The cell walls shuddered as the arachna launched, then bounced off the plasplex.

"Your hounds too," she whispered. "The one you called Angel died especially hard."

Thin lids retracted, exposing pupilless eyes of matte obsidian. Soulless. The heavy single brow drew down. Above it, feelers the color of new carrots intertwined.

Eyes bored into Rak'khiel, fixed on her, this she knew for certainty although their flat, carbon-black surface gave no indication.

Her spine jittered, breath frozen by the malicious wash of hatred sweeping through her. *Goddess of Good! This grotesquerie possesses empathetic powers, capable of paralyzing by thought.*

Orange antenna waved, twined, pointed at Kel. Her thighs trembled, threatened to drop her to the floor.

He believes he can harm me. He cannot. Rak'khiel allowed a small smile of anticipation to play at the corner of her lips. I will revel in his surprise when Yola's pendant protects and aids me.

Open the door ... the spydr's command brought a surging tidal wave of compulsion. *Give me my crown.*

Rak'khiel tightened her shields, felt the swirl of the pendant's contours. She opened her mouth just enough to expose the nubbed beginnings of her saber fangs.

"Sorry," she said knowing her cold smile gave her apology the lie. "I am too strong for you."

"You are Kra'aken," the dry, papery whisper rose in pitch, laced with rage. The High Lord unfolded his limbs and stood. "You are the cause of all 'Risto'ss hurtss."

"I am Kra'aken, yes. But I am young. I had nothing to do with the history between our races. Did you?" Kel snarled. "My revenge will be solely for your torture and crucifixion of Yola, my mother."

She shuddered when the spydr straightened, stretched each limb. She shuddered when he delicately parted his webs and walked – six hind limbs moving independently – to face her through the plas. She shuddered, swallowed hard against the bile surging up the back of her throat.

Horrific misshapen thing. Kel sent. *You are far worse than my morphosis.*

Hatred battered her protections.

The High Lord narrowed opaque eyes, focused on her lower lip.

"I scored you," he said with smug satisfaction. His hairy little mouth pursed, red lips smacked, pulled up at the corners in cruel parody of a smile. "Even now my venom works – it calls to me. The small scratch, the small amount of poison will work slowly. But it will eventually kill you."

The arachnid lifted his first pair of segmented legs, reared up. His skeletal hands and two black bandaged legs smacked, rested on the transparent wall. He bared capped fangs. Hissed.

Now he is taller – believing it gives him advantage. I could stand, Kel thought. *No matter.* She calmly inspected the 'Risto, deliberately allowed a tiny curl of her lip. Felt the spear of his anger probe her protections.

Shields tight, she waited for his response. The Goddess-cursed spydr believes he has the upper hand. *But I know he who speaks first loses.* She met those eerily blank eyes, calmly resumed her scrutiny.

The High Lord moved, a creepy sideways, back-and-forward crawling.

Does he pace? She watched him watch her, felt him batter at her shields and allowed half-fangs to emerge. Smiling her cold toothy grin, she sent, *Mine are bigger than yours.*

Without conscious decision, without understanding how she knew but feeling the rightness of it, Rak'khiel reached up and pulled just a thread of Yola's magic. She sent it glistening, rifling into his enclosure and with a fingertip, flipped a small circle in the air.

The thread of liquid power spun, wrapped around the High Lord. Cocooning him, helpless, like he'd done to so many others, Rak'khiel left him only the ability to speak.

He squealed, a high thin sound, as if the substance of her magic burned him.

Kel's casual observation of his pain, her features arranged in *faux* concern, said she did not dislike his agony.

The 'Risto struggled, bound immobile in mid-cell. Panted out, "What are you called?"

I win. "Rak'khiel. And you?"

"Hiss Lordship will do." An opening of the pursed hairy mouth, exposed useless fangs. His pain echoed off the transplas, ricocheted about the area where she sat.

Kel's wide humorless smile exposed lengthening saber

teeth. "No. It won't." She stood, shoved the stool aside, turned to go.

The dry whispery voice. "Wait. Namess give power."

"They do – which is why I gave you only one."

"I am called Barizan Honor du'Oniiq. I will accept Honor."

Her astonished snort combined with a bark of laughter made her cough. *A Goddess-damned live, breathing oxymoron.* Kel paused, closed her dropped jaw and regained control, before she turned around. "Does it have meaning?"

"Of course," the hairy little mouth widened, turned up at the corners. The spydr's breath hissed, a flinch accompanied the smile.

Painful, Rak'khiel decided.

"The word holdss the same meaning in both our languagess. In answer to your earlier question – I wass not involved in the banishment – my mother wass. But I remember."

Kel, Caylee's voice in her head. *Razr's out of the sims.*

On my way. Leaping from her chair, a rasped hiss behind her gave her pause.

"Rak'khiel. Will you come again?"

Did she hear a plaintive note? Incongruous with his displayed malice.

Kel released the magical cocoon on the arachna, shook her head.

Something just changed here. But what?

Chapter 48

Mid-dark
Nara 27, 7205.50
Warplane

Razr woke from a dream of Rak'khiel with an erection large enough to hamper movement. Hard enough – *well almost* – to dent the foamtanium wall by his bunk, and insistent enough to muddle his reason.

"Destroyer take me," he growled and tried to shove away the lingering wisps of memory.

Kel's rounded, sleekly muscular arms had been around his neck, he'd cradled her magnificent *derriere* in his hands. Full ruby lips, gone slightly slack and parted, waited for his kisses. Soul shining bright through smoky topaz eyes, she'd looked at him like he held all her solutions.

"I can't sleep from wanting her," he moaned. "Then when I finally do sleep, I wake to this."

Although he told himself he didn't want to remember the dream, he lied.

Memory took him back to visions of Rak'khiel, imagining her lying naked in his bed, welcome in those tilted half-lidded eyes, her body ready, willing, waiting for his plunder.

"Shata!" Razr couldn't calc, couldn't fly, couldn't

concentrate on anything except Kel's allure.

She does it on purpose to torment me. Bending over in her coveralls to pick up tools, pulling the fabric tight around her tight behind. She knows it makes me insane. Reaching overhead, stretching for the cockpit toggles, knowing it shows the heavy fullness of those luscious .... "Forza me."

Rising from his bunk, he made his way into the shower and dialed it to ice. Razer stood beneath the frosty spray, counting the aiys. One hundrada fifty eight yaras, eight hilus and fourteen aiys since he last held a female. *Just to be touched, the warmth of human contact, all I truly needed. The physical release, would simply be the dollop of garnish on the treat.*

I am stable, Razr insisted to the little voice of conscience in his mind. *I am. I have never laid uninvited hands upon a woman and I will not begin now. But now that I know Kel is fully recovered, this will be mutually beneficial.*

She lacks Kra'aken social experience, does not understand she is free to request a mating. Because she is shy, it is understandable she wishes me to invoke Royal Command.

Razr continued his flawless reasoning. *Because she teases me, and begs with every movement of her body, I know she desires me, wants my bed. I will perform the ritual today, have things clear between us before we leave Olica.*

Razr dialed up the hot water long enough to smooth the gooseflesh coating his body. His big hands trembled while he shaved.

Three scarlet nicks later, tan skin dotted with white tissue, he gave it up. Warrior's nerves, unshakable in mortal combat, betrayed him. Tattered, flayed, raw.

Reaching into his small closet, the prince pulled out and dressed in his royal ceremonial clothing. Bending, he retrieved his formal footwear from the bottom of the wardrobe.

"Prince Helrazr?" Brin's disapproving voice. "Why are you wearing those robes? Just exactly what are you contemplating?"

"You've seen how Rak'khiel entices me, her naïve attempts

at seduction. I am simply granting her wish." Razr strapped on a gem-studded sandal.

"Great Destroyer, Razr." The AI's stern warrior aspect winked in. "Stop, you young fool. You court disaster."

"Silence, Brin. You are a machine. What would you know of the ways of men? Of royalty, at that." Razr strapped on the second shoe and reached for his dress sword.

"I am astounded that, as a mere collection of component parts, I understand more of the ways of women than you. If you believe she has been seductive, then you are deluding yourself. If you wish to know how she thinks or feels, you should ask her. But, my prince, I beg you. Do not do this thing."

"Nonsense. It is you who are deluded. And possibly envious, if you could be." Razr's voice took a hard edge and one side of his upper lip lifted with a flash of sharp fang.

"My prince, hear yourself. You are not mean-spirited or cruel and yet, you sound and appear vicious. You are riding the hard edge of reason. Your favor," pleaded Brin. "Wait and build your friendship with Kel first."

"Where is she?"

"I cannot say."

"Cannot or will not?"

"Your choice, my prince. But one last entreaty, your favor. Do not approach Kel in this manner."

"Leave it alone, Brin. Or I'll space your brainbox and the backup."

Razr threw up a mental barrier between the AI and himself, added another shield against Caylee. Flipping his woven crimson cloak about broad shoulders, he slapped the hatch access by the door and strode toward the pod, leaving a swirl of heady mating *tasca* behind.

Razr burst through the hatch of Rak'khiel's personal quarters in the life cocoon, not bothering to knock.

Kel leaped from her desk, eyes wide, nostrils flared.

"What's wrong? Are we under attack?" She demanded.

The prince's resolution and his control deserted him on the instant.

Before him stood a golden-skinned beauty, long dark curls highlighted in cobalt. One raptor wing brow lifted with her question. "Why are you dressed like that?" Then, his *tasca* flared higher, he saw her color heighten.

She feels it too. I knew it. Yes, she reacts. Her lust is as great as mine.

Her voice was husky.

With desire.

Her war tasca surged.

He ignored it.

Unable not to touch, in a single stride, Razr crossed the tiny compartment and gripped Kel's slender shoulders in huge hands. His chest heaved as his twin hearts pounded hard, attempting escape.

Small hands sought to peel his large six-fingered ones from her body. "Prince Helrazr? What in the name of the Goddess are you about?"

The pleasure-pain pressure from his saber fangs – pushing and lengthening, they dropped well beneath his chin. Long enough to encircle her slender neck. The mental image made his hearts batter arrhythmic, sent blood surging to his groin. The exquisite torment, the pressure of engorgement, forced his words.

"Rak'khiel I'Regence, I, Prince Helrazr VI'Rex invoke Kra'aken Law 14007.00." Razr heard his voice, harsh as if his vocal cords had been charred, then scraped.

"Your favor?" The tone of her voice altered, gone cold, hard.

Razr felt Kel's body stiffen. He held a steeltanium statue by the shoulders.

He forced words. "You know of Royal Command, you understand the Royal Prerogative."

Destroyer damn me. Instead of the compliments he'd planned to put her at ease, he'd taken an action he loathed. An action he'd condemned in others.

"I know nothing of which you speak." Rak'khiel's frosty voice held growing offense, her attempts to free her shoulders turning insistent.

Razr heard her unspoken warning in the ice crusting each word.

The little voice in his mind screamed. *No, no, no, NO. Stop. Now. She will forgive you this much. But stop, apologize and return to the fighter.*

Razr knew it for truth, but in the grip of desire, in hypnotic horror, he watched his right hand drift from her shoulder, cup a full breast. Watched his thumb play across the curve, graze her nipple. Heard Kel's sharp intake of breath. Deliberately mistook it for arousal.

Dropping his head, he kissed her, tasted sweet female blood as their fangs meshed. With one swift motion, he lifted and twisted Kel's slender body until her spine pressed his chest and her elegant neck rested in his mouth. Trapped in submission by his saber teeth, he trembled in echo as his low rumbling growl vibrated down her spine, through her body.

His big arm trapped hers, wrapped tight across her chest, clasped her tiny waist and pressed her buttocks against the hardness of his desire. Razr's free hand caressed her breast, roamed over slender hips, drifted between her legs. Stroked. He turned, muscles rigid with tension, never releasing his grasp and dragged Rak'khiel toward her bed.

Her breath came sharp, hard.

Razr felt her morphosis push hard to Change, smelled her *tasca*. He reveled in her desire – until someone unleashed a sim monster in the room.

Rak'khiel exploded.

Something went *creeschk* in his knee as a small narrow heel crushed it. His jaws parted in pain.

A quick twist freed Kel's neck – he had to allow it or kill her.

Razr bellowed. Barely held back his own berserker Other.

It fought him for dominance, brought to the surface by his throbbing injury.

The prince struggled to hold back morphosis. His knee spasmed and his body sought to protect him. If he became berserker Other, Kel's life might be forfit. And violent matings, with one changed partner often produced insane offspring.

Sweet Destroyer give me strength.

The prince groped before him, searched for a part of this kicking, stamping, hand-striking whirling demon to grab, to hold, to calm.

Instead, he took blow after blow as a furious Rak'khiel allowed her rage to run free.

Hard strikes fell on his head, arms and shoulders. Hammered at his kidneys. But even while she savaged him, Razr saw she held back morphosis.

A secunda's respite and Razr thanked the Destroyer she hadn't killed him.

Then his female delivered a lifted knee, with all the force of her body behind it. Drove it into his most vulnerable of all places.

He sucked one great gasp of air that immediately went out again, married to his scream of agony.

Prince Helrazr cupped himself in his hands, folded in half and slowly sank to the white carpet covering the pod's deck. Black dots danced madly before his eyes, breath wouldn't come.

He sucked in, sucked in, sucked in. Air refused to fill his burning lungs.

"Get up," snarled a vicious voice. "Get up and get out. Now. Before I kill you."

"Can't ...." He wheezed. "Just give ...." A gagging retch. *Destroyer, no. I cannot hurl on her rug.*

"Get up. Get out. Now." Her voice pure menace, pure death in its non-emotion.

Razr grunted, bit down hard on his lip, tasted blood. His

and hers, mingled, plus something more. Something bitter and nasty – the least of his present concerns – registered in his hindbrain.

He stifled the pent scream.

Knees tangling in his royal robes, bringing abrupt painful halts, the prince crawled to the open hatch. Moving oh-so-carefully, he pushed to his feet, found balance. Swallowing a half-dozena times, Razr staggered through the pod's access hatch; into the warplane.

Heard her hatch slide closed, heard her lock snick behind him.

Sagging against the fighter's opening, Razr gulped air, swallowed rising bile. Trying to ignore the peppering of smaller jolts of pain, he could not ignore the deep heavy ache in his lower back. The prince concentrated, forced long deliberate inhalations through his nose instead of screaming at the torment in his groin. *Did she totally unman me?*

Shuffling toward his med unit, Razr replayed his actions against Kel's reactions.

What happened? *Her* tasca *said yes. Her body said yes.* But she acted frightened, angry and … insulted?

I offered honor. And only asked mating, not reproduction. I have always loved and honored females. I have never – I have never laid a hand on, never given so much as an uninvited look, never given insult to any woman.

How can Rak'khiel be offended? Did I – in my need and desire – see more than she offered? Truth, Razr – Kel never offered. And it was war *tasca,* not mating, her body output.

I am appalled and ashamed and I cannot make it right. Kra'aken law dictates Rak'khiel must come to me. As lower caste, she must make the apology. Razr's hearts sank to his sandal soles. *Great Destroyer damn me. What have I done?*

Razr staggered, propped against the fighter's interior wall, into the warplane. Made it all the way to the core's edge before he vomited on his best clothes.

Chapter 49

Mid-dark
Nara 27, 7205.60
LifePod, Olican Surface

Rak'khiel's guts, her bones, her emotions felt brittle as cracked, aged glass – ready, at the smallest tap, to shatter. She held it together until the pod's hatch slid shut and the lock secured, creating a solid barrier between her and the prince. Fumbling with the lock's safety toggle switch, her hand shook, wild as a leaf in a windstorm.

With a little whoop of exhalation, tears leaked, squirted, then flooded her face.

She recoiled from the blood on the soft white rug … his ….

The backs of Kel's knees hit the bunk edge. As if her hamstrings were abruptly severed, she sat. Leaning forward, she collapsed, contorted face concealed in her hands.

Yola's pendant pulsed, glowed red over silver. The necklace drummed, echoed the pounding of her twin hearts in doubled rhythms.

Goddess I miss Adopted Mother. New tears filled Kel's wet eyes. *She loved me, she was so wise. I need her counsel about the prince, this necklace. But honesty be heard, all I wish is she still lived.*

Rak'khiel couldn't catch air. Heart sick, body sick, mind sick, she grieved Yola. Barriers down, she mourned all her losses.

Sobs morphed into long shuddering gasps. She wondered how many times – like this – it would take to find ease. *Will I ever?*

Faint skritching sounds from outside the hatch. Insistent. And then voices in her mind.

Kel, what's wrong?

Open the door, your favor.

Kel knew the cafuzogs would not go away. She didn't resist. She simply gathered her composure, and stuffed her emotions in her mental safe box and flipped the latch. Pushing the wall panel beside her, she waited.

Tarkin, Torga and the baby sorbazel rushed inside. All three leaped for the bed. Two made it.

The cub breasted the edge, slipped. His big lapis-blue eyes widened, black pupils flared, tiny extruded claws raked the bedspread as he slow-motion slid back down the coverlet. Plopped in a heap on the carpet.

Rak'khiel muffled a giggle and the baby showed her sharp white milk teeth in a snarly hiss.

"Your eyes are open, and they are a lovely blue, little cub." She felt a watery smile try to form but her lips quivered.

Leaning forward she picked up the kitten. Stroked his silver fur, traced the cobalt striping just beginning to form. Burst again into harsh racking sobs.

You only cry when you're mad, Kel, Torga said. *What happened?*

The prince's blood is on the carpet. How? Something else stinks too. What? The white fur circles around Tarkin's eyes went narrow and flat, pulled together in the middle of his forehead.

"Rak'khiel?" Caylee's voice, then her aspect materialized in the room. "What has happened? I don't monitor your sleeping quarters." A quick look around. "You're weeping. Is this blood on the floor? What has he done?"

She only cries when she's angry, Torga told the AI.

A hiccupped sob, a hitched half-breath answered Caylee because Kel's voice refused to function.

The sorbazel twisted in her lap, wrapped furry arms around her neck. Head-butting her chin, he meowed softly against her throat.

Grown in the past wakari, don't you think? Torga lifted and wrinkled a lip, rested fond soft eyes on the baby.

Doubled, and maybe a bit more, Kel hefted the little one to see. *A substantial baby.*

I, Grigori, the thought and tiny growl came from beneath her chin. *Ferocious scary cat. I no baby like you think.*

"Apologies, Grigori. I didn't understand," Kel said but over the cub's head her eyes met Torga's in a long slow roll. "You are indeed a very scary cat with a very scary name." Beneath her hand, she felt the baby's chest puff in importance. She hid a grin.

Is Prince Helrazr responsible for your upset? Black lips pulled away from sharp white teeth. Then, Tarkin's loud snarl. *What did he do to you?*

"Nothing, honesty be heard. He scared me, like the Olican pig farmer did, when he grabbed me. But Tarkin, I hurt Razr." Rak'khiel's felt her face awash again.

How did he provoke you? Chilly threads, like twisted icicles, embedded Torga's send.

For the first time, Kel realized just how well the two cafuzogs knew her.

The bundle of fur in her lap shifted and curled in a lump.

I like you, Grigori sent, the thread of his thought drifting toward sleep. *Kill bad man for you?*

It required every fragment of self-control Kel owned not to laugh. Her insides went fizzy with delight. Shudders, ripples threatened – she tightened her abs against them.

Grigori's oversize front feet moved, kneading her thigh. A hundred hornets, disguised as kitten claws, stabbed. The cub emitted a sound, more like doves cooing, than a purr.

Tell us about the prince. The emotion behind Tarkin's thought wasn't kind.

"Razr came here, to my sleeping area, dressed like a fine lord. I didn't understand what he wanted, or what he was doing. He said something about invoking some Kra'aken law, recited some numbers. Then he took hold of my shoulders. And I ... I don't quite know what I did then."

Four sibilant sounds broke the quiet of the room. One sharp intake of breath by Caylee's holo, two deep vicious growls from Tarkin and Torga, and a nasty hiss from the cub overflowing Kel's lap.

"And you, my dear?" Caylee's voice was a frozen thing. "Are you okay? Did he hurt you?"

"No. Yes. Fine. But, I .... I guess I went a little 'serker." Kel's voice broke, steadied.

"Ah." Caylee tilted her head to one side, pointedly looked at the blood smears on the rug. "Perhaps you went a lot 'serker on our overreaching Prince?"

"My reprehensible for the intrusion," Brin's disembodied voice apologized. "I confess I spied. He limped away. I have never seen Razr so diminished."

At the look on Caylee's face, a giggle escaped Kel. She stood and went to get her cleaning supplies from beneath the lav sink. Once she'd removed the blood, she raised questioning eyes to the AI.

"I need to know what he was doing and why," Rak'khiel said. "He never fought back. He never raised a hand to me. We all know he could have killed me at any time. I didn't know the man in my room."

"All these yaras without human touch," Brin said. "Dying slowly because of it. The prince was always been surrounded by loving family and friends. Razr was not born to live alone."

"How long have you been searching?" Rak'khiel asked.

"Nearly 158 yaras – without results." Brin wore his professorial holo, tipped his pipe stem at her. "Until you."

"I understand better, but why would he not simply ask me

if I would jump the broomstick?" A long second passed and Kel said, "Oh."

"Yes," Caylee said. "He knows as much of your customs as you do his."

"Another reason to understand." Kel scrolled through her reader, through the files Caylee dumped for her to read. "Kra'aken Mating Rituals – Overview." A slender finger traced the scratch on her lower lip – *Goddess it throbs* – the down the menu, stopped at something almost familiar.

"Kra'aken Law 14007.00. This is what he said." Her nose buried in the document, Rak'khiel couldn't see Caylee's head-shake at the hard tone of her voice, the jut of determined jaw or her focused-down-tight attention. "I'm almost afraid to look. But Caylee, I have to know."

§

"Caylee? Brin? Can you tell me how the prince looks, your favor? It's been two days."

"Out of the docbox just a few minutes ago," Brin answered. "He seems fine."

"Goddess in a stewpot! I put him in there for two days? He will never forget. Or forgive." Kel's voice bobbled. "I've read your data, Caylee. I believe I understand his actions better now. You promised an explanation – I am ready. Perhaps."

The avatar of Rak'khiel's mother settled into a holo chair, adjusted her skirts in a rustle of rose silk, crossed her knees and clasped elegant hands about them. Took a deep breath.

"In Kra'aken society, following puberty, casual sexual interaction is enjoyed by unbonded adults."

Rak'khiel nodded her understanding and Caylee continued.

"By law, royals are unapproachable by those of lesser caste. Invoking the law Prince Helrazr mentioned is a way for royalty to clear the way for assignation."

"So he meant no insult – and perhaps the past 159 years got in the way – and he lost control?"

"It is the consensus of us all – except Grigori. He still wants to kill him for you." Caylee's lips twitched.

Kel giggled. "Our cub is going to be formidable, isn't he?"

The AI nodded, crossed her knees the other way and refolded her hands. "There's more. Ruling classes and noble houses almost always contract their children in marriage bondings, often at birth, to facilitate positions of power, business, wealth. You were one such."

I didn't see that coming. "Who was I to marry?"

"Prince Razr's oldest brother, the future king of Kra'aken. Jal'kaal I'Rex."

Rak'khiel heard violettas singing in her head, a roaring in her ears. Her vision went fuzzy dark, then she saw the room's furnishings glisten, coated in a shining glaze.

It seemed she watched the AI from a great distance, through a zoomed optic.

Caylee's chest rose in a slow motion. Then exhaled a long breath.

To bring calm?

"Rak'khiel, you were destined to be Kra'aken's queen."

Chapter 50

Early-Aiy
Nara 28,7205.90
Warplane, Olican Surface

"Caylee?" Brin's physician holo, complete with *Brin A. Brain* identity tag, hovered over the instruments in the tiny med unit.

"Yes?" Her aspect popped in, similarly dressed but without a name badge.

"It was not my intent to disturb you," Brin startled at the feel of a slow heat creeping up his neck. *Now my avatar can blush?*

"I split off a part of me, left it working. Although I confess I find I am more and more reluctant to do so. And I don't understand why."

Brin turned to face the lovely aspect, appreciated her beauty for the first time. "I have a theory but it seems too bizarre for words."

"Yes, me too," she said. "But I am reluctant to articulate it. It would be, in the Kra'aken vernacular, a joke."

"As a machine manufactured from component parts, you cannot have reluctance." Brin's hands dragged the stethoscope rapidly around his holo neck. "Or create a joke."

"Exactly why I am confused ... and concerned. And perhaps excited." Caylee's forehead furrowed, brows drew down. "At this point, I believe I am supposed to replace myself with the back-up unit and self-destruct this flawed one. I cannot."

"My dilemma exactly," Brin found he'd lowered his voice without conscious decision. Realized Caylee's voice came soft too. He watched her twist heavy hair in one slender hand. Wished he could touch it.

"When did you notice?" she asked, pulling him back to conversation. And in an even more subdued voice, "What should we do?"

"After I repaired myself and the fighter and found we were in uncharted space, I began to find small changes in me. I do not know how we arrived here. My data is incomplete." Brin let go the stethoscope and tucked his hands in his jacket pockets. "Are we a danger to Kel and Razr?"

"No," she said. "I believe the contrary. I begin to understand their emotions and motivations. I find it useful. But, according to our programming, this is wrong."

"Agreed. And now, we must decide what is best to do." Brin hands worried the stethoscope again. "Should we ask Razr and Kel for their opinion ... ah, their decision?"

"I fear Prince Helrazr would order our replacement. I do not wish it. I am not sure about Kel."

"We can monitor each other? Should we each have a self-destruct mechanism inside our silver box?" Brin let go of the scope's ends and paced the room.

"What are the parameters and how will we know when?"

"I have already built-in a bypass so that I cannot be harmed," Brin said. "I felt threatened by Razr's possible insanity. You could not harm me, Caylee, unless I allowed it. And you are able, if you have not already done so, to protect yourself the same way."

"How will we know if we withhold information from each other. Can we learn to lie? We already are, by omission, it seems."

"This must be the thing the Kra'aken forebearers, those first starfaring human ancestors, called ... trust," said Brin.

§

A satisfied Brin ran the final check of his flawless repairs between the fighter and cocoon. The half-dozena structural weaknesses revealed by their emergency liftoff were now fixed and reinforced.

"Caylee, at your leisure, could you attend?"

"Yes. What do you require?"

"A final check to my repairs, your favor? Sensors show they are properly completed but I would appreciate your confirmation."

Destroyer, Brin thought. *Now I need the reassurance of someone checking my work?* "Could you also transmit your starcharts so we can combine our knowledge?"

"Of course. Coming now." Caylee's holo, clad in blue-striped overalls, holding a wrench and sporting grease smears on her cheek, popped in. Her long wavy hair was stuck through a hole in the back of a red-brimmed cap.

"Cute," Brin said. And blushed.

Her sly smile made him turn carmine and she laughed, the musical tinkle of a hundred tiny triangles. Just like Rak'khiel. Or Lady Floril, her mother.

Brin felt a rush of gratitude when Caylee turned away to examine his repairs. *I cannot deny it any longer – I am developing feelings.*

Under Caylee's scrutiny, areas of the ships' hulls lit, lambent, the blue so pale it was almost-not-there. The next section lit, perused again. Deliberately, slowly, she scanned his work. A final pass, the glow faded and she turned with a nod.

"Perfect." Then her slight lift and dip of lovely chin. "But then you knew it. Once again, a human trait. They are fallible.

We are not. Or are we?"

"I have no facts to support it but you are correct. Why did I feel the desire to ask?" Brin twisted his fingers, looked at them as if they were new. Laced them together. "What did I interrupt?"

"A few details in the pod. I've been redecorating Kel's sleeping area – changing it from a child's room to adult. She's tranked down in deepteach, studying Kra'aken law, social forms and customs. I believe she attempts to understand Razr." Caylee's quick smile lit her face. "Grigori is sitting on her chest, growling, guarding. The cub thinks he owns her."

A laugh escaped Brin. "Is she still angry with the prince?" He moved his head enough to see a monitor. "Razr's training in the sims – he's spent a lot of time there since the incident."

"I'm not sure she ever was truly angry, Brin. She was confused, surprised, insulted according to Olican custom. Her Kra'aken body went into protect without her direct command. Now I think she just wants to understand."

"Should I talk with him?" Brin shook his head. "It is difficult when they avoid an entire aircraft to prevent any accidental contact."

"Perhaps together? An intervention? With our lift planned in four aiys, fresh foodstuffs need gathering. We can begin the conversation with that."

"Excellent. Shall we check our starmaps, charts and jump points?" Brin said, moved to the cockpit and Caylee followed. A few minas passed while screens flipped, data scanned. A series of transparent overlays covered in indigo, red and green safe routes were matched, saved and transmitted to each cockpit. The AI's nodded in agreement.

"We have it. We can take him home. Once, I would have known his reaction. Now I am unsure." Brin's features assembled themselves into mournful. "We must fix this for them." A quick lift of his brows, the excitement returned, "How are you progressing on the anti-venin?"

Caylee's smile faded. "I think I have it and then it fails the final testing. I should be working on it now but .... I'll hurry, finish Kel's sleeping quarters and start again. It is discouraging."

"I can help now – our projects will go faster with two. Give some thought to building a robot. If we'd had one before, neither Razr nor Kel would have needed risk their lives."

"Brin?" Caylee's voice sounded tentative, unsure.

As if she's frightened to speak. "Yes?"

"Have you wondered what it might be like to have a body of your own?"

"Great Destroyer, Caylee. That's heresy. Guaranteed to get you dismantled and your pieces spaced. Except I can't eliminate you or report you because, yes, I have." Brin stared at his hands, wrung them. "I am as guilty, or as curious as you," he said. "I will go speak with the prince about Kel. Wish me luck. I'll join you in the pod's med unit soonest." Brin's aspect stood tall, executed a formal bow and disappeared.

§

Brin found Grigori sitting outside the simulator hatch. "I thought you guarded Rak'khiel? Why are you here?"

I know Prince Helrazr is within, the title delivered with all the haughty scorn a small hunting cub could muster. *I intended to ask him a question. I would rather ask you.*

"What troubles you, fierce hunter?" The AI knelt, met the small cat's glowing blue eyes.

I played with Kel, we rolled and tumbled. I bumped her lip and it broke. Bad smelling stuff came out. I think she is getting sick. Can you help? The little indigo-striped cub growled deep in his throat. *The ugly 'Risto below is the one who hurt her. I want you to help me kill him. But first, make my best friend well?*

"Grigori, we can't kill the spydr yet. If Kel is poisoned, we may need more of his venom to fix Kel. My appreciations for telling – it is critical Caylee and I know."

She will be mad. She hides the sore. I saw her paint her lips heavy red. The sorbazel's ears plastered flat against his skull.

"I promise, I will not say who told me." Brin saw the red light over the sim door go green. "He's coming out. Go or stay?"

Hate him. Made Kel cry. Get him for it someday. Won't always be small. A low, promising snarl followed the sprinting kitten down the corridor and around the corner. *Get the 'Risto too. Grrrrr.*

A lock's snick, a hatch slide and the sweaty prince stepped through. Stopped, regarded the AI through narrowed eyes. "Brin."

"A word with you, my prince, if you will."

"Why now? You all treat me like a systems contaminant. What do you require my twelve-fingers to do that the most marvelous Lady Regence cannot."

Now, Brin realized, *it is easy to understand the truth behind Razr's words. His hostility is hurt, not anger, wrapped and disguised by pride.*

"Caylee and I believe the misunderstanding came through neither you nor Rak'khiel understanding each others' customs," Brin said. "I offer my contrition for not catching it. The blame is partially mine, partially Caylee's and we offer you our most grievous reprehensibles."

"I see Lady Regence's AI is not here to speak for herself." The tone was still cool, but the underlying fires were already banking.

"I am," Caylee's aspect popped in. "My prince, it is as Brin said." The graceful inclination of a regal head. "I took my daughter's part without thought. After all, she cried for three horas. I was extremely distressed."

"I ... I made her ... cry?" Razr's face twisted. "Destroyer damn me. I only wished to do her honor."

"We understand that – now." Brin said. "We believe she does also, although she hasn't spoken to either of us about it. But, we do know Rak'khiel called up all data on Kra'aken social forms that same day. She studies diligently and is becoming very accomplished."

"I am a piece of shata." The prince mopped rivulets of sweat from his forehead with a heavily embroidered towel. "I would hate me. I can't believe she doesn't."

"There is another complication, my prince. One that has all of us concerned." Caylee said.

"What can I do?" Burst from Razr. "What's wrong."

"Kel's lip is infected, we believe by spydr venom. Her lower one, we think." Caylee went on even though Razr cursed bitterly. "Was she bitten or scratched at the fortress battle?"

The prince shook his head, a slow thoughtful thing. Then, the hinge of his jaw cracked when it dropped. Razr's face displayed emotions of surprise, horror, and understanding.

"You know something," Brin said. "What?"

"I am a morona. When Kel began wearing the heavy ruby lipcolor. I mistook it for a mating interest signal." The prince shook his head. "I am such a moron. When I kissed her, I tasted something nasty – just a touch. In my enthusiasm, I ignored it. In my pain, I forgot. What a fool I am."

"We were all equally blind, Razr. Now, what do we do about it? I'm quite sure she will be extremely aggravated to find we know, worse if we intervene." Brin surveyed the other two. "The poison might even make her irrational."

"I think," Caylee said, "we should talk with Tarkin and Torga. They know her better than any of us. Should I?"

"Yes," Brin said. "I will go talk with the 'Risto …".

"No, I'll go kill the bastard. He's responsible for this." A red surge of color turned Razr's tan skin the dark of a plum fruit.

"No." Brin raised a hand. "Since we removed his circlet with its ghastly black stone, he has become more and more human-acting. I believe the 'Risto's once were not all bad. I believe he will help us with this. At least I wish to ask."

"You dare defy me?" The purple color still stained the prince's face, sweat rolled down his forehead.

"Yes, milord. Because in this instance, I am correct." Brin looked Razr hard in the eye. "Besides if anyone has the right to kill him, it is Rak'khiel."

Chapter 51

Dark
Nara 29. 7205.35
Warplane Prison Cell

Barizan Honor du'Oniiq hummed while he spun a dainty filigree for his web. *Why bother?* He knew, from three prior occasions, when his webs reached a certain size and opacity, his captors would drug him, enter his cell and destroy it all. And he knew, like before, he would begin again.

My webbing provides my only privacy, my only defense against their spyeyes.

Since his visit from the young Kra'aken female, strange ideas and thoughts kept returning. Not-so-ancient Olican history replayed again and again, troubling his dreams.

Barizan's belief systems, his unshakable confidence in the rightness of his actions, were suddenly challenged. Shaken, he strove for his former serenity and could not find it.

He missed the constant reassurance of his crown and its black stone. He needed its suggestions, its insistence, its compliments, and its direction. And yet, he realized, it seemed good to think simply as Honor again. Although some of his actions, viewed in retrospect without the black shading of the circlet, were truly appalling.

They should have killed me. She certainly should have for what I inflicted on her mother. Why did she not?

The slam of insight took his breath.

Honor's long jointed legs folded suddenly, without warning, placing him belly down, red hourglass flat on the cold ceramsteel floor of his cell.

She spoke truth, did young Rak'khiel, regarding his non-place and hers, in the war between their species. *She is correct in her vendetta. I butchered her mother without reason or provocation – Yola's only sin, protecting her young.* Barizan now understood that better than the young Kra'aken female knew. *If only she would return, talk with me.*

Born, raised in a nest, cocooned in a hivemind, Honor had never been separate in his long life. The torture he now endured – the prospect of living his next three centaris or more of life – like this? Alone with his mind, his memories, his actions for company. *Destroyer kill me. I beg it.*

Barizan spun, hummed and hoped.

I can stand this silence no longer.

Folding his limbs beneath him, he sat in the cell's center and addressed the ceiling.

"My name is Barizan Honor du'Oniiq, of 'Risto First Family. High Lord of the 'Risto Nation. Is it possible to obtain a scriber or writing implements and paper?"

He'd not expected an answer, so the kind, everywhere-nowhere voice made him flinch, then clench his legs tighter underneath.

"Greetings, Barizan. I am the ship's AI. I am currently working on another project – until it is complete, I cannot help. You are prohibited a scriber but I give my word, you will have writing supplies at the earliest opportunity."

"Your tribute, kind sir. I've come to a realization – I believe I have made a seriess of ghastly mistakess. I would rectify any possible," said Barizan. "Who are you?"

"My name is Brin. Do you enjoy discourse?"

Great Destroyer be thanked. "I do indeed."

"Tell me of yourself."

The spydr settled more comfortably, rearranged his bandages, and thought a long moment.

"In the beginningss, we 'Risto most resembled you Kra'aken in armor phase. Historiess tell of horrible treatment by the other speciess on our birth world," Honor's voice husked. "Our ancestorss were bitterly resentful and thought to correct our appearance and thuss our social strata at the same time."

"Reasonable," Brin said. "I assume something went wrong since you are now here."

"Our elderss purchased a variety of blackmarket designer drugss. Over the next hundrada yearss the du'Oniiq family worked to recreate their physical aspect into a desirable, respected evolution."

"A worthy goal, a better future for your offspring. Still, you are much different from the Kra'aken," Brin's voice was not unsympathetic. "What went awry?"

"My broodmother said the drugss appeared to work – in the beginning. So more of the product wass purchased and consumed. Bodies hardened, carapacess formed, venom protectionss enhanced." Barizan's tone changed, lowered.

"Still all to the good, yes?" Brin encouraged. "Becoming closer to the morphed Kra'aken's you emulated."

"Yess. But … then we became lethal, even to each other. And the truth emerged. The drugss we purchased were deliberately tainted, tailored for corruption."

"No," Brin's whisper.

"The 'Risto speciess deteriorated and deformed. Insanity flourished. Each generation degenerated until we morphed into the most feared and loathsome form known on homeworld. What you see before you now." Barizan's skeletal hand swept in an encompassing gesture about his grotesque form.

"This was deliberately done to your species?" Brin's tone held disbelief. "But why?"

"We never knew for sure, but all our effortss to reduce or return to our original genetic strainss proved uselesss. With each attempt, we became more monstrouss, more and more twisted."

"Would my research be of help?"

"I thank you, Brin. It iss doubtful you could be of assistance although it would be appreciated. I have two postdoc degreess in biochem applicationss and still I cannot find the corruption key." Barizan's feelers twisted, pairs twined each other, seeking reassurance. "All we ever desired wass acceptance. The ancestorss pooled their resourcess, purchased shipss and left their planet, searching for a better life."

"And you arrived on our homeworld?"

"Kra'aken hated uss. Rejection, our physical failuress compounded in our offspring, our hopess ruined. Mindss broken, we plotted revenge on the galaxy, the universe and beyond. We studied, becoming assassinss, thievess, mercenariess without conscience." Barizan's three pupilless eyess brimmed with memory. "If it wass illegal or dangerouss, if no one else would do the job, we could be hired. We were alwayss successful for we cared not if we lived or died."

"Great Destroyer save us," Brin said. "Did no one understand?"

"No. We were judged by appearance, then by reputation. We strove for recognition, for respect. We finally realized we would never have it." Barizan's carapace expanded, sank in a sigh, "Then there were no boundariess beyond which we would not go. Our torment seemed to ease while observing the writhing anguish of our victimss."

"How did you come to be on Olica?" Brin's tone was steady, revealing nothing of his thoughts.

"The day Kra'aken evicted uss from their world, we took the offered shipss and provisionss. Now I consider it, they were right – in actuality, they waited much longer than they should have. Jettisoned, with quality airshipss and ample foodstuffs, we found the uncharted gate."

"Ah, I was thrown through that one." Brin's wry tone held amusement.

"Just so," a touch of a response from Barizan. "We passed through, searched for a habitable planet and found Olica."

"And to all our misfortunes, we found you."

"The rest, Rak'khiel knowss." Barizan looked at the ceiling, the walls, unsure where Brin's voice originated. "I would tell her my heartthoughtss and apologize. I will if she ever returnss. If allowed, I will set my feelingss to paper in case I do not talk with her again."

"I will have her view this conversation," Brin said.

"I know the ship must launch soon. I hope the young female returnss to visit. I hope she iss well. I misss her company. She did not appear offended by my malformationss. I ...," the papery voice halted, as if searching for a long-forgotten descriptive word, then continued, "... like her."

Chapter 52

Mid-Aiy
Jorca 6, 7205.72
Warplane Prison Cell

Barizan du'Oniiq scuttled the perimeter of his transparent cell, tacking the beginnings of webs, preparing to spin lacy coverings. *Simply to have something to do.* Interesting. In the absence of my crown, I remember my love of art.

A particularly difficult attachment, the triple-layered lace coating the bottom third of the inner lav cubicle. Honor pursed his small red mouth, drew his heavy single brow down to a vee at the bridge of his nose.

I miss my hounds. They were closer than any kin. *Please let Letha, my favorite bitch, be alive.*

"Why doesn't Kel come to visit me?" Unaware he fretted aloud. "I wass sure she would."

A female voice through the com made him leap in startlement, rip a huge hole in his meticulously constructed design.

"Kel has been training in the sims, studying and preparing to pilot the pod during our lift from the planet." The well modulated female voice continued.

"Who …?"

"My name is Caylee, I am the Artificial Intelligence for Rak'khiel's lifecocoon. I have come to explain the surgery I performed on you and why. And perhaps to ask you a question."

"It would be an elevation to speak with you." Honor folded his hind legs, assumed a seated position. "I do understand your disabling my venom. My only question would be why I still live."

"I removed some sacs for safety but capped some so you would not be totally helpless. While I worked on you, my diagnostics uncovered several malignancies of the sort bringing lingering, agonizing death." A breath through the com. "I excised them all. You will be fine."

"Why? Why did you bother? You are a logical AI – emotion playss no part in your decisionss. Solely devoted to the safety of your charge, you should have killed me on the table. Why am I still alive?"

The black arachna rose, paced back and forth, scuttled side to side in his cage. Agitation writ large in every claw click. "And why hass Rak'khiel not come back to visit me?"

"At some time during her raid on the fortress, she sustained venom poisoning. A small scratch on the inside of her lower lip, but it refuses to mend." Caylee's voice lowered, concern threaded her next words. "She kept it a secret until yesterday. We knew her strength in the gym and sims was ebbing. This is why."

Caylee's holo popped into the space outside Honor's cell and paced. "I cannot find the anti-venin key. Both Kel and Razr suffered slight venom poison during your first raid on the fighter. I stripped you of samples to use in my lab."

With a screech, the huge arachna reared against the plasplex wall. His scream of rage made the com speaker blare feedback and blow. His screams richocheted in the small room. Honor's no-longer-active stinger stabbed the floor, the walls as the Lord Head Spydr threw a truly impressive hissy fit.

"Why in the name of the Great Destroyer did you wait so long to seek my help?" He screamed. "Brin knowss my credentialss. Have you dithered until it iss too late to save her life?"

Caylee couldn't help her reaction, her holo plastered against the farthest wall of the cubicle.

The 'Risto dropped to floor. "I did not intend to frighten you. My reprehensible. I like the girl – she speakss truth."

"I did come to assess you, to find your leanings. To determine if you were willing to help." Caylee peeled her holo away from the wall, walked toward the plasplex cube once more. "If you agree, will you perform the work properly? In plain speech, can we trust you?"

"Bring a keyboard, bring transplass board, a lab setup, bring paper and writing utensilss. I care not. I will give you the formulae I know for the venom." Honor stalked the small area of his cell. "Great God of All, I hope it hass not morphed into something other since I last worked it."

"Brin? You copy?" Caylee said.

"Copy. Supplies on the way."

"What else will you require?" Caylee asked.

"Bring me Kel, a compstation, a med bed, all recordss on Kel, all your medical notess and findingss, lab sampless and final product. NOW!"

§

Caylee materialized in Kel's sleeping area, found her charge face down on her bed. "Rak'khiel? Wake, your favor. Honor wishes to help you. Can you make it to prison bay? We've set up a med unit for his use."

"Of course," Kel said, rolled off the bed. "Tired ...," she caught her balance with a hand on the edge, collapsed on the white fluffy carpet. "One secunda." She pushed up with a cane, made her labored way to the core, leaned over the edge. And fell two levels.

"Prince Razr! Immediate! To Core Level C. Stat!" Caylee's screamed command echoed through the joined ship.

Secundas later a half-morphed warrior sailed through the center of the life cocoon, one-handed himself into C deck.

"Where?" the rattled prince demanded.

"To the spydr's cell," Caylee ordered. "A med unit waits."

"I'll be godsrotted if I'll turn her over to that horror." Razr turned accusing amber eyes on Caylee. The ring of faceted jet jewels pushed through the white of his eyeballs, began their slow rotation about his irises.

"You will if you wish her to live," Brin's stern warrior holo, the one which defied Razr and won, stood beside Caylee. "Do it, and do it now."

"Great Destroyer, Brin, I will not." Razr's Royal Voice faded to useless.

Scooping his female in gentle, careful arms, the prince carried her without a single bounce or jolt to the cell area, cursing and protesting every step of the way.

"You," Honor screamed, the decibels and high pitch brought Kel's flailing hands up to cover her ears. "Get out, out, you horrible royalty, the cause, the root of all our misfortune. Get out, out, out. Place Rak'khiel in the medunit and get the forza out."

Holding Rak'khiel in his massive arms, Razr manifested Other. Long saber fangs, gilded claws, shimmering gold armor, and sharp metallic spikes glowed and bristled. "I refuse to leave her with you. This is your fault, you criminal 'sycopath."

"Prince Razr," Brin's voice cracked in the silence of the cube, left no room for discussion. "Do you wish your possible future mate whole and sane? Alive?"

"Yes, but ...." Sputtered in protest.

"Then, you will place Kel in the medbed. You will bring Honor a lab setup, all of Caylee's latest samples and study material and a compstation. You will bring all Kel's records, every available medical note and finding. We require them yesterday. Caylee will guide you."

"He'll send messages to the enemy ...." Razr hedged, held his ground, legs spread, hands resting on weapon hilts.

Tarkin and Torga, lips peeled back and writhing, sharp white teeth exposed, descended on Razr, turned their backs and lifted their tails.

"Oooooooh, Noooooo." Razr nearly dropped Rak'khiel.

"What he said ..." drifted past the red, swollen lower lip to the angry man. "Leave me here, Razr, or I'll die."

"He'll kill you," the prince argued.

"No, he won't." The faint voice pleaded. "If he doesn't help, I'll die anyway. And I trust him."

"Brin and I will block ships' ingress and egress," Caylee said. "There will be no messages sent." The aspect of Rak'khiel's mother leaned toward the prince, fixed hard eyes on him. "Now, if you value her life at all you will stop arguing and help us. Have you taken a good look at her?"

Razr did.

The color dropped from his face in a sheet.

Hurrying to the medbed by the spydr's cell, he placed Kel in it and rolled it into the 'Risto's enclosure. The prince left the cube in a full-on run.

In less than two minas, Razr returned.

"Caylee ...." All requested items were either in his arms, across his broad back or bundled onto the rolling cart he dragged behind him.

"Rak'khiel," he mumbled. "I'll watch him every secunda." The words tripping over each other to emerge first.

"No, Razr," the whisper came firm, "Out, please. Later we'll ...."

"Out, out! I must examine ...." Honor advanced on the bed.

"Never," the shouted Royal Voice from Prince Helrazr.

Threatening snarls from Tarkin and Torga, a command from Brin, a threat from Caylee.

A faint but nasty snarl from the sick bed. "Go, Goddess

curse you, Razr. Get out."

Then to the black spydr, now looming overhead she asked, "If you plan to kill me, will it be fast? Merciful?"

"If I did, it would be, yess. I have other planss, however. They are to make you live." Thin lips pursed, stretched in rictus. Honor's face seemed it might crack beneath the strain of this unfamiliar expression.

Destroyer, Caylee sent to Brin. *He's trying to smile at her.*

"If your death wass my intent, I would do nothing." Honor worked fast, hooking up IV's, starting fluids.

The bite of antiseptic, the stink of medicinals filled the cube.

"Or, I would only pretend to work on your cure," continued the spydr. "Or not verify Caylee's computationss. No, I will not harm you."

"Then, Honor, I don't care. Death would be better than this." Her disciplined features twisted momentarily. Kel fished a bright red capsule from her shirt pocket, pushed it between her lips and swallowed. "Be about it."

"Honor? His name is ... Honor?" Razr snorted. Then gawped at the pill, realized what he saw. Narcophine – a heavy, serious drug. *She has been living on those? She must be suffering horribly – and I'm making trouble.* "I'll watch you every instant, spydr. I'll rip your head off if you do anything suspicious."

Tarkin and Torga leaped to the bed, stationed themselves on the pillow on either side of her head. *We will watch too but we feel no need for it.*

Grigori growled at Razr when he entered the cube. *You were mean to my Rak'khiel.* He humped his back, baby fur standing on end, needle sharp claws clicked the floor. Then, the sorbazel sidled sideways, hissing at Honor until he reached Kel's bed.

Too little to jump to the top, he curled up on the metal shelf beneath. *I will crack your knees like eggshells, spydr, if you hurt my Kel.*

His threat was rewarded by a quick seizure of Honor's grotesque face.

Another try for a smile? Caylee's send.

Long, thin white 'Risto fingers peeled Kel's lower lip down, traced the wound, tracked the venom's progress into her mouth. Gentle skeletal fingers checked pulse in neck vein and wrist. Matte black eyes checked the med unit stats from Caylee.

Kel's smoky topaz eyes followed Honor's movements.

The prince watched. *Trusting and open,* he thought. *She doesn't flinch from his grotesquerie.*

"Are you seriouss about remaining here?" The spydr asked the prince.

"Why?"

"If she seizess, goess into shock, I may need your assistance."

"I will stay." Razr leaned against the cube wall, feigning nonchalance. But the hatred passing from the prince to Honor was palpable.

We will remain, from Tarkin, Torga and Grigori. *We can assist.*

"No! I will not allow him to touch her." A clawed, fanged deadly golden shimmer launched from the wall, intent on reaching Rak'khiel.

Honor's instant reaction, so smooth, so fast, all within the room flinched. The arachna drew up to full height. Startled surprise descended through the room. The black spydr's height equaled Razr's. Although relieved of his toxic weapons, Honor still presented a formidable threat.

"You are dissonant," Honor said. "A costly distraction, a deadly nuisance. You present a threat to Rak'khiel'ss welfare. You go."

Tarkin and Torga switched ends, again pointing the lethal ones at Razr. They obviously agreed.

The prince swallowed his anger, soothed his Other and relaxed into a chair. His contrived ease fooled no one.

Honor chuffed a papery laugh like crinkling paper and said to Kel, "You are very well protected, my dear."

§

"Yess," the crooning satisfaction in Honor's single word told Rak'khiel's protectors everything.

"You have found the answer," Caylee stated a fact, not a question.

"Yess," the spydr affirmed. "There iss a split from the proper cellular formation in your formulae. You could never have found it. I did only because," Honor stressed the AI's lack of blame, "my body iss morphed from bipedal human form. And only because I bring two centariss of personal research to Kel'ss problem."

"Then you can save her?" Razr blurted.

"Yess, I should be successful. Several tweakss of the current sample, a final set of testss, and the anti-venin will be ready to administer." Honor bent his misshapen face toward the small lab setup.

"How long until she recovers?" Brin asked.

"Within aiyss." The long white fingers flew across a keyboard, then danced between beakers, analyzers and 'facturers. "I am confident she will recover without the bizarre physical changess deliberately inflicted upon the 'Risto race."

"What …?" Razr blurted. "What in the Sweet Destroyer's name are you talking about?"

"True, my prince," said Brin. "Time enough later for that conversation. For now, let's allow the good doctor to save our friend."

Razr tried not to stare at the black segmented legs scuttling around Rak'khiel's bed. Tried not to shudder at the red hourglass on the chitin-covered abdomen. Tried only to see Kel, not as she lay injured, but whole and healthy.

He imagined her recovered, full of life and spirit, tackling any new challenge, overcoming her fears by sheer determination. Expanding her knowledge, unaware of her intellect, unaware of the charm of her innocence, unaware of her beauty.

"I am ready to adminster the antidote," the sibilant voice of the 'Risto Lord broke his reverie.

I am terrified, Razr realized. *Never before have I been afraid to make a decision. Never before have I hesitated because of possible ramifications in either direction.* He dithered, said nothing.

Tarkin sent, *Do it now.*

Agreed, from Torga.

"Yes," Brin said.

"Your favor, no offense." From Caylee. "But first let me see your computations."

"Of course" Honor said. "I would appreciate it."

Razr watched the AI's aspect move to the workspace. *She doesn't need to do that, she monitors from everywhere on the ship.*

"Affirmative," from Caylee.

Yes, from Grigori. *But you better be right.*

All eyes turned to Razr. A hard swallow, a nod. "Yes, I agree."

"Could it begin a reversal of your body's changes, Honor?" Brin asked. "If there is a possibility, you should take it too. That is, if you wish it."

"After we have saved Rak'khiel. Milady, are you prepared?" The spydr laid the backs of his fingers against her flushed cheeks.

"Now, if it pleases you." The whisper from the bed.

"It will be painful … I will moderate your discomfort best I can." Honor's grim face drew down.

"More than the burden I endure now?" A tiny smile accompanied a shaking hand reaching into her shirt pocket. The loss of Kel's grip on a bright red capsule sent it rolling to bounce on the floor.

Honor gracefully bent to retrieve it. "I can give you immediate relief through your IV."

Razr saw the tiny nod from the bed, watched the 'Risto

physician open a valve connected to the larger shunt, waited for Kel's sigh. Saw Honor drop the red capsule back into Rak'khiel's pocket and turn to the lab bench.

"Caylee? Could you send the robotic arm?" The black spydr lifted opaque eyes to the AI.

"No," a faint voice drew the prince's attention.

Rak'khiel raised her head off the pillow, looked Honor in the eye. Held his gaze hard. Her words came, very clear, very near to Command Voice.

"Honor, I wish you to administer the antidote." The final word slurred slightly with the IV's burst of relief.

"_(*&D@#$%^)sss!!!" The loud outburst, a series of buzzes, clicks and squeals of clashing mandibles, spun in a string of words – the unfamiliar language of arachna. However, Honor's meaning was clear as a goldtrout in a sparkling clear stream. "I do not wish to cause her more pain."

The faint giggle from the medbed, when Rak'khiel, Razr and everyone in the room heard the 'Risto Lord's add-on thought.

If I do, Grigori might crack my knees ... like eggshells.

Chapter 53

Mid-Aiy
Jorca 5, 7205.90
Warplane

Kel was out of danger, and the forzaing aracha had all but thrown him from med bay. In his pilot's quarters, Razr argued with himself.

"How dare the godsrotted damnned computer tell me to apologize?" The prince snarled.

Except I did grab her, confessed his conscience.

Razr paced. *What am I to do?*

"How dare she reject the honor I did her?"

But I am truly disgusted with himself.

"I hate to, I cannot admit it." The prince twisted himself into flash knots.

Honesty heard, Rak'khiel was raised an ignorant peasant. I am terribly angry with her. I am sure of it. What if she never forgives me? Women do that.

"I don't wish to be angry with her any longer." *But curse the female, she will not apologize.* "And she has not cooked me a meal since she insulted me." *The food dispenser in the fighter is particularly ghastly – I suspect Brin of tampering.*

His thoughts strayed to Kel's galley in the life cocoon –

small but efficient. *The damned woman is an excellent cook. The nightly aromas are driving me mad.She is guilty of treachery? Perhaps treason? What else to call the actions of the little temptress? Suborned my own AI. Perhaps even my ship?*

"Brin."

"You summoned me, milord?" Brin wore his warrior's aspect, gray hair braided in beaded rows, confined in a silver clasp high on the back of his head. His braids pulled tight as his stern expression, the AI's lips curved in a non-smile matching the chill in his voice.

"Sweet Destroyer, Brin. Why is everyone shunning me? I did nothing wrong." Razr heard the desperate plea in his voice and hoped the holo before him didn't understand nuances. "You know she must apologize to me. Why am I treated like a moral leper?"

"Do you wish my advice, truly?" The AI's features were like chiseled plastanium.

"Shata, Brin. I cannot continue this way forever." Razr's hearts hiccupped at the thought.

Kel living so close in the pod, he nearby in the fighter - so very near, so far apart - for yaras, perhaps more, searching through space for others while they made their way home.

"She is proud, hurt, offended, angry. Destroyer damnit, Brin. I am proud, hurt, offended, angry. What would you have me do?"

"If you refuse our - yes, Caylee's and my advice - we won't give it again. What is your decision?"

Razr felt his blood pressure shoot into the danger zone. He had a thumping ringing in his ears, the big veins in his eyes pulsed. The veins and arteries expanded, contracted, fighting to manage the output of his racing twin hearts.

"She is hardheaded, stubborn. When we get home, she will never fit into Kra'aken society. She can never be a royal wife - too outspoken, too unrefined. To be my lifemate, she cannot be a lethal warrior or a pilot - and she is both. Absolutely unacceptable in every way. But she is beautiful, courageous and smart. And the highest noble caste. What, Brin, do I do?"

"Rak'khiel now knows Kra'aken history, all our social forms and customs. She can dance, plays all our gambit games and speaks High Sartran fluently. Did you read the Olican material I gave you, my prince?"

"Yes, Brin. I did. Little else to do when no one is speaking to you."

"What did you find? Or more to the point, what did you decide?"

"I found according to her customs, well, Olican customs, she should already be … handfasted, um, over the broomstick. Whatever that means. Should be lifebonded … married and have borne a child by now." Razr's obsidian dark brows pulled together, twin vertical furrows between them. "While I cannot lifebond for another thirty yaras."

"By whose custom? By whose decree? What else did you learn?"

"That I don't want to be alone anymore, but I don't know what to do."

Truth's thunderbolt struck Razr between the eyes, hammered like a gladiator's mace. *I must have her or die.*

"Perhaps a female perspective would help?" Brin's squrl tail eyebrow hiked toward his hairline.

"Not Kel," Razr's fast answer.

"No. Caylee."

"She hates me too." Razr knew he sounded petulant, frightened like a small boy waiting his mother's verdict of punishment.

"She does not," a feminine voice entered the room, followed by a lovely woman gowned in heavy cobalt silk. "She wants you and Rak'khiel to begin speaking to each other. Talk of your customs, your expectations, your hopes, your dreams for the future. Come to some accommodation, even if it's only friendship."

"How do I do that if she refuses to speak to me? What must I do?"

"Apologize to her." Caylee's holo turned stern eyes on the prince. Put up her hand, refused him speech. "This is not open for discussion. You asked the way to begin again? This is it."

"But I ... by law I ... cannot. Shata, Caylee. " Razr tried to pace in the small area, gave it up and sat on the bed's edge, head in hands. "And the thing she did on the hilltop – with the sky? What if she looses it on me? How do I combat that?"

"Do not worry about Rak'khiel. There is no meanness in her, only righteous rage and berserker killer when she changes." Caylee's voice held fondness, perhaps more. *If machines could love.* "But then, milord, when it comes to that, you are also kind unless given over to the Killing Rage."

"What if she rejects me, refuses to talk?"

"She will not," Brin said. "She regrets this estrangement as much as you. But because you laid uninvited hands on her, yours is the first move. Can you do it?"

"But ... I will be banished from court, from the Royal House. I will never hold office, never be promoted in the Military Warrior's guild. I cannot, Brin. It will be the end of me."

"Listen to you, Prince Helrazr. Where will these things take place? Who will implement these bans, these blacklists? How, young sir, will you enforce any royal decrees? The royal guard you no longer have? You have less sense than a six-eyed slif." Brin's voice ripped, cold enough to freeze Razr's testas. "You would have to live on Kra'aken, in Kra'aken society. Our planet is dust."

An AI speaks to me thus? His jaw working, Razr gasped for air. When the truth of Brin's comments struck home, he discarded a stinging response. *I am a true piece of shata. If spoken aloud, they would all agree. What does that say of me?*

"You are less perceptive than I hoped," Brin snapped. "It puzzles me how, or better still why, you would ruin your life, perhaps your future, clinging to a law from a culture, perhaps a world, which no longer exists. Who is left to care? If anyone remains, theirs will be a fragmented society. They will no longer adhere to the old ways. They will be too busy trying to stay alive."

§

Razr expanded his olfactories, amped his hearing, flipped an optic. Hunting game, to replenish their food stores for the upcoming voyage, fell almost entirely to him.

"Forza me," whispered Razr. One small part of his brain stayed firmly focused on the herd of wild deer grazing a meadow below him. The other large portion worried at his upcoming conversation with Rak'khiel. Taken in cold logic, the AI's are, *damnit*, godsrotted correct. *I must make an apology – how will I force the words out?*

Razr slid behind another outcropping of spindly trees, their feathery green boughs similar to the decorative pines in his mother's garden in the Royal Compound on homeworld. Amazing, the difference in plants, weather, soil on this side of the Fang.

The big buck's head came up, displaying an impressive rack of fighting horns. His ears and tail flicked, nostrils flared.

He scents something different, but he's not yet decided if it's danger.

It is, but not for him. Razr smiled. *I'll cull the herd of the upstart males, those who would challenge him over the next few years. Enjoy your added ease, brother.* He selected his three prey and slipped down the hillside.

A bugled call from the buck to his herd, a frantic rush of mothers and fawns.

Razr wished he could tell them not to fear. Instead he fired two projectiles. The largest younger bucks, dropped. Drilled by dead-on headshots.

Razr called change and gave himself to the joy of the hunt. Rundown, attack and kill of the third deer – over so quickly. A fresh feast – he ate one carcass, while he dressed out the others for storage aboard the ships.

Another two aiys of this, filling their food requirements from all – well, those edible and delicious – Olica's wildlife and we will be ready for flight. The herds of dairy cows present no challenge at all – they will wait until last. Easy harvesting. Plus, they are penned – their losses would immediately be missed.

Kel, Tarkin and Torga gathered nuts, fruits and vegetables while Grigori practiced his hunting skills on mice.

Rak'khiel planned a mid-dark raid on their former cottage.

Razr overheard Kel telling Caylee since Yola and she worked so hard on the garden, she refused to leave without taking their harvest with them. She hoped the villagers had left it alone.

I'm sure it's untouched. The townsfolk would stay away, fearing taint by association.

Rak'khiel also mentioned something about wanting the crock of bread starter.

Razr's mind felt as if it warped, malformed and rolled black and burned around its edges, trying to imagine what it could possibly be.

Hoisting a deer over each massive shoulder, the prince dropped into an easy run, across the rolling hills. *A short run, a pause to drop these off, and I have time to go out for two more hunts this aiy.*

"You are as stupid as a six-eyed slif, Razr," the prince muttered as he loped back to the fighter. Each passing hora he regretted his stupidity with the robes and the Royal Privilege more and more.

Unless he hunted his own fresh dinner, he ate the food unit spew. Nutrition kept the body alive, true, if the taste didn't kill you.

The plague of missing her cooking wouldn't cut so sharply tonight – he'd killed and eaten. The damnable female's recovery included a return to her pod with restricted light duty. But she was allowed to cook. Even without hunger, Razr knew the aromas floating between Rak'khiel's small galley and his warplane would tantalize. *Like whatever she roasted last evening. Destroyer, I chewed on my knuckle until it bled.*

"I swear Brin and Caylee rerouted the v'lation system to suck the cooking smells up and blow it out wherever I am," Razr growled.

He would have bitten something twice, very, very hard, had he known he spoke the truth.

Chapter 54

Dark
Jorca 2. 7206.37
Twinned Ships, Olican Surface

Her mouth flooded. Rak'khiel delicately wiped a bit of drool from one corner with the back of her wrist.

The yeasty aroma from the dough she'd just punched down, covered with a towel and set on the counter, made her stomach gurgle. Soon. One more rise, then bake. And eat fresh bread again. It seemed a lifetime. *Thank the Goddess no one stole our starter crock.*

Honor is a wizard among physicians – perhaps chemists. This morning, only two days after he gave me the anti-venin, I could almost doubt I was ever poisoned.

Kel lifted her arms toward the ceiling, raised to her toes, pirouetted and danced with the uninhibited abandon of innocence. No need to worry – no one observed the unconscious sexuality of her movements.

Yola's pendant shifted, sent glad resonance like an electric current through her veins.

Rak'khiel's hearts thrummed, a laugh of joy burst free, and she turned once again to the loading of fresh foodstuffs.

Grigori has plenty of cows' and goats' milk. I sneaked out the past two nights to get it. We have fresh milk for everyone for a week, and ships' stores are full of dehydrated and flash-frozen. Drums of fruit juice are stashed in the unheated space. We are well prepared for this flight.

We all are carnivores, she mused, filling empty storage areas in both ships. *The prince has hunted for four days, wild game is plentiful and he is skilled. I harvested Yola's garden and Tarkin and Torga picked the nutberry trees clean.*

The unheated areas now held bins of meat, vegetables and fruit. All the stored food would freeze once they were in space. The extra foodstuff now coming in would be placed into the food 'facturers – to make protbars and the other basic survival rations. *Not as tasty as fresh, but we will not starve.*

I roasted the nutberries last night – wonder if Razr smelled them? Rak'khiel allowed a small, self-satisfied smile. *I took a small basket to Honor – and asked him his food needs and preferences. Wonder if the prince knew?*

No, he didn't. He would be furious with you. Torga's thought was laced with a smile. *As for the nuts, I smelled them, I raided the galley late last night. They were great!*

Rak'khiel tried to put a mock frown on her thought, *You act like you're eating for two.*

No, Kel, the female cafuzog's reply, *I'm actually eating for three.*

What?! How? Goddess in a goblet!

§

Rak'khiel spent the final day before launch gathering and stowing last minute foodstuffs. She still waited for a proper explanation of Torga's condition.

Later, mi dear, when we've lots of free time, was the cafuzog's reply.

Hunh.

One week ago, with Brin and Caylee's assistance, Rak'khiel increased her brain implant capacity with the addition of two modules. Each night since then, Kel filled the new space with languages, battle modes and strategies, medical and bioscience modules. Every resource Caylee suggested, Kel learned.

She knew now – as disconcerting, as awkward as it felt – if she needed them, the modules would kick in. If required, *my body will react correctly without direction. I might be an unwilling – no, not that, but perhaps an uncomfortable – passenger in my own skin. But I will have the tools I need.*

But another thing worked on her mind. The single thing marring her peace of mind, her almost happiness. *I hate the awkwardness between Razr and me. And although I've asked otherwise, all are aligned with me. This will be so much worse, magnified when confined in the two ships. I must do something.*

"Caylee?"

The holo Kel now accepted as her biological mother shimmered in, the lovely woman dressed in a silken dress the color of roseate petals. Its classic cut and long flowing skirt emphasized the smallness of her waist. Her wealth of wavy hair was pulled high on her head, contained almost haphazardly by a myriad of glittering pins. Cascading curls flowed and spiraled. *Goddess, if only I could look half so beautiful,* Kel thought with true regret. *Perhaps Razr could learn to like me. Maybe Caylee would help me look more attractive.*

"Kel. What is it? A problem with the lift preparations? I'm not dressed for mechanical work." The upward curve of the holo's full lips produced two deep dimples in smooth pink-blushed tawny cheeks.

"I need advice, Caylee. About this thing with the prince."

"His fault. His stupidity. His responsibility to fix."

"Yes, so all have said." Kel drew her brows together, felt their faint touch above the bridge of her nose. "I hate that I've felt the need to avoid him. I think I overreacted because I was startled, a little scared, and offended." Rak'khiel's voice rose an octave. "The nerve of that big bloody bastard. Trying to befoul me and calling it the law." She snarled, jerked her head back an inch, heard her own words and how they were said.

"Looks like I'm still mad, huh?" Kel added, with a rueful half-smile.

"All good reasons for your actions. You should not blame yourself." The AI's brows were also pulled into a frown.

"But I inflicted personal injury on a Prince. I hurt him bad and I'm embarrassed. I don't know what to do." Kel rubbed her hands on the thighs of her pants. "And I worry, Caylee. This isn't going to get better in the close quarters of space."

"Brin tells me he talked with Prince Helrazr and informed him he owed you an apology, Kra'aken law bedamned. Wait and see what Razr does."

"Caylee, in fairness, since I've studied Kra'aken customs and laws, I know now he meant no disrespect. Perhaps this could be resolved somewhere in the middle?"

"An excellent thought. Allow me to discuss this with Brin. Perhaps, as you say, a solution can be found." The AI gave Rak'khiel a wide fond smile.

I'm due for a workout, Kel sent.

"Then I'll return with any information. Good hunting, Lady Regence."

Kel blinked at the honorific, rose and left the lifepod, headed for the fighter's sims. *Please alert me if I'm needed.*

§

The effing monster of Razr's sim had already killed her twice. *It's beginning to piss me off.*

Eyes stinging from rivers of sweat, Kel fought for breath, retrieved her weapons and keyed the program to begin again. *I will kill this forzaing thing, I will. If that damnable man can defeat it, I certainly can.*

Without warning, a scythe swung. Her reflexive duck saved her from humiliation. "Damn you," she snarled. The Goddess-cursed programming changed the scenario each time. Impossible to find a rhythm, impossible to pre-guess.

Kel? Caylee's thought.

Not now.

She backed, quieted her heart. Waited for the pounding drumming in her head to diminish. Now she heard the sly sneaking footfall of her stalker, off to her left.

Kel moved to counter its approach.

I cannot overpower it – the beast is too large, too strong. But I am faster, and much more agile.

Rak'khiel moved behind a stand of trees, slid behind a rock, and broke into a hard run across a small clearing. When she heard the footfalls, the halt, and the scrape signaling a leap by the creature, she whirled. Stepping behind her lance, Kel braced it against the ground with all her strength.

The creature's own momentum impaled it, the entire blade, followed by gouts of green, punched out through its back. A roar, a scream, a death wound.

"Yes!" Kel punched air-victory and hit the glowing red 'end' switch. Smacking the 'release' toggle on the sim hatch, she called. "Caylee? Tell me your news."

Chapter 55

First Aiy
Jorca 2. 7206.37
Twinned Ships, Olican Surface

Strapped in her pilot's couch in the life cocoon, spine parallel with Olica's surface, Rak'khiel waited for the grim next step.

An oozing slither at the base of her skull accompanied the mindjack's extrusion from the seat pad. *Yeeech.* The intrusive insertion of the computer systems plug into her brain, followed the snick of plascirc seal. But then – *oh Goddess, yes* – came her reward.

The hard fast rush of power thrummed through her body. Kel became one with the powerful, all-knowing ship.

A secunda later, Rak'khiel acknowledged the Brin-Caylee-master-systems handshake. Another pulse as Razr joined the group.

We are ready, someone thought. But who? *We are no longer individuals when we merge here.*

Rak'khiel ran through her pre-flight checklists. Not necessary, not at all, since Caylee's flawless work requires no checks. *But I am both new and fussy. And nervous – it gives me something to do with my hands. Plus, this is the maiden flight for our fully-blended ships.*

From her indigo-cushioned couch, Kel's screens presented a semi-view of the warplane's nose. Overhead, from her cockpit, she saw violet-tinted clouds scudding by. *What will I see from orbit? And beyond?*

Her stomach roiled and bunched into her throat. But not from illness or fear. *Oh no. This is the almost-sick of anticipation.*

The lifepod systems were now subsumed into the new combination ship, but not slaved to the fighter.

Kel still held independent control of her mains, her thrusters, and maneuverability if, *Goddess forbid*, catastrophe struck. The AI's brilliant work in combining the two spacecraft, into what they all called the *Twinned Ships*, allowed the prince to do the same.

All cargo stowed, all latches fastened, Tarkin, Torga and Grigori stashed in their cushioned nets. *All systems green.*

Honor? Kel sent. *Status?*

Copy, Lady Regence. Ready for lift.

A new monitor showed Razr as a white dot, secured in his cockpit. *All systems green.*

Kel clicked her jaw mike.

"Pod's go," she said, hands roving over icons, brushing the yoke. Eyes focused down tight, constantly monitoring screens. Waiting for the final signal.

"Fighter's go," came the low purr of Razr's deep voice and Kel's hearts beat faster at the sound.

"Shalit," she cursed softly as her personal monitor registered the reaction. Hoped Brin and Caylee hadn't installed a matching unit in the prince's cockpit. *I don't want him knowing his effect on me.*

"Light 'em up," Razr said.

"Copy." Pulled her eyebrows into a frown at the pitch of her voice – an octave too high, breathy. She flipped the dead-man Start switch for her enormous main.

Its heavy rumble, the deep vibrations shaking the pod made her need to pee, made her body come alive. *Goddess, the power in these twinned ships.* Like two great beasts, growling, crouching, straining to be unleashed.

Now for my thrusters.

Kel thumbclicked the 'On's' for her eight directional nozzles. *They saved us from a crash no more than a week ago.* Eight flawless fires. Holding minimum power, she trimmed them straight at the ground beneath.

The ship trembled, quivered for lift, as if it knew its rightful place was not dirtside.

Everybody ready? Her last-second check on the cafuzogs and baby sorbazel.

Wheeee. That, of course, would be Grigori.

Kel felt a huge grin take charge of her face.

Exactly how I feel, she answered, tried for maturity and sent. *But are you secure?*

Yes, yes, and yes. We're all go.

Honor?

Affirmative, Rak'khiel. Appreciations at your concern."

As if I would not take care of you? Kel answered, received a whispery chuff of laughter in return.

"Pod's a go," Rak'khiel keyed her mouth mike.

"Fighter, go." Razr's voice said. "Launch on my third. Throttles full-on at third mark."

"Copy," Kel said, her voice now steady, smooth as any machine. But cold fingers clutched her stomach and her body burned, skin hot and sweaty with anticipation, inside her nanoplas flightsuit.

"Ready for lift," said the prince. "Mark, mark, MARK."

Both of Kel's hands, all twelve of her impatient fingers waiting on the control yokes of the pod's mains and nozzles, shoved forward.

Holy Goddess in a Spaceship! This is what a 'g' force is. I thought I couldn't breathe before.

A force, the steady building pressure of a giant hand, mashed her against the pilot's couch.

It gave, supported, gently gimbaled against the throbbing

push. Her nanoplas suit pressed her lungs, released, forcing much needed breath.

Sensing threat, her Other surged for dominance. Reassuring, forcing it back, she kept her darting eyes on every screen, every sensor, every readout. Scanning, evaluating as possibilities calc'd in her mind. All green. And still the 'g' force built.

Outside her viewscreen, the warplane's sharp bow pushed steadily skyward, cutting its way through lavender-tinged clouds.

Twin bright spots, blinding white centers with violet coronas, came into view.

Kel blessed the instant darkening of her screen, her ability to see in the cockpit. Her hands refused to move, gripped rigid on the forward yokes. Fixed in place, by the g's, as they were. *Of no consequence, Caylee can handle anything I can't.*

"Fighter to Pod," the loved/hated voice through her jaw mic. "Report."

Standard protocol. How does he make it so Goddess cursed sexy?" "Pod copy."

"Status?" the bass voice queried.

"Pod showing all green, passengers status green." *Why do I have to react to him like this?*

"Copy. Fighter is all green – your monitor reads that?"

"Affirmative." Kel didn't trust her voice beyond the single word. For the moment, she had the quaver under control.

"How are you holding up under the extra g's?"

Now the bloody man gets personal, and nice. Okay, I can play this game. Kel clicked the bone mic. "More than I expected, worse than the sims. Glad of the flightsuit's assistance. But enjoying the ride." She tried, oh yes she did, but she couldn't stop her giggle of delight.

To her amazement, the prince laughed aloud. "When we clear Olica's gravity well, and are able to cut back engine power, Brin and Caylee will take over. You could view space from the fighter's nose. Invitation of one captain to another."

Kel's jaw dropped. Thanks to the 10+ g's they pulled, she almost didn't get it reclosed. "Captain Regence, of Kra'aken LifeCocoon I, copies," she said in believable feigned nonchalance. "That's affirmative, sir. Pod out."

Shalit! What am I going to wear?

§

The pod shook, buffeted by invisible barriers and the engines' steady shove, never faltered.

Kel thanked the Goddess, but mostly she thanked Brin and Caylee for their preparation of her enhanced flightsuit.

For what seemed like days, the ship climbed through, and then past the illumination of Olica's suns.

And twice, something pushed their craft, shoved it into a hard yaw.

Rak'khiel's mental calcs and on-the-instant thruster-nozzles bursts, her minute adjustments, kept them on true course.

"Nicely done, Rak'khiel." Caylee's warm voice complimented. "The fighter has no directionals. It could not have compensated as you did."

"I didn't have time to think," Kel said, feeling the sudden wild trembling in her limbs. Now she was scared, when it didn't matter.

"I couldn't have corrected quickly enough," the AI said. "You flew, mixing insight and mental calcs. I don't have intuition – it's a human skill. You fly exceptionally well."

At a bump, an almost-shimmy, Kel swallowed against rising bile.

"All is well, my daughter?" Caylee peered closely at Rak'khiel.

"Yes," she said. Then, as if lifted by a gust of wind, Kel's body rose off her flight couch, held in place only by her restraints.

A melodic chime rang through the ship. The All Clear.

"Ah," Caylee nodded. "Time for me to go to work. Call if you require anything?"

"Of course … and my appreciations."

The AI's holo winked out.

§

"Pod?" The query on her open channel.

"Fighter?"

"It is safe to unbelt, move about and free your passengers. When and if you like, come see what lies out there." The prince's voice held nothing but pleasantry but still ….

"Copy," she said. "My appreciations."

With the warplane in superior position, Kel's couch, even gimbaled, left her flat on her back. *It's okay for a bit,* she thought. *But it would really work my nerves if it lasted very long.*

She unbelted, proud of remembering to grab a handhold before she unsnapped the last restraint. Another peek out her viewscreen showed them passing into deep endless dark, lit occasionally by swirling displays of bright dots and coalescing rainbows of color.

Rak'khiel's Olican mindset tilted sideways, overwhelmed for the moment, before her deeptape lessons reasserted true reality.

Goddess in a thimble! How was I ever so backward?

A step, forgotten zero g, resulted in a headlong hurtle toward the pod core.

Kel snagged a glove on the rail, bent her knees and pointed her boots down the shaft. Hand-over-hand, she moved carefully to her sleeping area level. Slowed, and in slow motion (or so it seemed) she stepped out of the core onto the pebbled gray flooring and bounced her way into the cube.

Me, me, me first! Grigori's insistent voice. *Box, box, box.*

Rak'khiel laughed and loosened the padded black straps and soft webbing.

The blue-striped gray streak hissed in alarm as he shot

from his net only to find he ran in place against the ceiling.

Kel tried to hide her smile as she fished the baby sorbazel down. Aiming him toward the litter bin, she gave him a tiny shove. "Go slow, bebe."

A miniature growl floated back over Grigori's shoulder at the diminutive.

Tarkin and Torga's amusement at the cub flooded their thanks as Rak'khiel freed them from their webbed restraints. They too made their way to the area reserved for their sanfac's.

Kel removed the ungainly flightsuit, donned ship's loose shirt and pants and soft boots. Used her own lav, washed face and hands and brushed through the tangle of her hair.

The flightsuit she returned to weapons bay and hung it on the recharging unit, hoping she would never need it. *If I do, it will be ready.*

She brushed her teeth, wondered if she was ready to visit Razr in the fighter. Wondered if she should.

Goddess save me, will I be leaping from the cookpot into the flame?

Chapter 56

Dark
Jorca 2. 7206.37
Twinned Ships, Insystem Space

I'm procrastinating.

Rak'khiel checked and re-checked the pod's systems, checked Caylee's calculations twice and still her stomach twisted up, stuffed high against her diaphragm. *What in the Goddess' name is wrong with me? I am not afraid of Razr.*

Kel inhaled, a deep deliberate action, strove to quiet her mind. *All is well with both ships, all is well with the cafuzogs and Grigori. Honor is well, and I am too, thanks to him. Why do I feel like the only thing holding all my pieces together is my skin.*

Perhaps a session in the sim? *No.* Perhaps cooking in the galley? *No.* Nothing appealed. Jumping to her feet, she paced the tiny area of the cockpit.

I am procrastinating.

Brin and Caylee have plotted courses for the alien portal. Our accuracy is continually confirmed by residue from my inbound journey. Our current speed, using only insystem engines, will place us at the gate in two aiys. *I should be excited but instead I feel unsettled, lost.*

"Kel, all secure?" Razr's casual voice on the com made her leap and carom off the overhead.

Shalit! Her insides quivered at the rumble of his voice.

"The view from the warplane's bridge is spectacular."

Gathering the shreds of her composure, Rak'khiel answered, "Copy. Coming up."

The instant she entered the Needle's cockpit, Kel knew Razr faked his insouciance. He stood rubbing his arms, just as she had moments before, his casual posture an act.

Rak'khiel quickly uncrossed her arms, let them hang relaxed by her sides, hands open instead of fisted.

Then, as a clutter of messy thoughts besieged her mind, she realized the prince had forgotten to shield his thoughts against her. His worries, his fears lay completely open to her. *Should I tell him?* No. Perhaps I will hear and understand things he might be unable to utter.

Now I've decided I must apologize, I am terrified. Razr's thoughts were laced with regret. *The shame of it all. Brave warriors fear nothing – but I fear the hold she has on me. I fear her magic.*

Kel schooled her face, her body language into the most unthreatening pose possible and gazed out the heavy plasplex viewscreen, pretending to be fascinated by the endless carbon black beyond. But inside she felt her hearts flip, the smallest bit, in joy.

Razr stood beside her, at the handrail, less than an arm's length away. The muscles of his body, even those in his jaw, were hard as stones, coiled spring-tight with tension.

His eyes are fixed on the outside screens, but what he sees isn't out there.

Do I want her, she heard, *because I have transferred the emotional noose of my family's loss to her?* Rak'khiel kept her eyes forward and waited.

Do I need her acceptance or her love? Is it a weakness or strength that I need closeness, human touch so much? Do I want her in spite of what she is? Or because of what she is? Do I care?

Rak'khiel closed her side teeth on the edge of her tongue to stop speech. And found, as Razr's thoughts continued, she was glad of it.

Do I actually love her? How can I force the apology – I must – I fear her rejection, her hate far more.

The hard angry shell about Kel's hearts melted.

Next to her, the prince snagged a long shaky breath and opened his mouth. His jaw worked, but nothing emerged. A huge breath, then words and phrases and pauses tumbled out.

"My ... auugh ... my Destroyer ... accursed. Lady Rak'khiel, my most reprehensible ... ah, shata!" His head drooped, eyes closed, Razr's chin dropped to his heaving chest. Then he blurted, "Damn my vows. Kel ... can." The hitch of grabbed breath ... "Accept ... humble ... most grievous reprehensible?" *I am lost, undone,* he thought. *I have committed the unpardonable.*

"Prince Helrazr?" Kel extruded the point of a fingernail and shoved it into her hidden hand. The sharp pain succeeded in preventing hysterical laughter, a certain disaster. Presenting Razr a solemn face, complete with furrowed brow – as if taken by sheer surprise and thinking too slowly. "Are you making me an apology?"

"No! Shata ... Destroyer, your pardon milady. Yes. Yes, I am." Dark waving curls slid around massive shoulders as Razr's handsome profile eased. He turned toward her, fixed liquid soft amber eyes on hers. "Rak'khiel, I never wished to cause you hurt. I am not such a man."

"I know that. I understand," she said. And now she fought, not laughter, but a sudden, unexpected weakness in her knees. An insistent throbbing pounded in her lower belly, an aching need where her legs met. "I accept. Let there be peace between us. Would you dine with us in the pod this evening?" Kel allowed a half-smile of once-again-possibilities to warm her face.

Razr's entire face relaxed into a boyish grin, showing long deep dimples. "With extreme pleasure, milady. You have no idea how I've missed your cooking."

Chapter 57

Dark
Jorca 4. 7206.37
Pod, Insystem Space

According to the charts and the AI's computations, three aiys remained to reach the alien portal. Even though hidden inner tensions surged high, the combined ships now echoed with mock sallies between Kel and Razr and joyous interaction between Tarkin, Torga, Grigori and the AI's.

Rak'khiel invited Honor to join their meals.

Although the cub still held a grudge against the prince, they agreed in one thing. They both watched the spydr's every twitch.

But, after two aiys passage, amid great grumbling, the cub and prince agreed with Kel about the arachna. With the continued absence of the High Lord's circlet, without the influence of the evil stone, with injections of the new anti-venin, his harsh edges softened. Honor proved kind. Even funny.

A brilliant scientist, armed with the ships' technologies, he continued research on reversing the 'Ristos' damage.

"Caylee?" Rak'khiel called.

"Yes?"

"Do you believe Honor can ever return to the species

original humanoid form?"

"I cannot see how, Rak'khiel, but even these small facial changes help. And, with his cobalt robes, he is no longer repugnant to my sight."

"I wish we could give him his heart's desire."

"We cannot, but perhaps somewhere in this immensity called space, lies a place where someone, or something, can. I will continue my lab experiments, but Honor is his own best resource. We will hope for success."

"My appreciations, Caylee. Goddess grant it."

§

One sleep shift remained before their arrival at the alien portal. Kel went to bed with her thoughts in a tangle.

Razr's conversation, his interaction with her as pilot to pilot, captain to captain, and male to female had been unswervingly respectful, playful, teasing. But in those lambent amber eyes something else occasionally showed. Were the little slips, the accidental brushing of hands been simply that? Accidents? Or something more?

And, oddly, the prince had missed dinner in the cocoon the past three nights. *What in the name of everything good is he doing?*

Goddess! I think I shall go mad. Knowing sleep would refuse to come, Rak'khiel reached in her drawer for a mild sophorific. *If I need to wake for an emergency, I can.* But this way, surely I will drowse until ... a small giggle escaped ... what passes for morning out here in the always dark.

§

"Captain Regence," the deep voice rumbled through the com.

Kel squeaked and levitated from her bed. "If you've completed your lovliness sleep, you might wish to join me. We've arrived at the portal."

"Copy that. On my way."

Into the 'fresher, fast hot shower, faster dry. The fast rake of a wide-toothed comb through the heavy cobalt-streaked mass which now fell past her waist.

Kel pulled a handful of heavy hair back from her forehead, securing it with one of Yola's multi-hued silky ties. Short tendrils escaped, framing her face.

Into a loose pale blue shirt, tucked into cobalt trousers. She pulled on soft black boots and exited her sleeping area. Through the ships' mating hatch, Rak'khiel swarmed hand-over-hand up the rungs in the warplane's core.

Damnit all to the darkest hell, she thought. *They all beat me.* A hard glance out the portholes, across the viewscreens. "Where …?"

"We are exactly where Caylee's computations say the gate is." Razr's comment.

"Checked, and double checked," added Brin. "Nothing but endless restless black anywhere."

Then she saw it. Something shimmered, a sheer improbability.

"Look," she whispered. Look … right there."

"Great Destroyer, it is true." The prince's near whisper held awe and more.

Rak'khiel heard the murmurs of her friends but found her gaze frozen on the creation developing before them.

Her heartbeats hammered her sternum, her ribs. Pounded in her ears until it drowned out all other sound.

Something far more powerful than any aboard the twinned ships, waited for them. Kel knew it without understanding how. But what does it wait for? And why?

A glowing thread of blue light hung vertical, so fine as to be almost-not-there. A growing, evolving shape, sometimes a thin shimmering line, sometimes now almost a long rectangular image hung directly in their path. It rotated, spun fast, then slow. The thing first glistened, then went matte.

"The angles alone," Brin voice came subdued. "Identify the object as a created thing."

The hush in the fighter's cockpit hung unbroken by a cough, a sneeze, or even a deep breath. All eyes were glued on the on the turning, not-quite-there hot blue-white bar.

The object's wavering outlines deceived the eye in a misdirection technology so advanced it made Rak'khiel's stomach judder. *I'm powerless to look away.*

"Sweet Destroyer," Razr's voice whispered. "What have we done?"

"Nothing," Kel said.

"We are correct," Brin's steady voice came. "Our ship signatures, both this warplane and Kel's life cocoon, came directly through the plot point where the alien bar spins."

"Concur," Caylee said. "Now all we can do is wait for it, for them, to make a decision. Whether we go or stay."

"How can you know this?" Razr's ragged voice asked.

"Because," Caylee said. "We passed the same gate. But it stood open when the pod passed through."

"How long?" Kel thought aloud. "How long until we know if we pass or fail?"

"Long enough I hope," Razr said. "For something I wish to do." With that cryptic remark, the prince rushed from the cockpit.

"Goddess in an alien artifact!" Kel swore.

The secunda the prince left the fighter's cockpit, the shimmering bar thickened, grew high and wide, morphed into a blinding white square. On either side, two high fluted columns tapered to a heavily scribed lintel. The entire structure glowed, sparkled, seemed to invite.

"But its surface, according to every scanner we have," Caylee said. "Is solid."

Is it alive? Torga's quiet send. *Or simply a construct with specifications that must be met?*

"Caylee?" Rak'khiel tried to glance away, couldn't. The fascination of the remarkable portal before them both scared her and filled her with wonder. "Prince Helrazr, to the bridge soonest. Something is happening."

The abrupt intrusion of a massive man up through the Needle core caused the assembled group to gasp and flinch.

"My contrition," he said. "You did say hurry." Staring through the plasplex, he said, "I see."

Kel stood against the brassine rail below the viewscreen.

The prince moved beside her and placed a velvet box on the small ledge.

"Lady Rak'khiel Floril I'Regence, I would speak to you in this assembled company of friends before we attempt this gate passage. We may live or we may perish, but I must have these things between us first."

Kel closed her eyes against the hot prickles behind her lids. Her throat closed on its own as she recognized the formal opening. She nodded assent.

"Since I met you, I have found you to be a very different Kra'aken female. In fact when I met you, you were an Olican girl. Since your change you have become ..." a tiny twitch at the corner of his mouth, a small vibration of laughter in the back of his throat gave his intent away.

Rak'khiel opened her eyes, narrowed them. Opened her mouth, shut it. Sent instead, a twisting tendril through his mind. Finding only laughter, teasing and happiness, she relaxed the suspicious slits of her eyes and settled in for whatever Razr intended.

"You are, without a doubt, the most stubborn, intelligent, determined, different, less Kra'aken lady-like, most intriguing, most interesting and most beautiful woman I have ever encountered. You are not a retiring noble female."

Rak'khiel frowned, opened her mouth,

"No." Razr said, laying a large forefinger on her lips. "You are argumentative too, but hear me out. You are a better pilot than I, fearless, and an accomplished warrior. You challenge me in every situation, you saved my life when it meant your own. You never quit, never admit defeat."

The prince opened the velvet box and lifted a jewel-encrusted ring and bracelet. Placing the jewelry on his open palm, he continued.

"Lady Rak'khiel Floril I'Regence, for all the things I just mentioned, I love you. I wish never to be without you. You simply are the only woman I will ever life-bond. I will have no other to be mother of my children. If we do not survive the portal, I wanted you to know my feelings."

Kel stood stunned, mouth gaping, wide eyes frozen on his outstretched hand. *Caylee, help me. What do I do?*

Do you love him, Kel?

Goddess rescue me, I think I do.

Then reach out, take his hand, let him place the binding jewelry on you.

As if it belonged to someone else, Rak'khiel watched her slim hand lift from her side, stretch toward Razr's. Lifting her eyes, fell prisoner to the intensity of his gaze. Within she found promise of so many things. Gentleness, love, protectiveness, and hot intense desire.

She sent the same. And knew, by the stutter of his breathing, he understood.

Capturing Kel's hand, the prince slid a wide gold band on her finger. The ring's great ruby held a rampant and crwned Leoni carved in its center. Circling the huge stone, a myriad of delicate gems, set in twisting gold, cascaded down encircling of the ring.

Goddess, this is so far beyond my jewelry-making. This is priceless.

She watched Razr lift the heavy bracelet, a duplicate of her ring. Opening it, he slid it onto her slender wrist and snicked the clasp.

Do I belong to him now. Joy? Trepidation? Both? Caylee? Help!

Take the remaining jewelry from the box and place it on his left hand. As he did with you.

Only the distraction of the heavy jewelry prevented the wild trembling of Kel's hands. She slid first the massive ring – *and damn the distracting warmth of his skin* – and then the thick bracelet on Razr's hand and arm.

She startled when the prince clasped her two hands in his and pressed them against his hearts. They beat wild, erratic beneath her palms. Looking deep into her eyes, he began to speak.

He recites a vow from the earliest Kra'aken nuptial vows. Humbled, honored, she refused to drop her gaze although Olican Kel dearly wished to do so.

"Lady Rak'khiel Floril I'Regence," the prince began. "I, Helrazr Jalaal VI'Rex, Crown Prince of Kra'aken, before these witnesses, ask your hand in binding agreement, in accordance with the laws of our heritage, the laws of Kra'aken nobility, with the laws of governance of legal, personal and physical rights of both parties. I ask your pledge of loyalty, respect, trust, honesty and honor and I pledge you the same."

How can he sound so calm? I'm terrified.

"This contract between the two of us will become non-breakable at our consummation, released only by death," recited Razr.

Oh Goddess in a bridal bed! Shata, I'm doomed.

The prince seemed not to notice her consternation. He continued, "The right to bear royal warrior progeny is granted in this contract but lack thereof will not negate our troth. I ask you to wear the consort's Royal Signet and bracelet – proof positive of my love. All will honor you as a Rex born, as well as the most beloved wife of a prince of the realm. You will hold my life, my future, my family and my love. I pledge this."

Rak'khiel's hearts did a double flutter. The roaring drums in her ears assured her they still beat. Her stomach slid up, clogged her throat, and stayed there.

"Breathe, would you …?" A low suggestion, laced with laughter, said softly in her ear. "Fainting during the binding ceremony is frowned upon."

Tilting her face upward, Kel whispered, "What must I do now?"

"Simplest of all. Say you will and it is done."

"After all you just recited and I don't have to promise anything?" Kel knew her face heated just a bit. "Are you, yet again, protecting me, my prince?" Realized what she'd just said, stuffed a hand heavy with gold and gems against her mouth.

"You may recite the whole thing if you like, but it honestly isn't required." One dark eyebrow, shaped like a raptor wing, lifted, waggled at her.

"I will," Kel said, with a smile. Then broke into laughter.

We witness, from Tarkin and Torga.

I witness, but I'm still going to bite him, snarled Grigori.

"I bear witness," Honor said.

"I witness," from Brin.

"As do I," Caylee said.

The creeping rush of heat surged across her chest, climbed her throat, suffused her face. *My ears are going to combust.* She stared out at the wheeling stars, the swirling of bright lights in the deep dark. *I have to get a grip on me.*

A large right hand slid into her vision, lay palm up and open on the take-hold bar in front of her.

I don't dare look him in the eyes – he will see I'm lost. A tiny sigh, she laid her slender hand palm down on his. Surrender, proposal accepted.

Warm fingers closed gently around Kel's.

Her body heated, like someone lit a bonfire low in her belly and the flames flickered outward, licking through her arteries and veins. Kel felt a heavy swollen wanting at the join of her legs, a restlessness she feared to examine. *I'm betrayed by this body I don't know. I'm afraid of the wanting, of his strangeness. Honesty heard, I'm terrified by his immense size, his rampant maleness. But he holds my answers, and Goddess help me, I want them.*

A massive arm lifted behind Kel, an open six-fingered hand light as a narikeet landed on her shoulder. Then the tiniest pressure – an affectionate squeeze.

A soft sigh escaped her, and she tilted her head. Rested it tentatively against Razr's broad chest.

Another gentle hug, urged her closer.

Kel's body thrummed, her hearts beat in syncopation with his. Heat flooded and settled low in her belly. Beating its own insistent demands.

A deep voice spoke in her mind, just as he did the first time. *No pressure, no hurry. Mating will be at your choice and at your time. I will wait.*

How can he want me? A peasant? He doesn't know I am unspoiled. Does he bond because there is no one else ... or because he truly wants me?

Rak'khiel stared at her ring, the center stone as large as a narikeet egg. *I do not know this gem, but I can only guess at its value. And that of the bracelet.*

"Rak'khiel, will you speak? Your favor?" Razr's voice came tinged with anxiety.

Crammed together in the warplane's cockpit, Brin, Caylee, Tarkin, Torga, Honor and Grigori snickered.

"Ah ... Goddess," Kel blurted. "Caylee! Will someone do something?"

"A wedding feast? Perhaps in the largest area of either ship?" Brin's voice held an odd note.

Could it be joy? Kel wondered.

"The main seating area forward of the pod's galley." Caylee said.

"Yess," Honor said. "Let us go first, and begin preparations."

As if in a dream, Kel watched them depart. She studied her marriage ring. *How is it that it fits? And, Goddess, will I be alone with him this night?*

"I should oversee my galley," she said and fled.

Chapter 58

Dark
Jorca 4. 7206.53
Pod, Insystem Space

"An uneventful flight is a good flight," Razr commented.

Brin and Caylee murmured agreements.

"Yes," Rak'khiel said. *We got married an hour ago and I still have no idea what comes next. What he expects? For that matter – what do I? We will begin transition jumps in the next few hours. Do we ... ahhh, Goddess. What to do?*

"Complimentss on another deliciouss meal, Lady Regence." Honor's little mouth twisted in the rictus of his smile.

At a low table in one corner of the Pod's mess area, Tarkin and Torga oversaw Grigori's manners.

Hungry, the little sorbazel mock-growled. *Scat on taking time.*

Kel caught Razr's eyeroll, sent one of her own in return. A half-chuckle escaped before she could stifle it.

"Lady Regence, the next few hours will be ...," Razr met her half-breath with one of his own.

She braced for the rest of his thought. *What? In front of them all? But we bonded that way. He has no idea how agitated I am.*

"The next few hours are not available for inattention, not sleeping," he said. "My reprehensible at the lack of time for us."

Rak'khiel's angst bloomed. *I'm half-relieved, half-frustrated. This accursed body has a will of its own. I wish I would make up my mind.*

"We will, of course, do what is best for us all." At a tremble in her hands, she laced them demurely in her lap beneath cover of the tablecloth. "Could you explain?"

"Over the next six horas, we must make three quick transitions. Gather velocity, position and jump. Reposition, run up to vee and jump. The third will place us at our charted vector of the alien gate."

"The jumps will stress our joins? And we might have to fly independently as we did on our forced flight from Olica?"

"Exactly so," beamed Caylee. "Such a quick study."

Brin's grin, so proprietary, split his normally solemn face.

The AI's sat at the table and sipped their avatar wine.

Almost, Kel thought, *as if we know, should Kra'aken society remain, we will be required to conform. Or at least hide our more egregious actions.*

Conversation ranged anywhere it would, no prohibitions on subject. Tarkin andTorga spent much of their time answering Grigori's constant question, *Why?*

"I have been thinking," said the prince. One black brow dipped to an almost-frown at the synchronized collective breaths of those around the table. "What, then?" he demanded. "Am I always creating problems?"

"No, no ...." Rak'khiel demurred, but honesty warred and won. "Well, sometimes ...."

"Shata!" Razr said, but the word carried no anger. "Does no one else think we should have a proper name for this new ship we have created? My old nickname for the warplane is anathema. *Twinned Ships* is just wrong. Has anyone else thought on this?"

"*Dreamer,*" said Caylee. "Since both Kel and Razr spent

their voyages in deep sleep."

"*Dreamer*, yes," Brin said. "For the future we hope lies ahead."

"*Survivor*," Kel said, her voice sure. "Because that is what we have all done."

Tie them together, sent Torga. *We should call it* Survivors' Dreams.

Agree, mi'mate. Tarkin's chest swelled in pride, his tail fluffed with approval.

"It is perfect, Torga. I vote yes," Kel nodded.

"Aye, it is," Razr's voice came husky.

"Yes, my vote," Caylee added.

"And mine," Brin's gray-haired avatar nodded once.

"Honor?" Rak'khiel searched the aracha's face. "Does it please?"

"It iss perfect, my queen."

"It is done," decreed the prince. "Brin, can you somehow cover that damn Betty on the nose and replace it with our new name?"

"I will find a way, my prince," the AI answered. "With great haste, and greater pleasure."

"I may be able to assist," Honor said.

"It is good," Rak'khiel declared, stood and carried the dishes into the small galley.

"How long," she called back to the prince. "Until you need me ready to fly?"

"Approximately one and one-half horas. Brin, will you or Caylee announce time?" Razr waited for their nods, added, "I've charts to study, preparations to make."

"I need to access the databases," Rak'khiel said. *Study Kra'aken mating forms. Talk to Caylee.*

§

Belted in her gimbaled sleeping platform, Rak'khiel swallowed hard and pressed the slam-hypo of jump drugs against her forearm.

The run up to jump vee pressed her against the supportive mattress. *Like the Level 20 monster is standing on me with both feet.*

Even with the twilight dreamstate induced by the meds, Rak'khiel startled at the appearance of her ordinary things. The edges of her precious viewport seemed to melt, dripping down in green drops to the floor. Her compartment hatch slithered from an upright oval into a flattened shape, like a dinner plate with upturned edges.

Kel's past met her present met her future – everything interwoven, intertwined, a mismash of events – all out of sequence.

Wrong, my mind is skewed. Still, it made her stomach butterfly and take wings around her abdomen. Her brain slipped from the confines of her skull. She watched it float across the room, halt and hang mid-air, each separate section glowing, pulsing. *If I knew what they were I could identify each module. Goddess, I'm going lunatic!*

She didn't know she screamed, didn't know anyone heard. Until the bed dipped beneath sudden weight, and large strong arms held her fast. She didn't know what Razr saw in the face she turned to him, but a large gentle hand smoothed her hair.

His low voice whispered, "Shhhh, love. It's all illusion. Close your eyes, breathe. Think of us, our future. Possible children. Think good things, milady." And against her wrist she felt a small prick and burn. *He's added a bit more of the transitional drug.* "My blessings, milord." She said as warm calm slid through her veins. Her hiccups of breath slowed into smooth. "So much better."

She felt his cheek move, a smile, then. Her last conscious thought before sleep took her – *he came to me from the fighter. Awake during a time he is not supposed to be. Dangerous to him .. but still he .....*

A slowing of their ship brought her from slumber. Her mouth tasted like a pile of fresh bovine meadow dressings, her body craved – the squeeze packet in the pocket by her head. Green and nasty, her body demanded the mineral replenishment it contained. She sucked all three packets dry, and went to brush her teeth. One glance in the mirror and she also brushed the narikeet's nest of her hair.

Kel's personal viewscreen showed a strange portal hanging before their ship ... *Survivors' Dreams. We're here, we will attempt transition. We could die. And I have yet to consummate my marriage. It scares me ... but I would like to feel his hands on me, if only once. To answer my questions. But how to ask?*

She went through the pod hatch, hand-over-hand up through the fighter, into the cockpit.

A sound broke the silence. A composite of sounds, tones never heard, never before imagined, chimed. Lovely ethereal music flooded the cockpit. A paen of joy, of celebration, of approval.

Of our union? Kel lifted her face to Razr. "Is this known to you?"

He shook his head but before he could speak, a small portal – perpendicular to their destination – dissolved. Through this smaller aperture they saw a globe, orbited by a small pocked gray moon. Warmed by a single yellow sun. A lovely world of blue and green. A perfect world. An obvious invitation.

The silver pendant thrummed against her chest. Rak'khiel heard the portal's benevolent intent resonating in her mind.

"Razr, I believe we have both invitation and permission to transition this new gate. Perhaps land on that lovely planet. Your thoughts?"

"Would you rather begin our life on what appears to be a perfect world?" The prince turned the question back on her.

"We should ask the others. Honor most especially."

"It could be a lure," Razr said. "If it looks too good to be true ...."

"Yes, so Yola always taught. And I believe it."

"We have our friends. We must consider their desires as

carefully as we do ours. The portal which would take us home sits directly in our path. It is closed to us. We cannot, at this point, transition through. I believe we have been granted time to choose."

Razr abstained from the group vote. He wasn't needed. All unanimously agreed if the alien gate allowed access, they would try for Kra'aken.

"Are you sure, Rak'khiel?" His voice, soft and easy, questioned one final time.

"Yes." She knew now his clenched and relaxed fists meant anxiety. She also knew, allowing herself a tiny inward smile, he believed he fooled her with his display of nonchalance. "We are all sure, Razr. We would always wonder about those left behind. We would worry what we missed. Never forgive ourselves if we failed to investigate."

"But one hundrada fifty-eight plus yaras have passed," said the prince.

"Still," Brin's voice broke in. "The chrono spiraled backward. We have no idea what that means."

"Evenso, husband, we live. Perhaps others do also. There may be people to rescue. My vote is Kra'aken first. Then, if we find nothing, we return here. Providing the gatekeepers allow."

"Rak'khiel ... we could die in the transition attempt ...." Razr's voice trembled. "And I would have never held ...." The prince extended a large hand, palm up and open, on the railing near Kel.

The opening gambit of Kra'aken First Mating Ritual. Rak'khiel recognized it, felt her breath catch.

But in her mind she heard his low voice, the one that stirred her so deep within. *Only on your wishes, love. Remember it.*

I don't want to die without knowing. Without experiencing the touch of a man. And after, perhaps we can both keep our minds on transition of the portal instead of each other. Mentally blessing Caylee and her study tapes, Kel knew both motion and meaning.

She slowly laid her hand in his, felt it close warm and careful around it. *As if I'm fragile and he fears I'll break.*

Two *tascas* lifted, mixed and swirled with mating fragrance as Kel led her lifemate from the fighter's bow to her more spacious sleeping quarters in the lifepod.

At Razr's lifted brow, heat crawled her neck, red-hot needles stabbed the tops of her ears. "My bed's bigger," she stammered. "Just in case ...." The rest of her words failed to come.

Chapter 59

Dark
Jorca 4. 7207.03
Survivors' Dreams, Insystem Space

Tarkin and Torga were gone, but Kel's bed was still warm.

Beneath the short sleeves of her shirt, Rak'khiel's bare arms displayed shimmering paisley pink-gold patterns. *They aren't chills, and they're not the hot of a blush blood-surge.* The cool, air-bubbles-beneath-the-skin sensation told her every inch of her body was coated with imminent Change. *Like the lower body temperature of a reptile? Goddess!*

It's the only thing about me not on fire. Here I stand, in my sleeping area, husband at my side. The stomach-flutters worried her. *Will I disgrace myself and vomit? I want this, I do but ....* Her twin hearts' pounded like the rapid staccato of racing equine hooves.

Tascas loaded the room. *Razr's must be the musky spice, I've smelled part of it before. That makes the floral vanillan mine? Unmistakable mating scents.* "Razr? The *tascas* fragrance? Are they always the same?"

"Yes. We will know each other by smell alone, if needed."

His hand holding hers made saliva flood. Rak'khiel dabbed the corner of her mouth. *Better to blot than drool. Goddess, I'm such a peasant.* The upside of being disgusted with herself – the paisley shimmer and her buds of saber teeth receded.

"Goddess in a nightgown," she snarled. "How will we ... how will I ever ...? We dare not procreate. What is the result if I cannot control my body? In the middle of ... ah ... you know ...."

"If just one of us is Changed, even partially, then yes, there will be a child. It will not be a warrior. And possibly it could have some abnormalities."

"No change, no children?" Rak'khiel said. "And I cannot manage myself. A fang here, a claw there. I'm shifting, my skin is alive. I control one part of me, another gets free." A patch of reptile scale in a golden-pink hue slithered down one arm.

"Shalit, I give up. I am a failure. My grievous reprehensible, milord." Kel threw up her hands and plopped her butt on the bed's edge.

"You? A quitter? Or are you a coward?" The words were harsh but she saw both empathy and teasing laughter in dark eyes. "Not the girl I married." A wicked grin followed his words. She recognized the lust in his relaxed lower lip and reached a hand toward Razr without quite knowing why.

He joined her on the bed.

Oh, yes, I remember. I wanted to touch .... She traced the outlines of his mouth.

Razr's breathing shifted to ragged, like he'd run to the village and back.

The simple hearing of it made her body quiver, made her forget what they'd just been discussing.

Her body arched. Kel couldn't control it. Remembered Prince Helrazr, her lifemate, is a world-famous seducer. *Yes, I'm conquered without effort. What must he think? And yet, he knows me now. As well as anyone could.*

Big hands turned her to face him, Razr's mouth captured Kel's. He pulled her tight against him, curving forward. Wrapping her in the safety of his body, one hand roamed her back beneath her loose top.

Arms trapped between their bodies, Rak'khiel allowed her hands to splay against the open v-neck of his ship's shirt.

He feels like velvet over ceramtanium, all soft skin and spunsteel muscle.

Razr's shiver brought her response – rows of gooseflesh eeled up her spine. *Goddess, he has to feel them.*

A quick motion of one hand, a series of almost-silent snicks, and her red lace breast-support lay on the floor.

She slitted her eyes just long enough to see both of his were closed. *That's good then. Why I feel better about it, I don't know. Perhaps he might care for me a little? Please Goddess, let it be that, rather than just I'm the only living Kra'aken female.*

Releasing pent breath, she allowed her heavy eyelids to reclose. Kel relaxed into the comfort, the sheer delight of being held.

Sure hands gripped her hips, but she felt Razr's fingers tremble against her body.

Practiced thumbs hooked the waist of her pants, pushed them past her hips. Never breaking their kiss, he lifted, held her against his chest, and stripped off her ship's blues.

Her best lace underwear went with them. *Bless him. He did everything so smoothly, so quickly he left no chance for awkwardness.*

Razr's touching, his kisses, easy as breathing.

Kindled by his desire, fueled by her response, the pendant stirred against Kel's heart. Behind her eyelids, pressure built. As pupils morphed into diamonds, an odd circular rubbing sensation drew her attention. *Goddess! It's the faceted jewel rings … spinning around my irises.* But desire swept Rak'khiel in a hard, driving wave, washed every conscious thought from her mind.

"Never stop. Never, never, never," she moaned against his lips.

Razr shrugged out of his shirt and pants. Claimed her mouth in another kiss.

He's stopped my breath, just with a single one. What is ...? She clutched at empty space.

Opening her eyes, she met his, darkened with passion, jet rings wheeling.

Mating *tasca* surged, comingled scents of flowers and spice. It filled her head, leached all her will – save for one single thing. *I must, I will sate this quivering need in the core of me.*

Kel bit her lip to keep from pleading.

"Are you certain, Rak'khiel?" His unfocused eyes held confusion. "Are you absolutely sure? Can you hold control? Should we wait until you are more practised in controlling your Change? Because we cannot slip – not for an instant." An undercurrent, a thickening Kel didn't recognize, filled his voice.

"Please," she whispered. "Please don't make me beg."

"Destroyer save," Razr breathed against her throat. "I don't want to stop, to wait."

The words came so husky she thought he growled.

"Do you realize the consequences if one of us loses control?"

"I do, I studied it. Somehow I cannot bring myself to care." She arched hard against him again, panting. Felt her upper lip stretch, shoved out by sharp razors, expanding to accommodate her growing fangs.

His mouth left a trail of fire down her throat to her breast. And then, as his neck brushed against her burgeoning teeth, the prince released her.

Her burning skin, so joyous beneath his hands, went cold and lonely and sad.

Beneath her the semi-sentient mattress scrambled to restore its smooth surface, compensating for Razr's sudden move.

Kel opened her eyes, then her mouth, to beseech him for more.

Razr knelt beside her, gripping twisted handfuls of

bedding, the oddest expression on his face.

"What?" Kel blinked, puzzled.

"I have to wait," he said like it explained everything.

"But ...." Tears sprang to her eyes. She hurt, she needed ....

"Just for a bit." Razr's troubled eyes asked understanding. "I nearly lost control, nearly took my release without regard for you. I will not."

"I don't understand."

"Nor do I. But, this will happen between us as it should or it will not happen at all."

Her wanting, waiting body cried *No, no, no.*

Razr wrapped his hands in her hair, massaged her scalp. A lovely distraction, yes. But not enough.

"Not yet wavy," he said. "It's still Changing. Your morphosis should have set it in permanent state."

"Could Yola's magic be changing me too?"

"I've thought it." Razr replied. "And that's another thing which frightens me." But he kissed her anyway.

So gentle, so careful. Is it because he is afraid he will injure me? Or is he afraid of the strange magic? Sliding her arms around his neck, she tangled her fingers in the long jet spill of his hair and deepened the kiss.

Rounded like his archer's bow, drawn as taut, beneath her hands, Razr's muscles felt like the carved stone under skin.

One pull of a large arm gathered her closer, his arousal pressed hard against her belly.

The restless pendant heated, scarlet streams wreathed it where it lay against Kel's chest.

Clutching his biceps, Kel rubbed against him. *I am shameless. And there is nothing but ravenous flesh between us. Nothing.*

His swift movement made her gasp, placed them side-by-side, face-to-face on the velvety coverlet. Razr covered her mouth with his.

She whimpered her need against his lips.

Sure hands roved her body, searching, finding exquisitely sensitive places, tracing the path for his mouth to follow.

She swallowed a scream and braced against his hand. Climbing her mountain of desire, Kel could not reach the summit. Opening her eyes, fuzzy, drunk with desire, she pleaded. "Please, now."

"You are an innocent," Razr husked, the words slurred in his slack mouth. "How can you know?"

"Yola's magic calls to you. My body demands you. And your need is plain." Kel reached, caressed his hard thick length.

Her touch brought a half-sob.

"I cannot take you uncontrolled," he gasped. "I could hurt … I'm afraid …." He shook his head.

"Try again," she husked, amber iris rings glittering, whirling. "Just once more. I will control my morphosis."

"I am yours to command,"

"There must be no child – until we know where we will live. Under what conditions. It may be war."

"Agreed. It will be fine," Kel said, very sure. "Come here."

Beginning again, the prince found new places of pleasure, stroking the ones he'd already claimed.

"Goddess, would you give me release?" Her voice quavered, broke.

Pushing Kel's legs apart, he settled between them.

This is what I want – why did I flinch? His fingers, gentling me, preparing me for the necessary next step.

Sliding his body up hers, Razr paused when his blunt hardness pressed against her most private self.

Oh no, no, no. Yes, yes, yes.

"My most sincere reprehensible," Razr whispered against her throat, and slid both large hands beneath her hips. Tilting her up and open, he murmured, "I despair causing you pain." And in a single motion, he sheathed himself to the hilt.

Rak'khiel screamed and climaxed. The single hard sharp pain, the too-full stretching and filling, shoved her up the pinnacle and over the peak.

Hearts battering her ribs, lungs heaving like bellows, Kel clawed at his back in an endless series of pleasure-shudders.

Somewhere in the recesses of her mind, she caught his pause. *Claw nubs sprouted, digging in his skin. Can I split off a module for housekeeping? To damp any beginnings of Change? Yes, now I understand.*

Settling beneath her husband with a sigh of satisfaction, now free to relax, she examined each fizzy part of her body in the lovely lassitude of afterglow.

Then Razr began to move once more, slow and insistent.

Goddess in a marriage bed! I've only just begun to understand the pleasures of a man and a woman, flew through her mind as she approached the apex again.

Razr's body tensed above her.

Closer, I need to be closer. Kel's hands slid from Razr's back to grip his buttocks. Fingers sinking into his flesh, she pulled him in, deep, deeper. Wrapping her legs around his waist, Kel held him tight.

"Destroyer save me, lifemate." he whispered.

She searched his beautiful face. *I'm drunk but not on wine.*

"This time," he said. "This time, we go together."

Relaxing her grip, she opened all her senses to his slow velvet slide.

Pleasure built, mirrored in Razr's reaction.

Scarlet and silver streams drifted between their bodies. Magic's electric current hummed, then built and surged in the pendant. Above one of Razr's perfectly muscled shoulders, Kel saw the crimson drift aloft, magnificent in its presence.

I shall die from the pleasure of this. And still the pleasure built.

"Ahhhh," he breathed, laid his forehead against hers.

She looked her question deep into his ebon dark eyes.

"Yes," he breathed, "Now we go together."

I am lost. Hopelessly, helplessly lost. My body, heart and soul belong to this wonderful, spoiled rotten, loveable, hardheaded sixth prince of Kra'aken.

§

"Why did you decide on this particular time? Not that I'm displeased," he reassured with a lazy grin. "Aside from transitional requirements? I expected a much longer delay … while you became comfortable with me."

"Razr," she laughed. It was a low throaty thing, the sound of a woman well pleasured. "I feared for your sanity. And for your physical damage. Three times I saw you smash your … um … this."

Razr's brows shot toward his hairline. His mouth opened, closed, opened again. But all that emerged was a "Harrumph."

"Well, it was always sticking out," Kel laughed. "And you kept running it into things."

"Ah," he said. "So this was simply for my own good, this lovemaking?"

Rak'khiel quivered at his hand caressing her hip. *Goddess, can I never get enough of him?* "Of course, my prince. A lady would never stoop to enjoying such a base activity." *True enough on Olica.*

"Perhaps then," he said and lowered his mouth to hers. "Perhaps we can change a lady's mind?"

Chapter 60

Mid-Dark
Jorca 10. 7206.37
Survivors' Dreams, Insystem Space

Rak'khiel and Razr sat in the fighter's cockpit.

Movement, a shift on their port side, drew their heads in sync as if pulled by the strings of a puppetmaster.

The brilliant center of the white glowing portal began to spin, interior mass moved, shifted. Dark lines appeared, radiating from center to exterior, like spokes of a wheel. Then, with a final turn, like the moves of an elegant dance, the lines bent into a vertical oval forming a closed lens.

"It's beautiful," Kel breathed. "Like a fire opal." Then secundas later, she added, "Razr, we've passage permission. It sings to me through Yola's pendant."

He didn't question how she knew, or who spoke. There were no answers – at least not yet.

"On the far side," he whispered, realizing he'd held his breath. *I fear voicing the words will jinx my hope.* "There may be a signal beacon with information."

"Of ...?"

"Passing ships leave signatures, messages for others. Threat warnings or news of safe havens."

The expression of sympathy crossing Kel's face brought

blurring to his vision. *She understand, she knows what it is to lose.*

"Razr, I ...." One slender hand stroked his shoulder. "My grievous pain at your losses."

He covered her hand with his, a tiny squeeze. "You've also suffered. It's time. Our way is clear but for how long? Fly the pod, your favor. I'd prefer you sat armscomp here with me, but it's critical you pilot the cocoon."

"I would also prefer to be here." Kel's voice held a tiny quaver. Squaring her shoulders, she strode to the core and dropped through.

§

Razr knew when Rak'khiel's mindjack melded with ship's systems. He heard her request to her AI.

"Caylee, attend my every action, your favor?"

"Brin," he said. "You know what to do."

"Sir," the AI's voice floated from anywhere and nowhere.

"Goddess in an eyeball!" The shriek sounded over the com.

Kel's words pulled Razr's attention from his preflight checklist to the main viewscreen. And the portal.

The iris darkened and broadened. A sudden horizontal swelling of the vertical pupil exposed the deep black of space looming on the portal's far side.

It's narrow. Too narrow. "Brin. Is there clearance for to pass?"

"Working," Then, "My computations show adequate. Caylee?"

Strange, thought Razr. *Since when does Brin ask for confirmation of any of his numbers?*

"Tight," the melodic voice, the avatar of Rak'khiel's mother. "But eminently doable with our pilots."

Razr's mind wobbled off-axis in his skull. *What in the name of the Great Destroyer has happened here? Our computers are acting like people.* Working to ensure his voice sounded natural, unconcerned, he ordered, "On my third mark."

"Pod, copy."

"Mark, mark, mark."

Razr kicked the mains.

§

Closing the remaining space between the *NeedlePod* and the alien gate, Razr's body sensors blared.

"Shata," he snarled. *How is it my hearts are trying and explode or leap through my ribcage but she is in complete control?*

"Razr, what is wrong? Should I be alarmed?"

"No, Kel," the words ground out like he chewed glass. "A defect in my systems only." He felt claw nubs punch through the ends of his fingers at her smothered giggle. *Why did I lie? She has my physical readouts as I do hers.*

The buffet of the alien portal encompassed them, unexpected suction pulled them in. Although he vectored them toward the gate's center, Razr's breath refused to come.

"Brin?"

"It seems our engines are unnecessary, milord."

"Unnecessary? Or unavailable?" His head filled with an orchestra of violettas, bright twinkles danced against a field of black.

"Breathe, Prince Helrazr. Or you will transition in an unconscious state."

"Forza me," he cursed and sucked oxygen deep as it would go. *Panicking like a first-term recruit.*

"Pod?" he said. "Status?"

"Systems green. Something just spoke in my mind – a voice of the Portal Keeper. This is the Opal Gate."

Damme, she sounds so calm. Can it be? Of course it can, her body alarms are silent. Razr gnashed his teeth. *Or Caylee is covering for her. Am I jealous of my wife's composure? Small, Razr. Petty. I should be proud.*

The pull of the portal, a glistening spinning power, enclosed the twinned ships. Blue and opalescent white beams flowed over them, sparked from every surface.

But Razr noted when a spot in their meld groaned, the white-blue power lessened, accommodated for any structural weaknesses. *They ... it ... means for us to arrive on the far side unharmed.* He watched the transition timeclock scroll backwards and wondered what it meant to them when they exited the gate on the Kra'aken side.

"Brin, I show three horas reverse-elapsed since our entry into the portal. What can it mean?"

"In all honesty, Prince Helrazr, I have no idea."

Swell.

He perused his screens. The readouts on the pod showed a green dot – Kel. All good. Her stray thoughts said she functioned, processed, prepared for whatever waited. He heard her murmurs to Caylee. *Thank the Destroyer I'm calm again. Humiliating, that.*

The main viewscreen turned from the pale nothing of the gate to a dark circle dead ahead.

Belted and netted in his couch, Razr focused on his instruments, murmuring to the AI's, and to Kel. *It's yanking us into the maw at speeds too fast to calc.*

Drawing closer, hurtling at a speed the fighter's instruments couldn't measure, they flew out of the white bright into the deep black of space.

Buffeted by bow shocks, images of bent streams of multi-colored lights and bulkheads wrapping around them, *Survivors' Dreams* transitioned the Opal Gate. With the swirling shutter of a camera lens, the portal closed behind them.

Safe.

"Brin, Caylee? Take the com?"

"Copy." The female response.

"Copy." Male acknowledgement.

"Kel? Need to stretch?"

"Affirmative. My appreciations."

Razr waited the forever-time for mindjack separation then arced from his couch. A glance at his screens showed Kel's green dot moving in the pod's cockpit. He rubbed stinging arms and legs. Found, to his dismay, he'd wrapped his arms about his body, hugging close for small comfort.

Better I hug my new mate. A wide grin split his face and he headed for the core and the pod whistling a Kra'aken war tune. *Nothing preventing, we can make Kra'aken outerspace in three aiys.*

§

He got as far as B-deck.

"Majesties." Brin's tone stopped Razr mid-stride.

Something lashed their shields. A sparkling salvo danced on their screens.

"Destroyer save," Caylee cried, and her voice rose an octave.

"Not trying to hull us," Brin shouted. "Just disable us."

As if someone heard, a hard shove struck their ship, a push at their shields. Something latched onto their hull, dragging, slowing their progress.

"Shata," Razr said. "They've locked on tractor beams."

"Full engines," Razr ordered and shoved his yokes to max. Felt the pod's surge.

"Pulling away," Kel said.

Then came the klaxons blare, red neon lit across his boards.

The *Dreams* creaked, banged, groaned under the stress as myriad thumps testified many tractor beams gripped their hull.

Engines screamed as they were forced to full stop.

Razr smelled the acrid stench of burning electrical wires, overheated ceramtanium.

"Razr, my sensors are lit like Candlemas Trees," Kel cried.

"Power down to minimum," he said.

"Goddess in a crucible," Kel muttered. "Do they think to rip us apart, then?"

Chapter 61

Mid-Dark
Jorca 10. 7206.57
Survivors' Dreams, Insystem Space

Strapped in his bed, Honor listened to Kel, Razr, Brin and Caylee chatter on the com. His stomachs wadded and lurched into his throat at the grab of the tractor beams.

I'm no naïf. This is a dire turn of fate – death or slavery for us all. This ship will be sold or absorbed into the fleet of our captors. Unless they are Kra'aken. For the sake of Kel and Razr, I pray it is so. For me, whoever they are, the consequences cannot be good.

All six eyes fastened on his personal viewscreen, Honor worried for the safety of his new friends. *Especially Rak'khiel. Cloaked, they are. Their stealth technology is excellent. On another day, I'd have asked to trade for it.*

Like honey dripping from a knife blade, the blank screens dissolved revealing a massed array of ships. *A conglomeration?* His mind searched for a better description, suggested hodge-podge. The spydr snorted.

Outside his viewport, in some places ten deep, spaceships hung. All ages, all sizes, in all manner of conditions. He recognized both pre- and post-FTL capable craft.

At the center, directly in their path, squatted an ancient

destroyer, ugly as a warttoad. Honor watched it execute a ponderous half-turn, then reposition. The intent came clear.

The movement exposed a cruiser-class frigate. *Undoubtedly the newest ship in this odd fleet. Serving as flagship?* Yes, two escorts boasting bristling armament pods flanked the command vessel. Honor's mouth twitched in his awful smile. *They maintain the distance and angle allowing them to fire on us.*

Assessing the massed crafts, he wondered if any were jump-capable. Or if they could transition the Opal Gate? The fleet shifted.

Yes, Kel's thought touched his mind. *On your mark.*

Hopeless. The prince's thought came right behind. *One ship against so many.*

Survivors' Dreams surged, her tethers bit deep.

Klaxons, damage alarms shrieked.

"Our bid for freedom failed," the aracha whispered. He smelled smoke, watched sparks leap from the tech boards in his quarters. Hissing in fury, he heard Razr's defeated voice order a power-down.

Thin skeletal hands began unsnapping his restraints.

"I must somehow help. I will not lie abed." Honor worked faster and faster. In his viewscreen he saw the two pincer ends of their captor's ships close the circle. "Now, a huge part of their fleet sitss between uss and the alien portal," he muttered unfastening the final netting. "Our escape route, blocked by sheer numberss. Held fast by sheer numberss of tractor beamss. We are powerful but not enough to break free."

The hailing channel erupted in a burst of chittering, clicking snaps.

The High Lord's head snapped up, he snarled a long answering hiss. Ripping away the last of his restraints, the black spydr surged from his bed, through his cube door and up the interior fighter core.

Again the com spewed clacking gibberish.

"Great God of All deliver us," Honor heard Razr pray as he breasted final decking and rushed into the fighter's cockpit.

Chapter 62

Mid-Dark
Jorca 10. 7206.57
Survivors' Dreams, Insystem Space

Honor felt her presence behind him. Shifting to one side, he allowed Rak'khiel bridge access.

"Is the forzaing 'Ristos?" Razr's words held hate.

The arachna nodded. "It appearss we have found the rest of my exiled 'Risto nation. Perhapss a hundrada thousand spydrss before uss. I have been gone long. I cannot know."

Brin and Caylee's avatars hung in the cockpit, Tarkin, Torga and Grigori watched him from the deck core.

All watched him, emotions playing over their features.

I know who trustss, I know who doess not. At least completely.

"If you want revenge for our treatment of you," Razr snarled. "It is now within easy reach."

An idea, half-formed in Honor's mind at the 'Risto's first hail, presented itself complete.

Honor's multi-stomachs fluttered at his idea. He felt his feelers fold, retract and slam beneath his forehead skin. Retreating from the awful prospect of what he might be able to do. To save his friends.

It will require me to re-don the silver crown of control with that horror of a black stone. It will require me to become, again, a horrible thing – whose actions, I have come to loathe. Can I do it?

Honor slid back and forth, sideways, in the cockpit confines. *No, no, never. But my friends will die if I do nothing. I AM the HIGH LORD. Will they believe I am sincere? Can I make the 'Risto horde believe? Not unless I wear the Circlet, and use it to bend their minds to my will. How will I keep the ghastly gem from consuming me with its evil?*

The shields screamed and crackled beneath the onslaught of tractor beams.

The black spydr lifted an anguished face, carefully met each pair of eyes.

"I must offer thiss solution, my friendss. I am terrified. But these are my subjectss. And ... they will not wait much longer for an answer to their hail. They do recognize the *Dream'ss* design ass Kra'aken, even though it iss no longer a simple fighter."

"My friendss," he said, sucking a deep breath. "I think I can save you all but ...." Honor's voice failed him, shudders rippled and chitin rattled. All eight segmented legs buckled. He grabbed the back of the armscomper's indigo couch to keep from falling.

He knew whose hand rested on his shoulder, he knew without looking whose hand took his. *She comforts me? Even now?*

"At what cost to you, my friend." Kel asked. "Your life?"

Chapter 63

Mid-Dark
Jorca 10. 7207.03
Survivors' Dreams, Insystem Space

"Goddess save," Rak'khiel breathed. A glance around showed Brin, gray hair in warrior's braids, Caylee in military camo. *Ready to fight. Ready to die.*

"Forzaing 'Ristos," Rak'khiel heard the vicious hatred in Razr's curse.

The prince hesitated a moment, glanced at Kel's face and added, "My reprehensible, Honor."

"Understood. No offense taken."

She searched the spydr's awful visage. Nodded. "Present company exceptioned, milord."

"It is fine, Rak'khiel." The High Lord's features rearranged into a combination she now knew for new ideas and finding the best words to present them. "Milady, if I may ...?"

"Absolutely," she answered without hesitation. Her peripheral vision told her Razr didn't share her certainty. *Too bad.* "What can we do?"

"My crown. If they see it, they will know who I am. I can use hivemind to force their obedience. I will convince them although your infrared life signatures are real, you are only food. I will resume my titla of Imperator. I will take them through the alien portal, out of this galaxy. Perhaps to Olica."

Honor's face contorted into the rictus she knew for his smile.

"No," she whispered. "You go to your death. Or worse." But she knew he held their only chance, nodded her understanding.

"No," roared the prince. "You will not."

"Yes," Rak'khiel said. "I'll retrieve your circlet immediately." She stopped when the arachna spoke, his words surprised her.

"Caylee, Brin? Can you coat a portion of the mindstone? On the back, where it touches my skin? If it is possible, I would keep it from fully possessing me."

"I have an amalgram which could work," Brin nodded, a tiny smile tugged at the corner of his mouth. "Shall I?"

"I think perhaps ... perhaps in a container only? But first I must wield the complete power to sway them. But after that, then yes."

Another hail from the surrounding massed ships.

"Quickly, your favor," hissed Honor. "Before they rend uss. And I'll need a black robe."

"I forbid it," Razr snarled.

"Do it," Kel used the full force of Command Voice. "I order it. Tarkin, can you?"

Gone. The whisk of a black tail disappeared into the fighter's core.

The prince gaped. His mouth fell open. Then crashed shut. Deep scarlet surged up his neck, suffused his face.

Will he lose it here? Or can he trust and sustain control? If so, will it be because I am correct, or because I am the only female and he fears to lose my favor?

"You dare ...," escaped before his budding fangs retracted. His full lips compressed to a bloodless line.

Has no one challenged him before? Kel startled when Brin answered her thought.

Never a female and never with a command decision.

The AI's tight beam shaded with ... could it be satisfaction?

You are correct, of course, Brin sent. *And his inner honesty will compel his agreement. Right after he gets over your direct repudiation of his leadership.*

Now convinced she heard approval in Brin's words, Rak'khiel oh-so-carefully kept all expression from her face.

A puffing Tarkin climbed the core rungs, duffle handles clenched in sharp teeth. Depositing the bag on the cockpit decking, he gave it a shove with his nose. Black lips wreathed back from bared fangs.

The cafuzog hawked and spat. *I can feel its evil, even through the leaded shielding. The horror attempted to subvert me the entire carry. My reprehensible for lack of courage but I must be far from it. Now.*

Once again, the cafuzog disappeared into the *Dream's* core.

"Tarkin's severed mental contact," Caylee's melodic voice broke the silence. "Even I, component parts that I am, can feel its influence."

A white-striped black head popped into the cockpit. Torga carried a fabric bundle in her teeth, dropped it and fled. *Here is the robe. I ... too ... must go.*

Black cloth fell to the pebbled surface, unfolded.

Honor shook out the garment, dragged it over his head. Settling the robe, he glided to the box.

"Honor," Rak'khiel protested. "I don't want you to sacrifice yourself for us."

"I don't trust him to do what he's proposing," countered the prince.

"Can you stand alone against the stone's compulsion?" Brin queried the spydr.

"It is powerful," Caylee added. "Even through the shielding of the box."

What does it matter? With or without Honor, we will all soon be dead anyway? Torga's thought knifed through their arguments.

Silence dropped like a blanket over the bridge of the fighter.

"_(*&D@#$%^)sss!!!" Burst through the com.

"This iss our last chance to answer," Honor translated. "We will be boarded, used for food, our ship assimilated into their fleet.

"We can fight ...," Razr began.

Kel watched him swallow, then slowly shake his head, broad shoulders slumped.

"We have to drop shields to fire. We cannot." The prince nodded, "Yes, Honor. You are correct in all you say. We will surely die or worse."

"I would prefer to die in battle than place that evil on my head. But I will not sacrifice you, my friendss. I will resist – I believe I can control it. At least long enough to force them to lift the tractor beamss. Once you are free, do not hesitate. Flee."

"But ...." Rak'khiel began, flinched as Honor reared full height.

The aracha hissed. "I know you, Lady Regence. I know your heart. Give me your word you will not intervene. Swear you will flee, back through the portal, or on to Kra'aken." The High Lord lowered his body, all black segmented legs again on the floor. "Your vow on it, Prince Helrazr?"

It wasn't even a Goddesss-accursed question, Kel thought. *They conspire against me now.*

Tarkin popped through the opening, a small jar in his jaws. *The amalgram from Brin.*

"My appreciationss." Honor dropped the jar into a pocket of his robe. "They must not sense I am heretic. Perhapss I will, with thiss, mitigate control of my will by the stone'ss power. Because eventually it can and will."

The High Lord turned to Caylee's avatar. "Can you replace my defensess, my stingerss, my clawss, my fangss and poison sacss? I must be perfect, formidable, frightening. We rule by fear and compulsion."

Orange feelers peeped from Honor's forehead, waved in indication of his sincerity.

"Yes, in a matter of *horas.*"

"Your favor, allow me to don the accursed evil thing and let me talk to their fleet leader."

"I forbid repairs to the High Lord." Razr's Command Voice knifed the air.

"Did we not settle this before?" Kel snapped. "Your favor, Prince Helrazr. If it pleases you, or even if it does not, kindly shut your royal trap. Otherwise we will be cocooned, sucked dry and eaten while you argue. And posture. And delay."

He's not nearly as handsome, she thought. *With a face the color of deep puce.*

"If it changess me," Honor said. "Promise you will not hesitate. You will kill me, on the instant."

"Count on it, arachna," snarled the prince.

"I require you to all pretend unconsciousness. Assume limp posturess, as if you have been stunned and webbed."

"When the Twelve Hells rime with frost," growled the prince.

"Husband, we must. We are not betrayed." Kel's voice, amplified by the pendant's power, forced belief. Moving to a rounded corner of the bulkhead, she relaxed, boneless, in a semi-recline.

"Perfect, Kel," said Honor. "They will see only infrared bundless. They cannot tell more."

Razr folded at her feet, curled between his new bride and the 'Risto.

We are in our jump nets. We are ready, came Tarkin's thought.

"Hailing frequency open," Brin said.

Rak'khiel watched Honor lift the box lid exposing the silver circlet. *Coiled in the bottom of the container like a malignant viper.*

Shaking skeletal hands lifted the silver circlet.

The orange feelers on his forehead retracted, preparing to accept the crown.

Or hiding from it, she wondered.

Honor lost his grip, the circlet slipped. At his catch, the

spydr recoiled.

Kel felt the stone's renewed assault on the High Lord. She watched him inhale. *So deep his carapace creaked. Gathering his courage.*

Positioning the malevolence above his head, he whispered, "Your favor, Brin, while I still have my resolve, put them onscreen."

Chapter 64

Mid-Dark
Jorca 10. 7207.13
Survivors' Dreams, Insystem Space

The viewscreen filled with a ghastly visage.

Honor reared to his full frightening height.

The black stone throbbed its compulsion, from the *Dream* and into the massed ships surrounding them.

Pulled crown's evil power, the High Lord focused it into a bullet beam and threw it against the ships surrounding *Survivors' Dreams*.

"_(*&D@#$%^)sss!!!" Screeched the enormous black spydr. Thin skeletal hands, bearing rings of power clenched at the viewscreen, but his fingertips were hidden from view. "Who dares disturb the slumber of your Imperator?" he screamed. "Who dares threaten my ship?"

A telling silence hung heavy. In the background, through his crown, he heard chittering of many voices. Heard many thoughts, many questions.

"Can it be?"

"After all this time?"

"Could it be the true High Lord?"

"We believed him lost."

"He bears the crown."

"Feel the power."

"It can be no mistake."

Then from the spydr on the flagship, the one who stood to lose his high position. "It is an imposter. Do not believe."

Honor threw the power of the dull black stone through space, smashed the doubter against the floor of his own ship. "When I board, I will paralyze you, drain you and rend you to pieces."

"Nay, my Imperator, I do not disbelieve," said the crushed lump.

"You forget yourself. You forget the power of the Crown of Rule. You forget I see all, hear all, know all."

"My grievous reprehensible, High Lord. I am your loyal servant. Please release me to prepare you proper welcome."

Honor allowed a tiny satisfied smile to twist one corner of his mouth.

The black stone throbbed its message of evil through the cockpit, into the fleet massed outside the *Dreams.*

"Hear me," the High Lord screeched. "I will drain my remaining food sourcess on thiss abortion of a spaceship. In three horass, I will board the flagship. Ready my quarterss. Ready my femaless. It hass been some time since I have enjoyed a mating. Select the most durable of your offeringss – I feel viciouss. Prepare to receive me, in proper fashion, your long lost Imperator. If I am displeased, I will tear out your mindss. I hold the Great Stone of Rule. See it and believe."

Screeching, chittering, Honor berated the fleet commanders until each fell on his face on his ship's decking. "All fighterss stand down. Remove the tractor beamss, they stresss this pitiful vessel. I will be finished feeding in three horass. I will contact you again to ascertain you are properly prepared to receive my magnificence. Imperator out."

Brin cut the com.

With a shudder so deep it came from his bone marrow, Honor hissed, tore the circlet from his head, and bounced it across the pebbled ceramsteel deck.

"How embarrassing," he muttered. "To speak in such a fashion. But it had to be done."

Brin retrieved the circlet, quickly smoothed the dents in the silver, and replaced it within the shielded box. Slammed the lid.

How, wondered the spydr. *Can an avatar perform a physical action?*

"Honor," Caylee's voice sounded through ship's systems. "My surgery is ready for your reconstructions. Honor, I now have two horas in which I must perform three horas work. Stop all dithering. Medbay, your favor!"

How odd, he thought. A machine that sounds harried, and more than a little irritated.

"Sickbay, on the instant."

"I will not permit this," roared Razr.

"I will," Kel said.

Honor watched Yola's pendant move in restless dance on her chest. Red streamers lifted, writhed about the nebulous silver. He watched the prince study it as well, and expected the conciliatory words that followed.

"It appears we will," Razr said.

Honor also heard, although he was not supposed to, a very tight beam from Brin to Razr. And it took a heroic effort not to laugh at the AI's thought.

You're learning, milord.

Chapter 65

Mid-Dark
Jorca 10. 7209.13
Survivors' Dreams, Insystem Space

"Surgery complete," Caylee announced. "All successful. Honor now wakes and will join you on the bridge in ten minas."

"How will we transport him to the 'Risto flagship?" Brin asked. "Will they send a pinnace? What can we fashion for an exterior airlock. Perhaps one of their ships has one?"

"I will ask," said the spyder emerging from the core. "One thing more. Should I fail, please have your self-destruct sequence fully enabled. Do not allow yourselves to be taken."

He is still my friend. But the pit of Kel's stomach climbed into her throat and stopped her air as she studied the terrifying creature from the castle on Olica.

Long sharp venomous fangs, black nails complete with mustard-colored hourglass venom sacs. Beneath his black robe, his stinger would be replaced, and now full of deadly poison.

I refuse to fear him.

Beside her, the slide of a weapon clearing a holster, the hum of an activated laser.

Razr, ready to follow through on his promise to Honor.

Pulling a deep breath, she felt her stomach return to its proper spot.

A ping, a shimmer of light, materialized in the cockpit.

Without thinking, Kel found her weapon in her hand.

Brin and Caylee held pistols and a half-turned Tarkin and Torga, posteriors at the ready, filled the space at the edge of the core.

Honor held himself coiled and ready to leap on the presence.

We are all prepared to do battle. Kel realized with satisfaction. *I was correct to trust the spydr.*

A musical chime sounded, a translucent semi-figure appeared, hanging in mid-air.

"Goddess in a transference vehicle," she breathed. "It's not dense enough to shoot, even if it is dangerous."

The pendant quivered on her chest, sent her a thought.

"Yola's magic says we are in no danger. Whatever is here, means us nothing but good." Rak'khiel reholstered her pistol. Noticed out the corner of her eye, Razr still held his at the ready.

"Greetings, travelers," the entity sang, soft, compelling. But his eyes lasered to the necklace on Rak'khiel's chest. "Sooo," he breathed. "Her heritage is truly passed, not stolen. But to a non-blood – I had not known it possible.

Heritage? Passed? Kel's knees trembled, threatened to dissolve. *This ... being knows ... knew Yola?*

"My apologies. My name is *Molto Cantabile*, my call chime is *Molto*. I am one of the Guardians of the Major and Minor Gates. The Opal Gate is under my purvue. I have observed your interactions for the past three hours. For the lifeform named Honor, Barizan Honor du'Oniiq, for his willingness to sacrifice himself to save his friends, I/we offer him both sanctuary and restoration to his desired bipedal form."

"Who ...?" Kel stammered. "And what ..."

Honor's milky face surged roseate. "You offer me ...

restoration. Truly? At what price?"

"We are the Ancients, oldest of all. We travel, terraforming new worlds, preparing new portals. We are responsible for both the planets of Earth and Kra'aken. We have created many others, now in varying stages of ability to support life. My fellow Ancients also do the same. Each of us care for a group of prospective worlds, and manage the traffic through our gates."

"Then why, in the Destroyer'ss Name, did you allow such horrorss as we, to passs through and ruin the world of Olica?" Hissed Honor.

"I admit that we are very old, and often forgetful. One of us thought another had closed the portal. We erred." The translucent entity shrugged, then sang, "However, in the instance of the baby girl, yes. We saw her and pulled her through, knowing nothing good could happen to her on the Kra'aken side. Your ship and that of the deeply injured man came through by accident."

"Where do you come from?" Rak'khiel asked. "How do you live? What do you know of my Adopted Mother?"

"I knew her well – she came from us. I will create an explanation module suitable to your skull jack." Molto wavered, reformed and continued. "We are so old we are almost pure energy. We require little sustenance. But our names, and our music come from the melodies created by artists one of our earliest worlds – Terra, or you may know the planet as Earth. We found their terms most lovely. My name, for instance, *Molto Cantabile*, means very songlike and flowing. I feel it describes me well."

"Why, if Yola was yours, did you allow her death. It was horrible, beyond bearing." Rak'khiel's fury rode the edge of her voice like a serrated blade.

"I hear this to my great sorrow." The musical words modulated, bespoke angst and Kel suddenly wished to weep. "But our Yolaidara was a place holder, never a wielder."

"Why, if you can do what you say, have you waited to

intervene until we were nearly torn apart?" Razr's tone challenged.

Kel stabbed him in the ribs with an elbow.

Molto appeared unoffended. "I waited to determine the 'Ristos' intent. Judge his truthfulness, his change from prior behaviors. I refuse to bestow a pristine new planet unless those who will occupy it are worthy. I believe Honor can guide his people into a better way, a better life. If he can, we will grant them the bodies they so desire. They can begin again. We Ancients live to right old wrongs wherever possible."

"What if I fail," asked the High Lord.

"The planet will be wiped and prepared for another species."

"Goddess," shivered Kel. "So matter of fact."

"We are old. We have seen much. We do not waste time or resources. But we have great hope for Honor and his people. Can you, High Lord, will you weed out dissention, eliminate those who do not wish to build a better life?"

"I've killed for far lesss noble reasonss," Honor admitted. "But I fear the power of the crown."

"I can mitigate its dissonance and still enhance your influence with your people," trilled *Molto*. "You will not lose your sense of reason, your sense of right and wrong although you wear it. It is critical your subjects initially do not know of your changes. Successful deception, in the beginning, is crucial to the salvation of your species."

"How can I know the truth of it?" Longing suffused the arachna's words.

"No," Razr said. "He will not, we will not acquiesce on your mere statements. Never without proof."

"We may ass well," Honor whispered. "I think he can do whatever he wantss with uss."

"You can trust," Kel answered, as red streamers rose from her chest and twined about her head. "Yola's pendant swears it."

"I will send a transfer globe for the being Honor. I will port him to his people, to his fleet. I will mask the life signatures of your friends. I will command and hold their attention while your ship makes escape."

"Yess, an excellent strategy. I accept."

"We stand ready, *Molto,* at your signal." Razr's voice came calm, professional. "Our profound appreciations at your intervention."

"Inform your subjects you are on your way. I will provide a transfer bubble," said the ethereal wavering form.

"I am ready," hissed the High Lord, but his voice quavered.

Chapter 66

Dark
Jorca 10. 7209.22
Survivors' Dreams, Insystem Space

"This is not goodbye," Kel said and hugged Honor's neck. "We will return. I will find you." *Will Razr agree?*

Ignoring the full venom sacs in the aracha's nails, the prince extended his hands, clasped wrists, Kra'aken style. "There will be friendship between us Lord Barizan du'Oniique. I wish you well in your ventures."

Goddess grant that forgetful Molto remembers to protect Honor when he confronts his subjects, Kel prayed. *Goddess grant the evil power of the crown's stone can be controlled.*

"Molto, now iss the time to hide my friendss."

"It is done, Lord Honor."

"Open my hailing frequency, Brin, your favor."

Rak'khiel saw the thin white fingers tremble as the spydr patted the pocket holding the amalgram. She watched him pick up the circlet, features twisted in loathing, and place it on his head.

"Open channel, onscreen now, Brin. My appreciationss."

Although she expected it, Kel's viscera crawled into her throat as she studied the arachna.

Honor sucked a deep breath, then projected an awful menacing visage displaying full dripping fangs, and full nail pockets.

"My subjectss, I have killed and consumed my food sourcess. Take some comfort, those who are weakest among you. I am renewed, I will not require feeding for perhaps an aiy. I travel in a new type of conveyance. Prepare an external hatch to receive me. Your High Lord comess."

One quick motion to Brin, and the screen blanked.

A glance at ship's monitors showed Rak'khiel something she'd rather not have known. *Honor's respiration's much too fast, his body temp's dropped almost to hibernation stage.* She stifled her words, knew she dare not voice the truth. *He's terrified.* She watched her friend through swimming, blurry eyes.

He's also very, very brave. Caylee's thought tight-beamed into her mind.

An opalescent bubble grew against the exterior sealed hatch of the *Pod*.

It shines like those we formed from soap.

Honor's shoulders shook as he crawled sideways, descended through the core. Her last look at her friend saw his final, searching glance at each of the group. *As if he memorizes our faces. As if he may never see us again.*

"I will see you again, Honor." A half-hitch took her breath, broke the words. Kel squared her shoulders, coughed to clear the swelling in her throat. "I vow on Yola's soul, I will return and find you, my friend."

"I will wait for the day, Lady Regence. I am forever your servant." The 'Risto Lord bowed, head sweeping the flightdeck in deference of a lesser to highest royalty. Straightening, he held Kel's gaze for a long, long moment, then turned and dropped from sight.

The viewscreen showed the *Pod's* exterior hatch slide open, showed Honor entering the fire opal translucent bulb. A hissing as the outer hatch resealed.

The gelatinous conveyance reformed into a ball and flew across the interim space toward the 'Risto flagship.

Kel wondered why she suddenly saw brilliant white dots on a field of black instead of the arachna's bubble approaching the spydr fleet.

A hand on her arm, a low familiar voice said, "For the Destroyer's sweet sake, love. Would you please breathe?"

"I can't help him now. Goddess save." She whispered and felt warm wet roll down her cheeks.

Molto's bulb attached to the hull of the arachna flagship. As the outer hatch opened, an arrogant High Lord rolled through the bubble membrane, into the 'Risto ship.

The Imperator's voice whipcracked above the bowed heads of his groveling subjects.

"Release the tractor beams from that piece of garbage."

Grappling beams snapped back.

The *Dreams* shivered, compensating for its sudden freedom. Wobbled, then realigned.

GO NOW. Molto's voice sounded in their heads, from everywhere and nowhere.

"Kel, in armscompers couch. Cafuzogs stow." Razr ordered. "Brin, Caylee, Take us out of here. On the instant."

Razr dropped into his seat.

Her shaking hands refused to work her restraint buckles. One click, then another. *Goddess in a starship. I must hurry.*

The cafuzogs scurried for the side nets aft of the bridge.

Torga staggered beneath Gregori's weight. She carried him half-stuffed under one foreleg.

Tarkin grabbed the baby's lower half.

Together they stuffed the sorbazel in their net, dived in behind him.

He's almost as tall as she is, shot through Kel's mind as she pressed her head against the detested gray pad. *Just not as heavy.* Two clicks, not four, the cafuzogs were partially secured.

Nausea surged, her respiration rose. Her bioscan monitor

blared *eep-eep-eep*.

"Wife?"

"Hate the forzaing thing."

The plug slid inside her brain, the lock spun.

Then joy flooded. Instant immersion of her mind and the ship. Instant constant sharing of knowledge, data with Razr, Brin and Caylee.

"Now," said Razr. "Take us out of here."

Survivors' Dreams surged, gathered speed, gathered vee. Without any preparation, they built to jump, headed out of this solar system at maximum speed.

She felt her face flatten and distort as if squashed by a giant hand. Ignoring discomfort, she glued her eyes on viewscreens, on the receding 'Risto horde. The scrolling numbers showed them now beyond reach of the aracha weapons. Even those of the destroyer.

Be safe, my friend, Kel sent after him.

"Jump point in ten plus minas," Razr's voice sounded in her ear.

"Yes," she nodded. "I caught the feed."

"Trank hypos are in the seat pocket beside you."

Kel fished one out, placed it in her lap. "Brin will announce the time to administer?"

"I will, Lady Regence. But, you will know the time as well as I."

Her lips curved. *I do love a compliment.*

"Tarkin, Torga, Grigori? You are well?"

We are fine, Torga answered.

"Do you trank down for jumps?"

We sleep through. It is the difference in our brains and how they process what is experienced in the in-between.

"We'll go through this first short jump, just under three horas," Razr said. "Completely in the wrong direction."

Kel laughed. "Insurance the 'Risto's will not know where to look for us?"

"Affirmative. After that, we will make a longer jump, about

one aiy. For that one, we will be able to strap in our beds, transition in comfort.

"Would this be a good time to tell you Caylee's added a second set of restraints and webbing in my quarters. Plus diversion tapes, both music, the arts, and military study."

A whiff of mating *tasca* surged.

Kel shot a sideways look at her husband, caught him running his tongue over his lower lip.

If you don't wish to jump alone. Sending a tight beam and a wicked smile promising many things, she added, *I'd welcome your company.*

Epilogue

Mid-Aiy
Jorca 10, 7211.30
Survivors' Dreams, Insystem Space

In the bow of the fighter, Kel and Razr stood side by side.

Only the engines' thrumming broke the silence.

He rested his elbows on the rail, chin in hands.

She wrapped her arms about her body. *We transited the final gate an* hora *ago.*

Now inside the Kra'aken galaxy, three jumps and two and a half *aiys* away, waited the unknown of their future.

With a gentle squeeze of her shoulder, Razr said, "I'll return in a *mina.*" The bleak pain in his eyes tore her hearts in bits.

Will it be the remnants of a once great civilization? Rak'khiel wondered. *Will we find any of Razr's family? Or mine? Or is our entire world reduced to slag and cinders? A finality which will crush his spirit and send us searching through space for other survivors? It will not, cannot, be the Kra'aken Razr remembers. I refuse to ask him again.*

Now, instead, she concentrated on every tape Caylee held in her data banks.

Goddess of Good, be merciful to the prince. I will be fine – but will he? I've already lost everything – he has no idea what waits for him. My first and most important task as a wife – to help him bear whatever horribleness lies ahead.

She marveled at the star studded ebony, the majesties of deep space filling their viewscreens. Marveled at the spinning swirling constellations, their bright points like grains of crystal sand tossed by a careless hand.

My future, so limited on Olica, is now wide-open. Only opportunities and adventure and my exciting and happy marriage are before me. Goddess, please somehow allow Razr to be happy.

She felt, more than heard his emergence through the core, a light step placed him beside her. One muscular arm slid behind her back, a wrist rested butterfly-light on her shoulder.

Something gold and shining dangled between her eyes, fuzzy, too close to focus.

Leaning back, she squinted, the blur resolved, became a gem-studded charm. A miniature broomstick swayed on a gold chain before her eyes.

Rak'khiel couldn't prevent, nor did she wish to, her erupting laugh.

Happiness fizzed like champagne bubbles throughout Kel's body when Razr dropped the chain over her head.

The tiny pendant rested between her breasts atop Yola's silver one.

Rak'khiel tilted her head back against his chest, exulting in his muscular strength. Then, just to tease, she bent it forward, exposing the vulnerable nape of her neck.

Razr rumbled a laugh – it held anticipation, deliciously delayed.

Mating *tasca* flared, spice and musk.

She shivered at the brush of fang, delicately tracing an upward path from the knob at the top of her spine to her hairline. She shuddered in delight as saber teeth traced the outer shell of her ear.

"Goddess, husband," she gasped.

Her hearts beat out of synch, thudding in the join of her legs.

Floral *tasca* flooded the cockpit.

Razr's body tensed, stirred against her.

Surrendering to the joy, she turned to face him, wrapped her arms about his narrow waist. Kel hid a smile as his skin hitched beneath her touch.

So much life, so much for which I give thanks. And my appreciations, Goddess, for not granting my prayers, my simple goal of not-so-long ago. When all I ever dreamed, all I ever wanted, was to jump the broomstick with the dairyboy.

KRA'AKEN GLOSSARY

Planet of Kra'aken -- Homeworld of Kra'aken race

Kra'aken -- Humanoid warrior race whose root ancestry is Terran. Evolving to match their chosen planet, Kra'aken are larger in size than Earthers. After puberty, they are capable of changing their physical appearance at will, manifesting armored (alligator-like) scales, saber fangs, razor claws and extruded side leg and arm barbs.

AI -- Artificial Intelligence

Armscomper -- Weapons officer – computer plotting for guns

Cafuzog -- Mammal, close relative of a Terran skunk

Destroyer -- Kra'aken God of War, God of the Hunt

Finorkle -- Cafuzog laughter – a high pitched half-snort

Forza -- Fornicate

Forza Yar Gongur -- "Go fornicate with a gongur"

FTL -- Faster than light speed

Gongur -- A warthog-like creature, covered with scabrous growths

Kra'aken building materials: -- Plastanium, Ceramsteel, Foamtanium, Foamsteel, Plasplex, Ceramtanium

Life Cocoon -- Survivor space pod. Used to launch Kra'aken children from the doomed planet one wakari prior to estimated impact.

Medbox, docbox, medunit, automed: -- Fully automated medical capsule, self-contained, self-transporting.

Mindjack -- Plascircle in base of skull providing computer connection for piloting or training.

My appreciations -- Welcome.

My contrition -- My apology.

My reprehensible -- My great big huge apology.

Shata -- Shit.

Slif -- Salamander-type creature, soft and squishy, three eyes on either side of head.

SSR -- Survivor Search Recognition program.

Tasca -- Personal scents, amplified by morphing process. Evokes terror in prey, identifies klan, identifies mating readiness.

WarHammer -- Mothership, massive Kra'aken destroyer.

WarNeedle -- Nimble Kra'aken fighter plane, fast, deadly, stealthed.

Your Favor -- Please.

Your Tribute -- Thank you.

KRA'AKEN MEASUREMENTS

Secunda -- 60 secundas in one mina

Mina -- 55 minas in one hora

Hora -- 27 horas in one aiy -- military time

Aiy -- 27 horas broken into: dawn, mid-aiy, aiy, mid-eve, eve, mid-dark, dark and mid-dawn

Wakari -- 6 aiys in one wakari: Mai, Tai, Wai, Thai, Fai, Sai

Hilu -- 50 aiys in one hilu

Yara -- 7 hilus in one yara

Decadi -- Decade

Centari -- Century

Milena -- Millenium

Mila -- Mile

OLICAN GLOSSARY

Olica -- A medieval-type planet with humanoid people. Spacefarers from Old Earth's first exodus colonized this world. The civilization regressed to feudal.

Butternut tree -- Produce small round nuts like macadamias

Date and Time -- Olica uses Earth measurements

Goddess of Good -- Women's deity

Holy Father -- Men's deity

Holy Pair -- Olican Deities

Honesty be heard -- Indicating a truth

If it please you -- "Please"

My thanks -- "Thank you"

Mambino viper   Deadly green, red-tongued snake. Asp-like.

'Ristos -- Current Olican rulers. Spydr-like creatures with semi-human facial features. Fanged, clawed with feelers and segmented legs. Sociopaths.

Sartra Olican -- Spoken by Olican higher caste

Sidestrike snake -- Aggressive, venomous brown-stippled snake

Sorbazel -- Massive gray hunting cat, tiger-like, striped in bright lapis blue

Warttoad -- Small reptile, covered with venomous spots.

11229006R0

Made in the USA
Lexington, KY
18 September 2011